DIRTY *Lawyer*

NEW YORK TIMES BESTSELLING AUTHOR

LISA RENEE JONES

Playlist

In My Head by Brantley Gilbert

Unforgettable by Thomas Rhett

Slow Hands by Niall Horan

The Fighter by Keith Urban

They Don't Know by Jason Aldean

Take Me There by Rascal Flatts

Chapter One

Cat

Day 1: The Trial of the Century

Coffee is life, love, and happiness. Actually, it's just alertness, and on a day that I'll be covering the trial of the century along with a horde of additional reporters, I need to be sharp. That need is exactly why I've dressed in my sharpest navy-blue suit dress and paired it with knee-high boots before enjoying a fall walk to the coffee shop three blocks from my New York City loft. Only two blocks from the courthouse, it's bustling with people, but the white mocha is so worth the line, and I've allowed myself ample time to caffeinate. In fact, I have a full two hours before I have to be inside the courtroom, and I plan to sit at a corner table and draft the beginning of my daily segment Cat Does Crime before heading to the courthouse.

I step into a line ten deep that slowly moves, and google the name of the defendant, looking for any hot new tidbit that might not have been live before bed last night. I tab through several articles, and I've made it to a spot near the front of the line when some odd blog linked to the defendant's name called "Mr. Hotness Gets Illegally Hot" pops up in my search. Considering the defendant is a good-looking billionaire accused of killing his pregnant mistress, I buy into the headline and click. The line moves up one spot, and I move with it and then start reading:

I need help. I've done something bad. So very bad. I was told he would take care of me. Protect me. That was three months ago. I remember that day like it was yesterday. But now, it's today, a world behind me and in front of us. I enter his office and shut the door. We stare at each other, the air thickening, crackling. And then it happens. That thing that always happens between us. One minute I'm across the room, and the next I'm sitting in his chair, behind his desk, with him on his knees in front of me. Those blue eyes of his are smoldering hot. His hands settle on my legs just under my skirt, and I want to run my hands through his thick, dark hair, but I know better. I don't touch him until he tells me I can touch him.

I grip the arms of the chair, and his hands start a slow slide upward...

"Next!"

I blink out of that hot little number of a read and pant out a breath, feeling really dirty and gross, and with good reason. I'm hot and bothered over what I think is a fantasy piece about a man who is accused of pushing his pregnant girlfriend down the stairs and killing her. Correction, his pregnant mistress. Only the baby wasn't really his, and he says he wasn't her lover, and he was still charged over fingerprints on a doorknob.

"Cat!"

I jolt at my name as Jeffrey, who works the register as regularly as I visit, shouts at me from behind the counter. I take a step forward, only to have a man in a dark gray suit step in front of me. Frowning, I instinctively move forward and touch his arm. "Excuse me." He doesn't respond, and I am certain he's aware I'm now standing right next to him. "*Excuse me,*" I repeat.

He doesn't turn around, and now I'm irritated. I tug on the sleeve of what I am certain is his ridiculously expensive jacket and achieve my intended goal: He rotates to look at me, the look of controlled irritation etched in his ridiculously handsome face telling me I've achieved my goal. He now feels what I feel, and as a bonus: He now knows that despite my being barely five foot two, blonde, and female, I will not be ignored. "I was next," I say.

"I'm in too much of a rush to wait for you to finish playing games on your phone."

"Games? Are you serious?" I open my mouth to say more and snap it shut, holding up a hand to stop him from doing or saying something that might land me in a courtroom today for the wrong reason. "Wait your turn, like the gentleman you should be."

His eyes, which I now know to be a wicked crystal blue, narrow ever so slightly before he turns to the counter. "A venti double espresso and whatever she's having." Mr. Arrogant Asshole looks at me. "What do you want? I'll buy your drink."

"Is that an apology?"

"It's a concession made in the interest of time. Not an apology. You were the one on your phone playing—"

"I was not playing games. I was working, while you were plotting the best way to push around the woman who was ahead of you."

"That's the best you've got? I'm pushing around women?"

"No, you're not pushing around women today," I say. "You tried and failed. I can buy my own coffee." I face the counter. "My usual."

"Already wrote up your cup," Jeffrey says. "It should be ready any minute."

"Thank you," I say, and while I should just move along, I find myself turning to Mr. Arrogant Asshole because apparently, I can't help myself. "I'll leave you with a helpful tip," I say, "since you've been so exceedingly helpful to me today. The phrases 'thank you' and 'I'm sorry' are not only Manners 101, but failure to use them will either keep a man single, or make a man single." And on that note, I move on down the bar, which has a cluster of people waiting on drinks, but thankfully, I spot the corner table I favor opening up. Hurrying that way, I wait for the woman who is leaving to clear her space, and then murmur the "thank you" that Mr. Arrogant Asshole back at the counter doesn't understand before claiming her seat and placing my bag on the table. Settling into my seat, I have no idea why, but my gaze lifts and seeks out Mr. Arrogant Asshole, who now stands at the counter, talking on his cellphone and oozing that kind of rich, powerful presence that sucks up all the air in the room and makes every woman around look at him. Me included, apparently, which irritates me. *He* irritates me, and the only way you deal with a man like him is naked for one night, which you end with a pretty little orgasmic goodbye, and that *is all*. Anything else is a mistake, which I know because I've been there, done that.

Once.

Never again.

It's in that moment, with that thought, that Mr. Arrogant Asshole decides to turn around and somehow find the exact spot where I'm sitting, those piercing blue eyes locked on me. And now he's watching me watching him, which means I'm busted and probably appear more interested in him than I want to appear. I cut my stare and pull out my MacBook, keying it to life, and just when it's connected, I hear, "Order for Cat!"

At the sound of my name, I eye one of the regulars, a twenty-something encroaching on thirty, who got fired from his job and started some consulting business. "Kevin," I say, and when he doesn't look up, I raise my voice. "Kevin!"

His head jerks up. "Cat," he says, blinking me into view.

I point to my table and the coffee bar. He nods. I push to my feet and, not about to cower over Mr. Arrogant Asshole, who is now standing at the bar with his back to me, I charge forward. I'm just about to step to his side and grab my drink when he faces me, holding two drinks, one of which he offers to me. "Your drink," he says.

I purse my lips, refusing to be charmed. "Thank you." I pause for effect and add, "But you're still an asshole."

His lips, which I notice when I shouldn't, because *he really is an arrogant asshole*, curve. "You have such good manners," he comments.

"My mother taught me right. Manners and honesty."

"I won't argue the accuracy of your statement, considering the fact that I *was* an asshole."

"Well, good," I say, curious about this turn of events. "We agree on something."

His eyes light with amusement. "I'd apologize, but then this would be over."

I frown. "What does that mean?"

"Meet me here in the morning and we'll negotiate the terms of my apology." He steps around me, and I whirl around to face his back.

"You're an attorney, aren't you?" I say, because I know the lingo, the style, everything about this man. And I am, in fact, a Harvard graduate attorney myself, as are two of my three brothers and my father. Them by choice, me by pressure that I stopped caving into two years ago next week.

He stops walking and rotates to face me now. "Yes, Cat. I am. Which means that you can handle Manners 101 and I'll handle Negotiation 101." He smiles—and it's one hell of a smile—before he turns and walks away.

I watch him disappear in the crowd, knowing I have two options: Forget him or show back up. This is crazy. Men like that one are trouble, and I don't like trouble, so why the heck am I staring after Mr. Arrogant Asshole? I'm not meeting him. End of story.

Shaking off any other thought, I walk back to my table and glance at the computer screen, where I've typed "Mr. Hotness," and decide that hot little blog post is half the reason that Mr. Arrogant Asshole was able to get to me. I'm not meeting him. Of course, if I did, I'd do so with the understanding that trouble can be managed, and in this case, in his case, that would be with a *dirty, rich one night stand.*

Or by simply not meeting him again, but this is my coffee shop and I won't be run out of it.

An hour later, I've written my intro for today's courtroom activity, detailing what I know of the crime in question and the accused killer himself, before heading to the courthouse. I arrive forty-five minutes before the start of the trial, and it's a good thing I do. The outside of the courthouse is crowded with picketers and press. Inside the courtroom, cameras and people have hoarded ninety-nine percent of the space. I squeeze into the back row and remove my brand-new leather-bound notebook, open to the first page, where I write: *Murder: Guilty or Innocent?* I follow with random questions I hope to answer today and during the trial, as I did in the two major trials I sat in witness to prior to this one.

I've just finished my list when the courtroom activity begins. The jury enters. The defendant and his counsel enter, but the stupid cameras block my view. The judge enters next, and we all stand, which means I have an even worse view. Finally, we all take our seats and the lead counsels for both sides approach the bench. They are only there for a minute at most before they turn back to the courtroom. It's then, as Reese Summer, lead counsel for the defense, takes center stage for opening statements that my lips part in shock, and with good reason. Reese Summer is Mr. Arrogant Asshole. I sit there, staring at him, dumbfounded for the first five minutes of his opening before I even remember that I need to take notes. I start writing, studying him as he walks, talks, and presents not just his case, but himself, to the jury, audience, and cameras.

"Nelson Ward met Jennifer Wright when she was scared of her boyfriend and he didn't look away like most people would. He looked at her. He saw her instead of seeing through her or past her. He told his wife about her. And together he and his wife, helped her seek shelter and a job. Nelson did not have an affair with Jennifer Wright. The DNA has proven that the child Jennifer Wright was carrying was not his, but rather her boyfriend's, who was abusing her. The prosecution wanted to make the public happy and they needed a victim to convict. And that's what my client is: A victim. The prosecution will present fingerprints on the doorknob of Ms. Wright's house as evidence. That was the bombshell that landed Nelson Ward in this courtroom. My fingerprints are all over this courtroom. Did I commit a crime here? No. I did not. Has a crime been committed here? Yes. In fact, there have been three murders on this very property. According to the prosecution's handling of this case, you all must now need lawyers. Why? Because that is the only evidence they have against my client, fingerprints on a door. I don't know about you, folks, but I'm terrified at the idea that we can be convicted of a crime off nothing but our fingerprints on a door. Not on a weapon. On a doorknob used over and over by many people."

He continues, and there are quips, and murmured laughter, and intense scowls. He takes everyone on an emotional journey. When he's done, I sit back to assess his skill, and I judge him as a man that can seduce a courtroom as easily as he seduced me.

He's trouble.

Big trouble.

And it's now my job to make him my obsession for the remainder of this trial. Which means a dirty, rich (naked) one night stand can't happen until there can be that pretty little orgasmic goodbye. Anything else would be a mistake I've already made. Once. Never again.

Chapter Two

Cat

Day 2: *The Trial of the Century*

I wake up the next morning with no intention of meeting Reese for coffee. Any personal encounter with him would be inappropriate, and I'd risk my credibility as a reporter with a potential scandal. Which means, instead of my normal routine that would include showering and dressing before heading to the coffee shop, I'm still in my PJs when I walk into my kitchen and put a chocolate-flavored pod in my Keurig. While it brews, I proceed to think about the man I'm avoiding. If I were another reporter, I would take him up on the invitation and corner him for an interview, but I'm not big on the sex-for-information kind of reporting, and that's how that reads to me. Besides, no one likes to be stalked by the press, and while Reese Summer might be an asshole, I'm not. Nor am I chasing headlines, but rather meaningful, objective commentary that has often been the reason I am awarded interviews I would not otherwise be awarded.

Steaming cup in hand, I sit down at my white marbled kitchen island and proceed to finish two cups of coffee, while doing what I do every morning. I read my *Cat Does Crime* write-up in hopes that I won't hate what is now published, and today, thankfully, I do not, though sometimes I do. And I didn't have much to work with to start. There were opening statements, some heated words between counsels, and the judge pulling them back behind closed doors, in what became the end of the day. But reading over my published piece, I made it work. There is a nice mix of personal insight into the case, the judge's general attitude and presence, as well the jury's engagement in the courtroom events. Additionally,

I share my opinions on what should happen, has happened, or has not happened. Finally, I end with a closing statement of my own:

The prosecution's opening statement promised to prove a good-looking billionaire to be a monster in disguise. The defense, led by Reese Summer, in turn, promised to prove them wrong. It's a predictable narrative, of course, except for one thing. The sensationalism in the courtroom for the defense, in what appears to be the JFK effect of good looks and charm, wins the day. Summer slays the jury and the audience, convincing them that the prosecution is on a witch hunt. And since the prosecution chose to present their case with over-the-top drama akin to a B-rated, poorly shot, Friday the 13th movie, they better have facts as backup to win. Until then, —Cat

I left out the part about me having met Reese, finding him to be an arrogant ass, and that he still had me actually contemplating getting naked with him. I don't even know where my head was. Reese personifies the very man who has always been a problem for me. I know Reese is trouble. If the prosecution doesn't know that by now, they will. Just to arm myself with facts, to back up those statements, I google him now. In the name of research, of course. I write down the details in my notebook:

Age: 35
Yale Law School graduate, eight years ago
Single
Never lost a case

God, the man has a résumé that matches that of my father, two brothers, and Mitch, my ex. If only I'd stuck to fucking that man in his office, I might not have minded that he'd also fucked his secretary in his office. Funny how that works. And on that insightful note, I shut my computer. Time to shower, dress, and head to court, sans a stop by the coffee shop for a white mocha and a brush with Mr. Arrogant Asshole.

By the time I'm out of the shower, I start to wonder if I've let my irritation and attraction to Reese Summer cloud my judgment about meeting him. In an effort to not appear unprofessional, have I decidedly acted unprofessional? I'm going to want to interview him. Why would he grant an interview to a woman who stood him up? Of course, I didn't agree to meet him and it wasn't a date, but still...

By the time I've dressed in a fitted black suit-dress with a V-neck, and have pinned my hair neatly at the back of my head, I'm certain I've misstepped. Determined to fix that problem and catch Reese before he leaves the coffee shop, I pull on a black blazer and my knee-high black boots, and then slip my briefcase and purse across my chest on my way to the door. I've just finished the fifteen-floor elevator ride and stepped into the lobby when my cellphone rings.

I cross the lobby while scooping it out of my unzipped purse to note my friend Lauren Walker's number.

Waving at Adam, the doorman, I exit the building and answer the call. "How's the baby?" I ask, answering the call.

"Are you talking about the one in my belly or the one in my bed?" she asks.

"You're the only person on this planet that would call your beast of a husband and ex-FBI agent a baby."

"Baby is the wrong word," she concedes. "Protective bear is more like it. He hovers worse than the DA, and I know you know what that means."

After three years of working with her and under said DA's operation, I do, but I get it. She miscarried last year. Her husband is worried. Still. "Royce can't be that bad."

"He is. So are his brothers. Soon I will have a drone following me to the bathroom."

I laugh. "That would be bad. Really bad. But sympathy aside. How *are* you feeling?"

"Sick. I hear that's actually a good thing. But me aside, I have a client meeting in a few, but there was a purpose to this call other than drones and hovering men. I thought you'd want to know that Royce got a call from the defendant in the case you're covering."

I frown. "Nelson Ward wants to hire your husband's company to protect him?"

"He isn't pleased with the company he's using to handle the threats he's getting."

"And?"

"Royce immediately declined. He just feels it's bad mojo to aid in the defense of a guy who might have killed a pregnant woman, especially with a pregnant wife of his own."

"I think he has a point."

"Of course he does, but I know Reese Summer. I don't believe he'd take this case if he believed Nelson to be guilty."

I turn a corner and keep walking, weaving through the crowd. "You've met Reese?"

"Yes. I know I told you that."

"No. No, you did not tell me that, though I suppose it's logical, since you're both working criminal defense attorneys. Are you telling me now that you're going to talk Royce into taking the case?"

"No," she says. "I tried and failed, and I know what battles to pick with the Walker men. And I read your rundown on opening statements, which was not only excellent, by the way, it cements my belief that Mr. Hotness wins again."

"Mr. Hotness?" I ask, stopping dead in my tracks only a few steps from the coffee shop. "What does that mean?"

"Oh gosh, you don't know Mr. Hotness? What kind of reporter are you?"

"What are you talking about?"

"Reese was on TV last year, and it sparked all kinds of fantasy blogs about him. It's insanity the way it took off. He hates it."

"Reese Summer is Mr. Hotness?"

"Yes, but like I said. He hates it. He feels it degrades his skills. He's a good guy. And he *is* hot, but don't tell Royce I said that. He's been very jealous since I got pregnant again, which is just silly. I'm pregnant, for God's sake."

"Like you have eyes for anyone but Royce anyway."

She sighs. "I really do love that man. Anyway, I have to go. But for the record, I'll bet you a Chocolate Avalanche Sundae at that ice cream place we found a few months back that the woman's ex-boyfriend killed her." There are voices in the background before she says, "I need to go, but I expect courtroom gossip you tell no one but me." And on that note, she hangs up.

I lower the phone and blink with the realization that right now, the biggest gossip I have to share, or withhold, is me meeting Mr. Arrogant Asshole while reading about, and admittedly living, a mini-fantasy about Mr. Hotness, both of which are Reese. How is this even possible?

I glance at the time on my phone and realize how close I have to be to missing him before he heads to court. Shoving my phone back inside my purse, I hurry forward and open the door just as Reese is exiting. Before I can even blink again over this man, his hands come down on my shoulders and he turns me to the side of the door. "You're late," he says, his hands scorching my arms, while a fall breeze is now tinged with the spicy, masculine scent of his cologne.

"I don't remember setting a date or time."

"And yet we did," he says. "But you obviously had to talk yourself into showing up."

"I came for coffee."

"Liar," he says.

"I came—"

"For me," he says, his voice a low rasp as he adds, "*Come for me* again. Tomorrow. An hour earlier than today."

"I need—"

"Good," he says. "And I want to hear more. *Tomorrow.* I have to go." He releases me then he's walking away. I rotate to watch him depart, and Lord help me, the man really is Mr. Hotness and I can still feel him everywhere, and he didn't touch me anywhere but my arms. He's also gone before I've confessed my identity, and I consider chasing him down and explaining myself, but he's headed to court. I'm the last thing that he has on his mind today. And yet he was here. For me. I'm not sure what to do with that little tidbit of information. But then, men like him love the chase, and I didn't fall at his feet.

It's about the chase.

Until he decides I set him up to get the interview I still need from him. This really can't end well, or even naked. No one is going to come, at least not Reese and myself together.

Chapter Three

Cat

I arrive to the courthouse an hour before start time, but, frustratingly, the picketers and crowds are pure insanity. I push through it all and by the time I make my way to the courtroom, I end up in the same back row as yesterday. Then again, I think, as I try to get comfortable in the hard seat, maybe I need to keep a low profile until I deal with the Reese Summer situation. *Situation.* There's a way to describe what's happening between me and that man.

Pulling my journal from my briefcase, I open it to my writing from yesterday, and grimace at my scribbled note about women who fall in love with convicted killers. Mr. Hotness isn't the defendant, but the story idea is still a good one. Setting that aside for now, I start jotting down notes related to Lauren's comments, with a focus on who might be guilty of the murders, if not the defendant. I'm pages into my thoughts when the action in the courtroom begins, and it's not long before Reese is at his table, and I find myself remembering his words, spoken all gravelly and low: *You came for me. Come for me again.* There had been a glint in his eye, I realize. Cocky bastard knew exactly what he was implying about me and my, well...orgasm. And holy hell, as he walks to the bench to greet the judge, I'm fairly certain a number of women sigh for no reason other than that he is in the same room. I really hate that I'm one of them, but I'm not going to deny that he's a good-looking man. That isn't the point in all of this. His attitude and my job are.

The trial begins, and the prosecution claims the reins, continuing its opening statement narrative, painting a picture of a selfish billionaire who wanted his cake and to eat it too, a.k.a. a wife and a mistress. It's dirty, gritty, nasty legal work. It's also delivered clumsily, filled with empty spaces, and theories that have no factual support. And from where I sit, Reese does an incredible job of tearing down every witness that is presented.

So much so that by lunchtime I set aside Lauren's praise for Reese and decide that my original assessment of the man is correct: He is most definitely the kind of man who will fuck you and fuck you over, unless you fuck him and fuck him over first. Professionally speaking, of course, and as a general observation, made objectively by a woman who has not gotten naked with him. Which brings me to who *is* actually naked and exposed right now, and it's not me or Reese, but rather everyone else in the courtroom.

As if proving every mental point I've just made, he approaches a witness for the prosecution and proceeds to turn the woman into a silly schoolgirl, who fidgets, smiles nervously, and bats her eyes at him. She also proceeds to look like a liar when she can't keep her story straight. It seems that her claim to have seen the defendant with his "alleged" mistress, as Reese calls her, proves less than reliable. Apparently, she's not sure what she saw after all.

Unsurprisingly, once she's off the stand, the prosecution asks for an early, and long, lunch break. "One hour," the judge allots, giving nothing but the standard break, which to me says that he believes the witness list is not only long, but destined to be drawn out.

The gavel is clunked on the wooden block on top of the judge's desk, and the courtroom becomes a gaggle of people standing and moving toward the door. I don't get up. I can't. The walkway is packed and I'm trapped. I try to make good use of my captive position, watching the front of the courtroom for a story. The prosecution scrambles to a back room while Reese lingers at his table, conversing with his client and co-counsels. Interestingly, Reese stands close to the accused. He leans toward him. Lauren is right. This is a man who believes his client is innocent. Or Reese simply loves everyone who pays him and pays him well.

The courtroom doesn't just begin to thin out, it empties out like a suction draining a swamp, and suddenly, I'm out in the open, exposed, a woman watching Reese Summer in a sea of empty seats. It's in that moment that he leans in close to his client to say something in his ear. In doing so, he faces the courtroom, and me, and his gaze seems to fall on me: The woman who almost stood him up for coffee, who is now sitting in his courtroom, staring at him. This feels like a scene out of a stalker movie, and I'm the stalker.

He doesn't react to my presence. Maybe he doesn't recognize me. Maybe his mind is elsewhere. Whatever the case, he continues to stare at me with no external reaction before pulling back to look at his client, his attention back where it belongs: Not on me.

"Miss," a security guard greets me, suddenly towering above me. "We need you to exit the courtroom."

I frown and look at grandpa in blue, wondering if the man is serious. How was I supposed to leave when I was blocked in? My walkway is clear now, and I leave my comment in my head. "Of course," I say, as he steps into the aisle in a fashion that prevents me from walking in any direction but the door. Maybe he thinks I'm a stalker, too.

I move in front of him and exit the courtroom. And that is how my thirty-second encounter with the man of the hour, Mr. Arrogant Asshole, Mr. Hotness, ends: With me escorted to the door by an armed guard. So much for professionalism and discretion.

Reese

I exit the side door of the courtroom, Nelson Ward walking in front of me, Elsa and Richard, my co-counsels, beside me, while I have one thing, the wrong thing in the middle of a trial, on my mind: A woman. They reach the private room where we'll have lunch and talk strategy, and I watch them enter before turning on my heel and heading the other direction.

"Reese."

I turn to find Elsa, who is a stunning older version of Cat by fifteen years, standing at the door. Only I don't want to fuck Elsa. I've never wanted to fuck Elsa, and not because of a ten-year age difference between us. Because the woman has the personality of cardboard, despite her brilliant mind. But I have wanted to fuck Cat. From the moment she tugged on my sleeve and cast me in an irritated, green-eyed stare that told me at least ten things about her personality, all of which became: I want to fuck her.

Instead, she was already fucking me.

Fucking reporters, and that has to be her story. It's the only thing that makes sense.

"I'll be back in ten minutes," I say to Elsa, already giving her my back and walking down the hallway.

I exit to the main corridor, happy as hell that the press has rules to follow that don't include accosting me and security has a tight handle on the boundaries. Of course, some of them might decide that equates to a challenge, I think, with Cat in my mind. I scan the corridor and get lucky. I spy my little blonde game player headed down the hallway to my left. I don't need encouragement to follow. I'm already making tracks in her direction, and when she turns right, I step up the pace. Her path leads me to a set of stairs, in a less-populated part of the courthouse. The sound of her footsteps leads me up the stairs, and I reach the top just in time to see her enter a room to my right.

I pursue her, and when I discover that room is a bathroom, I don't care. This woman played me, and I don't like to be played. She finds out *now* that it ends *now*. I follow her inside.

Chapter Four

Reese

I find Cat standing at the sink, three open stalls behind her. She whirls around as I enter, her pretty pink painted lips that I wanted to kiss this very morning parting in shock. "You do know you're in the bathroom, right?" she demands.

"Since the door said *bathroom*, yes. I know." I close the space between us, and she doesn't back away. She stands her ground, her hands settling on her curvy, but slender, hips. Her perfume flowery, roses, I think. Sweet, like I knew she would taste, right up until a few minutes ago.

"The sign says *women*," she says, "not bathroom. Not *men*. And unless you have unexpected equipment, or you simply identify as a woman, and that's what you're telling me, you can't be in here."

"Good to know you understand limits," I say. "Unfortunately, you don't know how to use them in your job. And stalking the defense is not how you get a story."

She glowers. "Stalking you? Last I heard, stalkers do the following. You were in line behind me when we met, not the opposite. And you were the one who cut in front of me. *And*, in case you didn't notice, I'm well known in that coffee bar. I didn't just show up there because you were there."

"You mean my choice of coffee shop near the courthouse worked out for you."

"I live right by it and I'm there all the freaking time, and we both know that you are not."

"You expect me to believe that you didn't know who I was?"

"Believe what you want," she says, "but no. I did not know you were there. I didn't even know who you were until opening statements."

"Then you aren't a well-prepared reporter."

"Look here, Mr. Hotness," she bites out, immediately adding, "Mr. Arrogant Asshole. Knowing who you are and knowing what you look like are not the same."

I arch a brow at the irritating territory this has now entered. "And yet you know about Mr. Hotness?"

"Because Lauren Walker is my friend and she told me about your female following this morning. She also told me you hate that name, which may or may not be believable, since she also told me you were a nice guy."

"I *am* a nice guy. When it's deserved. How do you know Lauren?"

"How is that your business?" she challenges.

"You were talking about me with her."

"The entire planet is talking about you right now, so no. That does not make anything about me or my conversations your business. And for the record, I wasn't going to meet you this morning at all, which is why I was so late."

"Why not?" I demand, that reply hitting me in all kinds of wrong ways. "You knew who I was by then, by your own admission."

"Because I didn't want some scandal to come out of it or for you to think I was going to get naked with you for an interview. I still need and want one, but not that way. And yet here you are. In the ladies' room of the courthouse. Seriously? What are you thinking? You have reporters following you around."

"Says a reporter following me around," I counter.

"I'm not following you. That isn't my style."

"And yet you showed up this morning," I say.

"I decided that I needed to tell you I was a reporter before you found out, but you left before I could. And I didn't want to hurt your big-ass freaking ego by making you think I didn't want to meet you."

"Did you?" I ask.

"Did I what?"

"Want to meet me."

"Does anyone ever want to meet an asshole?" she snaps.

"Did you want to meet me, Cat?" I press.

"Does that matter at this point?"

Good question, I think, and yet it does. "Answer," I order.

"I would have if you were just another good-looking asshole, because then I could have—" She stops herself and repeats, "If you were just another asshole."

"Good looking?"

"Asshole," she replies.

"Then you could have fixed me?"

"You don't fix assholes."

"Then why consider meeting me if you didn't know me and you thought I was an asshole?"

"You get naked with assholes and then you say goodbye."

My cock is instantly, readily on alert. I step closer, a lean from touching her. "That was your plan? To fuck me and say goodbye."

"It was an option."

I arch a brow. "Was?"

"Now you're my job, and I can't cross that line."

We'll see about that, I think. "Who do you write for?"

"The *New York News*. The 'Cat Does Crime' column."

"And what makes you qualified to write that kind of column?"

"A Harvard law degree, five years of practice, and a family of attorneys."

"A Harvard law degree," I say, surprised, though now that I've sparred with her, I shouldn't be.

"And Harvard trumps Yale," she says, pitting her degree against mine.

My lips curve with that obvious jab and challenge. "And yet I'm practicing and you aren't."

"Being good at what you do doesn't matter if you're miserable."

"If you were miserable, why did you do it?"

"None of your business," she says.

"What if I want it to be my business?"

"Give me a real interview, and you can ask me as many questions as I ask you," she negotiates.

"I'll think about it."

"An interview with you and an interview with your client," she adds.

"Now you're pushing your luck."

"You get nothing you don't ask for," she says.

"Do you think he's guilty?" I ask, sizing her up to decide what I will, or will not, grant her.

"What I know," she says, "is that you're winning so far."

"Let's hope the jury agrees with you."

"Because he's innocent?" she asks.

"Yes. He is. And yes, you can quote me on that, and on this: If he wasn't innocent, I wouldn't be defending him." My cellphone rings in my pocket. "That would be the end of our time together. At least for now."

"What about my interviews?"

"Give me your business card."

She reaches into the side pocket of her purse and hands a card to me. I accept it, my hand sliding over hers in the process, that touch between us is electric, and I stare down at her, assessing her. My phone stops ringing and then starts back up again, my gaze flickering over her lips and returning to her beautiful green eyes. I believe her. She didn't know who I was when we met. And in hindsight, of course she did not. We fought, and I wanted to have make-up sex with a woman I didn't even know at that point.

"I'll call you," I say, heading toward the door, pausing to look at her. "I won't be your job for long."

Cat

The rest of the afternoon, I watch Reese work the courtroom, and he is no longer a stranger. He's the man who just had a conversation with me in the bathroom of this very courthouse. He is the man who touched me on the hand, *just* the hand, and made me feel it everywhere, inside and out. I *really* felt that touch, probably because those blue eyes of his were burning into me when it happened.

All that aside, he is still the lead counsel on this case, whom I need to interview to do my job properly, but at least I've set the stage to get past our initial encounter, by being upfront about that request. The air is clear. I've been honest and professional. Well, honest. I'm not sure telling him that he's an asshole that can't be fixed can be called professional any more than me telling him that I considered getting naked with him, even if that tidbit was mostly implied. But as far as I'm concerned, the questionable professionalism of those confessions should be cancelled out by him following me into the women's bathroom. After that encounter, I'm not convinced he's the nice guy he and Lauren claim him to be, but *I am* convinced he's trouble.

By the time the courtroom closes for the day, I'm also convinced that he's one hell of an attorney who hasn't earned his perfect track record of all wins and no losses by luck. He's picked his clients wisely and defended them just as wisely. By the time I've left the day behind, and I'm back home in my PJs, with Chinese food and my MacBook both in bed with me, I'm convinced that nothing he said in that bathroom was accidental. I replay the conversation and focus on four significant words from our exchange: "*You can quote me,*" he'd said. Was that a test? To see what I would or would not write? I frown and decide that even if it wasn't a test, it's a message that he wants delivered.

With that in mind, I start working on my column, writing up my detailed outline of my day in court and then using my closing statement to deliver his message and summarize mine: *With more horror-show antics that lacked evidence, once again the prosecution came up short and the defense made their case by simply pointing out the weakness in every witness that took the stand. I expected physical evidence, which hasn't been presented. But tomorrow the medical examiner takes the stand, and that will be the real test of guilt or innocence in the eyes of the courtroom, at least from where I sit, which is admittedly pretty far back. As for where that will leave the defense once the torch is passed to them and they take the floor is yet to be seen, but I find Reese Summer competent and convincing.*

On a side note, I've been told by those who know Summer that he won't defend anyone he doesn't believe to be innocent. In a short, unexpected encounter with him, that is exactly what he told me. He believes in his client's innocence. I'm not suggesting that means that he's right and the prosecution is wrong, but in our court system, you are innocent until proven guilty, and thus far the prosecution has not shown guilt. Will tomorrow prove a different story? We shall see. Finished, I sign off with: *Until then, —Cat.*

I reread and edit my work and then send it off to my editor before I close my computer. It's done. I'm done. I've delivered a message to the general masses and the prosecution for Reese Summer, and I've sent a message to Reese Summer: He can trust me enough to grant me those interviews. The question is, can I trust him? With that question in my mind, I plop down on my back on the bed and stare up at the ceiling, replaying my encounter with him in the bathroom, and damn it, I am remembering how good he'd smelled: Spicy and woodsy. How good he'd looked up close and personal.

He's still an arrogant asshole, but he's also dirty, sexy trouble that I can't escape as long as this trial is a live media charge. In other words, I have to be willing to play whatever game he plays with me, and games are how you get burned.

Chapter Five

Cat

Day 3: The Trial of the Century

I wake to my phone ringing, and a dark room, with a quick look at my clock that reads 6:30 a.m. I answer without even looking at the number. "Who died?

"You quoted me."

My eyes go wide. "Reese Summer?"

"You know my voice."

"Don't let that go to your head," I say, scooting up to lean on my headboard. "Even if I hadn't been listening to you talk for two days now, which I have, you're the only person I quoted. And before this goes any further. You said, 'You can quote me on that,' twice, and so I quoted you."

"Yes. I did. I liked your insights."

"Because I said you were winning."

"Admittedly, that did help."

"Did you call to tell me I'm getting an interview?"

"If I say no, what will you write about me tomorrow?"

"The truth," I say, "just like I did today. I want to interview you and your client, but I'm not a child who will throw a literary tantrum if I don't get one. There will be another case. Another time. A little less coffee to fight over."

"Yes. Coffee. I'll see you at the coffee shop in an hour."

He hangs up.

I lift the phone in the air and stare at it. Coffee. Reese. The mistakes I could make because of how good he smells. The way he just ordered me to show up. The way I have no idea the purpose of this meeting. I call him back. "Hello, Cat," he greets me.

My name is like silk on his tongue.

I love it.

I hate it.

"Am I meeting you for an interview?" I ask.

"No."

"Then I'm not meeting you for coffee."

"Why?"

"One," I say, without missing a beat, "you didn't ask. I don't take orders. Two, if I met you, you wouldn't know if I'm there for the interview or sex or your stunningly humble personality. And I wouldn't know if you were trying to sway my coverage. Three, even if you did ask, I would not say yes until this trial frenzy was over."

I hang up, throw away the blanket, and twist around to settle my feet on the floor. My phone rings. I answer again without looking at the number. "Hello, Reese," I say, mimicking his greeting.

"I'll call. I'll ask. I'll impatiently wait until after the trial."

He hangs up.

He is making me crazy. He's making me want to know him.

I don't want to know him.

Only maybe I do.

I head to the bathroom and remind myself that there is a reason I just had a six-month relationship with an artist. Powerful, money-hungry, controlling men like Reese Summer are not my kind of guys. Then again, neither are artists, since the whole live in the moment with no planning thing drove me nuts, and no amount of sex, which the man called his "creative outlet," could change that. But my newly crossed-out artist boyfriend isn't the point. I've been here with a man like Reese, done this simmering burn before, and I cannot forget how this plays out. The sex is wild, the connection explosive, and then the crash and burn is hard, fast, and painful.

I will not fall for Reese "Mr. Hotness" Summer.

Three hours later, I am dressed in a black pantsuit—meant to fight the chill outside and inside the courtroom, which had everyone shivering the afternoon before—and heading out the door. With plenty of time to spare, and since that coffee date with Reese is on indefinite hold, I stop by the coffee shop. I endure the line and grab my white mocha, hoping the earlier hour will allow me to get a closer seat to the action. I fail miserably. I work my way toward the front door and the picketers and the camera crews seem to swell by the moment. My press pass is the only saving grace but I'm still delayed entry into the courthouse. Once I'm finally inside the building, I'm through security, and to the courtroom quickly. I'm also stuck in the back row again, but just as I'm pulling my things from my bag, a security guard steps beside me. "If you'll follow me, miss," he says, "I'll be relocating you."

"Did I do something wrong?"

"Not that I know of," he says, motioning me forward.

The next thing I know, I'm being shown to a seat just behind the families, sitting with the high-powered television news media and not far from where Reese is seated. The court is brought to order, and we all stand. The normal order of events takes place and Reese and his counterpart do as they have every morning: Approach the bench for some argument they are both already making. When Reese turns back to walk to his table, his eyes land on me, and while he shows no outer reaction, I feel the silent nod. The confirmation that he put me in this seat. And I'm not sure how to feel about it. Yes, I want the seat. Yes, I want an interview. But I don't want the sex for an interview thing. That isn't who I am, and maybe this has gotten so far out there with us that I just can't ask for an interview.

It's not a thought I hang on to for long, as Nathan Miles, the medical examiner on the case, is called to the stand, where he proceeds to deliver a convoluted testimony. The prosecution keeps him tied to the stand for hours, and I take pages of notes, but find no proof in anything presented. There is simply gore meant to drive the jury to convict. Come lunchtime, Reese hasn't even been given the chance to cross-examine, though he's had his share of objections.

The court dismisses everyone for an hour break, and I stand up, waiting for the crowd before I can exit my row. I'm stopped dead in my tracks and end up scanning the courtroom, where Reese remains by his table, and my eyes lock with his, the instant punch of awareness between us something I feel to my toes. My God. What am I doing with this man? Someone knocks into me and bodies fill the space between us, breaking the connection but I still feel it. I'm hot all over despite the courtroom being an icebox again today, and I waste no time hurrying through the building to exit the front door. Security has the picketers and the cameras pushed to one side, while a pathway is clear for the rest of us humans. I walk down the dramatic concrete steps and to my right, where there are food trucks parked. I'm starving and I want to stop, but there are hordes of reporters everywhere. I hurry away, take another two right turns, and head to a small park down the way that is my secret courtroom escape.

Once I'm there, I'm free from the crowds, and I have food trucks and even a bench when I'm ready to eat. I stop at a place that has candies and nuts and order two bags of the latter.

Once I've paid, I turn around and walk straight into a hard chest. "Oh God. I'm sorry. I—" I blink up and into Reese's eyes, that spicy scent of him now becoming familiar. "How are you here?"

"I was about to ask you the same thing," he says.

"You were behind me again, remember? I was trying to escape the crowd." And suddenly I'm aware that my hand is on his chest. I pull back.

He catches my hip, his hands settling just under the hem of my jacket. "Seems we were both trying to escape the crowd."

"Right. Of course." I hold up my bag. "Nuts?"

"No, but I really want to kiss you right now," he says, his voice a low intense rasp, his eyes a simmering hot invitation.

"That would be a bad idea," I say, when I really want him to just do it. Kiss me right now.

"Make your case, counselor."

"For the same reason your hand shouldn't be on my hip. We are most likely being watched, and you're feeding your Mr. Hotness reputation."

His entire expression sharpens. "I hate that damn name," he says, his hand sliding from my hip. "I need a hotdog. You want a hotdog?"

"No, but *thank you,*" I say, making a point of showing off my manners.

His lips curve. "*You're welcome,* Cat. How was that for manners?"

"You're learning."

"Maybe I won't end up single and alone after all," he teases, before motioning to a truck a half block down. "Walk with me."

I nod, and we fall into step together. "You're really getting a hotdog?"

"Yes. What's wrong with hotdogs?"

"I once worked for a concert venue, as a teen, of course, and the hotdogs we were putting out were green before they were heated."

"I love concert hotdogs," he says.

"I don't even know what to do with that statement."

"Cover those dogs with mustard and relish, you won't know anything but how good they taste." We stop at the truck and he glances at me. "You want something else?"

"A bottle of water, please," I say.

Five minutes later, we're on the opposite side of the truck, on a bench just inside the park, and out of easy view. "You don't seem like a hotdog kind of guy," I comment, tossing some nuts in my mouth and watching him devouring his lunch.

"I'm a Texas cowboy, sweetheart," he says. "Hotdogs around the campfire at the ranch used to be gourmet."

"My brother lives in Texas, but he doesn't like hotdogs."

"Is he an attorney?"

"No. He hates the legal profession. He's an engineer and went to school in Austin and just stayed. I thought your parents were law professors, not ranchers? And yes, I read up on you."

"For the record, I looked you up as well, and yes. My parents are professors. My grandparents owned the ranch. They passed and my younger brother took it over a few years ago."

"How old is your brother?"

"Twenty-eight. And to be clear, this conversation is not an interview."

"I'm not a tabloid or even a scoop reporter," I say. "I write opinion pieces and I've written a true crime novel, and have a second coming out in a few months. I don't do this for money."

"Because your father is Mike Maxwell."

I arch a brow. "How do you know that?"

"I told you I checked you out." His lips curve. "I called Lauren."

"You called Lauren," I repeat. "That wouldn't surprise me if she would have actually told me."

"It was right before court."

He was thinking about me right before court instead of his work. "And what did she tell you?"

"Good luck."

My brow furrows. "Good luck?"

"She said I'd need it to get anywhere with you."

"She's right," I say, and quickly turn the topic back to him. "Why didn't you run the ranch with your brother? That has to be a big job."

"I need more than horses and hay. He didn't, and I didn't miss how you just deflected from you back to me."

"How old are you?" I ask.

"Thirty-five."

"Ever been married?"

"Never," he says. "Must be my bad manners, right?"

"Exactly," I say. "They say you can tell a lot about a man based on his manners and his mother."

"So says my mother when she calls me three times a week, usually to bitch about my father. They've been married forty years and hate each other. I'm not inspired to fall in love. What about you? What's your story?"

"Thirty next month. Never married. If my mother was still alive, your parents and mine could be best friends, based on what you just told me about yours. And as for the interview, I don't want it anymore."

He crumples up his paper and tosses it into the trash before turning his big body and the full force of his blue-eyed stare on me. "Why?"

"Okay, I do want it but I don't want it because you—we—whatever this is that we're doing."

"Whatever this is wouldn't be happening if I thought that's why you wanted the interview. You still have a job to do, and this case will be over soon."

"You're going to move to dismiss, aren't you?"

"What would you do, counselor?"

"Move to dismiss, but there's pressure on the judge and cameras on the court. It will be declined. But I'd then quickly establish another suspect, point out that the lack of evidence just as easily points to that person, and then move to dismiss again and quickly."

"Why aren't you practicing?"

"I never wanted to practice. It was just what was expected."

He studies me for several intense beats. "I have to get back to court, but I'll call you for coffee and that kiss, sooner rather than later. For now." He picks up my hand and kisses it. "I'll settle for that."

He stands up and leaves.

Hours later in court, the prosecution rests. There is a quick-held breath as everyone waits to hear what the defense will do next. Will they move to dismiss? And, of course, he does. But the judge declines his request. The court is adjourned, and it's not long before there's a press conference outside, put on by the prosecutor while the defense stays in hiding, most likely preparing for tomorrow.

I stand on the sidelines and listen to what amounts to more of the courtroom conversations. Hours of the blown-up nonsense, and I'm sad for one reason. Right now, there will be no justice for a dead woman and her unborn child.

Twenty minutes later, I'm in my favorite coffee shop, at my corner table, heading to the bar to collect my order. It's then that I notice the prosecutor, a tall, lanky man in a basic blue suit and tie, sitting alone at a table and working on his MacBook. Seeing an opportunity, I walk up to his table.

He glances up at me. "Cat from *Cat Does Crime*," he says. "I was a fan until you dogged my performance. I read your true crime on the Piaz murders. It was good, but I'll write my own book on this. Move along. I'm busy."

Okay.

Reese just lost his title. He's no longer Mr. Arrogant Asshole. This guy stole it from him.

I walk back to my seat, sit down, and spend the next hour working on my column. My closing statement is this: *When you charge a suspect without proof to satisfy the public, you disappoint that very public when you can't deliver a conviction. But it's not just the public you fail. It's the charge when you have proof, and not sooner. And so, I'm going to challenge the defense to do more than protect their client. Give us the killer. Give that woman and child, and their family, justice. Until then, —Cat.*

I look up to realize that some time along the way, the new Mr. Arrogant Asshole has left, and I grab my phone and dial Reese. His voice mail picks up and I leave a message.

"Hopefully that hotdog didn't kill you and you get this message. Here is my closing statement, which I'm not changing, but I want you to know about it." I read it to his voice mail and then add,

"Good night, Reese." I end the call and pack up, heading back to my apartment.

As I enter the building, I stare at the fancy tiled floors and glance up at the towering ceiling. I inherited my apartment when my mother died. It had been her getaway. Her escape from my father, and he knew about it. I was unsure what to do with that little piece of information when I found out about it, but I tucked it away and pretended it didn't exist. Or I thought I did. Now, tonight, something about that encounter with Reese has stirred old feelings I don't want to feel, back to life. I don't even know what to call the feelings. Betrayal. I'd felt betrayed when I realized nothing about my life was exactly what I'd thought it to be. My parents were not happy.

And so I do what I do when I feel lost. I enter my luxury apartment, pour wine, and find my way to my favorite spot. A claw-foot tub hugged by windows, the moon and stars sparkling outside the window. I waste no time running a hot bubble bath, stripping down, and climbing inside. I'm halfway finished with my glass of wine when my phone rings. I glance at the number I now know to be Reese's and, with wet, bubble-covered hands, answer on speaker.

"Hello, Reese," I say.

"I'm going to tell you what I told Lauren, when I told her I was going to pursue you."

"You told Lauren that you were—"

"Yes. I did. And she wished me luck. To which I replied: Challenge accepted. Which brings me to your closing statement: Challenge accepted, Cat. Good night."

He hangs up.

I sit up and forget how wet I am, calling Lauren. "I wondered when you were going to call," she says.

"Did Reese—"

"Yes. And I told him good luck."

"And he said?"

"Challenge accepted. But I know you. He's the kind of man you're drawn to and fear. And he's your job. What are you going to do?"

I don't deny anything she's just said. We worked twenty-hour days together at the DA's office. We talked. A lot. Lauren knows me more than most. More than anyone, really.

"Cat?" she presses.

"What am I going to do?" I repeat. "I'm going to get naked with that man and say goodbye."

She laughs. "Then I'm going to tell you what I told him. Good luck."

I scowl as if she can see me. "Challenge accepted."

She laughs louder, and I hang up.

Chapter Six

Cat

Day 4: The Trial of the Century

I wake up exhausted and in need of caffeine, which is Reese's fault. He was on my mind last night, keeping me awake, which is unacceptable unless we're naked and together. Thinking means I'm getting too involved with him emotionally, and I'm not doing that now or ever. Deciding my coffee stop is safe today, or rather necessary for everyone else's safety, I pull myself out of bed and hurry to the shower, then put my Keurig to use to make a cup of coffee, which I drink while drying my hair, then flatiron it to a sleek shine. I don't tie it back, and tell myself that has nothing to do with Reese. It's the tired thing motivating this decision. I need the attention off my puffy-ass face.

I dress in a favorite outfit, a burgundy pantsuit with pants that hit at the ankle. I pair it with stilettos, and the shirt beneath the jacket is white; I then head to the coffee shop, where I read my newly posted column, as is my routine, and I do like my routines. The fact that I'm pleased with what I've written helps take the edge off my crankiness. And the fact that every other headline is about a baby killer, and headlines make my fact-based commentary stand out. Finally, it's my turn in line, and I order my white mocha, while trying not to admit that I'm a tiny bit disappointed that Reese has not shown up.

Once I'm at the courthouse, I wade through the gaggle out front. Once inside, I discover that I'm seated near Reese again, and when he enters, his eyes find mine and his words are in the air between us: *Challenge accepted.* At the moment, they're about him and me and me and him, not this case. But as he takes the courtroom reins, it becomes clear that he's up to that challenge as well. He calls the family and friends of the victim to the stand, and one by one, proves that no one knew his client was someone involved with the deceased. His client knew her, but he wasn't sleeping with her. He was trying to help her out of an abusive situation with her boyfriend.

Come lunchtime, I head back to the same food trucks I'd visited yesterday, and I've just gotten my nuts again when Reese reappears. "You have to eat something other than nuts."

"My nuts are healthier than your hotdog."

"Yeah, well, I only do hotdogs during trials," he says as we step to the hotdog truck.

He orders, and a few minutes later we're sitting on the same bench as yesterday.

"Why only during trials?" I ask, finishing off a handful of nuts. "Is it like a superstition thing?"

"It is," he confirms. "I ate a hotdog at lunch the day I got my first jury win. It's superstitious, but in this line of work, you take any advantage you can get."

"You're winning," I say.

"Juries are unpredictable," he says. "You know that."

"I do. I worked for the DA for several years, and even when you believed you should win, you didn't always win."

"The DA with a Harvard law degree," he says. "You could have been banking and you chose public service."

"I come from money," I admit. "I make my own living, but I inherited my apartment, and that gives me the freedom to do what I want. I can't say I'd be different or the same in my choices if that wasn't the case."

"I came from nothing," he says. "You should know that about me."

He says those words with a hint of that arrogance that I don't read the same way I have in the past. It's as if the arrogance is a wall to protect him from those who might judge him unworthy. "You seem to be doing pretty well now. And you know that what you do have, you created."

"And you don't?"

"I do now. I walked away from law. I embraced what works for me and I'm better at what I do now because of how I started. So I can't regret it."

"Why the DA? Why public service?"

"I thought I was helping those who needed help. Instead, decisions are politics, and then pregnant dead women don't get justice served on their behalf. And innocent people end up with a stigma attached to them that they don't deserve. I don't like it. Not one bit."

"You underestimate me if you believe that's how this ends."

"You'll have to hand over a damning case against someone else to end it differently."

"And I will. If my client lets me keep going. He wants this to be over." He balls up his wrapper and tosses it before taking my hand in his again. "Until tomorrow, Cat," he says, using my little goodbye in each of my columns before standing and walking away. Leaving me with that spicy scent of him lingering in the air, and a date for lunch tomorrow.

I could no-show.

But I don't want to.

Later that night, I am in bed with a pizza and no man. Just me. I've been alone like this for years, really. I mean, yes, there was the artist, but we had sex. The conversation was convoluted at best. Maybe that's why I chose him, and stayed with him way too long. He'd never really known me. He'd never threatened my heart. But I got to have an orgasm. I got to feel a body next to mine. It had seemed like enough. Which brings me to my column, which I write carefully on this day, because I dare to talk about domestic abuse. My closing statement reads like this:

Who killed Jennifer Wright and her unborn child?

That is the question in the courtroom now, and as the defense presents their case, more and more the answer doesn't sound as simple as who has been charged. Interestingly, I believe the defense could ask for a dismissal again at any time, and based on evidence, he should be granted that request. But I find myself wanting this trial to continue. I want to know who the killer is, and I want to see that killer brought to justice. Tomorrow is Friday. My assessment is that as much as I want this case to continue, it's expensive financially and emotionally. If the defense plans to ask for that dismissal, Friday is the day. Until then, —Cat.

I shut my computer and stare up at the ceiling. If the trial is over, then what?

Do I dare my one night, followed by a goodbye with Reese Summer?

Or do I just say goodbye?

Or is it really hello?

No.

What am I thinking?

Day 5: The Trial of the Century

I have trouble sleeping again, and I wake up with butterflies in my stomach as if I'm the one who has a high-profile case to close today. With the potential dismissal of the case, today feels like it should be more formal. I dress in a light blue suit dress that I pair with a black jacket, tights, and stilettos again, and despite drinking coffee at home, my white mocha has to happen. I reach the coffee shop and the line is predictably out of the door, but I'll get my white mocha and a better mood with it. I'm reading my own column on my phone while standing in line when I receive a text from my literary agent: *Loving your coverage of the trial. So is your editor. She wants to contract your coverage as a new book. Are you in?*

My mood is instantly better, and I type: *Yes, x 1000*

My agent answers with: *I'll email you the offer when I get it.*

Smiling now, the rest of the line is short, and I wonder if yet another book deal will finally win my family's support instead of their ire over my career choices. I'll share the news once I sign the contract. I'm already thinking about how to structure a book, and how today's happenings might impact my choices, when I finally get to the register. I head to the end of the bar and spy broad, perfect shoulders in an expensive suit: *Reese.* Reese is here. And I know he's here for me. I stop walking, and that's when everything changes. The woman next to him, a pretty blonde, is flirting with him. He looks down at her and laughs that charming laugh of his. Apparently, he likes blondes. Just how many is he pursuing? *Asshole.* Why did I even think all this interaction we had was about me, rather than the obvious—him getting laid?

Suddenly, Reese and the woman turn in my direction, and the woman is still looking up at Reese as his attention lands on me. The woman starts walking, and her destination is: *Into me.* Her iced coffee explodes all over me. I gasp with the shock of the cold beverage, and I'm pretty sure some of it just drained down my pant leg. "Holy hell," Reese murmurs, while the woman panics.

"Oh God. Oh God. I'm sorry."

Reese hands me napkins while he starts wiping my dress. I grab his hand. "Stop."

"Cat—"

"Don't say my name."

He frowns. "What?"

"Deal with your other woman. She's upset." I rotate away from him and into her. "Please move."

"I—Yes." She backs up, and I charge past her and down a set of steps that lead to the lower-level bathroom, and there is no question that I have ice between my damn boobs.

I reach the bottom of the steps, and luckily the bathroom is empty. I open the door, step inside, and shut myself in there. I'm a mess. A complete, sticky, horrible mess. I dig the ice from my bra and try to dry off enough to just get me out of here and back home.

Reese

I take a step to follow Cat, but the woman who was talking my ear off while I waited on my coffee steps in front of me. "I'm so sorry," she proclaims. "Obviously you know her. I want to make this right."

"It was an accident," I say. "And I'll handle it." I step around her, weave between bodies at the crowded bar, and head down the stairs that Cat had been rushing toward.

At the bottom level, I find the bathroom and knock on the door. "Cat."

The door flies open and she points at her coffee-stained dress, while I try to focus on the stains, not the curve of her breasts and her discreet but lush cleavage. "You did this," she accuses, pulling my gaze back to hers, while her verbal attack reminds me that she is hard to get in every way but a good fight.

"I didn't do this," I say. "I—"

"You were flirting with that woman and she was staring at you with her panties melting, and she just walked right into me. You did this. Move. I need to go home and change."

She's jealous, and I can't help but be a little pleased about this, but I bite back a smile and a laugh sure to get me hurt. "Panties melting?" I rest my arm on the doorframe above her. "Sweetheart, since I met you, the only panties I want to melt for me are yours."

"Really?" she demands. "Prove it."

"Name the time and place."

Her cheeks huff. "Forget I said that."

"No. I won't forget that you said that. Challenge once again accepted."

"Move. I need to go home and change because you ruined my dress."

I decide not to point out the inaccuracy of that statement yet again, and settle on a peace offering. "I'll buy you a new dress."

"Seriously? *You'll buy me a new dress*? Is that supposed to melt my panties? You think you can buy your way past your bad behavior? First you cut in line and want to buy my coffee, and now this. You really are an arrogant ass, and I can't be bought."

I grab her and pull her to me, my hand at the side of her face, the other on her hip, when I want my hands everywhere, all over her. "I was not flirting with that woman, but *you* are another story." I close my mouth down on hers, my tongue licking into her mouth. At first, she resists, but I deepen the kiss and she moans a sexy little moan, and then she's melting into me, kissing me back. The taste of her is chocolate and coffee. Temptation burns through me, thickening my cock.

But she suddenly pushes on my chest, tearing her mouth from mine. "Like I said," she pants out, "I can't be bought."

"You think that kiss was bribery?" I ask.

"Yes," she says. "I do."

"Did it work?"

"A little, but once you let go of me, I'll get over it."

"If I give you the chance, but I won't."

"I told you—"

I kiss her again, this time a long, drugging, deep kiss before I say, "If I had time," I say, finishing the sentence in my head with multiple choices: *I would fuck you, lick you, punish you with an orgasm you want but can't have until you see me again.* "I have to get to court."

"If you had time," she says, "I still wouldn't let you do any of the things you're thinking about doing."

"Like I said: Challenge accepted." I release her and start up the stairs, turning back to add, "You taste as good as I knew you would," before I turn away and head back up the stairs.

"Reese," she says from behind me just before I reach the top level.

I turn to find her standing at the bottom of the step. "Yes, Cat?" I say, and holy fuck, she's gorgeous with her hair down like this.

"You have my lipstick all over your mouth and face."

I reach up and run my finger over my mouth to find a shade of pink on my finger. "Is it at least your lucky shade?"

"I just had coffee spilled all over me while wearing it."

"And I kissed you."

"Yes, actually, there is that."

I have a brief moment in which I contemplate charging down the steps and pulling her back into the bathroom, where I would set her on the counter. Next her skirt would go up her gorgeous legs, and I would settle a knee in between her thighs, and rip off her panties rather than melt them. I would then lick her until she moans, tugs on my hair, and begs for more. But I have fucking court.

Instead, I simply say, "See you in court, Cat," before I turn away and head into the coffee shop again, where I stop for napkins, and head for the door, motivated to win my case, *and* Cat. And *I am* going to win with Cat. One lick at a time, if that's what it takes.

Chapter Seven

Cat

Reese is making me crazy. Since I met him, I can't think straight. I can't sleep. I can't even get a cup of coffee without it ending up all over me. He's trouble. He's my job. He's an incredible kisser. I hate him. I want to hit him. I'm all over the board with this man.

These are the thoughts I have over and over as I rush to my apartment to put on a pink dress I don't often wear to court. But I somehow end up in it anyway. Just like I somehow ended up with Reese's lips on my lips. Maybe that is the value of pink. It's innocence and sweetness. If I look the role, I'll behave the role. I'll scare off the deviant, arrogant assholes like Reese. Whom I hate.

I don't second-guess the dress as I step out of my building again, but I do in fact second-guess just how I allowed his hands to end up on my body, *in a coffee shop*, in the middle of this trial. I hurry toward the black sedan Uber I've prearranged and climb inside, greeting the middle-aged man behind the wheel. "Hello."

He gives a wave but doesn't speak, and perhaps I should question the weird triangle bald spot on his head that cannot be natural, but this is Manhattan. Antennas on the man's head wouldn't even be as weird as some of the things I've seen in my almost thirty years in this city.

We make it all of one block before we're in a dead stop and my cellphone rings in my purse. Digging it out, I note Reese's number. "Shouldn't you be with your client?"

"That implies a crisis to manage, which also implies the prosecution, not me or my team. Do you always taste like chocolate and coffee?"

"Do you always taste like arrogance?

"Better arrogance than an inability to please," he replies.

"That was a ridiculously arrogant answer."

"Back to the kiss. Better yet, let's talk about you and your confessed desire to get naked with me."

"I did not say that."

"You did."

He's right. I kind of did. "That was then," I say.

"When you hated me."

"I didn't hate you," I say. "I just didn't like you."

"And yet you wanted to get naked with me?"

"I said I considered that option. A one and done."

"Sweetheart, the fact that you believe that's an option tells me you've never been properly fucked. So let's be clear. If a man fucks you, and you have the ability to be one and done, he did it wrong. And I don't intend to do it wrong. Until later, Cat. And Cat, I can still taste you on my lips."

He hangs up.

My phone rings again almost instantly, and I answer with, "You know what they say. A guy who talks big—"

"Has a little dick. Don't I know it."

At the sound of my agent's voice, I cringe. "Liz. I thought you were—"

"A man who pissed you off. I hope there's incredible make-up sex to follow. After the trial. Stay focused. What you're writing is working for you and me. The publisher is preempting you with six figures to ensure you don't go elsewhere," she says. "But they want a lot of creative control."

"What kind of control?"

"They want to attach portions of your money to specific interviews that have to be included."

"I don't like that. That isn't how I work. And if that's how they want to play this, I'll write the book and then let you take it out to publishers when it's done. Then it's done my way."

"I knew you'd say that, but I needed to confirm. But there is more. They're in talks with Dan Miller for a book. They want you to consider co-writing it."

"The prosecutor? You have got to be kidding me. He's going to lose this case and he's a jerk. No one wants a book from a jerk and a loser."

"It plays out like this: The real story. What the jury wasn't allowed to know but the prosecution did."

"That's not my style."

"There isn't just more money in this for you. There's the establishment of your true crime brand."

"Which is not what you just described."

"Talk to him," she says. "Appease the publisher."

"Being forced to appease others isn't why I started writing."

"You'll meet him tonight," she says, as if I haven't spoken. "After court. The boutique hotel on the corner by the courthouse. The Johnnie—"

"Walker," I say. "I know it. It's popular with the insiders. When?"

"Seven," she says. "That's safe, right?"

"Yes. Seven works." I think of my encounter with him in the coffee shop and his comment about writing a book. "And he knows who I am?"

"Yes."

"I approached him for an interview and he told me he knew me and he'll write his own book." That made no sense at that point in time, but now it does.

She laughs. "Obviously the publisher had been talking to him."

"So tell me again why we're meeting? Because to make matters worse, I haven't been favorable to his trial skills."

"I'm aware of that fact. We all are aware of that fact, but the publisher seems to believe your present tone only makes you two teaming up all the more interesting."

"They're just looking for scandal on top of scandal," I supply.

"They're looking to sell books," she says, and without giving me time to respond, she adds, "Call me after," and hangs up.

I blow out a breath. I could be partnering with Reese's adversary, while I'm presently trying to recover from Reese's hands on my body and his mouth on mine.

Could this get any more complicated?

I'm still asking that very question as I reach the courthouse and discover that I'm running so late I need a guard to allow me inside the courtroom. The judge, jury, and legal teams are in place, which means I am forced to claim a back seat, or walk down the aisle and in front of all of the cameras. I'm not a newscaster for a reason. I don't like the invasion of the cameras lenses on ten different levels, which is something that someone other than me can analyze, preferably *never*.

The court is called to order, for once without counsels taking a walk to the bench. Reese works the courtroom, an edge of control and determination about him. He calls his first witness. The victim's boyfriend, whom Lauren is certain is the killer. He cries. He shouts. He cries some more. Guilty or not, he's painted himself as a victim, and I believe him. Right up until Reese turns the tables on him.

"Was it true that Jennifer was afraid of you?" he asks of the victim.

"Of course not."

"Are you certain that no one I put on the stand will say that Jennifer was afraid of you?"

"There are people who don't like me. I can't know what they will say."

"Which people?" Reese asks.

"Her mother, for one. She doesn't seem to even consider that I lost the woman I love and my unborn child. That is punishment enough without her attacking me. I can't deal with her attacking me, too."

"You've been accused of being abusive."

From there it doesn't get better for the witness, but it does for the accused. Reese doesn't produce a confession, but he opens the door to another suspect, and does so artfully in every way.

The prosecution is just about to cross-examine when the judge calls a short break. "Thirty minutes for lunch," he says. "It's Friday. I want to get people out of here and to their families tonight." The gavel hits the wooden block. The break is barely long enough to scarf something from a machine and pee, and, I reluctantly admit, my disappointment at the absence of a meetup with Reese. I'm leaning on a wall, watching people pass by and shoving a bag of peanuts down, when my phone buzzes. I dig it out of my purse to find a text message from Reese that reads: *You taste as sweet as you look in that pink dress, but not quite as innocent.*

I glance up and my gaze pulls right, to find Reese leaning on this very wall, a good ten feet away. Those blue eyes of his fix on me, and for just a few moments I think of what the witnesses feel on the stand. The steel force of his attention consuming them as it is me now. We stare at each other for several beats, but he doesn't move toward me, he keeps a distance, respecting the professional lines I've established between us. And then he's gone, walking away before we become obvious, and I watch him join one of his co-counsels and disappear down a hallway.

I could type a reply, but I have no idea what to say. None. Zero. Zip. I write words for a living and I can't find any words to type. This man really is making me crazy. And exceptionally warm. I guzzle my water, but what I really want is a long, tall drink of Reese Summer. I glance at my watch and confirm that *The Reese Summer Show* is about to start again. That means I'm one step closer to removing my no sex during the trial rule.

Chapter Eight

Cat

Four hours later, the courtroom of jurors, press and observers, has endured the tedious cross-examination of the victim's boyfriend and the tears of her mother. The testimony drags onward, and the day does not end early because it's Friday. But ultimately Reese tries to give us all an ending to the trial. Come nearly six o'clock, he stands and addresses the court. "Judge," he says, "the defense respectfully requests the dismissal of all charges. There has been no evidence presented to support charging my client. At this point, I think we can all question why my client was charged at all. With the obvious lack of evidence against my client, and a number of suspects, did the prosecution simply pick the one that gets them the biggest book deals?"

The courtroom erupts in murmurs and chaos, while I cringe at the personal note this has hit for me. I've been flirting with Reese. I've all but promised to get naked with Reese. I have a meeting about writing a book with the prosecutor, this very hour, perhaps. Turns out I know the answer to my earlier question: Yes. It can get more complicated.

The judge bangs his gavel and shouts, "Order!" pulling me back into the moment as he looks directly at Reese. "Unless you get me a confession by someone other than your client, the jury will decide this case, not me. Don't argue. You won't like the results. Court adjourned."

And just like that, the trial will continue on Monday, and I have drinks with the prosecutor instead of coffee followed by sex with Reese Summer. This day needs a do-over.

I don't wait to find out if there are press conferences after court. I analyze and opine on crimes. I don't push and shove. I don't hide in bushes or around corners to get stories. In other words, I don't wait to find out if there is a press conference after court that will include nothing more than more of the same huff and puff I listened to all day. A short walk later, I arrive at the Johnnie Walker bar, on the ground level of the Johnnie Walker Hotel, before the clusters of tables are filled. I glance around the spacious bar, the décor all brown leather and wooden masculinity, the lights dim.

I cross the room and settle into a seat by a window, away from any other tables, allowing for a private conversation with Dan that could include sensitive and confidential information, if we can get past our dislike for one another. It also allows me to see the door, at least at the moment, before the crowds erupt. For the time being, I ignore the entrance, and the menu on the table that I know from previous visits sports a wide variety of Johnnie Walker scotch. I'm not a scotch girl. I'm not a drinker at all—at least, not when I need my head on straight. Which means I will never drink with Reese Summer.

I'll order coffee.

It's safe.

Or not.

It's not safe, but it is lucky. Coffee is how I met Reese. Coffee is how I ended up kissing Reese. I'm not writing a book with the prosecutor. If I'm going to write a book with anyone, I'll write it with Reese. I'll propose that idea to him and the publisher. I just need to do the obligatory meeting I have set tonight.

Instead I order a White Russian with a half pour, which ensures I drink more cream than alcohol. While I wait for it and Dan, a television nearby has been tuned to the news and a familiar broadcaster is standing in front of the courthouse, where there is nothing but picketers being reported. I get one look at a "kill the baby killer sign" and I think I need the rest of that pour. But too late. My drink is here, and so is Dan Miller, and he looks as angry tonight as he does pretty much always.

Dan locates me quickly, proving once again that this day needs a reset button. He crosses the room: Tall, lanky, and in his forties, with a hint of gray in his brown hair. Too soon, he sits down by the window opposite me. "I assume you chose this location to be seen. The reporter that scooped the prosecution."

My anger is instant, but my legal training and debate skills remind me to clamp it down. "First," I say, biting out a controlled reply, "I didn't choose this location. My publisher did. Second, I don't scoop stories. Ever. I write expert analyses and true crime novels."

"Right," he says. "And I gave in and agreed to meet you. No more need to stalk me at coffee shops. Now what?"

I give an incredulous shake of my head. First Reese with the stalker thing. Now him. "I live by that coffee shop, so perhaps you were stalking me to get a true crime book deal."

"I don't need you for a book deal."

"And yet you're sitting with me. Have you ever written a book?"

"No, but—"

"It was a yes or no question, counselor. And now we both know why you're here. The publisher believes you need a skilled co-writer to write a decent book. I don't want to be your co-writer. Now we can say we met, we did this, and we won't work together."

He studies me several beats. "Who wins this case?"

"No one, because justice is not going to be served. You acted rashly. You didn't wait for the evidence to tell a convincing story."

"You don't think he's guilty."

"I'm an attorney. I honor the court system, and he's innocent until proven guilty. As for the book, this meeting is over. We can say we did it. We can say we aren't compatible."

"But you're writing a book anyway."

"Yes."

"You'll need my input."

"If you choose to let Reese Summer speak out while you do not," I counter, "I'll deal with that fact in my book and you'll have to as well."

"Is that a threat?"

"It's a statement of fact."

"This meeting was a joke from the get go."

He says something else, but I tune him out with the sensation of being watched I'd felt at the courthouse repeating all over again. My gaze pulls wide and lands on a table across the room, where Reese sits with his co-counsels, and my eyes connect with his, his narrowing, a question in their depths. He isn't sure what to think. I'm not either. My palms are sweaty. I feel guilty. This is crazy. I did nothing wrong. He really is making me crazy. My fingers curl into my palms. Why did I agree to a meeting at a courtroom hotspot? I've tried to be discreet with Reese, but I happily meet with his opposition in public?

"Look," Dan says, "I don't need or want—"

"I get it," I say, looking at him. "I'm not writing a book with you. And frankly, I hope you decide to spend your time finding the right person to prosecute, rather than writing a book about the wrong one." I grab my bag, stand up, and head for the door without looking in Reese's direction. I'll text him when I get out of here and explain, or not. This is my job.

I start walking, and I swear Reese's gaze burns through me. I weave through the now-occupied tables and the group of people that enter as I'm trying to exit the bar, pushing past them to travel through the lobby. Once I step outside, the temperature has dropped about ten degrees, while I feel downright hot. "Wait one moment."

At the sound of Dan's voice, I cringe and turn to face him. "The publisher wants this to happen," he says, standing in front of me, crowding me now. "We need to be on the same page when addressing them."

"I'll talk to them," I say. "I'll move this in the direction we both obviously want it to go." *Which is nowhere,* I silently add.

"When?"

"They'll contact me tonight. I'll let them know our decision."

He glares at me for several seconds and then scrubs his jaw and walks away. And that is when I realize that Reese is standing just outside the hotel door, close enough that had Dan turned just right, he'd have seen him. Close enough to have heard everything. For several beats, neither of us move, speak, even breathe, it seems, the overhang attached to the building shadows his face. But I don't need to see his expression to feel the anger in him. He thinks he knows something he does not know.

"Whatever you think you saw, you didn't," I say, and my voice seems to set him into action.

He walks toward me, Mr. Tall, Dark, and Angry at the moment, a man of power and control, but that anger is palpable. He stops in front of me, so damn tall and broad, a chilly breeze lifting that spicy scent of him, which wraps around me. Everything about him in this moment is overwhelmingly large.

"What I saw isn't what pisses me off," he says. "You have a job to do. You have interviews to do. I get that. It's what I heard that pisses me off. A book deal with that man? Were you feeding your book partner information?"

"No," I say quickly. "God. No. Reese, this isn't—"

"Were you going to fuck me for information?"

"That's not what this is. Why would I wait, if that's what I wanted?"

"You got me talking. And I admit it. You were good, sweetheart. You look good. You taste good. You fuck people over real damn good."

"Don't be an asshole because you think I'm an asshole. Because I'm not an asshole, and that makes you a really big asshole. And the very fact that you're going off the deep end like this tells a story. You've been burned, and guess what? Whoever she was is not me."

"Maybe you can put that in your book with Danny boy. Maybe you can even turn me into a monster defending a monster."

"No," I breathe out, hit hard by those words, and I don't even know why. "I don't think you're a monster."

"But you need to sell books. However you can sell them, right?"

"That's not who I am. I know you know that."

His voice softens ever so slightly. "I barely know you, Cat."

"Then don't judge me. My publisher set this up, and—"

"You *should have* warned me."

"This is my job. We aren't *dating*."

"Right. Just fucking. No. Wrong. We aren't even fucking. We were waiting while you milked me for more than an orgasm. And now I know where I went wrong with you. The minute I heard you were a reporter, I should have pulled your skirt up and had my one and done, and got you the fuck out of my system."

"Stop being an asshole."

"It's who I am, per you."

"You're reading this all wrong, and you're—"

"I don't want more information," he bites out. "Let's keep this simple but not sweet. Hard and fast. Hard and long. As long as it ends. I'm in. If you want to fuck. Let's fuck."

"You ruined the joy of that little adventure."

"Fine," he says. "If you change your mind, if you want your one and done, call me. Otherwise, don't." He turns and walks away, leaving me on the sidewalk, staring after him as he re-enters the building.

I take a step to follow him and quite possibly punch him, but several high-profile lawyers walk into the hotel behind him. And I amend my earlier statement. Meeting here wasn't stupid. I have nothing to hide with Dan. With Reese, it's different. We're one big, combustible ball of angry, sex-driven tension that's hard to miss if you're in the same room with us.

Rotating, I start an angry walk toward my apartment, and with every step I take, that anger vibrates through me. Being pissed off morphs into images of my ex screwing his secretary and a playlist of his lies. Reese didn't deny being burned. He didn't deny that it was driving his reactions to me now. Damn it, I've seen beneath the asshole. It's a wall. I get it. I have my own. My anger plummets.

I make it one block and I dial Reese's number. He doesn't answer. I walk another block and try again. He doesn't answer. I start getting angry all over again. This emotional rollercoaster and attempts to contact him repeat for seven blocks until I stop walking. At which point I realize that he must think that I'm actually calling for sex. Now he's toying with me the way he thinks I've toyed with him.

I turn around and start walking back toward him.

This ends tonight, one way or the other.

Chapter Nine

Reese

If she calls and suddenly wants to fuck right now, I'm right about her. She's a fame-grubbing bitch.

Those were my thoughts when I left her outside the hotel and rejoined my legal team. Elsa, who is strong-willed, and Richard, who will never be strong-willed enough for lead in a case like this one, but makes up for it with his genius. Tonight, though, both are worried, fretting over the client they too believe to be innocent. "Focus on what we can affect," I say, and in the next fifteen minutes, we review what that means, while Cat calls me three times, leaving no messages.

I don't answer. She's obviously freaking out. She wants to fuck. She wants to work herself back inside the story with me. Every second that passes, I get more pissed. I don't let anyone trigger my anger, but Cat has me churning anger like it's fuel. I'm also at my wits end with Elsa, who is rehashing the day over and over.

"Focus on what we can affect," I repeat. "The future we can control. Ideally, you two find me the real killer by the time we get there." They gape at my massive demand, but I've learned that you don't get anything you don't ask for. Maybe that's my problem with Cat. Until tonight, I never outright said, *let's fuck.* I never outright pushed her to get naked with me, and I know from that kiss that I could have. But I wasn't all about one and done, for once, but then neither was she, no matter what she claimed. That wouldn't have worked out for her.

I offer my credit card to the waitress, and glance between Richard and Elsa. "Go get some sleep. We'll meet at my apartment at noon tomorrow and we'll stay there until Monday morning, if that's what it takes to find our confession." I glance at Elsa. "Get that private eye we hired to meet us there."

"He sucks, Reese," she says. "What's the point?"

"I have to agree," Richard states. "We're on our own. I have a tech bud who can hack—"

"No," I say. "Illegal activity does not make for legal evidence. I'll make some phone calls. Both of you leave now. Go home. Do what you do to rest, because it's the last rest you'll get until this is over."

They both stand up and murmur their goodbyes, while my phone rings with yet another call from Cat. Her desperation just fucking pisses me off. I had to work for it until now. Now she has to work for it. Proof I never had to work for it at all. *You were burned,* she'd said. Damn straight I was. By her. Before her. I should never have let her get under my skin. Maybe I won't fuck her. She's a damn witch who makes me stupid drunk.

My phone starts ringing again, and I decline Cat's call and dial Royce Walker, who, of course, is married to Cat's friend, Lauren. Because I can't fucking escape Cat right now. "Royce." I greet.

"I'm not taking on your client," he says.

"Hello to you too, asshole. He's innocent."

"I don't care," Royce says, but he gives a heavy sigh. "But my wife does. She's pregnant and obsessed with this case. And emotional about the victim, who was pregnant as well. She thinks a killer is on the loose."

"She's right."

"Who did it?"

"I know who I think did it, but I have to prove it and force a confession by Monday or face a jury decision. And once my client is convicted, you know how hard it will be to get real justice."

"By Monday," Royce says. "That's a tall order."

"My client is a very rich man," I remind him. "He can pay for a tall order."

"Why come to me now rather than sooner?"

"The judge outright told me that I need a confession to shut this down or this rests in the jury's hands. My client didn't do this. I would stake my career on it."

"You have," he says. "Which is why you should have hired me for this, not a protective detail, a long time ago. Hell. If you were paying, and not your billionaire client, I wouldn't make you pay. I want the person who killed that woman and unborn child to be caught."

"Which is why I took the case. If he goes down, the real killer goes free."

"Agreed," Royce says. "And I make no promises ever, most definitely not this late in the game. But my team is the best. If there is a hole to find, a killer to catch, time is our only holdback. I'll be in touch by Sunday night."

He hangs up. The waitress sets my bill beside me. I sign the receipt, and I'm about to stand up when suddenly Cat is sitting across from me. Her cheeks are flushed, her lips glossy pink. "I'm sure you thought all those phone calls were me saying, 'Yes. Let's fuck.'"

"Weren't they?"

"No. No, I was not. But the idea that you would think that, was driving me nuts. So I'm here to say what I had to say on the phone, because you *wouldn't answer.*"

"I told you not to call unless it was to fuck. So this conversation is over."

Her lashes lower, hiding whatever reaction I've just created. "Right," she says, inhaling and exhaling as she looks at me again. "Right. Coming here was as stupid as me convincing myself that you weren't the person you showed yourself to be the day we met." And with that, she gets up and starts walking. And fuck.

Fuck. Fuck. I can't let her go.

I push to my feet and follow her, my damn eyes on her hot little ass in that pink dress. She weaves through the crunch of bar bodies, and I step up my pace, catching up with her just inside the hotel lobby, grasping her arm. She whirls around, jerking out of my grip to face off with me. "I hope," she bites out, her voice low, but fierce, "for the sake of your client, that the jury doesn't judge your client the way you have me, without facts and evidence."

I close the space she's put between us. "I know what I heard."

Her hands go to her hips, her stance that of challenge, not defense. "You know what you *think* you heard."

"You said yourself that your publisher set the book deal up for you with Dan."

"My publisher forced the meeting on me."

"I might not know you well," I bite out, "but I know you have enough money and freedom not to be forced into anything."

"I inherited my apartment, and I don't live on family money. I have goals. I have dreams, and, frankly, it costs me money, a lot of money, to dare to live those things."

"And your goals and dreams, I assume at this point, include writing a book and making bank by screwing me over."

"Do you think that I would rip on Dan's handling of the case, and praise you, if I ever intended to have that meeting with him tonight? Let alone write a book with the man?"

"And yet you took the meeting, Cat," I say, not even sure why I'm still standing here with her. Why I care how she answers, I don't know, but I do.

"Laying groundwork for the moment I declined an offer made by my present-day publisher, which is much like you walking away from a client mid-trial. It's a big deal. But you know what? I don't even care about the book anymore. I just want the respect of my readers following this case through my eyes and thoughts. Which means I shouldn't be standing here with you right now, probably making a scene. I hate scenes." She walks away.

I catch her arm again and guide her deeper into the lobby, toward the security booth. "Where are we going?" she demands.

"Someplace where you avoid your scene and I get my answers," I say, giving the security guard a nod, and turning us down a hallway toward the private elevators I know well.

"I'll leave," Cat says. "Then there is no scene to avoid. And I've told you everything I have to tell. Stop walking. Reese, damn it, stop walking. There's no one in this hallway anyway."

"Not yet," I say. "Not until I get us out of the eyes of the courtroom crowd."

"Let go of my arm."

I stop at the elevator bank and hit the button. "I'm not letting you go," I say, walking her to stand in front of me as I step into her. "Not yet," I add, the warmth of her body radiating into mine. "You haven't told me everything you have to tell."

"Just because you haven't heard anything to justify your attitude, it doesn't mean that I haven't told you everything."

"Have you, Cat?"

"Have I what?"

"Told me the truth?"

"Yes," she says. "I have."

"Make me believe it."

"I don't have to make you believe anything," she says, her voice a little lower, a little raspier. The air between us is thicker, harder to breathe in, but then all I want to inhale right now is her sweet floral scent.

"But you want to," I say.

"Yes," she dares to admit. "I do. And I hate that I do. I shouldn't care, because you're—"

"I'm not an arrogant asshole."

She studies me a moment, and I can feel a subtle softening of her body, see a warming in her eyes as she says, "Make me believe it," and with that statement, she lets me know that she's in this with me. That she still wants her one and done.

My lips curve and my cock hardens, pressing against my zipper when I want it pressing between her thighs. Holy hell. I've wanted those thighs wrapped around me from the moment this woman pissed me the fuck off in the coffee shop. It made no sense then. Nothing with this woman does, but it doesn't have to. One and done.

The elevator dings and I hold on to her. I don't want to let her go. I want to take her upstairs, when that is not a place I welcome women, not ever. And yet I brought her to this elevator. It's a realization that has me releasing her arm, and not because I've changed my mind about my one and done. But because I want the control this woman has taken from me. She doesn't get to hide behind my choices and my decisions.

"Come upstairs with me," I say, and while the words are not a question, I back away and lean against the inner frame of the elevator, holding the door open, forcing her to make the next move. To change the dynamic with her actions. She stares at the car, not at me, seconds ticking by before her gaze finds mine, her green stare piercing. I arch a brow in question.

"What's upstairs?"

"The top floors are residential. I own an apartment here."

She laughs without humor. "I had a meeting with Dan in your building."

"Yes. You did. And for the record, he knows I live here."

"You thought I knew." She doesn't give me time to respond. "You thought—I didn't know."

I want to believe her. *Too fucking much.* I want to fuck her. *Too fucking much.* "Come upstairs with me, Cat."

She answers by walking to me and joining me in the doorway, but she doesn't touch me. She tilts her delicate little chin up, but there is nothing delicate about her will when her eyes once again meet mine, as she says, "I did not plot against you. I did not ever plan to write a book with Dan. I do, however, regret not texting you about this meeting, when you don't deserve that regret right now. And I meant what I said. I really am going to bow out of this book deal. If you really don't believe those things, I need to go home."

"Why does it matter what I believe if we're just fucking?"

"Because you just told me to make you believe it, and that is a clear statement that you are fucking me just to prove to me and you that I can't hurt you. I have no impact on your life whatsoever. I'm just a fuck. And that's fine. I'm just a fuck and so are you to me, but that's supposed to equal an escape that feels good."

My hands go to her waist, and I walk her into me, her legs now pressed to mine, her hands forced to rest on my chest, where I want them willingly. "Sweetheart," I say, "I promise you that I'm going to make every lick, kiss, and touch as good as the moment before you orgasm."

"I don't doubt that you'll make me feel good *in the moment*, Reese. I don't doubt that this will make you feel like you won in some way I don't fully understand. And I think you might enjoy that feeling in the morning. I don't think I will. And not only does that defeat the entire premise of a one night stand, but I just talked myself out of this." She presses against my chest and tries to move away. I don't even think about letting her go. I don't just *want* her. I *crave* this woman.

Voices sound in the near distance, and I react instantly, not about to create a moment that embarrasses Cat or loses her. "I was an asshole," I say, and my hands come down on her hips. "I judged you." I maneuver her into the elevator and into the corner. I punch in my code to the elevator and focus on what matters. *Cat*. My hands go to her face. "I'll make it up to you."

"You *were* an asshole."

"*I'll make it up to you,*" I repeat, pressing my cheek to hers, my lips at her ear, as I say, "I promise you, sweetheart, that every kiss, every touch, every lick, will be as good as the moment before your next orgasm."

Her fingers curl around my lapels, and I can feel the subtle softening of her body as she replies with a raspy, "Does that promise include the words 'I'm sorry'?"

I ease back to look at her. "I'll say I'm sorry, Ms. Manners," I assure her, "if you'll say *please*."

"You have a reason to say I'm sorry," she counters. "You haven't given me a reason to say please."

And there it is. Yet another challenge by this woman that stirs ten levels of heat in my blood. The elevator dings and the doors begin to open. I lace my fingers with hers and tug her against me. "You do know that you can't issue a challenge like that one to a man, and not give him a chance to make good on it, don't you?"

"I'll stay, but you do know that 'please' is a word that, when used in this particular context, has performance implications, I assume?"

I laugh, and my cock twitches. "We'll let *your manners* decide my performance."

"I guess we will," she says, and it's officially game time: The kind where she's naked and eventually I will be, too. *After* she says *please.*

Chapter Ten

Cat

Time and mistakes have taught me that success and winning don't equal control, as my father and my two of my three brothers would have me believe. Making your own choices is what gives you control. Owning those decisions, and your own happiness, your own *pleasure:* That is control.

As Reese and I walk down the long hallway to his apartment, and he pulls me close with his big, powerful arm, I'm aware of where we're headed. I know that the warmth pooling in my belly and the heaviness in my breasts is a prelude not just to sex, but to me willingly allowing him the kind of control that enables him to *make me say please.* That's my decision. That's me owning my pleasure. And despite Reese being everything I don't want in a man: Arrogant, rich, and powerful, and too good looking to live amongst us real humans, somehow he is exactly what I need. I don't analyze why. I don't have to understand.

It's one night.

And that is what I want. It's freedom from inhibitions and complications, and yet as we draw to a halt at his apartment door, and I watch him unlock it, nerves flutter in my belly. I never get nervous with men. Not since law school, when winning mock-courtroom battles had meant finding a comfort level in my own skin and on my own. The problem is perhaps that I've let Reese get too far under my skin as well. I know him. I've talked to him. I've enjoyed engaging conversations. I've looked forward to our little encounters and exchanges. And since I'm still talking to myself in my head, I tell myself that all of that was just foreplay, the lead-in to a good show. Nothing more.

Reese opens his door, but I don't turn to face him. I stare into his dark apartment.

"Cat," he compels softly. "Look at me."

"No," I say, and it's not defiance. That's not what I feel. It's simply a negative that is perhaps an inherent need to challenge anyone who might have the ability to control me without me realizing I've allowed it to happen. Reese is one of those men who sneaks up on you and does such a thing, so yes, I decide. I need him to know that every bit of control I give him tonight is my decision, not his.

Which is why I move forward, entering his apartment on my own, my feet traveling a dark hallway. I make it all of three steps before a light illuminates a path paved with mahogany hardwood floors, which curves left and forms what is nearly a half-circle. On either side of me there are arched alcoves filled with books, and my mind craves a peek at each title, but that would mean discovering more about this man outside pleasure. I know this isn't what we're about, but I still find myself glancing at a shelf filled with books on art, a few of my favorite artists featured.

I shake off the idea of mutual interest that could be more show for him than it is enjoyment for me. I exit into a living area that is a wide tunnel of floor-to-ceiling windows framing gray couches, a round coffee table in the center. A flat screen television hangs from a built-in drop in the center of the front window. The room is stunningly elegant and decidedly masculine. A room decorated simply, with no place to hang a painting. Nor are there photographs of family anywhere in the room. Despite this, it feels like Reese.

I ponder why this is, but without a definitive answer, as I walk to one of the two white pillars dividing the glass left and right, and rest my hand on it. Stars speckle the sky with white lights, while below them the colorful painting that is New York City's lights in the night sky. Music begins to play, a song I do not know, soft, sexy, edgy. Reese could be described as hard, sexy, and edgy.

Those nerves I'd hoped to leave in the hallway are alive and well, in residence in my belly with a few flutters rising to my chest. It's adrenaline. It's anticipation, which we've worked as one might believe an artist would work to master the colors on a canvas. And we've done so with apparent attention to dramatics, considering the turbulence of our week-long connection. Goosebumps rise on my nape, beneath my hairline, a prelude to Reese stepping behind me. I face him to find that his suit jacket and tie are gone, and there is a drink in his hand. "Johnnie Walker?" he asks, offering his glass to me.

I stare down at his hand where it holds the glass, a strong hand that is free of any jewelry, anticipation fluttering through me with the certainty that it will soon be on my body. With that thought, my gaze pulls up and collides with his, the impact of that connection not only stealing my breath. I can't just look at him and not feel him everywhere. I can't just speak to him and not want to know more.

He arches a brow, indicating the glass he's still offering me. "No thank you," I say, shocked at how breathless I both sound and feel. "I don't drink well." *And I want to remember this night,* I add silently. Every moment.

"Meaning what?" he surprises me by asking, when I'd expect him to just get on to the naked part of this encounter.

"Meaning I'm a cheap date. Half a glass of anything and I'm on my ass."

"A few sips will calm your nerves."

"I'm not nervous."

He leans in, and suddenly his breath is warm on my cheek, his hand right there with it. His lips are a lean from mine. "Liar," he whispers, before his mouth caresses mine, a barely-there touch before he pulls back, one hand on the pillar above me. "A few sips," he urges.

My hands press to the concrete at my sides, rather than to his chest, where they'd rather settle. "I don't like whiskey."

"You don't like feeling out of control," he accuses.

"No," I say. "I don't."

"You know what that tells me?" His hand is suddenly scorching my waist, his cheek against mine as he says, "I'm not the only one who's been burned."

"That's not what you said earlier."

"I was wrong, Cat, and I'm sorry. See?" His lips quirk. "I have manners. All for you. But if you're honest with yourself, and me, you've been just as guilty of judging me like someone in your past."

Guilt stabs at me, and I think of my many assumptions about him the first time I met him, and actually since. And because he's being honest, I don't deny him the same from me. "Yes," I admit. "You're right. And I was wrong. And I'm sorry. Since I said that, does this mean I get to make you say please, too?"

His lips curve. "Sweetheart, when it comes to you, you got it. Please. And I repeat—please to everything." His voice lowers, turns gravelly. "I want you. Really fucking bad."

There is something so raw, and yes, again I think, *honest,* about this man, and I want to believe that's real, not a façade. I really want it to be real. "I want you, too," I say. "*Please.* And now that you have your please, what next?"

"The hard part. Trust." He shakes the ice in the glass. "Just a few sips."

The drink is a request for that trust he's just mentioned. I know it. I see it in his eyes. Or I'm overthinking one night. I suddenly decide that taking the edge off might be just fine right about now. I reach for the glass, and the touch of our fingers is a charge up my arm. And for the first time since I met him, I cut my gaze and tilt back the glass, letting the rich, spiced liquid touch my tongue. I manage all of two deep drinks and his hand is on mine, pulling the glass from my lips. "Enough," he says roughly. "I want you to relax. I don't want you numb. I don't want you to forget." He downs the drink and sets the glass somewhere. I don't know where. Maybe on a ledge wrapping the window, before his hands are above me on the pillar.

His eyes are fixed on my face rather than my body, and while there is no place where we are touching, I can feel the warmth of his body radiating against mine, which promises heat where there is a mere simmer.

"One and done, right?" he asks.

"Yes," I whisper.

"How many one night stands have you had?"

"One and done means you don't get to ask those questions," I counter.

"We aren't strangers who just hooked up without knowing each other."

"We are strangers," I insist. "Most people always are, in fact, strangers, and you're too good an attorney not to know that."

"Explain."

"Why are we talking?"

But he doesn't allow me to dodge my meaning. "Explain," he insists.

"People live in our worlds, but never really see beneath the surface. They never even try. It's how passion hides lies and love hides hate. How sex is an escape and not a confession of the soul."

He studies me, his expression unreadable while the music changes, and I know this song. A Jason Aldean duet with Kelly Clarkson, "Don't You Wanna Stay," which is somehow an unexpected choice for Reese, but it reminds me that I've started to know the man beneath the lawyer and asshole. A country boy with a family ranch, who is more than the suit he wears as armor in a courtroom. Perhaps in life. But as the words fill the air, it's not his past that speaks to me or us. It's the now, the here, the possibilities.

Don't you wanna stay here a little while
Don't you wanna hold each other tight
Don't you wanna fall asleep with me tonight

That last line quakes inside me, and suddenly Reese's fingers are tangling in my hair, his mouth lingering just above mine. "Sleep is overrated," he says, obviously referencing the song, a moment before his mouth crashes over mine, his tongue doing a wicked, smooth slide against mine, and then it is gone.

He lingers close a moment, breathing with me, and then, without warning, he turns me around, pulling my backside to his front, our bodies melded intimately together. And for just a moment, or two or ten, I think...I think he just breathes me in, and it's quite possibly the sexiest thing I've ever experienced. My body responds as if he's touching me, goosebumps lifting on my skin. My nipples are tight, aching buds. My panties clingy and damp. Suddenly, and yet not sudden at all, he is dragging my jacket away, his hands caressing my bare arms along the away, his touch light, but every part of my body is now laden with a warm, needy sensation.

He tosses my jacket aside. I don't know where and I don't care. I try to turn to face him, but he catches my hip. "Not yet," he says, his voice a low, sexy rasp I feel straight to my toes.

His fingers caress my hair to the side, over one of my shoulders, his lips touching the delicate skin of my nape. A tiny kiss that leaves me tingling all over as he reaches for the zipper of my dress and, with deliberate laziness, slowly tugs it downward. Inch by inch, it travels from my shoulder blades down to my lower back, the cool air of the room contrasting the combustible heat of anticipation: What comes next? What will he do? What will I do?

Questions that Reese answers when his deft fingers unhook my bra. He kisses my neck again, a whisper of a touch that shivers through me. His hands find my shoulders, and in a blink I'm naked to the waist. In another blink, he's caressing the material over my hips and my clothing pools at my ankles. Instinct has me ready to untangle my feet, but, showing he does have manners, he doesn't leave me a tangled mess. His powerful arm wraps around my waist, and he lifts me, his foot scooting aside my clothing.

The moment my feet are back on the ground, I am aware of my naked body being the only naked body in this room. Seeking to remedy that fact, and maintain some semblance of control, I twist around to face him. In the process, his arm has managed to remain around my waist, my hands have settled on his chest, and our eyes have collided. I forget control. I forget everything but these few seconds in which this warm blanket of intimacy wraps around us and steals my breath.

And then in the next moments, in which his eyes lower to my naked breasts, where they linger for countless seconds, my aching nipples pucker beneath his inspection before his gaze returns to mine. "You're as perfect as I knew you would be," he says, his voice managing to be both sandpaper and silk on my nerve endings, as he adds, "and almost as naked as I want you to be."

The idea that he has wanted me as much as I have wanted him does funny things to my stomach, but more so, delivers an unexpected wave of illogical vulnerability. This is sex. The end. I don't want or need to feel anything more. I want and need him naked and fucking me now, fast, hard. That's safe. Desperate to find that safe place, to shift the control from him to me, I push to my toes, my breasts molding to his chest, and press my lips to his lips. They are warm, and he is hard everywhere I am soft.

And his response to my kiss, the answering moan I am rewarded with, is white-hot fire in my blood that he ignites further with a deep, sizzling stroke of his tongue. He slants his mouth over mine, deepening the connection, kissing me with a fierceness no other man ever has, but then some part of me has known from moment one that he is like no man I have ever known. Which explains why he is everything I want. And nothing about this night is what I expected, any more than this man is anything I can control.

But there is something intensely arousing about the idea of trying.

As if claiming I am reaching for the impossible, he molds me closer, his hand between my shoulder blades, his tongue playing wickedly with mine, but I meet him stroke for stroke, arching into him. He cups my ass and pulls me solidly against his erection. He wins this one. Now I am the one moaning, arching into him, and I welcome the intimate connection. I burn for the moment he will be inside me.

But I also want him to burn for this just as much as I do, and I need to touch this man. Really, really, need to touch him. My hand presses between us, and I stroke the hard line of his shaft. Reese tears his mouth from mine, pressing me hard against the pillar supporting the window again, and when his hands leave my body, when his palms press to the concrete above me again, I sense his withdrawal is about control. I was winning. I confirm that as reality when our eyes lock, and the dash of fire in his eyes is lit by one part passion and one part challenge.

"If I slide my fingers between your legs right now," he says, "would you be wet for me? Are you ready for me?"

"Why don't you find out for yourself?" I dare him, testing him, pushing him, and I don't even know why.

"If I lick your clit, will you moan for me?"

"Is that a trick question?"

"Answer, Cat," he orders, his voice low, gruff. Aroused. And God, I love the way he manages to be power and control, and yet, intentionally or unintentionally, he doesn't deny me the understanding that I do this to him. It empowers and emboldens me. So when he pushes, when he says, "If I lick your clit—"

"Please," I say. "Is that where this is going? Can we get it over with and just have you get to it?"

His lips curve, with just a hint of wickedness to them that tells me he plans to make me say that word about ten more times before this night is over. And I'm okay with that, I realize. Because that is the glory of one night. I can enjoy every moment of challenge with this man, but I don't have to be in control until tomorrow. And he doesn't get to be in control tomorrow.

Chapter Eleven

Cat

As if he's heard my mental push and pull over control, Reese stakes his claim on those rights. His fingers close around my panties and he rips them away, leaving me in only my thigh-highs and high heels. I gasp with the unexpected action, and then inhale with the anticipation of what comes next. Only it doesn't happen. He doesn't touch me. His hand returns to the pillar above my head, and he stares down at me with half-veiled eyes. Waiting on my reaction. Maybe he wants me to say, *Please touch me.* Maybe he wants to frustrate me into finally hitting him. I aspire to give him the calm that is unexpected.

"You have on too many clothes," I say, pushing off the pillar and reaching for the buttons on his shirt.

He doesn't stop me, but still, he doesn't touch me, which leads me to more questions. I don't know if this means he intends to allow me to have more control than I'd believed he would, or if this is all part of a power play—the latter, I assume. Whatever the case, I want him naked, and I'm already working button number two out of the hole. Once I finish with number three, intent on reaching for number four, he rewards my efforts by pulling the shirt over his head. He takes a step backward and tosses the shirt behind him, toward the couch, while I admire his broad, well-muscled chest. The dusting of dark hair I find there leading my eyes along a downward trail to my intended below-the-belt destination.

I step toward Reese at the same moment he steps toward me, and he wins the battle of what comes next. Suddenly he's turned me to face the pillar again, forcing me to catch myself with my palms against the concrete before me. And then he is at my feet, fingers wrapping my ankles, lips on my backside. Hands caress a path all the way to my hips, until one hand flattens on my belly and he stands up again, cradling my body with his. His lips are at my ear as he says,

"After tonight," he says, his hands cupping my ass, "I won't be the stranger you claimed me to be anymore." His hands curve around my hips, his palms coming back to explore my backside, tracking the curve in the most intimate of ways, trailing lower, down my thighs and back again, until he gives my backside a quick smack. My lips part in surprise, and I am panting. I arch forward, pressing into his hand that now cups my breast, fingers pinching my nipple, a bittersweet friction that is part relief and part tease.

His palm flattens firmly onto my back, holding me in place, and oh God, the fingers of his other hand slide between my thighs, curving so that he cups my sex and strokes my clit at the same time.

"That's right, sweetheart," he murmurs, his leg pressing between mine, inching them apart, his fingers teasing the sensitive, swollen flesh of my sex. "I wonder if you'd let a stranger make you this wet?" His hand on my back caresses over my ribs, and he moves to palm my other breast this time, flicking my nipple.

"You *are* a stranger," I murmur, but I'm not exactly sure if I say the words or think them. I'm lost in sensory overload, his teeth scraping my shoulder, lips pressing to my neck, his breath a warm tickle, and his fingers are doing such spectacular things between my legs and to my nipples that I might shatter any moment.

His teeth that were on my shoulder are now nibbling my ear, and that tweak of sensation radiates through my sex, where I ache to feel him inside me. "Am I still a stranger, Cat?" he demands. "Or do I need to lick you to orgasm before I become a friend? Because I'm going to, you know. I'm going to lick you until you don't even know what one and done means anymore."

I moan with his words, and I'm no longer leaning into the pillar. I've somehow arched against him, and he's holding my weight, one hand cupping my breast, my hand over his hand. His other hand strokes my sex, and with the next flick of my clit, I gasp and then tremble into release, my body quaking with the impact.

Reese doesn't stop touching me, and he seems to instinctively know just what I need. He slows, softens, eases me into that moment when my legs might give out, but he's holding me, anchoring me. I expect, even want him to just bend me over and fuck me then, but nothing with Reese is that one and done. He turns me, stroking my cheek, my hair, and then he is kissing me, a slow slide of tongue that is so damn sexy. I moan into his mouth. He responds with this low, guttural sound, deepening the kiss as he does. And just like that, we go from slow and sensual to hungry and intense.

"I need to be inside you," he growls near my ear.

"Yes," I say, "*please.*"

He pulls back, and when he looks at me, I expect victory in his stare, but that's not what I find. His expression is unreadable, those gorgeous blue eyes probing mine, searching for some unnamed something. Suddenly, the fingers of one of his hands curl around my neck and he pulls my mouth near his. I think he will speak. I can almost taste his words on my lips and I want to know them, to understand them the way he was just trying to understand me. But he never speaks them. He kisses me, and I kiss him.

He reaches into his pocket and produces a condom, and for just a moment I consider tossing it away. I'm on the pill, and the delay that a condom gives is already too long, giving me time to feel how out there on a ledge I am with this man, how into this man I am. But he's unzipping his pants, and being the logical, smart person I am, I also remind myself that condoms protect us from many things. Clinical isn't emotional.

I reach for his pants, but it's like this man senses and shuts down the roadblock my mind throws between us, because he doesn't put the condom on. He scoops me up into his arms and starts walking. In those moments, naked and cradled in his arms, I am again aware of how affected I am by this man, how vulnerable that makes me. He cuts between the couches to an oversize plush gray cloth chair and ottoman. It's large enough that he goes down on it with me, behind me, my body curled in front of his.

He shifts behind me, and I can I hear the tearing of foil, that condom now in place, his pants disappearing. Once he's naked, his cock thick between my legs, and his big, wonderful body curved around mine, that condom doesn't feel so clinical. I don't feel it at all. I feel his hand on my breast, his erection up and down in the wet heat of my aching sex. It's torture. I need everything I don't have right now.

"Reese—"

He thrusts into me, hard and deep, burying himself to the hilt and moaning with the impact. I moan with him and gasp when he shifts my hips, finding a deeper spot. There is no time to revel in the fullness of him inside me, the completeness my body needs. He thrusts again, and the movement radiates through me. I grab his hand where it holds my breast. I arch into him, against him, pressing toward the next pump of his hard body inside mine.

In a remote part of my mind, I think of the absence of his mouth. I want to kiss him. I want him to want to kiss me. I know the irony of this. I want barriers. I don't want to be vulnerable, but I want his mouth. I want all I can get of this man right now, and that is when he does that thing he does again, where he reads my mind. He pulls out of me and turns me around, his leg between mine, his hand under my hair around my neck. His mouth is a breath from mine as he presses back inside me. His cock thrusts inside me at the same moment his tongue strokes my tongue.

With him touching me, kissing me, pressing inside me, the bloom of orgasm is swift. I want to hide from it. I want to stay here, in the middle of bliss. I want to die here, a happy woman, but he is pumping into me, hands on my body, driving me wild, and I am weak. I stiffen, frozen in the moment before I shatter, my body clenching the hard length of him and shooting darts of pure, white-hot bliss to every nerve ending I own.

A guttural sound escapes his lips, and he buries himself deep and hard inside me, shuddering his own release. I want to move, to push against him, to be a part of his pleasure as he was, and is, mine, but I am paralyzed in the aftermath of back-to-back orgasms.

For a few moments, the world fades and we are lost in a bubble that consumes only us, where no one else can intrude, and where nothing but satisfaction exists. When we finally return to the present, it's not a bad place to be. He's still inside me, his forehead pressed to mine, his breathing mingling with mine. He reaches up and gently drags his knuckles over my cheek. "Am I still a stranger, Cat?"

"You're still an asshole," I murmur.

He smiles.

"Of course I am. But am I still a stranger?"

I don't answer. It's feels like a trick, or a door that wants to be opened, one that I shouldn't open, only I really want to kick it down. He tangles fingers in my hair and gently tugs until my gaze meets his. *Am I still a stranger, Cat?*

"Fucking me changes nothing. You're still a stranger."

"And if I want to change that?"

Another trick question. Another door I want to kick open, but I'm not a sadist. I don't like pleasure that becomes pain. But when I open my mouth to tell him no, I can't get myself to say it.

Chapter Twelve

Cat

I'm saved from defining Reese as a stranger or otherwise when my cellphone rings and jolts me back to reality. "My agent. I was supposed to call her about that meeting with Dan. I'm sure he's already called the publisher." I try to roll away, but Reese doesn't allow me such an easy escape.

He releases my hair but catches my leg. "You can call her back in sixty seconds. To be clear, we're not done. We've barely gotten started." He rolls off the chair.

I will my racing heart to calm and do the same, oh so aware of just how naked I am right now, and how my dress is a very long walk away. Actually, I really don't know how far. I have no clue where it landed, but it's nowhere I easily spy. My phone starts ringing again, which is a clear sign someone, most likely my agent, really needs to reach me. Reese hands me my purse and I grab it, also oh so aware of how naked he is. "Thank you," I murmur, accepting my purse and retrieving my phone from inside.

"My agent," I confirm, as Reese scoops up his pants and delivers me a view of his bare ass, so delicious that it could feed fifty nations.

"Hey, Liz," I say into the phone as he covers the view with his pants, and I answer my call.

"Dan called the publisher and said you were a bitch."

I scowl. "Did Dan actually say that I was a bitch, or did you add your normal colorful wording in the replay?"

"I'm quoting Dan, according to your editor."

"He's such a gentleman," I snap sarcastically as Reese grabs a blanket from the couch and settles the soft gray material around my shoulders. I glance up at him, but he's walking away, all loose-legged male swagger that was just pressed next to me in all the right ways.

"No comment?" Liz asks.

"I think he said it all for both of us, don't you? It's done."

"What happened?" Liz presses. "I need details."

"We can't work together and I'm going to make this easy on all involved. I'm out. I'm not writing a book about this trial."

"What? Are you insane? This is a six figure deal. In New York City, you don't walk away from that."

"This has never been about money to me," I say as Reese reappears, a black T-shirt stretching over that incredible chest of his, another draped over his shoulder, and that loose-legged swagger of his is rather addictive to watch.

"No, *but*," Liz says, snapping my attention back to the call, and sparing me the embarrassment of staring at Reese, as she adds, "smart people with money keep their money by never walking away from large sums of money. Especially when that money is a gateway to much more money."

"You're not getting it," I say. "This is wrong for me," and it's then that Reese joins me, and I silently add: *Just like the man now sitting on the coffee table in front of me, staring at me, only feels pretty right every time I'm with him.*

"We need to meet. Where are you? I'll come to you."

"Now isn't a good time," I say, and sit up straighter. "I have to write my column."

"Tomorrow, then. We'll have lunch."

I firm my voice and attitude, which is the only way to win Liz over. "I'm not changing my mind, therefore, I'll call you Monday."

"They'll drop you if you shut this down," Liz says of my publisher.

"I don't like being bullied," I say, my voice going from firm to angry. "And if you support me, then don't participate in bullying me. I'll call you Monday." I hang up without looking at Reese, who is part of why I feel cornered right now, professionally and personally. "I have to write my column." I start to get up, but I'm not holding the stupid blanket, and it slides away, straight to the ground.

I grab for it and drop my phone. I'm exposed and truly so very naked in every way with this man, but rather than looking me over, Reese produces that extra shirt he'd been holding. "I brought it for you," he offers, his eyes meeting mine in one pulsing moment that steals my voice.

I nod my appreciation, but when I would take the shirt from him, he's already pulling it over my head. It drops around my body and I slip my arms inside the oversized sleeves, which aren't oversized for him at all, I'm sure. "Thank you," I manage now, and dare to meet his stare, and that pulse is back, this charge between us that I've never experienced with any other man. I can't breathe. I can't think. I'm so affected by him, I don't know if I'm coming or going.

I'm falling for this man. I'm going to get hurt. "I need to go," I say, but when I would move, his hands catch my legs, under his shirt, scorching me with the touch.

"Don't go," he says.

"I have to work."

"You can work here. I have to work, too. We'll order in dinner. Cat." He softens his voice. "I *want you* to stay."

He says these words as if they are a confession, but a confession of what? Needing me? Wanting me? He's already said those things. I search his face, looking for an answer, when I don't even know the real question, and for the first time since we met, I see the shadows in the depths of his stare: the hints of damage, maybe even pain, that he's hinted at but I've dismissed. I don't dismiss them now. I wonder if I've missed them or if he's chosen to show them to me now. My chest tightens with this possibility, with the idea that he might be willingly exposing a piece of himself to me, no longer allowing me to call him a stranger. Yes. I believe he is, and this matters to me. I am naked with this man in ways I did not intend to be, but I'm still sitting here, wanting more of him.

"Stay," he repeats. "I want you to stay, Cat."

"Yes," I whisper and I could leave it right there, but for reasons I don't understand, it doesn't feel like enough. "I want to stay."

His eyes warm with my response and there is a shift between us in that moment. I feel him becoming more to me than I planned, and maybe I am to him as well. I can't be sure. I don't know. All I know is that my guard is too easily falling, and every warning I'd issued in my mind about "men like Reese" feels as wrong as tonight, and this man feels right.

He reaches up and brushes hair behind my ear. "God, you're beautiful, Cat," he murmurs, a raspy, tormented quality to his voice that says more than the compliment.

I am shaken by the spontaneity and emotion in his words and the rush of emotion I feel in response. I reach forward and curl my fingers at his jaw. "Everyone starts as a stranger," I say, and this time I don't go on, I don't tell him how easy it is to be naked and still alone. I don't tell him how easy it is for lies to read like truth.

He cups my hand and leads it to his lips, where he kisses it. "And everyone who matters once did not." His lips curve, the mood shifting between us once again, lightening with the mischief that is suddenly in his eyes. "Will you tell me your secrets, Cat? Pepperoni or no pepperoni?"

I laugh. "Most definitely pepperoni," I say, not sure any man has taken me on a whirlwind of emotions like this one. "What about you?"

"Double pepperoni," he says quite seriously, before kissing my hand and setting it on my leg. "There's a place on the corner that can have it here in thirty minutes."

"I'm in love with the idea of pizza," I say, "but I hate I'll have to work while we eat." I grab my phone and look at the time. "Yikes. I can't believe I've left myself two hours to make press deadline. I'm not used to a Friday deadline. This is a special edition for the trial this week."

"Because of the trial and my failure to nail a dismissal," he murmurs under his breath before adding, "I need to work, too. Do you want to order now or wait until you're about thirty minutes from finishing up?"

"Do you mind waiting?"

"Not at all. Better yet, the restaurant downstairs makes a killer sandwich tray I order on later nights. Why don't I order that? It has, like, six different options. Then there is no pressure as to when to order or eat."

"Even better," I say. "I like that idea."

"Do you want something to drink? Wine or—"

"No alcohol, please," I say. "Just water if you have it. I don't want to get sleepy."

"I most definitely don't want you to get sleepy. I'll order a pot of coffee."

I laugh at his extreme swing. "That actually sounds good."

He tugs his phone from his pocket and punches a button, and quickly orders. "Done," he says setting his phone on the coffee table. "Do you want to work here or do you need a desk?"

"Where are you working?"

"Right by your side, sweetheart."

I'm surprised by how much I like this answer. Maybe more than I should. But "more than I should" could be my theme song with Reese. "Do you need a desk?"

"I'm going to catch up on e-mail, so I'm fine here."

"I'm eying a spot on the floor in front of the coffee table."

"I'll grab my MacBook and join you." I think he will get up, but he's suddenly leaning in and cupping my face, his breath a warm tickle on my lips. "Just so we're clear, Cat. I don't invite women to my house. You wouldn't be here if I planned to stay a stranger."

"And if I say you have no choice?"

"Then I'll kiss you a little deeper and fuck you a little harder, until you want to know me the way I've decided I want to know you. And that's just for starters."

He stands up and walks away, leaving my mind reeling with the most important question of this moment: How much deeper and harder?

Chapter Thirteen

Reese

I don't invite women to my house.

When I'd said those words to Cat, I'd meant them, and yet here Cat is, sitting on my floor in front of my couch, in my house. Here I am, sitting on the floor next to her after setting our food on the table in front of us, damn glad she is. Though I'm not sure she's actually aware that I'm here anymore, considering I stood up, walked to the door to grab our food, and rejoined her, and she hasn't looked up from the screen of her MacBook. Her focus and intensity over her work, paired with her educated and thoughtful written words, tell me what I already know without the research I could do: She was a killer attorney, just as she's a phenomenal writer. The truth is that, despite my momentary frustration during our coffee shop encounter, Cat had me at "hello," or perhaps "asshole."

I smile and turn back to my computer, remembering the way she'd tugged on my sleeve at the coffee shop and then scowled at me: beautiful and fierce. My obsession for this woman had started then, when my only obsession has ever been my work. I answer a few e-mails and absently reach for one of the homemade potato chips that had been delivered right along with the sandwiches. Apparently, Cat has the same idea at the same moment, and our hands collide. Cat laughs this feminine, sweet laugh and gives me a sweet, green-eyed stare, both of which are as good as foreplay. I'm there. I'm hard. I want to fuck her all over again. "Oops," she says. "You first."

"Ladies first," I say. "Manners are important, after all." I smile and add, "Especially the word *please.*"

Her cheeks flush a pretty pink, but she still answers without missing a beat. "Please *is very* important."

I give her a wink and we both return our attention to our computers. I answer a few more messages and we both munch on sandwiches and chips as we work. An hour later, Cat sighs and says, "Done." She glances over at me. "Can I help with trial research? I'm good at it. I still do it for my work now."

"Right now," I say, shutting my MacBook, "I'm done." I face her, my elbow on the table. "I've just been answering emails that are mostly a gaggle of press requests."

"I'm not one of them," she says, facing me as well. "You know that, right? I don't chase a scoop or even a story. I know I've said that but—"

"I know that, Cat." I reach over and trail my fingers down her cheeks. "There is a way you can actually can help me, though."

"Okay. Great. I want to help. How?"

"Read me your closing statement. I need some outside perspective for mine."

"Of course. I wanted you to read it before it publishes anyway." She moves from the floor to the couch and sets her MacBook in her lap. "Just the close, right?"

I nod and join her, claiming the cushion next to her. "Yes. Right now, I want to home in on where you landed by the end of the week, good or bad. That will tell me where the jury might have landed as well."

"The jury should be with me on this," she says, and shakes her hands. "Okay. I know it's silly but I always get nervous when I read my own words and when I know it's too late to change them. And it is. I sent this in to my editorial team last minute."

"I get it. I get nervous during opening and closing statements, especially in these televised trials."

"But not in the middle of the trial?"

"Once I clear the opening statement, I'm in a comfort zone right up until closing."

"Your opening was brilliant, by the way."

"As much as I appreciate that, we both know the only thing that matters is the outcome. And nothing you do in a trial is brilliant enough unless you get the outcome you want." I tap her MacBook. "I want to hear your closing."

"Right. Okay." She starts to read:

This trial has highlighted the tragic end to a woman and child. What it has not highlighted is evidence. Not once have I been given a reason to give my own personal verdict of "guilty." And yes, I know it's easy to hate a man who is good looking, rich, and seems to have it all, which sums up the defendant. That is what the prosecution seems to be counting on. That you will hate him for having it all. But I certainly hope the jurors remember that among the many reasons America is the greatest country on the earth is our court system. We are innocent until proven guilty, and we can't take that for granted. That is not how the system works around the world. And we must all think that if somehow, some way, you or your loved one was charged with a crime, would you want yourself, or them, to be convicted based on the court of public opinion? If there is no evidence, the jury must acquit. Don't be appalled and horrified when they do what is right. Be appalled and horrified that we wasted time and money, and that the killer, whoever it might be, is still free to live and enjoy life. There is one woman and unborn child that cannot say the same. Too often prosecutors lack the courage to wait for the evidence they need to convict a suspect, and rush to charge too soon. When they do, they fail us all. Until then, —Cat.

She sets her computer on the coffee table. "That's it for tomorrow, which you know, but I have until Sunday night to submit a follow-up that prints on Monday."

I sit there a minute, digesting her closing and scrub my jaw. "You might not need a drink, but I do believe I could use another."

"I thought you'd be pleased with my closing. It favors you."

"It drives home every failure I've had in this trial."

"Failure?" she asks. "What failure, Reese? You're the one who's nailed this trial."

"If I had nailed it, we'd have gotten that dismissal I asked for today."

"That's the judge caving to the court of public opinion. And between you and I, I got the impression from my agent that both your competing counsel and the potential publisher of his book believe he will lose this case."

"And yet they want the person who has hit him at every turn, journalistically speaking, to help him write his book?"

"I thought it was insane as well, which is why I asked that very question. They said it was because of the framework of the book pitch."

"Which is what?" I hold up my hands in a stop sign fashion. "You don't have to tell me."

"Of course I do. I'm wearing *your* T-shirt in *your* house, and I'm not writing a book on this trial anyway. Nor have I signed any confidentiality agreement. The angle will be 'what the jury wasn't allowed to know.' They wanted me because it would be more scandalous if it was written by someone skeptical about the guilt of the accused."

My brow furrows. "What the jury didn't know? What the defense attorney didn't know, apparently. I have no idea what that's about. Do you?"

"No. In hindsight, I wish I would have asked while I was with him. Dan is just such a jerk that I couldn't get past hello and goodbye. But I can find out from my agent."

I study her a moment. "I heard you talking with your agent. Of course I heard you, since I was sitting in front of you. I don't want you to turn down this book deal because of me."

She doesn't immediately respond, her expression unreadable, as if she's sitting in front of a jury, not me. "Right," she says. "I should go." She twists around and starts to get up.

I catch her arm and close the space between us, turning her to face me, my legs trapping hers. "I was not implying that we are not important. You have to know that."

"One and done, Reese. I get it. We agreed. And don't worry. I'm not making life decisions based on getting naked with you."

"We didn't agree on one and done."

"We said—"

"*You* said, sweetheart. Not me. I simply confirmed your position, but never stated mine. And if I have my way, one night is the beginning and not the end. And why would you say no to that book deal?"

"My God," she says dramatically. "You're such an attorney. You just threw a snowball at me and then hit me with a loaded question while I'm trying to recover."

"Recover with me this weekend. And yes. I *am* an attorney. I'm curious as to why the word attorney is an insult to you, especially since you are one as well."

"Because every challenge in my life that spiraled to a place I didn't intend involved that profession." She looks away. "And I don't know why I even told you that."

"I'm glad you did," I say, and, having no intention of letting her run or even look away, I take her down on the couch with me. Settling her on her back and me on my side, I rest on my elbow, my leg between her legs. "Tell me more about these challenges," I urge, my hand under her T-shirt, on her belly.

"I can't think when your hand is under your shirt on my body."

"I'll provide leading questions," I say. "It's the only time I can get away with it. I assume at some point you wanted to be an attorney, since you graduated from one of the toughest schools in the country?"

"I didn't want to go to law school at all," she says, rotating to her side to face me and grabbing a pillow to rest under her head. "It was expected. I know you know who my father is, and I have two brothers who are also corporate attorneys. I also have a third brother, an engineer, who went to Texas to go to law school, and changed majors without telling our father."

"How angry was your father?"

"He was a hurricane. I stayed in law school."

"But went your own direction. Is that why you chose criminal law? Because your father and brothers are corporate?"

"Yes and no. I mean, yes, I wanted and even needed my own identity, which makes another field of law logical. But I also wanted to make a difference, which is how I ended up at the DA's office with Lauren, but you know what I found out. Politics rules, not justice. You're doing more than I was in public service, and you're getting paid."

"You could go into private practice."

"I don't need a lot of money. If that's what motivated me, I'd be working for my father like my two brothers, raking in five hundred thousand a year. And I like what I'm doing now. I still get the high of the courtroom energy and the challenge of solving each case. And I'm actually able to bring attention to the right and wrong in a courtroom in the justice system."

"How does your family feel about your new career?"

"Daniel is supportive. He's the brother that started the hurricane. He takes pictures with my book every time he sees it in stores and tells everyone that his big sister is a *New York Times* bestselling author. He's proud of me and happy for me. My older brothers think I'm throwing away a career."

"And your father?"

"Paid for law school for nothing."

It's the answer I expect, and I shift gears, wondering who else in her life has affected her decisions. "Why haven't you ever been married?"

"I suck at relationships. Didn't you get that from this conversation?"

"You don't suck at relationships because your family wants you to be an attorney and you want to be you, not one of them."

"I was engaged and he slept with his secretary, or rather, fucked her right on top of his desk while inconveniently forgetting that I was coming by that night. So see? I suck at relationships."

"He was a bastard that didn't deserve you. That isn't on you. How long ago was this?"

"Two years ago."

"How long ago did you leave your legal career?"

"Two years ago. Am I on the stand being questioned?"

"He was the catalyst that changed you."

"Yes," she says solemnly. "I knew it was time to live for me."

"He was an attorney," I decide.

"Yes. He was."

"And so the picture begins to reveal itself," I say. "I have a stacked deck, don't I?"

"Pretty much." She reaches up and touches my face. "You're good looking, rich from what I can tell, powerful in person and on camera, and you're learning manners. You're the perfect heartbreaker. That makes you a perfect one and done."

"In other words, you want someone unattractive, with a small wallet, and no skills at pretty much anything. Is that right?"

"I guess I'll just stay single," she says. "What about you? Have you ever been married?"

"No," I say. "I have not. My obsession with my career hasn't exactly been conducive for relationships, but that's not a problem for us, Cat."

"Because I am one and—"

"My new obsession," I say, shifting our bodies to roll her to her back, with me half on top of her. "From the moment I met you, Cat."

"Because you thought you couldn't have me," she says. "Now you do. Now—"

"I want more." My hand caresses up her waist to her breast and I lightly tease her nipple. She pants and arches her back, pressing against my hand as I cup her breast. "Remember that word, Cat," I say. "*More*. I want more." I kiss her, and there is this crazy tenderness I feel for her that I don't understand, that I don't feel with women. I fuck. I move on. But holy hell, as my tongue strokes hers, I savor the taste of her, so wickedly addictive and yet so sweet, somehow vulnerable, when she is everything but innocent.

I work the shirt over her head, and my mouth lowers to hers, but I don't kiss her. I linger a breath, and two and three, from a touch. Her hand goes to my face, fingers curling on my jaw. "More is better achieved without your pants on. *Please* take them off."

I'd laugh at her use of the word "please," but I want her too fucking bad right now to do anything but feel that word in my groin. Fuck. Every moment since I met this woman, I have wanted her. And somehow she's not a distraction from my world, but already a part of it. Maybe it's her career that works for me. Maybe it's her personality. Right now, it's her fucking amazing breasts. I cup them and lick her nipples. She rewards me with these sweet, soft sounds that are so damn feminine and sexy that I want to bury myself inside her here and now. But then I'd miss the next sweet sound she makes just because I touch her, or lick her.

I lick a path down to her stomach, her fingers stabbing into my hair, her stomach trembling as I kiss it. And when I finally settle between her legs and blow on her clit, she grips my hair like she's holding on for dear life, arching into me, to my mouth, to my fingers, all over again. I give her nub a tiny lick and trail it down her sex, my cock responding to the salty-sweet taste of her with a lockdown that has my balls so damn tight they ache. My hand goes under her sweet little ass and I suckle her nub now, sliding my fingers up and down her sex. Apparently, that's the magic we're both after. She gasps, jerks, and then starts to quake. Her orgasm is here, and so damn quickly that I know one thing for certain: No matter how tough and one and done she wants to play this, she isn't any more done than I am.

I slip two fingers inside her, giving her spasming body something to hold on to until my cock finds its way to where my fingers are now. I ease her into that sweet spot that follows release, and my willpower is shot. I need to be inside her, *now*. I kiss her belly and she pushes to her elbows, and when her eyes meet mine, there is just a hint of that vulnerability in her stare. As if I've torn down some wall she didn't intend to tear down and she's not sure what to do about it and me. Perhaps she is thinking about how to run.

I decide to give her one of the many reasons to stay. I slide up her body, cup her head, and kiss her, letting her taste *her* on my lips. "Now I'm not just obsessed," I say. "I'm addicted to how you taste, which means I won't let you come that fast next time." I leave her with that to occupy her thoughts, and push off the couch to grab the condom in my pocket before I step out of my pants and sit down on the couch beside Cat. But when I would roll on the condom, Cat is on her knees in front of me, her hand around my cock, and holy hell, I want her mouth on me, too.

She takes the condom from me, my cock jutting between us, thick and heavily veined with arousal. "Should I put it on now or after I find out what you taste like?" she asks.

"I'll let you decide," I say.

Her reply is to lick my cock and send a shock wave of bliss through my body. "More?" she asks.

"Please," I say, without hesitation.

She laughs that sweet laugh again, and holy hell, she is everything: Smart. Funny. Sexy. I might be in love, especially since my cock is now in her mouth.

Chapter Fourteen

Cat

Reese. Naked. Hard all over, especially his cock. My tongue licking and stroking the soft skin covering hard steel. That is where this night, and a coffee shop encounter, has taken me and us. He watches me with half-veiled eyes, or he tries. I know the moment I've taken him to that blissful place where you just feel and don't think. His lashes lower, and his face and body tense with pleasure. Now I've reached my wanted destination, that place I'd planned to travel with him when I settled on my knees before him, where I'm the one in control, but suddenly, it's more about his pleasure. He affects me deeply, and the validation that I do affect him as well calms me and turns me on at the same time. That I need validation says I'm a mess of complicated history, and I hate that about me, but I don't hate him.

I tuck the condom under his legs, ensuring it's not lost, and one of my hands settles on his thigh, the springy hair there tickling my palm in a surprisingly erotic way, but then I am ultrasensitive, my body tingling all over. My hand is still at the base of his cock, and I drag my mouth back, no longer suckling or licking. His eyes open and I lick the salty-sweet drop of arousal pooling at the tip of his erection. It explodes on my taste buds and he moans. The sound of him turned on ignites my desire. I lick a circle around him and suckle him between my lips.

His thigh tenses beneath my palm, and I am now the one obsessed with this man and his pleasure, but I want him to reach for me, to need that release so badly, that he can't help himself. With this goal driving me, I begin a slow glide up and down his length, and his hips lift with me. I can almost feel his need to hold me in place, but still he does not. I draw him deeper and inch closer to him, pressing my breasts to his legs.

He groans and leans forward. "Enough," he orders, reaching for me.

I intend to resist, to take him all the way, but he's too strong for me to fight. I am in his lap, flush against his chest, his fingers tangling in my hair, his lips on my lips. Tongue licking into my mouth in a sultry, deep kiss. His erection is at my backside, and somehow the condom manages to find my fingers.

I close my hand around it and press it to his chest. Somehow our lips part and I don't think. I just ask what comes to my mind. "Why didn't you let me finish?"

He pulls back and looks at me. "We finish together, sweetheart," he says, his mouth crashing down on mine again. *Together.* I don't even know what that word means. I thought I did. I wanted to know, but it feels like fiction, a story that ends badly. I don't know why I'm even thinking about this. I don't know what this man is doing to me. Even now, his hands traveling my back and his touch on my body affect me in a way I have never experienced. Every inch of my skin, every nerve ending, is tingling and alive.

"I need to be inside you," he growls near my ear, his breath warm on my neck, before his lips brush the sensitive area.

My body reacts to those words, my sex tightening, aching. "Yes," I whisper. "Please."

I move, or he moves me, I don't know which. I'm so damn aroused I can barely think straight. All I know is somehow, that condom gets where it needs to go, and so do I. He shifts my weight and presses into me. I pant as he enters me, stretching me, pushing deeper and deeper.

"Holy fuck, woman," he murmurs, his voice low, nearly guttural, and he kisses me, fingers tangled roughly, erotically, in my hair. My hands are on his chest, my body arched over his, and when our lips part, our gazes collide, the impact stealing my breath. The air seems to thicken around us, the connection I've felt with this man on every one of our encounters, swelling between us, controlling me, and I think him as well. I see it in his eyes, his need, his passion for me. For us.

"Come here," he orders, and I don't really remember moving, but his hand is under my hair, around my neck, and our mouths collide in a kiss that feels different now, less about sex and more about emotion.

I feel this kiss in every part of my body, and those butterflies in my belly are back, but they don't feel like nerves anymore. We begin to move *together*, a sexy sway and dance, our hands all over each other, and I can't get close enough to him. I lose time. I lose the ability to worry or fear where this leads. I just want to drink him in, to inhale that spicy scent of his and taste him on my tongue. I don't want it to end, but he cups my breast and pinches my nipple at the same time that his tongue strokes mine and his cock drives deep inside me. It's done then. I can't stop the white-hot fire he's created or the orgasm that overtakes me.

I sink against him, my face buried in his neck as my body quakes, my sex clenching, pulling against him while he drives into me. He moans as my sex clamps down on him, a hand between my shoulder blades, molding me close. His big, powerful body shakes with release. Time is too fast, and too slow. I fade away, going deeper into the sensations rocking my body.

When, finally, I come back to the present, I feel him there with me, his body relaxing, mine with his, and against him. I'm numb, my limbs heavy, and Reese lays us on the couch, stroking hair from my face. "I'll be right back," he says, planting a tender, lingering kiss at my temple before departing. A moment later, the blanket is over me, but I'm still in the previous moment and that tender kiss. Of the many ways this man has affected me this night, that kiss, and even the blanket, affects me the most. I've barely had time to process these facts before he is back, condom-less, no doubt.

"The fireplace is on now," he says, lying down next to me and pulling my back to his chest, my gaze landing on the flames that seem to somehow be inside the window directly across from me.

"I should go," I murmur.

"I don't want you to go," Reese says, hand settling on my hip, his face in my shoulder, by my neck. "*Stay*, Cat."

I know I should go. One and done and all. It's the way you deal with men like Reese. Only he's holding on to me really tightly. And my lashes are so very heavy.

Chapter Fifteen

Cat

A muffled ringing has me blinking my eyes open, immediately becoming aware of Reese's big body wrapped around mine while the sound seems to be coming from somewhere on the floor. I blink again, sunlight beaming from around us. Reese is unmoving, completely knocked out. And just as good looking sound asleep as he is wide awake.

I know it's the morning after, and goodbye should have been last night, but this is over, and I can't help but touch him one last time. I reach up and trace his lips and then let the rough edges of his one-day stubble brush my skin. He blinks awake and I start to pull away, but he catches my hand. "Good morning," he says, those blue eyes flecked with amber sunlight, his lips that I was just touching, brushing my knuckles. "How are you?" he asks.

"Better once the awkward morning after is over."

He laughs. "There is no awkward morning after, Cat. There's pancakes and coffee, and possibly, no, *absolutely*, more sex. And I can't seem to find the awkwardness in any of that, can you?"

One and done, I tell myself. "What are we doing here, Reese?" I ask, but as he shifts slightly, I become aware of an impending need that takes precedence over my question. "Hold that answer. I have no choice but to announce that I have to pee. Really badly."

"Is that right?" He chuckles.

"Yes. Which means I must request that you immediately remove your leg from my leg and, before I stand up, which always makes these situations worse, direct me to the bathroom."

"That bad, huh?"

"Yes. I didn't go all night last night. Get up!"

"All right, all right. The bathroom is immediately to the left by the stairs right off the entryway." He lifts his leg and releases me.

I roll away, immediately aware of how very naked I am and since I don't exactly have time to dress right now, I tug on the blanket that we've been covered up with. I start to walk, taking it with me, but after one step I realize that I've left Reese naked and uncovered. I rotate to find him shifting to a sitting position. And yes, indeed, he is one hundred percent as naked as I thought and it's a beautiful sight.

He arches a brow in my direction, mischief and understanding in his eyes. "I thought you had to pee?"

"I do."

Mischief lights his blue eyes, sprinkles of sunlight in their depths. "Then why are you standing there?"

"Because you're naked," I say, seeing no reason to deny the obvious. He *is* naked. And perhaps the most perfect male specimen I've ever seen up close and personal.

"If you *keep* standing there," he warns "I'm going to pull you back over here, make sure you're naked as well, and say good morning properly."

"Oh," I say. "No. That's not possible at this very moment." His phone starts to ring, and he snatches up his pants. "That's the second call," I say, dashing across the room as I hear him say, "Hello," into his phone.

I hurry past the couches and think about my clothes. I backtrack and scoop up my bra, dress, and shoes, though my panties appear to be missing. I have delayed my relief so long that I need to pee ten times worse than moments before. So much so that I have to walk cautiously, but quickly, toward said relief. I enter the hallway, and sure enough, there is an archway just to the left of the living room entryway. I dart through it and find the winding stairwell covered in the same beautiful mahogany hardwood as the rest of the house. To my left beside those stairs is a doorway. I pull it open, and sure enough, it's the bathroom.

Hurrying inside the small room that just has a toilet and a fancy white ceramic sink, I drop the blanket and do my business. Once I'm done, I walk to the sink, wash my hands, and look in the mirror, and good grief. My hair is standing on end. And, of course, day-old makeup minus lipstick is never flattering. I dare to open the medicine cabinet behind the mirror and find toothpaste, floss, and a toothbrush. I grab the toothpaste and use my finger and the floss to do a pretty good job on my mouth. There is no hairbrush to save the mess on my head and I'm not washing my face with hand soap.

I grab the white ceramic sink and try to process the fact that I'm naked in Reese's guest bathroom, the morning after having all kinds of wonderful sex with him. And I'm not really sorry and I don't think he is either. I am, however, confused. This isn't how I thought this would play out, and I don't really know what I feel right now. I should go. Or should I stay?

I decide clothing gives me options. I quickly dress, and I've just stepped into my shoes when I hear, "Cat," at the door.

Inhaling, I'm nervous all over again, which is silly. I've been naked with him. I wanted this as a one and done. I force myself to open the door, and I'm rewarded with another wonderful view. I find him shirtless, his pants from last night on but unzipped. His eyes are hot as they look me over.

"I liked you better in the blanket," he says, resting his arm on the doorframe above his head, all that springy, dark hair on his chest, hard to not track here and there and everywhere. "Even better without it."

"I liked you better without it, too," I dare. "That's why I took it."

He snags my waist and walks me to him. "Stop trying to make this an awkward morning after."

"I'm not."

He arches a brow.

I say, "Okay."

"Okay?"

I go back to my pre-bathroom thinking. "I don't know what we're doing."

"We'll figure it out. But we do have a slight situation. I called Royce Walker last night to ask for some help on this trial. He and his brother seem to think they found something. They're on their way here now."

"Oh," I say, because I'm brilliant like that. Real words that mean things come from my mouth.

"And," he adds, "we slept later than I thought. It's ten thirty. My co-counsels will be here at noon to work on the case." His cellphone rings in his pocket. "Give me just one minute, sweetheart." He kisses me, a quick, minty-fresh brush of his lips against mine that tells me he found the toothpaste too. "One minute," he says again as if it's a promise, digging his phone from his pocket, which pulls his pants down to a spot that is dangerously distracting. "Hello," he says into his phone, and then covers it with his hand to look at me. "Come to the kitchen. We'll make coffee." He doesn't wait for a reply, but rather turns around and says, "What's up?"

I don't follow him. I'm feeling too incredibly awkward again. I exit the bathroom and head toward the living room, grabbing my bag, purse, and computer and packing up. I've just made it to the front door when I hear, "Cat," and Reese snags my arm and turns me to face him. "What are you doing?"

"I'm leaving," I say, when, of course, we both knew that before this exchange.

"Without talking to me first?"

"It's awkward after all, and you have your trial and—"

"Help me with the trial. I know it's not the most exciting weekend, but spend it here, and help me catch a killer." He steps into me and slides a hand to my face. "I need you here. I want you here."

"You don't need me."

"I do. It's illogical, I know. We just met, but I do need you here." He backs me up until I'm pressed to the door. "I can't help what I have going on in my life right now. Be a part of it. You *are* a part of it. It's how we met. It's your job, too. Let's do our jobs together."

"Reese, I—"

"You're good at closing statements. I need to deliver a killer closing to the jury and, apparently, to you. Say yes. To helping with the trial and to finding out what this is between us. I need to know. Don't you?"

Somehow, this man, who I've called an asshole and wanted one and done, has turned everything around. He made me want and need him, and then said everything I wanted and needed to hear and didn't know I wanted and needed to hear it. "Yes and yes," I dare, because there simply isn't another option I can live with. "But I have to go home and shower and change. Preferably before the Walker clan gets here."

"That's any minute now."

"Oh God. I have to go." I turn toward the door and Reese opens it so I can exit, but then catches my arm and turns me back to him. "Don't run. I know you were burned. But I'm not him and I don't chase women, Cat, but I'll chase you." He strokes my cheek, and I can't breathe as he repeats, "I'll chase you." He releases me.

I turn away and start walking as his words ring in my head: *I'm not him.* The idea that my ex-asshole is controlling me right now stops me in my tracks. He is. He can't have that control. I turn back around and find Reese still standing in the doorway. I march right back to him, press my hand to that gorgeous chest of his, and kiss him. "I'm coming back. I want to. And I am good at closing statements, and you have to give a killer one. This isn't your opening. You can't be your client and win over the jury."

"What does that mean?"

"Arrogant, rich, and good looking, and you are those things." I rotate and start walking, with his soft, sexy laughter trailing after me. And I'm smiling. God. This man makes me smile. I reach the elevators, step inside the car, and sink back against the wall. This man is making me crazy, but I feel the most alive I have in forever. It's terrifyingly wonderful. And he's right. I have to know where it leads.

Chapter Sixteen

Cat

By the time I exit the elevator in Reese's apartment building, my smile hasn't disappeared. That is until I see the two big, intense men walking toward me that my departure was not fast enough for me to escape: Royce and Blake Walker of Walker Security. Both are the proverbial tall, dark, and deadly mix of attitude and good looks in jeans and Walker T-shirts. Both with long, dark hair tied at their napes. And both are in a direct collision course with little ole me. My only saving grace is Kara, Blake's wife, who is walking next to them, who I have met numerous times and find really likeable, tough, and yet sweet.

With no other option, I charge toward them and stop in front of them as they do me. "Hi there, Cat," Kara says, while both men have knowing smirks on their faces.

"I distinctly remember seeing you on camera in that dress yesterday," Royce says.

I scowl, stunned that he would point out my obvious overnight stay with Reese, considering he's usually the quiet, brooding Walker brother. "Why are you even noticing my dress?" I demand.

Blake laughs and Kara elbows him. "Sorry, Cat," she says. "Not even his wife can teach him manners."

"I noticed the dress," Royce says, scowling at her and then at me, "because my wife complained that she couldn't fit into it because she's too fat, when, of course, she's not fat. She's just pregnant. But I can't get her to see that."

In other words, he couldn't care less about my overnight. He's thinking out loud about his wife and not sure how to be there for her. "Just love her, Royce," I say as if he's really asked the question. "And from what I've seen, you're doing just fine." I pat his arm. "More than fine. I'll let you all get to Reese. I know he's eager for whatever you found for him." I don't wait for the knowing smirks that might follow. I start walking and exit to the street, the cool morning air going right up my dress to my naked crotch, which, of course, reminds me of Reese ripping my panties off me. Why was I even looking for them? I can't actually wear them again.

I smile and sidestep a group of passersby, with my mind back on Royce and how he dotes on Lauren, how all the Walker men are that way with their women. They are arrogant and sexy, but they love just as big as they make the art of walking into a room. I know that kind of love exists out there, maybe thanks to them. It's just not how my father was with my mother. He had his women. She let him. I can't be her. And maybe seeing those Walker men right now was more well-timed than it was poorly timed.

I'm reminded that real men love their fat, pregnant women. I laugh and dig out my phone and dial Lauren. She answers on the first ring. "Hey, you big, fat, pregnant woman," I say.

"That is not funny," she chides, and I can hear her scowl. "I might even unfriend you."

"You're not fat," I say, barely dodging two men who almost run me over and never even notice I'm there. "You are however, quite possibly losing your mind, though, if you think you're fat. I just ran into Royce and he told me you were saying you are."

"Royce has a big mouth. And I am fat. None of my clothes fit me."

"You're *pregnant*. And tiny."

"I carry it all in my hips, not my belly. Some women are all in their cute baby belly, but no. Not me. All ass and hips. I want a cute baby belly. And how did you run into Royce? He was going to— Reese. Cat. Were you—"

"Yes. He apparently took your challenge and mine, and won."

She laughs. "As I knew he would. He has a lot of the Walker men traits about him. He sees. He wants. He goes after that target."

"Hold on," I say, running across a street before the light turns. "Okay. Sorry. I'm hurrying home. I need a shower. He's a good guy right, Lauren?"

"A very good guy. And you really like him, or you wouldn't be on the phone with me."

"He's never been married."

"Neither have you."

"He's never been engaged," I counter. "Or...I don't think he has. Why not? He's good looking and successful."

"Did you ask him?"

"Yes. He said he's a workaholic."

"He's in his thirties, probably a self-made millionaire or at least on his way there, and one of the top defense attorneys in the country. You and I both know what that takes." Her line beeps. "Hold on." The line clicks over and a few seconds pass. "I need to go," she says when she comes back. "I have a female client divorcing her abusive husband. It's a nightmare for her more than me. I want to talk about the trial. I'll call you back later tonight."

She hangs up, and I enter my apartment building to find my second oldest brother, Gabe, at the desk. The security guard says something to him and he turns to find me standing there. And, as usual, he's looking his blond, preppy man-self, in his weekend jeans paired with his favorite Harvard shirt that has a collar, of course.

"Why are you wearing the dress you wore in court yesterday?" he asks.

"How do you even know I wore this yesterday?"

"You were on camera."

"I repeat. How do you even know what I was wearing yesterday?"

"You're my sister."

"You've made my point," I say.

"That I'm not stupid? Thank you. Your hair is all over the place and so is your makeup. Who is he?"

"Why are you here?"

He reaches for the cups on the security desk. "I came to have coffee with my little sister."

I accept the cup and give him a curious look. "What are you up to?"

He laughs. "Stop already. I just came to check on you. And—"

"Cat!"

I rotate before he fills in that blank to find a petite and pretty brunette, who is about five feet tall and wearing five-inch heels and a black pantsuit, hurrying my way. And officially, this morning just keeps getting better. Not really. "Who is that?" my brother asks.

"My agent," I say a few beats before Liz stops in front of me.

"What are you doing here?" I ask her, and then hold up a hand. "Never mind. I know what you're doing here. No. End of conversation."

Her brow furrows. "Why are you wearing—"

"Do not finish that sentence," I warn her. "I don't need to hear that question again."

"Right," she says. "Let's talk upstairs, so you can fix yourself. You're a mess."

I throw my hands in the air. "Of course I am. Let's go."

I start walking, and my brother and my agent are quick to keep pace while I sip my coffee, which is actually perfect. "Thank you," I say, glancing at my brother as I punch the elevator button.

"You're welcome, little sis."

"This is your brother?" Liz asks, giving him a once-over with a little too much interest. Granted, he's good looking, but she's my agent and he's my brother.

"Yes," Gabe answers for me. "I'm the older brother."

"Age?" Liz asks.

"Thirty-six."

"Married?" she brazenly asks.

The elevator opens and I roll my eyes and enter, while the two of them go to opposite walls but keep talking. "Never married," Gabe says.

"Why?" Liz asks, as if replaying my conversation with Lauren about Reese. "What's wrong with you?"

I watch the interaction, which has forgotten me and with each floor turns more and more direct, until finally I can't take it anymore. I glance at Liz, who is all red-cheeked, and say, "Seriously? You're flirting with my brother in front of me."

"I am not," she says indignantly.

"You're not?" Gabe asks. "That's too bad."

The elevator doors open and I exit the car and just leave them both there. Once I'm at my door, I enter my apartment and leave it open. Kicking off my shoes in the entrance, I really want to just go shower, but I walk to the kitchen instead. After setting my bags on a red leather barstool, I walk to the microwave and stick my coffee inside. By the time it's out, the two of them are standing on opposite sides of the island looking at me.

"Cat," Liz begins.

"No," I say. "I decline the book deal."

"Why are you declining a book deal?" Gabe asks. "You hit the *Times* with your last book."

"How do you even know that?"

"Of course I knew that," he says.

"You did not," I accuse.

"I did too," he insists.

"You did?"

"Yes," Gabe says. "I'm not the ass you are apparently remembering me to be."

"You hate that I left my legal career."

"I'm over it. Your column is damn good, and so was the book. Why are you turning down another deal?"

"Wait," Liz says, glancing at Gabe. "Did you congratulate her when she hit the *Times*?"

"No, but—"

"And now we know why you're single," she says. "Next time send her flowers and chocolate. And no. I was not flirting with you." She refocuses on me. "Back to his question. Why?"

"No," I repeat.

"Why?" Gabe presses.

"Yes," Liz says. "Why?"

"Dan is an ass," I say. "He also represents everything I hate about the system. I'm not writing a book with him."

My cellphone rings, and I'm quick to pull it from my purse in hopes that I can just end this meet-and-greet in the kitchen. I glance at Reese's number and answer, "Hey."

"Did you walk home?"

"Yes."

"It's chilly out and I have your panties. You must have felt that."

I laugh and cut my gaze as inquiring eyes suddenly study me more intensely. "I survived."

"Come back and get them."

"They aren't exactly usable at this point. But I'll be about an hour. My brother and my agent showed up at my house."

"Take the book deal, Cat," he says, turning serious on me.

"I can't have this conversation with you right now."

"Just don't decline it officially until we talk. Promise."

"No."

"Cat—"

"No."

"Right," he says. "We'll talk about this later, naked. But soon. Get back here or I'll come after you." He hangs up.

I set my phone down and look between Liz and Gabe. "You both need to leave. I have someplace to be."

Gabe cuts his stare and looks frustrated, like he wants to say something but thinks better of it. "I'll see you later," he says, heading out of the room.

I glance at Liz. "I'm fine. Go see him off. I'll make coffee. I know where everything is."

"No to the book deal," I say, trying to get her to leave, too.

"Okay. I'll make a cup of coffee and stay awhile."

I sigh and follow Gabe to the exit to find him waiting on me with the door cracked open, his expression stern. "Why are you really here?"

"How good is Reese Summer?"

"He's good. Really good. Why?"

"The best?"

"Yes. The best."

"A killer?"

"In courtroom terms, yes. Why? Are you thinking of contracting him?"

"It's complicated and you have company." He turns and leaves, and I have this urge to chase after him and demand answers, when I'm not sure why, but he's right. I have company.

Frowning, I walk back into the kitchen and find Liz leaning on the counter by the pot, sipping from a cup. "We can set rules and guidelines for the book. You are in charge. You control the content, title, and cover. It's insanity to walk away from this." She sets her cup down and walks to the island, where she sets her phone down. "Are you fucking Reese Summer?" She taps her phone, and I go all hot and cold inside.

"What?"

"Look at the photo," she instructs.

I walk to the counter and stare down at a photo of me with Reese at the hotel last night, his hand on my arm. His body very close to mine. "How did you get that?"

"From your editor, who got it from Dan."

"That bastard," I say. "I had a fight with Reese last night just as I did with Dan. I tried to leave and Reese wasn't done with the fight."

"Are you fucking him?"

Damn it, she isn't giving up. "I plead the Fifth."

"Cat," she breathes out. "Why didn't you tell me?"

"It didn't happen until last night."

"The publisher, the person above your editors, wants to see me Monday, but I can already hear her now." She lowers her voice. "This situation creates a wave of tabloid-like gossip that doesn't do justice to true crime." She returns to her normal voice. "I hope that man is worth your career. I'll let you know what happens."

She heads to the door, and I let her go. I don't move, but I listen as the door opens and closes. I'd already turned down the book deal. I don't know why I feel so bad right now.

Chapter Seventeen

Cat

I spend the short time I'm in the shower fretting over Liz's claim that I've ruined my career. By the time I'm out and drying off, I'm starting to get over it. Just as I've dressed in a pair of black jeans, a thin, long-sleeved teal sweater and boots, my phone buzzes with a text on the bathroom sink. I grab it and sit down on the vanity chair to find a message from Reese: *Bring clothes. Stay the weekend. In the name of justice and all that is good and right about our court system.*

"Justice and all that is good and right about our court system," I laughingly murmur, and after a moment of considering my reply, I text back: *What if we hate each other today? Then the whole weekend thing could get awkward.*

His reply is quick and all man: *We'll fuck until we get over it. Doesn't sound awkward to me.*

He's right, I think. We will.

That's not awkward.

Which means that maybe it's okay if we hate each other and make that happen. Or even better, just don't hate each other at all and do it anyway. I think I'll pack a bag and just consider the options. I don't have to stay. I do so quickly, feeling good about my decisions as I apply my makeup, but as I dry my hair, Liz's words quite unfortunately replay in my mind. *Is he worth ruining your career?* Obviously, I'm not as over her saying that after all. No, I'm not, but by the time I've finished with my flat iron, I know why. Liz is doing exactly what my father did to me every time he and I disagreed. And I did exactly what I did with my father: *I doubted myself.*

I swore I was done with that kind of thinking, yet I get questioned about Reese, and I've reverted back to old habits and I'm second-guessing myself. I walk to my closet in the back of my bathroom, and in between beating myself up and replaying Liz's words, I pack my rolling computer bag with some personal items and a change of clothes, then stuff my computer inside. Now I can stay or go, and it won't look like I planned the opposite of either. I grab my purse, and in about two minutes, I'm inside the elevator and really fuming at myself, not Liz. I let her do that to me. That's on me.

I pull my phone from my purse, planning to call her once I'm street level. It beeps with a text from Reese. *I sent a car for you. He's there when you're ready.*

I frown and text him back: *How do you know where I live?*

He replies with: *Arrogant, sexy assholes know all.*

He asked Lauren, who is going to get her pregnant booty whipped, and not by her husband. I glance at the text message and type: *I said arrogant, good-looking asshole.*

He replies: *I like my version better.*

I laugh. Again. That matters. I don't usually laugh much. And I kind of like it. And I like this man. But stay the weekend? Am I really going to stay with him? God. I packed a bag. I think I am. I exit the elevator, and sure enough, there is a car waiting for me. Once I'm settled into the back seat, I dial Liz, who doesn't answer. I leave a message. "Call me."

I'm bothered by her not taking my call. Really bothered by it, and by the time I'm inside Reese's apartment building and clearing my entry with the security desk, she still hasn't called back. I dial her again on my way to the elevator with the same results. I try once more as I exit the elevator to Reese's floor and decide to just set aside my Liz issues. It's time to go help find real justice for an innocent woman and child. And this trial, and Dan, haven't done that.

I'm just arriving at the door when it opens, and he appears, and boy, does he make an impression. In ripped jeans and a simple black T-shirt that is not simple on him, he looks like sex, sin, and just what I need in my life, aside from a real purpose. Right now, that purpose is to help him with this case.

"Hey," he says as I stop in front of him.

"Hey," I reply, deciding he always smells wonderfully masculine. "Is your team here?"

"Yes," he says, but he doesn't back up to let me inside. His hand slides under my hair at my neck and he tilts my face to his. "But before we join them..." He kisses me, this slow, seductive, drugging kiss that has me softening against him before he pulls back and looks at me. "What the hell are you doing to me, woman?"

"Hopefully encouraging you to do that again."

"What happened with your agent?" he asks, his lips still a breath from mine.

"You really know how to ruin the mood," I say, pushing against his chest with hardly any movement on his behalf. He's still holding me. His mouth is still close to my mouth. "That's not important."

"We both know it is."

"It's not. Let's go inside and do something that is."

"Right. We'll have that naked conversation when we're alone." He kisses me fast and hard before releasing me. "Come on." He takes my bag and gives me a pointed look. "Kind of small."

"Big enough," I say, breezing past him and into the hallway before turning to wait on him. "But I need to get my computer out of it so that I won't be dragging other things out with your crew."

He shuts the door and sets my bag against the wall. "We certainly wouldn't want your clothing all over the house, now would we? For instance, hanging off a lampshade."

I'm already squatting by my bag, unzipping it, and my gaze jerks upward to his. "That's where my, ah, garment was at?"

"Yes," he says, his eyes alight with mischief and amusement. "That is exactly where it was at."

I grab my MacBook and zip up my bag before standing back up, at which time I decide to find out how much trouble awaits me in the other room. "Has the Walker clan left the premises?"

"Yes," he says, his hands settling on his hips. "They came in like a hurricane, asked a ton of questions, and then left."

"Didn't you say they had a lead?"

"Yeah. They think the wife did it."

My brow furrows. "The wife? You mean the victim's boyfriend had a wife?"

"My *client's* wife."

"Oh. Wow. Do you think she did it?"

"They have me leaning that way, but what I think doesn't matter. What I prove or what she admits does."

"All you need is reasonable doubt."

"I have reasonable doubt. You know that isn't enough in these cases."

"It's supposed to be," I say.

"Would have, could have, should have," he says, motioning me toward the archway that leads to the kitchen and the parts of the house I have yet to see.

We walk through that archway and pass the kitchen to enter the room on the other side of the stairwell, which is not so unlike the living area. The room is rectangular, wrapped in windows, with the same mahogany hardwood, only in this case there is a thick gray pile carpet covering most of the sitting area. On top of it is an L-shaped gray sectional with several low cushioned chairs. Reese's co-counsels are each on the floor, on opposite sides of the gray marble rectangular coffee table, their computers in front of them. "Cat," Reese says, his hand at my lower back, "meet Elsa and Richard."

"Hi," I say. "How's it going?"

Elsa and Richard give me steady, unreadable stares. "Hi," they say in near unison.

"I'm Richard, not Elsa," Richard says, with a completely straight face. And it is a handsome face, with sharp features, hard, and framed by longish, wavy brown hair.

Elsa, on the other hand, is pretty, blonde, with a heart-shaped face and about ten years older than me. With manners, too, it seems, as she says, "Nice to meet you, Cat."

"You look like Elsa," Richard comments.

Elsa snorts. "If only I were so young, but I'm not, so thank you, Richard. I'll take that comparison." She looks at me. "Come sit. I've read your column. I'm a fan."

"Agreed," Richard states, his tone dry and unexcited, but I've had the impression from his courtroom presence that this is his normal.

"Thanks to both of you," I say, chatting with them just a short bit about nothing much.

Reese breaks up the nothing chit chat by having me sign a confidentiality and consulting agreement before paying me one dollar for my services. "We'll work out compensation later," he promises.

I smile and he smiles, because we both know what I want, and it's not money. It's him, naked, and in all kinds of ways. That shared moment doesn't pass without notice but I don't really care. At this point, it's over, and we all get to work. I'm settled on the floor at the end of the coffee table and Reese moves to stand at the window with his back to us while he stares out over the city, most likely seeing nothing but what's in his head. "I still think it was the boyfriend," Elsa says, as I'm reading through the Walker notes.

"It was the wife," Richard states, almost matter-of-factly.

Neither myself nor Reese comment as they proceed to debate their points of view. I half listen, reading through all the Walker notes, which include some phone calls between the wife and the victim, as well as a few emails about meetups. "There's nothing that proves the wife is the killer," I say. "But I find the meetings curious. Reese, does your client know about those meetings?"

Reese turns to face us. "Good question," he says, walking to a chair right by me and sitting down. "He's not answering his phone."

"The boyfriend did it anyway," Elsa interjects. "We have police reports of a violent history. Fights. Domestic disturbances."

"None with the victim," Richard points out. "And all years ago, when he was a punk kid."

"In the absence of evidence," I say, "we have to make the suspects believe we have it."

"Exactly," Reese says. "Let's get a list of questions and cover every possible way they might be answered."

"We can't predict where the questions will lead," I say. "But we can come up with scenarios."

"The challenge," he says, "is that I don't want the jury to simmer on the heels of a hot testimony that helps us. I need to get a closing ready that I can tweak slightly based on courtroom action, and go in for the kill fast and hard."

We all agree, and for the next two hours, we work on prep for the wife. Reese is focused on his trial, not on me, but when our eyes collide, I feel it in every inch of my body. And I like watching him with his team, the way he interacts with them, the fierceness of his beliefs in each communication. We've all just filled room service cups with coffee from the pot Reese ordered when Liz calls my cellphone I have sitting on the coffee table. I inhale on the memory of her words, and pick up my phone and myself from the floor. Reese, who has been reading through his notes, looks up, and I look away before he reads something in me I don't want him to read.

Crossing the room, I feel Reese watching me, curious, perhaps too intuitive about my present mood, which is tense and fired up. I pass the stairwell and answer the call. "Just a minute," I say, even as I exit to the hallway and cross through to the living room, where

I will have privacy. "Are you there?" I ask, stepping to the window I'd stood at with Reese last night.

"Yes," Liz says. "I'm here. I saw you called. I had a meeting this afternoon."

It feels like a fake excuse, and that just drives me to get right to the point. "Dan stands for everything I don't like about the legal system," I say. "I'm not writing a book with him, and nothing you say to me is going to change that."

"The damage is already done," she replies. "The publisher is not happy. But I have to ask, because I have to explain this when asked. How is Dan a problem for you, but you'll sleep with the guy defending a killer?"

"What? Did you really just say that to me? Have you read my columns at all? There is no proof that the defendant is guilty. You don't convict an innocent man just to please the public." I remember Reese's courtroom statement. "Or to get a book deal. You know what, Liz? I think you need to represent Dan, not me."

"What? No. I'm just being frank."

"I'm glad you are. It tells me that we don't match up. And I've learned that when I expect those kinds of relationships to improve, they don't. They become poison. I'm sorry." I hang up, and the reality of what I just did hits me hard and fast. I fired my agent. Oh God. I *fired* my agent. That's a big deal.

I press my hands on the rail around the window and replay the conversation. My mind races so fast I don't even hear Reese approach. Suddenly, he's behind me, his hand on my belly, his body cradling mine. My body warms everywhere he touches and everywhere I instinctively want to be touched by this man. "How long have you been there?"

"I heard the call," he says. "All the important parts."

I face him, leaning on the rail around the window. "You're nosy."

"Concerned, and you were talking louder than you realized."

"Oh. I was?"

"Yes. You were. And back to me being concerned."

"No. Yes. I mean, firing Liz was the right choice. She has different priorities than I do."

"Are you sure? Or have you made this personal?"

I think about her reprimanding my brother over ignoring my *New York Times* achievement. "I think she cares about my career, but only when it pays her well. And I get that, too. She needs to get paid. I'm just not willing to get her paid doing what she wants me to do. It's just one of those decisions that you make, and then you get drunk on ice cream and chocolate afterward and move on."

"Okay. Then we'll have chocolate and ice cream for dinner. But you should write the book, just do it your way. It'll sell."

And just that easily, he becomes the first man in my life that has told me to do something my way, not his. Especially when it might affect him, and this will. I'd be writing about him to a rather large extent. "Maybe," I say. "I'll think about it. Right now, let's go win your trial."

"You're good in there, Cat. Really damn good."

And he gives compliments. I do like this man. "Thank you."

He cups my face. "And really damn good with me."

"Yeah?"

"Yeah."

"I think you might be good with me, too."

"Think?"

"That's all you're getting right now."

"Guarded. Understood. Challenge, once again, accepted." He takes my hand, and we start walking across the room. Mr. Arrogant Asshole is *holding my hand*. And I have the realization that no one was holding my hand a few days ago. In fact, had they tried, I would have shoved that nonsense aside. Only, it's not nonsense with Reese, and really, it's incredible how life changes in a blink of an eye. One minute, you have an agent. The next, you don't. One minute, you call a man you just met Mr. Arrogant Asshole, and the next, he's something so much more.

Everything changes, and that thought is what has me trying to pull my hand away from Reese's. But I can't. He's holding on too tight.

Chapter Eighteen

Reese

It's nearly eight when I walk my team to the door, and finally I have Cat to myself, in my house, and soon, in my bed. I return to the den to find her still on the floor beside the coffee table, pecking away at her computer. "You have to be tired, Cat," I say, crossing to join her.

She glances up at me. "Not yet. I get wired when I work."

"And when you drink most of a pot of coffee?"

"The pizza made me do it. It was heavy."

I lie down on my side on the rug next to her, fully intending to have her next to me in the near, anytime now, future. "What are you working so feverishly on?"

"I'm actually writing my column that is due tomorrow night."

"You could work on it tomorrow. Do it over morning coffee."

"I know, but—"

"You have a plan and you have to make it happen."

She twists around to face me, her green eyes lighting. "Since you mention it, I do. My opening statement starts with: *Who killed Jennifer and her unborn child?* I never name names, but I present investigative angles. I can't reach the jury. That's up to you, but I can affect public perception. Get them thinking about options. Get them involved beyond convicting an innocent man. Now, here is why I think this helps you. Or I hope it does. I'm thinking that the real killer gets news of my column and is on edge. That means nervous on the stand. What do you think?"

"It's brilliant. You're brilliant. I'm lucky to have your help." I lower my voice. "I want to feel you next to me, Cat. *Come here.*"

"I—Don't look at me like that, or say my name like that either, until I finish my work." She tries to turn back to her computer, but I don't let her.

I snag her arm and pull her down next to me, aligning our bodies, my hand sliding under her sweater to rest on soft, warm skin. "I need to work," she says. "I think this will be good for you."

"*You're* good for me," I say. "Must be why I keep feeling like I need you."

"You keep saying that."

"Yes. I do. Maybe one day you'll believe me."

"You just met me."

"You keep saying that, too. Soon it won't be true." I nuzzle her neck. "You always smell like fresh flowers in a city of smog and crime." I brush hair from her face. "I haven't smelled anything but that smog in a long time, Cat. And I didn't realize until I met you how much I needed something else."

Her hand settles on my shoulder. "You do know that I'm the one who called you an asshole, right?"

"Called? Or Call?"

She laughs, and it's that sexy, sweet sound I feel like a rush of adrenaline. It makes me hot and hard, and my mouth slants over hers, tongue pressing past her lips, and the heady taste of her, all sweet honey, coffee, and temptation, fills my senses. I deepen the kiss, drinking her in like a drug I cannot get enough of. *I can't get enough of her.*

She moans and slides her hand under my shirt. That sound, the touch of her hand on my skin, pushes me to the edge. A raw, low growl escapes my throat. I want her naked. I want to be inside her. For twelve fucking hours, I've wanted to be inside her, but not here and like this. She tangles her fingers into my hair and when her hand presses to my zipper, I catch it. "As much as I want your hand on my body, not here. Not yet." I stand up and pull her with me. "Upstairs." I scoop her up and start to carry her across the room.

"You don't have to carry me."

"And you don't have to run," I say starting up the stairs.

She doesn't come back with one of her witty replies. She doesn't say anything at all, which tells me I've hit about ten nails on the head. I walk us into my bedroom, but I don't turn on the light. My bed is on the wall immediately to the right, but I continue on to the foot of the bed and set her down, not facing it, but rather the view: A room that is all glass, the night sky alight with stars, and beneath us the city that never sleeps, aglow in a rainbow of colors.

She turns to me. "I'm not running."

"Prove it."

She studies me for several beats and then takes a step backward, just enough to allow her to start undressing, and I let her. I watch her as she does. I drink in every moment. Every slash of skin. The first pucker of her pink nipples. The curve of her breasts. Her hips. The V of neatly trimmed hair between her legs. And when she's done, she closes the space between us and stands in front of me. "Do I look like I'm running?"

I don't immediately touch her. I know now what she's doing. I see it now. "I effectively manipulate people for a living." I pull my shirt off and toss it and then pull her to me, molding her close. "And I know when I'm being manipulated."

"I have no idea what you mean."

"Yes, you do. Sex is your wall, isn't it, Cat? I can fuck you, but I can't have you."

Her hand rests on my chest, her gaze on her hand before it lifts to me. "Yes. I set limits for myself."

"And for those with you."

"Yes."

I tangle my fingers in her hair. "How's that working for you with me?"

"It's not. Because you're an asshole that won't let me finish my work."

I laugh, but it fades into something darker, far more possessive than I've ever known myself to feel with a woman. "You're in my bedroom, Cat," I say. "That is about more than fucking, but right now, fucking is exactly what we're going to do."

I rotate her and press her against the tall post of my heavy wooden bed. "Don't move," I order, stepping back from her to undress. She doesn't resist the command. She relaxes into the post, her hands at either side of it, her breasts thrust high, nipples higher. She's comfortable naked. She feels in control, like she can grab a man by the balls and twist, and they will be just fine as long as they get off. Not me. That's not how this plays out. She just doesn't know it yet.

I toss my boots and remove the condom from my pocket before I strip down. I'm about to open the package when she says, "You don't need that. I'm on the pill. And if we give each other something we can sue each other. We're attorneys and I'm still licensed, just so you know."

If she means to pull me out of my head and hers, and turn this into just a fuck, she fails.

In a blink, I'm there in front of her, my hands on the post above her in two seconds flat. "I thought *he* was two years ago," I say, and I don't even try to soften anything about my tone. I don't like games. I like facts.

"He was," she says. "There was someone else. A fuck buddy that wanted to be more."

Fuck buddy usually works for me. It's all that works for me but not this time. Not with Cat. I pull her to me, my hand under her hair, at her neck, my mouth a breath from a kiss I'm not ready to take. "I want more," I say. "And I am not your fuck buddy, and if you don't know that yet, you will." I don't give her time to reply. My mouth slants over hers, my tongue pressing past her lips, stroking and stroking again in what is instantly a deep, passionate kiss. She moans and pushes against me, and I swear the sound of her moan is like a renewed challenge. Submission that isn't submission.

But as if she's replying to that very thought, her arms wrap around me again, and she is small and delicate yet somehow bold at the same time. The touch of her, the taste of her, steals my anger and feeds my hunger for this woman, hunger that I feel in her as well. One minute, I'm kissing her and she's kissing me. The next, we are on the bed, her tight little nipples in my mouth, my cock buried deep inside her, and I am thrusting into her. I let myself be lost in her, in this, when I never lose myself. But I do in Cat; there is no time. No ending. There is just us, kissing, fucking, and she is just as fierce, just as hungry.

"Reese," she whispers, and my name is exactly the right thing for her to say. It tells me she's present. She's with me, not some nameless fuck buddy, and I pull my mouth from hers, and say just that.

"I am not your fuck buddy."

"Okay," she says, "but you're still an asshole."

I take that asshole comment as a wall she still needs, and answer by making damn sure she feels me the way I feel her. I mold her close, my mouth closing down on hers, tongue stroking her tongue. This isn't nameless sex. This is us. Me. Her.

She arches into me, and I wrap her leg with mine, holding her, allowing her no chance to hold back. I'm different with Cat. I feel it. I don't understand it, but I don't care. I'm in this, I want this. I want her and I cup her perfect little ass and angle her into me, thrusting as I do. She gasps, arching upward, her fingernails digging into my shoulders, her sex clenching around me, and it drives me wild. I press deeper inside her, and suddenly her body is clenched around me, pulling me into that same sweet spot she's drowning in, and I am shuddering with release. Everything goes black, but I can smell that sweet floral scent and feel her body next to mine. Time stands still and I come back to the present with the wet, warm feeling of me buried inside her, with no condom between us.

I reach behind us and grab a tissue, which I offer her. "Thank you," she says, and when I would pull her close again, she rolls away. "I need the bathroom." Which happens to be on her side of the bed, and she hurries in that direction. Running.

My natural instinct is to pursue her, and I'm up in an instant, rounding the bed with just that intention, but I stop for my pants, and the control they offer. I reach for them and my gaze catches on the condom I've apparently dropped on the floor, so I snatch it up. I never go condom-less, but I did with Cat. In the blink of an eye. This woman has me by the balls, and that should be a problem, but it's not, part of the problem is that she doesn't know it. The condom thing was just her way of deflating the emotional context of what just happened and making it about sex again. I shove the condom into my pocket and note the closed bathroom door. That's a clear message, and I give her space.

What she does next tells me everything.

Chapter Nineteen

Cat

Naked.

Leaning against the door of Reese's fancy bathroom, gray and white checked tile beneath my feet, I am naked in every possible way. What is this man doing to me? What is this crazy, wild emotion in my belly and in my chest? I don't remember feeling this with Mitch, the little cheating bitch. Not even before he was the little cheating bitch, though I suspect he was always that, I just didn't know it. I don't remember feeling this with anyone I've ever met. Really, truly, how does an asshole that cut in line become this, whatever this is?

And he thinks I'm running. I'm not running. I'm protecting myself. I'm making sure I don't make the same mistake twice. That's smart. That's not scared, which is what the word "running" implies. *Scared.* He called me scared. My father calls me scared anytime I do something that doesn't fit his agenda. Suddenly I'm angry, and I shove aside the whole feeling naked thing. I decide I need to draw lines with Reese. I need to tell him exactly what I think, despite the fact that at this moment, I have no clue what that is. I do, however, have complete confidence that it will come to me, and then out of my mouth it will flow. To him. Probably loudly.

I yank open the door, and my moment of confrontation is quite anticlimactic, considering the fact that I don't actually have a visual of Reese. He's definitely not on top of his massive four-poster bed, which isn't all bad, since that would likely distract me. I walk out into the room and snatch up his shirt because I'm not going anywhere. I'm not running. But maybe he is, since he's not here. I don't like that thought, but I stay the course. I pull his shirt over my head and let it fall to my knees. That's when my gaze lifts right and

I realize that Reese is sitting with his back to me, in a giant oversized chair in front of the wall of windows.

I inhale, and all those words I was certain I'd have at the right moment, I don't have. At all. What I have is honesty that just decides to smack me right in the face. I did run when I darted to the bathroom. In doing so, I lost the chance to read him in the aftermath of that steamy encounter. I regret that. I don't like regrets. I have too many of those, which finally led me to where I am now. To him. I still don't know what I am going to say to him, but I decide I'll know when I look into his eyes. One of the things I love about being with this man is how easy conversation is with him. How straightforward he is with me. How comfortable I am with him. It's my past that is uncomfortable for us both.

I round the giant, oversized chair and join him, sitting down next to him, but I don't touch him. I am so hypertensive with this man, though, that I have this sensation of touching. I can feel him everywhere, from my head to my toes, inside and out. I can almost taste him. Seconds tick by, and we both stare ahead, the connection we have shared from the moment we met expanding, intensifying, and then, proving how in tune I am with this man, at the same moment, we turn to look at each other. And in that first connected moment, he steals my breath and ravishes my resistance. He's not overbearing or brutally alpha, like many of the men in my life have been. He doesn't have to be those things. There is an inner strength about him, and a natural charm that allows him to own everyone around him. The way he *owns* me right now.

"You didn't run," he says softly.

"Actually, I did," I say, giving him a small smile. "Right into the bathroom."

"Yes," he says, caressing my cheek. "But you're still here. That's what matters."

I catch his hand. "Do you know why I called you an asshole?"

"Tell me."

"Because then I didn't have to be surprised when you turned out to be an asshole."

"Guilty until proven innocent?"

"Yes, actually. I know. I'm a hypocrite, but it's been working for me."

"It doesn't work for us, Cat."

"Then I guess it doesn't work for me."

His eyes warm and his arm wraps around my shoulders. "Come here," he says. Inching me closer.

I let him. I want to be closer to this man, so I snuggle into the shelter of his big, warm body. And maybe that idea is what shakes me more than anything with Reese. That he feels like a safe place, when I've spent so much time making sure I'm my own safe place. For right now, he is, though, and I decide to enjoy it.

For at least a full minute, we sit there in silence, staring out at the city, the quiet between us comfortable, and somehow a test that says this, whatever this is between us, is right, not wrong. "The view is incredible," I murmur, snuggling closer to him. "There's something about the angle. It's like we're floating and no one can touch us."

"This view is why I bought this place and why I haven't left this building. Well, this view, and that bar downstairs. It's the view that helps me come up with answers to ten thousand questions."

"What questions are you asking now?"

"Who was he?" he asks, and I don't have to ask for clarification. He's not talking about his trial, as I'd expected. He's talking about me, and my past, and the history that I've forced between us.

"No one," I say, but I know he wants more than that, and at this point, he deserves it. I settle and add, "His name is Mitch Welk."

He's silent several beats, in which I suspect I haven't given him the answer he wanted. "Reese—"

"I know Mitch, Cat," he surprises me by saying.

I twist around to face him. "What? How? Are you friends with him?"

"Relax, sweetheart." He pulls my leg across his. "I went to school with him. I've run into him a few times since, but he was a dick in school and apparently still is."

"He is what he is."

"No trash talking?"

"Not my style," I say.

"Good. It's not mine either. For the record, him being a dick is a statement of fact that I could back up with evidence but I don't have to. You know." He moves on. "How did you meet him?"

"A party at my father's offices. His firm partners with my father's on occasion."

"Did you love him?"

"If I did, I can honestly say that I don't remember it now. And I don't think you forget love."

"What about the fuck buddy?"

"Did I love him? No. Who was he? Lance Parish. A professional sculptor, and where Mitch was a shark, Lance was a goldfish."

"How long did your sculptor stay your fuck buddy?"

"He wasn't *my* sculptor, and six months. It was sex. I told you that. He got the job done."

"That is *not* the way a man wants his bedroom skills to be remembered."

"You have nothing to worry about, and you know it."

"I get the job done."

"Yes." I laugh, stroking his jaw. "You do get the job done, and for the record, I'm avoiding a joke with a certain nickname right now, despite the opening you're giving me. Because I know you hate it." I dive past the joke and turn the topic. "There has to have been some woman in your life."

"In my early career, there was someone. But to her, my work was king, and that left no room for her."

"Was she right?"

"Yes."

"Did you love her?"

"If I had loved her, maybe my work wouldn't have been number one. If she had loved me, maybe my work would have been more important to her, and less important to me. She wanted more. I didn't understand her version of more."

"And since her?"

"I don't bring women to my apartment. I don't take them into my bed. I don't share this view. I don't talk about my work or my life. I don't fuck without a condom." His hand slides to my face. "I don't just want more. This *is more* to me, and I want to know where that leads. If you don't—"

"I do," I whisper. "But please don't turn out to be an asshole."

His eyes light with mischief, a hint of starlight in the depths of his blue eyes. "Since you said *please*." His cellphone rings. "What do you think the odds are that this is my client actually calling me the fuck back?" he asks, pulling his phone from his pocket to glance at the screen and then me. "Royce. Let's hope he has some good news." He answers the call. "What do you have for me?"

He listens a minute, his leg tensing under my palm and calf that has landed on top of it. "When?" he bites out, followed by a pause, in which more bad news must follow, since his next reply is "Fuck," followed by "*Fuck.*" He stands up, pressing two fingers to his temple to once again ask, "When?"

Feeding off his energy, I stand up, listening to the rest of the short exchange, with little understanding, on pins and needles, waiting to hear what has happened. Finally, Reese ends the call and looks at me. "Nelson Ward decided to leave the city by way of private jet."

"Oh my God. You don't leave on a plane while on trial for murder. What are his restrictions?"

"He had a liberal travel agreement compliments of me," he says, "but it did not include traveling during the trial."

"What does your gut say? Is he running?"

"He hasn't returned any of my calls all day. He has to be running." He shoves fingers through his dark hair. "Holy hell, Cat. I would not have defended him if I believed he was guilty."

"I know that. Everyone who knows you knows that. Maybe he's just taking a quick overnight flight and returning tomorrow."

"Or he's running."

"He could be," I concede. "But that could be about fear, not guilt. This is scary stuff he's facing. How did Royce find out?"

"Walker Security oversees a huge portion of the airport security now. He got a flag. And he's also got a private plane I can use to follow the asshole when we figure out where he went."

"I know you want to talk to him for about ten different reasons, but if you follow him, you might look complicit."

"That won't happen. If necessary, Royce's team will take him into custody and I'll arrange for him to be taken into police custody. Unfortunately, it's too late in this trial for the judge to allow me to get the hell off this ship." His hands come down on my arms. "I want you to come with me, but I won't put you in the sights of a man who might be a killer. Stay here at my place. Be here, in my bed, when I get back."

"I'm in your bed for you and with you, not without you. Not yet." I push to my toes and kiss him. "I'll come back when you get back."

"I'm not going to win this argument in the ten minutes I have before I have to leave, am I?"

"Not when you have to pack and leave."

His phone pings with a text. "As if making your point," he says, pulling his phone from his pocket and reading the message. "Royce is five minutes out, per his wife." He slides his cell back into his jeans and kisses me. "I need to get ready, but know this, woman. I am going to come and get you when I get back." He turns and starts walking away.

"You need to pack an overnight," I call after him.

He pokes his head back into the room. "Can you grab me a razor and a new shirt?"

"Yes. Of course."

"Thanks, sweetheart." He winks and disappears into the hallway, and I'm left in his room with his trust.

It matters.

And every single time he calls me "sweetheart," I feel it with a flutter of my belly. I'm like a silly schoolgirl, and I was never a silly schoolgirl. I'm not sure what that says about me with him, but I'll analyze it later. I change out of Reese's shirt, put my clothes and shoes on, and then refocus on Reese's overnight bag, which needs more than a shirt and a razor inside. I dart into action and cross to what I assume to be the closet. Flipping on the light, I find an incredible, wonderful closet fit for a hundred pairs of high heels with a few modifications, like actually buying that many heels. It's all gray wood with a center dresser and rows of clothes framing it, with drawers and shelves stacked between rails.

Once I've spied a small leather travel bag, I snag it and head to the bathroom. I pack the razor first, a few random toiletries, and the cologne that smells the most like him today. I return to the closet, opening random drawers until I locate socks and, yes, underwear, of which he has a color assortment. I choose blue and red because, hey, I'm patriotic. I then grab a pair of jeans and pack them as I debate a suit but rule it out. He just needs a few shirts. I rotate and walk to the T-shirt row and reach for one in black and another beside it in blue, but pause when my eyes catch on a pink shirt. Pink? I grab it and my throat goes dry. It's a female-cut T-shirt with flowers on it and a V-neck. Nothing to hide, my ass. He said he didn't invite women here.

"That's not my size."

I whirl around to find Reese standing in the doorway, still bare-chested, but his pants are zipped and his boots are on his feet. "I noticed," I say.

"It is, however—or was, rather—just right for my sister, who was here right before the trial started. She left it in my closet, because I *shrank* it, which, she says, I need to repent for by calling her more often."

"Your sister," I say, my throat dry all over again.

"Yes, Cat. My sister." He walks toward me and shows me his phone. "Look."

I feel like I shouldn't look, but since he's offering, I accept. I glance down at the screen to find a photo of a pretty brunette that favors him, wearing this exact T-shirt. "My sister," he says. "She sent that photo to me today with this message." He pushes a few buttons and then presents me with a text message. "From my sister."

This time I wave off the phone. "I don't need to read that, Reese."

"I'll read it to you," he says. "She says: *You owe me a phone call, big brother. I know, I know. The trial. So call me after. Kill 'em while you can.*" He glances up at me. "She has a horrible sense of humor," Reese says. "Almost as bad as you."

"Yes," I agree, "she does, but I'm the one who is bad. I won't pretend my mind wasn't in the wrong place. It was. I'm sorry." I hang the shirt back up. "Did I mention that I suck at relationships?"

"You called this a relationship, not a one and done, Cat. You were honest about what you thought. In my book, those are wins." His phone starts to ring, and he kisses me. "Sorry, sweetheart." He pulls his phone from his pocket and answers the call. "We're on our way down, Royce." He listens a moment. "Yes. Got it." He ends the call. "Royce is picking us up. He's downstairs."

"Us?"

"I'm not leaving you to walk home or struggle to get a car," he says, grabbing a shirt and pulling it over his head. "We'll drive you home."

"Right. Thanks. That works. I didn't pack you a suit," I say. "Surely you won't need it."

"I won't," he says. "And if we're lucky, I'll make it to the airport, figure out what the hell is going on, and get to turn around and come back home to better things, and that means you." He eyes the contents of the bag I've packed, and then me. "You're officially the first woman since my mother to choose my underwear." He pulls the bag onto his shoulder. "I like the red, by the way."

We both laugh as I say, "I favor the blue," and we head out of the room and down the stairs, but despite his humor, I sense the edge to him, how bothered he is by the idea that he is representing a killer. And it's just one more reason to fall for this man. "Does Royce have any idea where Nelson is headed?" I ask as we reach the den and start packing up our work from earlier.

"Nothing on that yet," he says, zipping up his briefcase, "but we're a little too close to the Canadian border for comfort. It's a common jumping spot to another country."

He's right. We are, and this isn't looking good. We walk to the front door, and as I pull the handle on my roller bag, Reese turns to me, wrapping his arm around me and pulling me close, his eyes searching mine. His expression is indiscernible. "What is it?" I ask, my hand on his chest, and I can feel his heart thundering beneath it.

Suddenly, his hands are at my face and he's tilting my gaze to his. "Don't get spooked while I'm gone and run. I'll just run faster, because I don't give up when I want something." He kisses me then, a deep, drugging kiss, and when it's over, he adds, "And I want *you*, Cat." He doesn't wait for an answer or allow that statement to become negotiable. He opens the door, and in a few moments, we're walking down the hall, side by side, my hand in his again. Soon he'll be leaving, while I'm staying, but it's not goodbye. After tonight, it's a whole new beginning. One where you are innocent until you prove yourself guilty.

Chapter Twenty

Cat

Reese and I step into the elevator, and as the door closes, a switch flips in my head. "I forgot to tell you," I say, turning to him. "I can't believe I forgot this. My agent had a picture of you and me, obviously together."

"What picture?"

"In your lobby, when you held my arm and we were walking toward the security area. Dan sent it to my publisher."

"How did you not tell me this, Cat?"

"We've had a lot going on. Your staff was waiting on us, and I really, truly set this aside, but I'm thinking about it now. Dan is the asshole."

The elevator opens. "Let's talk in the hallway," he says. I nod and we step outside. "Am I right to assume that your agent felt this hurt your book deal?" he asks.

"I turned down the book deal, Reese. It was never an option with Dan involved. I swear to you."

"I'm not questioning you. I'm just thinking she has some agenda with Dan. Because that photo says that you could have a book deal with me any time you want it, if a partnership is what they want. And win or lose, my side of the story is half the story."

"I'm close to this. That never crossed my mind, but it should have. And whatever game she might have been playing, it backfired. I fired her. And that's not my concern right now. Dan is devious. I don't know what he might do with that photo."

"I've dealt with press exposure, including speculation about my personal life, for years. I'm thick-skinned and used to the gossip. It's you I'm worried about. I don't want this to affect your work any more than it already has."

"The trial is over soon," I say.

"You were worried about us being a problem for you before, Cat."

"We were one and done."

"We were never—"

I press my hand to his chest. "I know. I'm just telling you where my head was. I was protecting myself. I had a wall between us and I believed it to be real, because I needed it to be, but the book deal is done anyway, and I'm not going to lose my column if readership is high, and it is. I only brought this up for you. You needed to know. And right now, you need to leave."

"I don't want to walk into that lobby pretending we aren't seeing each other. We are. I don't want to hide it." My heart squeezes with how vehement those words are, before he adds, "But if you want to wait..."

"No. I really don't." I take his hand. "We need to get you to the airport and find out what's going on with your client."

He cups my head and kisses me. "I'm not leaving unless I have to, so don't get comfortable for a while." And with that, he laces his fingers with mine and guides us down the hallway.

I realize then that he leads often, but not in the wrong ways, and at the wrong times—so far. He worries about my career and makes it easy for me to worry about his. We enter the lobby, and Reese motions me to the security desk. "Let's stop here a moment."

We approach the counter, where a fifty-ish, stocky man in a burgundy jacket with dark, wavy hair with sprinkles of gray awaits. "Mr. Summer," he greets Reese upon our arrival.

"Newt," Reese says. "This is Cat. I need to put her on the approved list."

I glance up at him. "Do you have time for this?"

"I'm making time. I can't go anywhere until we know where I'm going anyway." He points to Newt. "Let him set this up."

"Okay." I look at the other man. "Hi, Newt."

"Nice to meet you, Cat. I'll need identification."

I fill out a form and show him my driver's license, during which time Reese has his hand resting on my back. It's during this stop that a prickling sensation forms on my neck, like I'm being watched, *we're* being watched. Thankfully, the security process is quick, and in a matter of three minutes, we're walking through the main lobby.

The slight tensing in Reese's grip around my hand tells me he feels it, too. We head toward the front of the building, and a glimpse to the right toward the bar shows it to be packed. Reese must follow my attention, because he answers my unasked question. "Sunday Night football is also big here."

"Do you ever join in?"

"Never. I like football, but in my own living room, and not for a few years. I never have time. What about you? Are you a football lover?"

"I follow along, mostly to cheer for the team going up against my brother's love, the Giants. The Cowboys will work just fine for me."

He laughs and holds the door for me. I exit into a gust of cold wind, as what is clearly our first cold front of the year is in full force. "Oh God," I say, trembling and hugging myself as Reese joins me. "What happened out here?"

He slides his arm around me. "Winter is coming." He points to a black Escalade. "That should be Royce."

We hurry in that direction, and Royce rolls down a window just long enough to confirm he's the driver. Reese ushers me forward and opens the door. I climb inside and all the way over. "How's Lauren?" I ask, as Reese joins us and shuts the door.

"Sick, and everyone that is normally close to her is out of town," replies Royce.

"Even Julie?" I ask of his brother's wife, who is a friend of mine, and darn near a sister to Lauren.

"She and Luke went to Paris on business they plan to turn into pleasure. Kara and Blake are meeting us at the airport to travel with Reese to get his client."

"Oh. Well, you want to just drop me there and I can stay with her?"

"Already planning on it," he says, glancing in the mirror at me. "Because I assumed your concern."

"I think I just got rolled over, but it's acceptable," I say. "I love her, too."

"I know that," he says, and he glances at Reese. "Vermont."

Reese follows his lead instantly. "Nelson went to his place in Vermont?"

"We assume," Royce says. "He hasn't landed, but his wife arrived there this morning. I'd bet my right hand, and I really fucking like my right hand, that he's going there."

"They both have to be in court next week," Reese says. "What the hell are they thinking?"

"Let's hope they don't plan a jump to another country," Royce says, pulling us into traffic. "However, at this point, I'd bet my left hand she's your killer."

"And what better way to take attention off yourself, but to bait your husband into looking guilty as sin," I provide.

"Exactly," Royce says. "Even Lauren, who was on the boyfriend team, has come around. In between throwing up."

"That bad, huh?" I ask.

"Yeah," Royce says, "That bad, which is why I'll be staying here. Blake and Kara are a kickass team. A pain-in-the-ass team, but kickass nonetheless. And Blake is the one who's been hacking a trail on these two."

"Anything else on that?" Reese asks.

"Not yet," Royce says. "But Blake and Kara feel like if they can pick your brain, and even meet your client and his wife, they will close in on the answers."

"The silver lining to this fuck-up," Reese says. "Yeah. I'm in. I'll talk their fucking ears off if they can help."

We turn onto the street where the Walker family owns a small building they remodeled as home and offices, and Royce glances in the mirror at me again. "I can't promise how late I'll be. You can have our spare bedroom if you want for the night."

"I'll take good care of Lauren," I say.

"I need this baby to get here," he grumbles.

"So you have two to fret over?" I ask.

"I can't even think about that right now," he replies.

I smile at his sweet version of grumpiness and Reese gives my leg a tiny squeeze, a calling card. I turn in his direction, and he leans in, lips at my ear, his breath a warm trickle on my neck as he whispers, "I really want to be in my bed fucking you right now."

My fingers flex into his arm I'm now holding, and suddenly, I am ridiculously wet, while my nipples ache. That's how easily this man seduces me. Reese eases back, and we share this crazy-hot—a "make me tingle where I'm already hot"—look. And then we smile, together, in the same moment. God. I'm crazy for this man.

"And we're here," Royce announces, as if warning us that our hot little moment, which he must have witnessed in his mirror, has come to an end.

That's when I realize that we're pulling beneath the Walker building and into one of the few attached garages in the city. "Lauren is expecting you, Cat," Royce adds, halting the Escalade in front of the elevator. "I took the liberty of assuming you'd be joining her, and told her as much, when I found out you were back with Reese tonight."

I don't comment. He's being a mischief maker, like his brothers. Reese opens the door and exits, taking my bag with him. I follow, and he helps me out of the car, like a perfectly, well-mannered gentleman. "I'll walk you up to Royce's apartment," he says, holding my bag.

"No," I say. "You won't. Thank you, but go deal with your case. I'm going to pick Lauren's brain for ideas, too. We were good at solving cases together at the DA's office." I push to my toes and press my lips to his.

He sets down my bag, and the next thing I know, he's tangling his fingers in my hair and staring down at me with a wicked-hot look. "I'm going to need to fuck this hell out of my system when I get home. Be ready." He kisses me, and it's short, but fierce, and then he's gone, leaving me breathless and weak in the knees, as he climbs back into the Escalade and shuts the door.

I watch them drive away, and according to the ache between my legs: I'm already ready for that fuck session, while according to the flutter in my belly, I'm falling hard for Reese Summer.

Chapter Twenty-One

Cat

Lauren is hanging over the toilet about three minutes after she answers the door, and I grab a clip from a drawer and pull her brown hair back from her face. Finally, she calms and lies down on a big, fluffy cream-colored rug. "How often are you doing this?" I ask, sinking down on my knees beside her.

"I should just camp out here in the bathroom," she murmurs. "That's how often."

"What does the doctor say?"

"That sickness is a sign of a healthy baby. Which sounds ridiculous, except for the fact that I wasn't sick before my miscarriage at all."

"You're miserable. Can they give you anything?"

"I have random drugs that he's prescribed. But the options are limited, and none that are approved for pregnancy seem to work for me. Do you know how hard it is for me to do my job like this?"

"I'm surprised you're even able to try."

"I have people counting on me," she says, "but Julie helps me a lot."

"Isn't she a divorce attorney?"

"She's burned out and working with me on criminal cases more and more."

"Divorce isn't pretty," I say, "but neither is crime. Are you eating at all?"

"Yes. Häagen-Dazs ice cream. It's all I can keep down. I'm going to be the size of a ship when this is over."

"You barely have a belly," I say, eyeing her flat stomach through her T-shirt and sweats.

"Right," she says. "I have four months of baby in my butt right now."

I laugh. "You do not. I checked out your ass already. It's as cute and perky as ever. Are you any better?"

"Yes. I need ice cream."

I laugh again. "Do you have some?"

"Royce bought, like, twenty pints. And I'm not kidding. He really did."

"I've met him," I say. "I believe you." I stand up and help her do the same.

A few minutes later, we are on the couch in the living room, the television on mute, the fireplace crackling in the corner, with a selection of six ice cream pints on the table in front of us. "I told you he bought twenty pints," Lauren says, finishing a bite of ice cream. "Did you know that one of these pints is, like, seventy percent of the calories we're allowed to have in a day?"

"Thank you for that," I say, as I try a spoonful of some kind of chocolate ice cream that is incredible. "Thankfully, I haven't eaten much today, and neither have you."

"I ate a pint," she says. "Maybe I ate two. For some reason, after I eat one of these, I'm not sick for a while."

"The baby wants what the baby wants," I say. "Eat the ice cream."

She grabs a stack of files sitting on the coffee table and sets them between us on the couch. "Has Reese talked to you about the trial, or is that off-limits since you're press?"

"I'm not press. You know I hate being called press as much as Reese hates being called Mr. Hotness. And I was with him and his team all day, working on the questions and closing for next week."

"Really? He trusts you already, then."

"I— Well, yes. I guess he does."

"How's trust working on your end?" she asks, giving me a knowing look, considering she weathered the Mitch storm with me.

"Better than expected," I say, "and for now, that's all you're getting."

"How did you meet him?"

"You didn't hear what I just said, did you?"

"I heard and chose to ignore what you said."

"Fine. He cut in line at the coffee shop and accused me of playing games on my phone while holding up the line. When I was, in fact, reading a Mr. Hotness blog without even knowing it was him."

She laughs and scoops a spoonful of ice cream. "That's priceless," she says, taking a bite. "Then what?"

"I checked his bad manners and told him he'd be single the rest of his life if he didn't."

She laughs and shakes her head. "That's the Cat I know."

"And I called him an arrogant asshole."

She presses fingers to her forehead. "Oh God. You just gave me brain freeze." She scrunches up her eyes and face for a minute and then refocuses. "Okay. It's gone. Back to you and Reese. All the women pining for that man, and you figured out the secret code. Just call him a manner-less, arrogant asshole. It's your charm, Cat. I've always admired your charm."

"Men want what they can't have."

"But he has you."

"Maybe he thinks he really doesn't."

"Does he?"

"Yes, actually, he does."

She squeezes my hand. "I'm glad. You really shut down after Mitch."

"I didn't shut down. I focused on doing me my way, instead of my father's. That meant getting to know who I am. I needed time and space to do that."

"And now, Cat? Do you know yourself now?"

"Okay, let me backtrack. I knew me. I just didn't allow myself the freedom to be me. That's still a work in progress."

"Has your father come around at all?"

"No. I haven't spoken to him in months. You know that."

"I hoped it had changed."

"It hasn't. We fight when we communicate and we both needed a break. But oddly, Gabe came by to see me and told me he's proud of me."

"Wow. That's huge. He *should* be proud. They make me so angry."

"It is what it is," I say.

We talk about Reese, my family, and her plans for the baby's room, and after I've returned what is left of the ice cream to the freezer, we move to a work session. "I changed my vote to the wife being guilty," Lauren says.

"I heard, and I'm curious as to what changed your mind."

"This morning, Walker Security had someone watching Nelson Ward's house when she left. She and her husband were fighting and he didn't want her to go. He tried to stop her." She grabs a folder and hands it to me. "Look at that while I go pee for the hundredth time today." She stands up and walks away.

I flip through the file and see many shots of the Ward house, as well as shots of the couple this morning. They were fighting, all right. "Royce is on his way back already," Lauren says as she returns. "Reese just got on a plane with Blake and Kara. One way or another, Reese will have his man back here by early tomorrow."

"Unless he had a new identity waiting on him in Vermont and he and his wife have now left the country."

"Unfortunately, we don't have men on the ground in Vermont, so we can't stop them without alerting the police. And that would be best avoided. Did you look at those photos? The two of them fighting and her leaving—it all reads to me like manipulation. Like she wanted to make him break his travel rules, which implies he's running from his guilt."

"Or she was trying to convince him not to run," I say. "Or she could have found out that he really did it, and she left him."

"You think he did it?"

"No," I say. "I think she did it, too, but I'm playing devil's advocate. And I hope like hell he's innocent. Reese won't just take a hit to his reputation. He'll start to question his instincts."

"Spoken like a woman who has seen inside his mind," she says. "What's happening with you two?"

"I don't know yet," I answer honestly. "But it feels kind of wonderful."

"So you like him."

"He's nothing that I expected and different from anything I've ever known."

She narrows her eyes on me. "You just walked around that question."

"It wasn't a question. It was a statement: *So you like him.* That's a statement. But yes. I like him, but it's new. Don't go marrying me off just yet."

"Just yet. That's an open door, so I'll take that answer. Just don't let Mitch's actions get in front of you with Reese, Cat."

"I'm not doing that."

"Reese trusts you or he wouldn't have you helping with this case. Trust him, too. And before you say anything, let me add this. I know it's scary, but if you don't take the risk, you will never know what might have been."

"I do. I trust Reese. And I'm a bit stunned by how much I mean those words."

Lauren swallows hard. "Oh God."

"What? What is it?"

"It's happening again," she says, covering her face. "Make this stop."

I go down on my knee beside her. "What can I do? Do you have crackers or soda?"

"No thank you. Those things are from the devil. They make me sick. Apparently now the ice cream does, too."

I get her crackers, soda, and more ice cream anyway, and my efforts fail. We land in the bathroom again, and when Royce finally gets home, we are both on the floor on our backs, talking about the trial. But I don't think Royce even knows I'm there. I stand up and he is quick to sit down on the floor and pull Lauren against him. They're talking and he's fretting over her, and my heart squeezes as I watch them together. They are so in love, and suddenly I'm thinking of me and Reese, reliving moments in my head with him: The coffee shop, the food-truck stops. *The sex.* The man knows how to get the job done, for sure. And that kiss goodbye...

I suddenly can't breathe, and it's already eleven o'clock anyway. I sneak to the door and leave, calling an Uber that I wait for in the parking garage. And too soon it seems, that car arrives and delivers me to the front of my building, which is not a thought I'm used to having. I like my apartment. I like being in my space. But tonight, it feels like this isn't where I belong. Nevertheless, a few minutes later, I walk into my apartment, flip on the light, and then lock the door. Leaning against the wooden surface, I stare down the hallway, when I would be normally racing to my sanctuary tub or bed. But tonight, it just feels empty.

I blame Reese, who's filled up my life too easily and too quickly. Reese, who I already know could hurt me, and yet the idea of walking away from him guts me. I can't do it. It's too late to turn back.

"Asshole," I murmur under my breath, but I remind myself that he's innocent until proven guilty.

He trusts you, Lauren said.

He tried to leave me at his apartment. He cleared me with security. He told me things that a member of the press would expose and knew that I would not. He *does* trust me, and I trust him. We're also at that sweet spot in a relationship: Untarnished, a diamond in the rough with endless possibilities.

I push off of the door and walk across the hardwood floors, before cutting left and up the stairs to my bedroom. I've just flipped on the light and walked to my sleigh bed, setting my bag and purse beside it, when my phone rings. I quickly retrieve it from my purse, and there is no denying the punch of disappointment I experience to see Lauren's number, not Reese's. "Hey," I say, walking toward my bathroom. "How are you?"

"You left."

"Yes," I say, flipping on the bathroom light. "I left you with your hot, doting husband."

"You're home safe?"

"I am. Thank you for checking. Are you doing okay?"

"There is a reward at the end of this, so I'm okay. Thank you for staying with me. And, Cat? He'll call."

"What?"

"If Reese feels what you feel, he'll call. I promise." She disconnects, and I want to throttle her.

Now if he doesn't call, it will mess with my head.

I walk to the bathroom, strip down, and take a long, hot bath in my massive tub, which is the best feature in any bathroom. I sit there in the hot, bubbly water, with my phone on the ledge, of course, because now I'm obsessed over the call I might miss. I hate that I'm obsessed. Once I'm in my Victoria's Secret pajamas, I grab my MacBook and take it to bed with me, where I work on my column that is due tomorrow. My closing statement reads:

If this trial ends in a guilty verdict, it won't be based on evidence. If the trial ends in an acquittal, don't blame the system. The system didn't do this. The prosecution did, by charging too soon. They should have taken the time to back up their case. We all want justice for a woman and her child, but deep down, we all want to believe the monster who did this is no longer free to do it again. If nothing changes, I for one will not leave this trial with the comfort of knowing a killer is behind bars. Until then, —Cat.

I study the page and have second thoughts about the content. If I point the finger at new suspects, as I did in the first part of this column, what happens? I believe that, yes, it puts attention on suspects other than Reese's client. Maybe it puts those suspects on edge. But after tonight, Reese may prefer to sideswipe those people on the stand. I need to find out or just write another version of my column in the morning to have options.

I glance at the clock. It's two in the morning. Reese isn't going to call tonight. I shut my computer and lie in bed, in the darkness. Alone. He might not be able to call. He might be in hell right now. God, I want to know what is happening. I want to hear Reese's voice. I want to know he's safe. But I don't need Reese to call for some kind of validation, and he has no obligation to call. It's not like I'm married to the man.

I just wish he would call.

As if I've willed him to do just that, my phone starts to buzz. I register Reese's number. I grab it with a relief that says I wanted this call more than I want to admit. "Hello," I answer.

"Hey, sweetheart. Were you asleep?"

"No. I've been too worried about what was happening there."

"You were worried?"

"Yes. Very much. What's happening?"

"Well, he was at his house, as we hoped, and so was his wife, Kelli. I'm calling you from the rental car, while Blake and his wife each question the husband and wife one on one. I've spent the last hour talking to them myself."

"And?" I prod.

"Kelli supposedly got spooked by the press, or rather 'suffocated,' as she called it. She needed out of town. He followed."

"She was suffocating, so she left her husband to fend for himself the weekend before he learns his fate? That doesn't sound like a loving wife who believes her husband is innocent."

"No, it does not, but then, we all think she did it."

"Lauren showed me the images they took of the two of them fighting."

"Yes, there is trouble in paradise for sure. The question is, did that trouble originate from the trial pressure, or is it long term?"

"I know you stated in your opening statement that the baby is not his and he adamantly denies ever sleeping with the victim. Do you still feel that is a truthful statement?"

"I do. I was afraid I wouldn't after tonight, but nothing has changed."

"Why didn't he call you before he did this?"

"He knew I'd tell him not to go and he wanted me to have deniability," he says.

"Does his wife believe him?"

"Yes, which she says she will state in court."

"Is it safe to let her testify? What if she sets him up?"

"It's a risk that I have to take to try to get a confession from her, because I damn sure don't have any evidence. Hell, it might be the boyfriend. I am flying blind."

"The prosecution has no evidence either," I say. "You're going to create reasonable doubt. You have already. When are you coming back?"

"As soon at Blake and Kara finish up, we'll all fly back, including Nelson and Kelli, in the Walker plane."

"You'll get back here early in the morning, without any sleep, and you have to be fresh for court Monday."

"I have to be prepared Monday, which means sleep is a luxury I can't afford. Call me when you wake up and I'll come pick you up."

"No. You have to sleep and focus on your Monday game plan."

"I'll do those things with you, Cat. I'll see you soon." He hangs up.

I let the phone drop to the bed, and I'm back to staring into the darkness, but this time, I am not fretting. Lauren was right. That call means something. It tells me that I am a part of his life now, and it's terrifyingly wonderful.

Chapter Twenty-Two

Reese

By the time Blake, Kara, and I follow my client and his wife back to their house, it's seven. I leave them with two of Royce's men watching the house. I walk them to their door and Kelli goes inside, while Nelson and I stand on the porch. "You're paying for the plane, and the services I found necessary today. That's non-negotiable."

"Understood," he says. "I know I fucked up. Are you telling the judge that I left?"

"No, but I should," I say. "Just like I should ask to be recused from this case, but it's too late in an expensive trial. The judge won't let me. But be clear: If you give me one more reason to doubt you, my closing statement will get the job done, and nothing more."

I turn, walk away and climb into the back seat of the Escalade Blake is driving instead of Royce this time. Once I'm inside, I shut the door and watch as Nelson heads back into his house.

"She did it," Kara says. "I spent the entire flight talking to her, and she did it."

"I don't disagree, but we're all speaking on gut instincts," I say. "I need more."

"Unless you have a problem with it," Blake says, "Kara wants to talk to Nelson's secretary."

"I don't have a problem with it at all," I say, "but why? Where are you going with this?"

"A secretary knows the boss's secrets," Blake says. "I can't tell you how many times a secretary busted open a case for me."

"And women share dirty secrets more readily with another woman," Kara adds.

I'm reminded of Cat's history. Her ex fucked his secretary while he was with her. The secretary definitely knows a man's secrets. "Do it," I say, "but do it quickly. I'll push Kelli's testimony to Tuesday, but I can't push it any further."

"We'll go see her today," Kara says. "After we sleep a few hours."

Blake turns toward my apartment, and I think of Cat in her bed, instead of mine. "Take me to Cat's building." I give him the address.

"So you two are really a thing, then, huh?" Blake asks.

"Yes," I say. "We are most definitely a thing."

Kara turns and smiles at me. "A man who knows what he wants and is going after it," she says. "Are you sure you don't have Walker blood in you?"

I don't comment, and she doesn't expect me to. She turns and faces forward while I silently agree with her. I am a man who knows what I want, and that's Cat. And I'm going to make sure she knows. For the remainder of the drive, I switch back and forth between trial details and Cat, finding my desire to talk through everything that happened on this trip with her. That's a first for me. But not only does she want to help, she actually does.

By the time Blake drops me at Cat's place, it's nearly eight. My brilliant plan to talk my way past the security desk and surprise Cat doesn't go as planned. "Call her," I tell the guard, a man with gray hair, wearing a blue jacket and a big attitude. "Tell her I'm here. The name is—"

"Reese Summer," he says, disdain in his voice. "I know. We all know who you are."

The man defending a baby killer, I think. That assumption after what I've just dealt with irritates the fuck out of me. "Don't spread that around or Cat will end up with reporters chasing her and you'll get to handle the gaggle of people that will appear in your lobby. And I'll make sure the right people know who made that happen, which would be you."

"I don't run my mouth, sir, or I wouldn't have a job."

"Call Cat," I order.

His lips press together, as if he's biting back a retort, but he dials Cat's apartment and I'm given immediate clearance. I walk to the elevator, tension radiating throughout my body. I'm ready for the fucking hellish trial to be over; that seed of doubt about Nelson's guilt eating me alive. He can't be guilty or I can no longer trust my instincts. I ride the elevator to the fifteenth floor and I swear, just knowing I have a bed with Cat in it waiting on me punches back some of that edginess the guard has stirred in me, right along with the weariness of no sleep. Once I'm at her door, I knock with impatient insistence. I need to see her, to hold her naked body in my arms. It's irrational. It's nothing I've ever felt with a woman, but it's real. It's now and I want the walls between me and this woman gone, literally and figuratively.

She opens the door, looking adorable in pink pajamas, with her blonde hair in disarray. "You should be sleeping," she says. "Why are you not in bed?"

I'm already hot and hard from just seeing her, but the minute I hear her voice, as insane as it sounds, I'm over the edge. I want to feel her close, her breasts in my hands, and my cock buried inside her. And damn, I want those soft moans she makes. I drop my bag, and step into her, hands on her waist as I walk her into the foyer of her apartment and kick the door shut. "I told you I was going to need to fuck when I got back. And I do." I tangle my fingers in her hair. "Do you have a problem with that?"

"Only the part where you want to but haven't yet."

I kiss her, my mouth closing down on hers, my tongue pressing past her teeth, stroking her until she rewards me with one of those moans I craved every minute I was apart from her. That sound undoes me all over again, and nothing undoes me but this woman. I'm suddenly so damn ravenous for Cat that nothing else exists but one goal: More of this woman. I deepen the kiss, drinking her in, demanding everything she holds back. I undress her in between kisses, touching her everywhere I can touch her in the process, and it's not even close to enough.

"Damn it, woman, you are making me crazy," I murmur, this hunger inside me for Cat damn near painful. I press her against the wall, my fingers sliding between her legs, stroking the wet heat of her sex.

She pants and I swallow the sound, licking into her mouth, the hint of toothpaste in her mouth ridiculously sexy. She tugs at my shirt and I pull it over my head. By the time I've tossed it away, she's dealt with my zipper and is closing her hand around my cock. Fuck. I need to fuck. I lift her leg, and between the two of us, my cock presses inside her. I cup her sweet little ass, and her legs wrap my waist. I thrust into her and pull her down on top of me. She clings to my shoulders, and I wrap my arms around her waist.

"I have you, Cat," I say, and those green eyes of hers meet mine, and I know the minute she understands: I want her trust. She nods as if I've asked for it with words, and she leans backward, taking more of me, rising to me as I thrust into her, her beautiful breasts swaying between us. She watches me, too, like I am her, and that connection between us is there, burning a path between us. We are moving again, her driving down against me, me thrusting into each push she delivers. I'm on edge, almost there, when she suddenly leans forward, burying her face in my neck, and I can feel her fighting what comes next. But I don't let her.

"Come for me, sweetheart," I murmur. "Give me what I want."

And what I want is to feel her clenching me, trembling in my arms, and that is exactly what happens. She tumbles into orgasm and I drive into her until I'm going there, too. I thrust one last time and nothing else exists. There is just me, her, and the quake of our bodies.

I come back to reality with my legs burning, and the two of us holding on to one another, breathing together. Somehow, my pants are still in place. "Where's the bathroom?"

"The door right next to us," she says.

I walk us in there and set her on the white and red checked vanity, slipping her a towel to clean up. I quickly return to the hallway and bring her my shirt. She tosses the towel, and I help her with my shirt before pressing my hands to the counter on either side of her. "Good morning."

She blushes a pretty pink. "Good morning." She touches my face. "I can't believe you came here."

"I can't believe you thought I'd go any other place, Cat. Take me to your bed."

"You need to be in your own house and your own bed. Tomorrow is court. You need the familiar."

"Come home with me."

"You need to sleep. We won't sleep."

"Sweetheart, we just fucked. I can sleep a few hours, I promise you."

"Is that the way to put you to sleep?"

"Every night," I say. "Are you up for the challenge?"

She laughs. "I think you're trying to fuck me out of your system."

It's a joke, but there's a serious undertone. "Here's what I say to you on that, Cat. I can, you should let me, and I should let you do the same. And then when we fail, we'll talk about what comes next. Deal?"

"Yes. Deal."

"Good." I pick her up and set her on the floor. "Take me to your bed, and later I'll take you to mine."

Chapter Twenty-Three

Cat

"It's time for bed," I say. "*To sleep.*" I grab Reese's arm, pulling him out of the bathroom off my foyer.

"I'm not going to argue," he says. "I'm officially done for a few hours."

I slide my palm down his arm, my fingers lacing with his, the first time *I've* ever held *his* hand, not the opposite, and when I look at him, the warmth in his eyes tells me he knows this, too. My cheeks warm like his eyes, which is silly, because I've done all kinds of naked things with this man. I cut my gaze, my throat thick with just how connected I feel with this man. How emotionally exposed I am with him. I am so very naked with this man in every possible way, and now he's about to sleep in my bed, with me, by my side.

We cross through my living room, which is decorated in navy blue and grays, the navy of my curtains a shade darker than his gorgeous blue eyes. I guide Reese inside the doorway just off that room, and he stops inside the entrance, scanning the gray and pink décor. Lots of pink, actually, a color choice I made after I left my law career and Mitch behind, a kind of kiss off to everyone I felt had masculated me in my life. I can be more than flat and one-dimensional, and with my writing, I in fact, must embrace variety to be interesting.

Reese walks straight for my bed with the puffy pink comforter and pink pillows, his exhaustion showing in how quickly he strips off his shoes and pants before slipping under the covers. I join him, and he pulls me under his arm, onto his chest, and that's when he murmurs, "Pink suits you, Cat," his voice laden with grogginess, and when I glance up at him, his eyes are shut.

Warmth fills me all over again as I consider that statement, which means more to me than he realizes. Pink is poison to my father. Weakness. A tool a man would use to classify me as woman, not an equal. Reese is my first, in every way. I could love this man and that terrifies me, but it's not a feeling you can walk away from. It's a feeling that consumes and seduces, a drug you can't get enough of, like this man. I can't get enough of him.

I smile and shut my eyes, letting the earthy, rich scent of Reese consume me as my body relaxes into his, the heaviness of sleep reclaiming me.

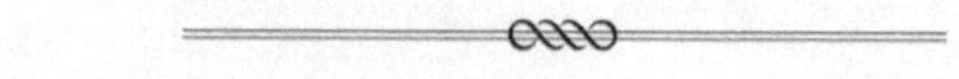

Reese and I sleep for four hours. We wake to the buzzing of my cellphone as Liz texts me and wants to talk. "Important?" Reese asks.

"No," I say. "Go back to sleep."

He doesn't argue. He's out again in a minute, and I snuggle closer to him and do the same. We finally get out of bed at two o'clock, shower together, and dress. Reese dresses in the clothes I picked out for him, including jeans, a black T-shirt, and the blue underwear he points out, since they were my favorite, though I really couldn't care less about the color. They're on him. That's what counts. I myself decide on the New Yorker look of all black, including my jeans, my knee-high boots, and a sweater, considering a cold front has officially arrived, per the weather app on my phone.

I've just finished flat-ironing my hair when Reese appears and leans on the counter next to me, his thick, dark hair still damp, his blue eyes bright and focused on me. "Stay with me for the rest of the trial."

Stay with him, at his apartment, for the rest of the trial. It's almost like living with him. My first instinct should be caution, but I don't seem to have any left with this man. In my mind, I know that I should slow things down. We're moving fast, but the truth is, I don't want to slow down. "Yes," I say. "I'd like that."

Approval fills his expression. He's pleased with my answer. I like this reaction. I like that I never feel like I am in a power play with this man. We are simply together in what is such unfamiliar territory for me, and I can only navigate it by acceptance. "That was easier than I expected," he comments.

My lips quirk. "How can we fuck this out of our system if I'm not with you?"

"Indeed," he says, his expression amused. "I do think we'll both enjoy that process, but Cat," his voice softens, "I've never met a challenge I wanted to fail, until now."

A knot of emotion fills my chest. "I'm okay if you fail this one, too, but, of course, you should see the challenge through."

"Of course," he says, smiling, and he has such a devastatingly sexy smile. "*Of course.* That will take energy for us both. We need to power up. Do you want me to run and grab us food while you pack?"

"Oh, I have an idea. Kind of a ritual. If you like waffles and omelets, there's a place I order from that has the best Sunday brunch. The menu is on the fridge. They deliver, and you can tell them Cat's usual and then whatever you want."

He leans down and kisses me. "The usual. Got it. I'll wait on you by the coffee pot."

He disappears, and I sigh, the spicy, sometimes borderline earthy, but always wonderful scent of him lingering in the air. I did good when I packed his cologne. He smells so good. He always smells good, and that will never get old. I stand up and pack a bag, enough for a few days, at least. Once I'm done, I set my bag in the living room, just outside the bedroom, and carry my MacBook with me.

I find him at my island kitchen, his computer in front of him, coffee beside him, his hair almost dry, a wave to the thick, untamed strands that is almost curly. "Twenty minutes for delivery," he says. "The menu looked good."

"It's so good," I promise, setting my computer down, as well as my phone, before making coffee. "I save calories for Sundays just to pig out on brunch." I rejoin him, claiming the high-backed barstool directly across from him. "Anything from Walker Security?"

"Nothing."

"Are you still putting Kelli on the stand tomorrow as a follow-up to the boyfriend?"

"As much as I want that back-to-back presentation of additional suspects, I'm going to hold off. I told Blake he could have time to get me evidence. I actually told him he could only have two days, but I'm rethinking the timeline."

"What are the factors you're considering?"

"Now that I've convinced the Walker team to come on board, we might actually find a bombshell I can use. I'm going to save her for the last bombshell testimony, but I dislike placing distance between her testimony and the boyfriend's."

"I know you said that you wanted to wrap this up this week. Is that still going to happen? And why were you winding it down that quickly?"

"My initial decision was made when it became obvious that the prosecution was going to rest their case quickly."

"Which told you what?" I ask.

"That they were hiding from a weak case and didn't want to risk me tearing it down. That's when I decided that short and efficient is the way to go with my presentation. I can't give Dan a chance to make the prosecution look good."

"If I were the prosecutor and the judge told the defense they had to get a confession to avoid a dismissal in a case I was prosecuting, that would add fire to that strategy. I'd try to speed things up and keep that ruling in the jury's minds. And I'd do that simply because at least some of those jurors will take that as the judge's assumption of guilt."

"Good point," he says. "And if I'm right about my assessment, Dan the man already needs me to be speedy to avoid highlighting his weak-ass case. The man didn't even call the investigative officers. He knows they have no evidence to present. I don't think he's going to hold things up."

"But maybe *you* need to slow things down, Reese. Dilute the judge's ruling."

"If I dilute that ruling, I dilute how pathetic the prosecutor's case is."

"Not if you grind the right points to death. Even consider recalling some of their witnesses to refresh the jury's minds."

"Maybe. I need to think about this."

My phone rings, and I grab it. "The security desk," I tell Reese before I answer. "Yes. Please. Send them up." I end the call and refocus on Reese, going right back to our conversation. "I'm surprised they didn't drag everyone who knows Nelson Ward to the stand and try to paint some nasty character profile."

"Nelson is beloved by everyone," Reese says. "That's one of the reasons I was willing to take this case. That and the fact that the baby wasn't his and there is no DNA evidence. And I believe he's innocent."

"Even after last night?"

"Yes. His wife was behind that, and he needed her back here to testify."

"He should have called you," I say. "And taken your calls."

"Agreed. And I threatened to scale back my defense to the basic requirements, and definitely not aggressive. But I still believe in him."

"Okay, then back to buying time. You could call on the list of character witnesses."

"Each of which could suddenly present me with a problem," he counters. "I keep every trial simple for a reason. I don't create new problems while trying to solve another. Hell, I could spend weeks and maybe even months building his character, but I go back to the two key points: Every witness is a potential backfire, and I dilute the weakness of the prosecutors' presentation."

"What about putting Nelson on the stand?"

"You said it yourself. No one likes a rich, successful, good-looking man who has everything they don't have. I think it's risky."

"But you say he's loved by all."

"It's too risky."

"Okay," I concede. "It's risky. Are you still calling the investigative officers tomorrow?" I ask, remembering his list from our work session yesterday.

"Yes. That plan hasn't changed. Dan isn't going to avoid that hit. And they will be."

"You're sure they have nothing to offer to hurt you?"

"I have their written statements. If they deviate, they look like liars."

A knock sounds on the door, and Reese stands up. "I'll grab the food."

I nod and grab a couple of bottles of water from the fridge, and a few minutes later, we are both pigging out on waffles and eggs. "Set aside the case for a while," Reese says. "Any regrets over the agent firing this morning?"

"None. Though she was the one who texted me while we were asleep. She wants to talk."

"Are you going to talk to her?"

"I'll talk to her, but I'm not rehiring her. I'll start looking for a new one to deal with my option when the trial is over."

"How do options work?"

"I signed a contract and they optioned my next true crime novel. They get first right of refusal. But I know the terms. I'm not legally obligated to accept the deal with Dan. I am legally obligated to present a proposal for my own book, though they can decline, because I turned down the partnership with Dan. But that's fine.

Once they pass, and I get another agent, I can go to another publisher."

"A lot of people would have taken the deal, Cat."

"And I have my mother to thank for leaving me my apartment and a trust fund I'll inherit at thirty-five. I'm not in a position where I have to do what I don't want to do."

"I didn't know about the trust," he says.

"I don't talk about it. It's hard to look forward to money you get because a parent died."

"How did she die?"

"She had untreated high blood pressure that triggered a massive stroke."

"That's rough."

"It was hard. She wasn't all that happy. My father treated her like crap. She and I fought a lot because I wanted her to get out, or at least force him to do right by her."

"I understand. My parents have struggles. At times, I think they'd be better off apart."

"If it weren't from watching the Walker couples, I'm not sure I'd even believe marriage can work," I admit. "But they don't seem like normal human beings."

"And what am I, Cat?" he asks, studying me, watching me for a reaction.

What is he? It's a complicated question that I answer as simply as possible. "Not an asshole anymore."

"I'll take that," he says. "For now." He moves on. "Didn't you tell me your brother came by? I got the impression you weren't on good terms."

"We haven't been but the whole visit was odd. He wants something. He actually asked about you."

His brow furrows. "What about me?"

"He just asked if I would recommend you as the best of the best. Or something along those lines. I said yes and he dropped the topic."

"Does he know about us?"

"No. I think it was because of the trial. You're on everyone's radar. And apparently, he actually reads my column, which highlights your trial skills."

"Which brother?"

"Gabe. He's the second oldest and he works for my father's firm. Oh, and since we're talking about my column. I think I should save my 'who done it' angle in my column for later in the week, right before Kelli's testimony. If you agree, I'll reframe the pages I've written for tomorrow, which I need to do soon."

"I agree," he says, his eyes narrowing on me. "You're not worried about journalistic integrity by colluding with the defense?"

"You're not worried about corrupting a journalist?"

"I'm counting on it, sweetheart," he says, his eyes filling with mischief. "How am I doing?"

"I'll let you know," I say, but the truth is, he's corrupted everything I thought I knew about what I wanted in a man, and made it all about him.

Hours later, Reese and I walk into his apartment, and he carries his bag and mine into his bedroom. "I'll put these in the closet," he says. I join him and he motions around the room. "Pick a section and make it yours."

My stomach flutters, and I'm suddenly overwhelmed with how fast we are going. "Reese—"

He's kissing me before I ever finish that sentence. "I plan for you to be here often. Claim your space. I'll share everything but you, Cat." And with that loaded comment, his phone starts ringing and he snags it from his pocket. "Blake," he says, kissing me. "Save that thought. I want to hear it," he adds before answering the call.

He listens a minute and says, "Let me dig out my files. I'll call you back." He ends the connection and looks at me. "Nelson's secretary said she'd talk to him, but she's with her mother today and doesn't want to upset her any more than this trial has already."

"Haven't you already talked to her?"

"Yes, but I talked about Nelson. Blake and his wife are going to find out what she knows about Kelli. But Blake is asking for some information I have in my files. I'm going to go look it up for him." He cups my face and kisses me. "I'm glad you're here, Cat." He turns and leaves the closet, and I stare after him with that stupid ball of unnamed emotion tightening in my chest.

I rotate and scan his closet, deciding on a spot to hang the items I brought with me. I consider leaving the rest of my things in the suitcase, but decide that means leaving it out and in the way. I open his drawers and pick a couple of spots to place my things. I empty out his bag and mine completely and store them. And for a moment, I simply stare at my dresses next to Reese's suits and have no thoughts. I just have feelings. So many feelings I can't even name. I don't want to name them. It's too soon. I grab the toiletries and head to the bathroom. I place my items at one of the two sinks, hoping it's not the one Reese uses. I'm just finishing when my neck prickles and I turn to find Reese in the doorway, one of his broad shoulders leaning on the frame. "Did you ever live with Mitch, Cat?"

"No. I've never lived with anyone. Have you?"

"Never even considered it," he says.

"Not even with—"

"Karen was her name. And no. I was focused on my work, and to be completely honest, her living with me felt like it would be a distraction."

"And what am I?"

He studies me for several moments, his expression indiscernible. "Come here," he orders softly.

I think about that command, not because it's a command, but because it doesn't bother me as it would with anyone else. I walk to him and he takes my hand, lacing our fingers together and leading me out of the bathroom to the chair in front of the windows. We sit down and he pulls me under his arm, and I rest on his shoulder, as the sun splashes the sky with rainbow colors as it disappears at the horizon. "Ask me again," he says softly.

I don't ask what he means. I know. "What am I?"

He looks over at me. "The only person I've ever watched a sunset with and had it matter."

Those words alone might not mean more than a seduction, but I don't miss the relevance of him saying them right here, in his room, in this chair, after asking me to stay with him. So when he asks, "What am I, Cat?" I shift and climb on top of his lap, straddling him, my hands on his face. "Someone who matters," I reply, pressing my lips to his.

He cups my head and kisses me. "Ask me again."

"Who am I?"

"Mine," he says. "You just don't know it yet."

Chapter Twenty-Four

Cat

The next morning is a morning of revelations.

I wake up in Reese's bed, with his arms wrapped around me. We're spooning. That's revelation number one: I'm *spooning* with Reese Summer, formerly known as Mr. Arrogant Asshole, commonly known as Mr. Hotness.

"Morning, sweetheart," he says, clearly aware that I'm awake. I'm also naked, and he's naked, and when he rolls me over and settles between my legs, kissing a path down my belly until one of my legs is over his shoulder, I have revelation number two: Sleepovers are underrated, especially since I shatter into complete, utter bliss. When Reese carries me to the shower, where we then have hot sex against the shower wall, revelation number three is a big one for me: I decide my dislike of mornings, which has been with me most of my life, has been cured.

Once we're out of the shower, both of us wrapped in towels, we each claim a sink and I try to focus on my hair and makeup, but he's shaving, and I'm kind of obsessed with watching. He catches me and winks. Revelation number four: While I've never really liked a wink from a man, I like it when Reese winks at me, which clearly proves that the source of a wink matters more than I once thought. Namely, that it's delivered by Reese Summer.

Revelation number five: Reese has a lucky suit, a gray power suit with a matching gray silk tie, a detail I learn when he asks me to pick out a suit and tie for him, and I choose the lucky suit. "That one is for closing arguments," he says. "Pick any other."

I grab a blue pinstriped suit and a blue tie that matches the stripe. "Why is the gray one lucky?" I ask as I pull a black jacket over my long-sleeved turtleneck, that I've matched with my flared skirt.

"I won my first jury verdict in it," he says. "And if I'm really lucky, as I was that day, the verdict is the same day as my closing."

I step into a pair of black stiletto heels and when he's fully dressed, except for his jacket, I knot his tie. "You're skilled at this," he says. "Whose tie have you been attending to?"

"Three brothers," I say. "One of which, Gabe—the one who stopped by my place—still can't tie a tie. I used to pre-knot them for him."

He laughs. "I had a friend in law school like that. I couldn't teach him. He bought a machine to do it for him. The guy could debate the hell out of you in the classroom, and he's a damn good attorney now, but a tie brought him to his knees."

I pat his tie. "All done." I step back and watch him shrug into his jacket. "You need another lucky suit. I think you should actually buy a suit for every trial to be 'the' suit."

"Why is that?" he asks, sticking a tie pin into place.

"Because then you can see your successes line your closet, and you know why I think that's important."

"Why?"

"Because you're not lucky. You're good. You don't need a suit for luck at all."

He snags my hip and walks me to him. "Maybe I should make you my lucky charm."

"You'd have to give up the suit then."

"I'll take you over the suit any day, sweetheart."

I'm still smiling over that comment when we head to the kitchen and grab a cup of coffee. After which, I open my MacBook and read my new column while Reese answers emails. "Are you happy with it?" Reese asks, closing his computer.

"I am," I say. "Are you?"

"You're the one who counts."

"I wanted you to read it last night before I sent it in."

"And I told you, I don't want to influence your writing." He sticks his MacBook in his briefcase and gives me his full attention. "Read me your closing statement."

I like that he wants to hear it. I like that he doesn't want to influence me. The problem is that he didn't and I'm not sure I want to read it to him. "Tonight," I say. "I'll read it to you tonight."

"I don't want to know what you wrote, do I?"

"I don't want to influence you."

"When have you ever held your tongue with me?"

"The morning before you walk into court. Reading it to you last night was different than reading it to you ten minutes before we have to leave for court."

"Cat," he prods. "Read me the closing. Influence the fuck out of me. If I need to hear what you wrote, I need to hear it."

I inhale and breathe out. "All right." I start reading: *When a prosecutor spends all of three days presenting his case in a trial this massive, you have to ask: What is he afraid of? Why not call character assassins to the stand? Why not call the investigators to the stand, and how did they end up on the witness list for the defense, not the prosecution? Why not spend days or weeks with medical experts on the stand? I'm baffled and have only two conclusions I can draw: Either the prosecutor charged rashly, and planned to build a case later, one that simply didn't exist, or he has a brilliant plan, perhaps a trap set for the defense, that has yet to be revealed. Until then, —Cat.* I look at Reese. "Well?"

"A trap," he says. "Why the hell would you let me walk into court and not bring that to my attention?"

"It was a random thought right before I hit send. I mean, what trap could he really have set?"

"One of the witnesses on my list is going to burn me. Maybe one of the investigators I'm calling today. And that burn will be deeper because I called them, not the prosecution. I'll look ill-prepared."

"You said it yourself. They have signed statements. Don't back down."

He taps his finger on the island. "You've validated my plan. Short and effective. I'm not calling anyone I don't have to call."

"See why I didn't want to tell you this morning?"

"I don't rattle, Cat. If you have an opinion, share it."

"I will. I promise."

"Good." He glances at his watch. "If we go now, we have time to stop at the coffee shop."

"Let's not. I saw Dan there. You don't need that kind of distraction before the trial."

"I won't be distracted, sweetheart, but I have a feeling he will be, and after your closing, that won't break my heart. I vote for coffee."

"You're looking for trouble," I accuse.

"That's the name of the game during a trial."

"We can get coffee but not there. Pick another place." I grab my briefcase, stuff my purse inside with my MacBook, and head for the door.

Reese joins me, but he doesn't reach for the door. "Let's get coffee at our place, Cat."

"Fine, but let's set some groundwork. The days you are heading up a high-profile trial, or really any trial, you will get your way eighty percent of the time. The days you are not, I get my way eighty percent of the time."

"I can live with that. Do you need a coat? Do you have one with you?"

"I brought one, but I don't want to deal with it in court. I'll be fine. I'm ready."

He doesn't move. He reaches in his pocket and pulls out a key. "For you."

My lips part. "What is that?"

"You're staying here," he says, taking my hand and closing it around the key. "You should have a way to come and go."

"Reese—"

He leans in and kisses me. "It's yours, Cat." He brushes hair from my face. "And don't go getting spooked on me."

"I'm not. I'm just—surprised."

"Then you must not get it yet."

"Get what?"

"I play for keeps, sweetheart. And I'm keeping you." He motions to the door. "Come on. Let's go win a trial."

He says those words like we're in this together, and we are. I'm in this with him. I'm holding his key in my hand. He opens the door and we step into the hallway. While he locks up, I stick the key in the zipper pocket of my briefcase and we head to the elevator. Once we're inside, both our phones buzz with a text. He laughs at his and shows it to me.

I read it: *Don't be a loser, pretty boy. No one likes a loser.*

I arch a brow at him. "My sister," he says.

"She's brutal, but funny," I comment.

"Yes, she is." He sends her a quick message, and I show him my text message that reads: *We need to talk. I've talked to the publisher on your behalf because I care how this ends for you.*

"Your agent," he says.

"My *ex*-agent."

The elevator opens, and we start our walk toward the exit. "Call her while we walk."

"I'll call her tonight. You need to focus on you and the trial, not my agent drama."

"Cat. This is your career."

"This trial is my career. I'll call her." It hits me that he's the only man, of the many in my life, that actually presses on matters that concern me. We stop at a stoplight and I turn to him. "I promise. And thank you for pushing. I know it's because you want to look out for me."

"I owe you. Your input on this trial has been invaluable."

The light turns and he motions us forward. A few steps past the intersection and we arrive at the coffee shop, and avoid talking about the trial while we wait in line. Instead, we talk about his parents. "Tell me more about the ranch your parents own."

"They have stallions. Do you ride?"

"No," I say. "But I've always wanted to."

"I'll take you up there. We'll figure out when and do it."

He wants to take me to his parents. "You want to take me to your parents?"

His eyes soften. "Yes, Cat, I do. Just be prepared for a cranky married couple. And my brother, who rivals my sister in attitude."

"I'm used to brothers."

"You'll like my sister."

"Does she work at the ranch?" I ask.

"No. She's an interior designer, but she only lives an hour from the ranch. She'll show up if I show up."

It's our turn at the register, and it's not long until we have our coffee and we're finishing the short walk to the courthouse. I stop him a block away. "You don't need to walk in with me, Reese. Mr. Hotness gossip isn't what you need right now."

"Cat—"

I push to my toes, lean into him, and kiss him. "Please. Go on without me. And go Team Summer. Kick ass."

"Are you Team Summer, Cat?"

"You had me the minute you cut in line and earned your temporary Mr. Arrogant Asshole title."

He laughs and kisses me again. "I'll see you for lunch unless some hell breaks loose."

"See you at lunch."

"Call your agent," he says, and starts walking.

"Ex-agent!" I call after him, but he's right. I need to call Liz.

I glance at my watch, and it's actually early. I have time to call her. I walk onward to the courthouse, and since the picketers have already started, I round the corner and sit on a bench. I punch the autodial for Liz and the moment is rather anticlimactic, since I get her voice mail. I text her: *I'm headed into court. I'll try and call you at lunch.* I disconnect, place my phone on vibrate, and head inside. A few minutes later, I've claimed my spot in the courtroom and pull out my notebook, not sure if I did the right or wrong thing when I wrote that closing statement and read it to him.

It's a half-hour later when Reese walks into the courtroom, and he's relaxed, confident, charismatic. The room expands with his energy. If he's rattled, it doesn't show. It's not long before the trial is underway, and Reese sticks to his plan. He calls the investigator. A man named Kevin Smith who is in his mid-forties, an air of confidence about him, with gray streaks at his temple and speckled through his dark hair. He's good looking. If he's articulate and smart, he's dangerous.

"Detective Smith," Reese says. "I have here," he holds up a document, "your written statement. Please read the last paragraph to the court."

Detective Smith shifts in his seat, looking uncomfortable. Reese walks to him and hands him the document. The detective picks it up and reads from the paper. "In closing, Nelson Ward knew the victim. He had frequent communication with her, but there is no physical evidence to point to him as the person responsible for the murder of Jennifer Wright and her unborn child." The detective sets down the document.

"There was no evidence to point to him as the person responsible for the murder," Reese repeats. "And yet my client is on trial today. Did you have new evidence presented after you wrote that statement?"

"None that I'm aware of," Smith says.

"I'm finished with the witness," Reese says, walking back to his table and sitting down.

Dan stands up but stays behind his desk. "How many hours of behavioral studies, psychology classes, and special training have you had, detective?"

"Hundreds."

"In your expert opinion, based on your interviews—"

"Objection," Reese says without even standing, and smartly before Dan is able to connect his client with the word "murder" in that question. "The word 'opinion,'" Reese continues, "calls for conclusions not based on evidence."

"Sustained," the judge says, eyeing Dan. "Move on, counselor."

"I'm done with the witness," Dan states, sitting back down, which is a huge win for Reese. If there is a surprise coming, it's not here.

Reese stands up, clearly not done yet. "Redirect, your honor?" After the judge's nod, Reese continues, "Detective, how many times in your career have you thought someone was guilty and discovered they were not?"

"A number of times."

Dan stands up. "Objection. Irrelevant and immaterial."

I smirk. He should have said that before the detective answered the question.

"Sustained," the judge says.

"Understood," Reese says. "I won't ask the detective how many times he was wrong."

"Counselor," the judge chides.

"My apologies, judge. I'll move on." He eyes the detective. "Did you have enough evidence to convict my client?"

"As I stated—"

"Yes or no," Reese presses.

"No."

"In other words, your opinion, no matter what it might be, was not enough to convict my client."

"No. It was not."

"And right now, all you have to offer myself and this jury as evidence is your opinion."

The detective's face tightens. "Correct."

Reese sits down. "No further questions."

Reese calls a second detective next, and the morning is his. He owns it. Come lunchtime, I head out of the courthouse, eager to meet up with Reese and talk about the morning. The sun is high, warming the day, and with my boots, turtleneck and jacket, it's perfect, like Reese's performance this morning. I'm just walking down the steps when my phone buzzes. I pull out my phone and find three missed calls, all from my publisher. This can't be good. I dial them back as I walk, assuming it's my editor trying to reach me, since I didn't actually listen to the messages like I should have.

"Melanie," I say when she answers. "You called? I've been in court."

"Yes. I called. Liz says that you two parted ways."

"Yes. We did. It happened yesterday. I was going to let you know, but the courtroom has to be my focus this morning."

"I understand, but that's why I called you directly. A representative for Reese Summer called our office this morning."

I stop walking, an instant knot in my belly. "What? Why?"

"Reese Summer says that he will not write a book, but he won't talk to anyone else who might, except you."

My God. What has he done?

"Are you there, Cat?"

"Yes. I'm here."

"We're prepared to make you a five-hundred-thousand-dollar offer."

My jaw drops to the ground. "Can you repeat that?"

"Five hundred thousand *dollars.*"

I don't let myself react. "Liz is still the agent on record for my option. I'll need to talk with her, coordinate my new representation, and get back with you."

"When?"

"By Monday."

"It's already Monday. Wednesday."

"I'll try. I make no promises. If you want to pay me that kind of money to write about this trial, I can't miss it."

"Fine. Monday."

We disconnect and I start walking, trying to calm down. It's a huge offer, but it's not an offer for me. It's for Reese. I can't accept it. He's effectively made my career about him. It's not even my money. I remind myself that he was trying to protect me. I know he was, but it's a big red flag. Every man in my life has tried to protect me by taking control. And you don't just take control of my career. I'm angry. I'm hurt. I'm grateful. How do I feel all of those things at one time?

He's taking over my life. I'm losing my independence. And part of me doesn't care with this man. What is wrong with me?

I arrive at the food trucks and pass them right by, walking to the benches I normally sit on with Reese. "Cat."

I rotate to find him walking toward me, all loose-legged swagger and confidence that I can't dare rattle right now, right before he returns to court. I don't know what I'm going to say or do.

Chapter Twenty-Five

Cat

Reese stops in front of me, and when he reaches for me, I step back. "No. I think I'm angry with you."

His brow furrows. "You think?"

"Yes. I might be. I need to think. I'm confused right now, and when I'm angry, I prefer to have that anger fully vetted. And I know I can't have an angry conversation with you right now, anyway. Not before you go back to trial. So I'm going to leave now, you can have your lucky hotdog, and I will see you after court adjourns."

"Why are you angry?"

"I said I *think* I'm angry. I *need some time* to think about what I feel right now. I mean, why would you— No." I hold up my hands. "No. No. This is not the time. Eat and go back to court and win your case." I try to walk around him.

He catches my arms and pulls me around to face him, and apparently my body is not one bit angry with this man, considering I'm warm where he touches, and pretty much everywhere I want him to touch. Bottom line, I'm warm. All over. "Talk to me, Cat," he orders softly, stepping into me.

Now, I'm really warm. "Not now," I say, wishing he didn't smell so good and feel so good.

"Now," he says. "I want to know now."

"You know what you did."

He narrows his eyes on me. "Sweetheart, I'm getting to know you, but I'm not used to you walking around things."

"You have court."

"Cat," he bites out.

"Why would you call my publisher?"

"Well, that was fast. I thought I'd have tonight to talk to you about this."

"This involved me. You talk to me first, not after you do something, so yeah. I've clarified how I feel. I'm angry."

"I wasn't going to let Dan fuck with your career."

"So you made my career about you?"

"Of course not. It's about you. And if you think it's about me, then that's you being insecure and letting your past settle between us again."

"The offer is because you're involved."

"They wanted you for Dan, Cat. You were already offered this deal. Only, Dan would have taken your money."

He's sort of right. "It's feels different."

"Because you're making it different. It's not."

"You should have talked to me."

"You're right."

My brow furrows. "I'm right?"

"Yes. You're right. Come out of the walkway," he says, lacing the fingers of one of his hands with mine, before leading me to the back side of the food truck and pulling me close again, hands on my waist. "I should have talked to you, but in my defense, and to be clear: You are my woman now, Cat. I will protect you and I won't apologize for that, and I don't know why you would want me to. But I'll communicate better."

I'm his woman. I try to get my head around why those possessive words don't stir a pushback from me. I close my hand around his tie. "No one takes care of me but me."

"Until you had me."

"This is still new, Reese. We're new."

"And that means what? Because I can tell you, I know what is real. We are. And I know this because I haven't wanted to take care of anyone but you. You're different in every way, and I can't not take care of you."

A million emotions pound at me, and I decide to just be honest and say what comes to me. "I don't know how to reconcile how much I like what you just said to me and how much I need you to let me be my own woman."

"I love who you are, sweetheart, and I don't want you to change, but you have to let your guard down. Let me in."

"I am. I have, but we *really* are new."

"You're right. We are. I told you, though, when I want something, I know it, and I am in a one-hundred-percent charge forward."

"Charge with me, not at me, Reese."

"Point made. Point understood." He strokes hair from my face. "Let's sit down and talk."

"You need to eat and go back to court, which is why I didn't want to do this now. We'll talk tonight."

"I have time. We have a long break. Let's grab some food together."

"Yes. Okay."

We grab our usual, my bag of nuts and his hotdog, and claim our regular bench. "You made your sister proud this morning," I say. "You killed it in there."

He finishes off a bite of his hotdog. "My team had a good morning," he says. "But that doesn't mean there isn't that surprise you mentioned waiting on me."

"There has to be a surprise," I say, facing him. "The prosecution can't be this unprepared."

"It's an election year," Reese says. "A trial makes a big splash, and we both know the public is going to convict my client, and the jury if they acquit, no matter what the evidence says. That's a win at the voting booths." He takes a bite of his hotdog and I open his water for him. "Unless," he says, accepting it, "we come up with that confession we need." He guzzles his water.

"Anything from the Walker crew?"

He finishes off his hotdog and tosses the wrapper in a trashcan. "The secretary put them off."

"Interesting. She must know something and can't decide what to say."

"Agreed. And I don't know if I should be worried or impatient, or both."

"You need to stick with believing in your client," I say. "If you falter, the jury will know."

He sets the water on the ground and changes the subject. "Take me out of the equation. If you didn't know me, would you be excited about what your publisher had to say?"

"Yes, but I can't take you out of the equation. I don't just know you, I'm sharing your bed, you gave me a key to your apartment, and I don't know how to separate that."

"Take the deal or use it for leverage to move to a new publishing house and get the agent you want."

"They offered me five hundred thousand dollars. If I do this, I'm splitting the deal with you."

He inches back and arches a brow. "Half a million. Not bad." His hand comes down on my leg and he pulls me to him, and I scoot closer. "I don't want your money, Cat. I just want you." He cups my face and his mouth slants over mine, his tongue stroking against mine in a slow, drugging kiss. "I can't wait to get you home tonight." He brushes his lips over mine. "I'll see you soon." He stands up and leaves me with so many thoughts that I have to weed through them. I focus on one word.

Home.

He called his apartment home, and, of course, it is. He just used it in a way that felt inclusive, like his place is my place.

But it's not.

Could it be?

Do I want it to be?

Maybe.

Which leads me to the only thought that matters right now. I'm not just falling harder and harder for this man. I'm falling in love. I'm vulnerable. I could get hurt in a way Mitch could never have hurt me. But I trust Reese. He did everything right today. Said everything right. And he meant it.

He's not going to hurt me.

Not on purpose.

I stand up and stuff my water and nuts into my briefcase before heading back to the courthouse. Rounding the corner to the front of the food trucks, I stop dead in my tracks, to find Reese in a confrontation with Kelli Ward, the wife of his client, and, of course, a possible killer. "How do we know what we say to you won't end up in one of her columns?" Kelli demands, that question clearly about me. "How?" she demands. And without giving him a chance to reply, adds, "This is malpractice." She turns and walks away.

It's not malpractice, I think, that's just silly, but I don't want to cause Reese trouble.

He turns toward me and motions me forward, away from the people in line at the truck who had to have heard Kelli's outburst. "That wasn't good."

"She's afraid of you. Which tells me she's afraid of a whole lot more."

"Is this going to be a problem for you?"

"I told Nelson about us this morning. I wasn't giving Dan a chance to shake my team up with some sort of bomb that isn't even a bomb."

"And he said what?"

"It was a non-issue. But do me a favor, sweetheart. Call the Walker team. Tell them Kelli is rattled. She's set up for a misstep and I want her to go down, even if that means I have to take a few risks in the courtroom and draw this trial out."

"I'll call now."

He kisses me. "A longer trial means we're going to need to pick up more of your things and bring them to my place." And with that, he leaves again, and I don't let myself think about the fact that he's pretty much moving me in with him. Right now, it's about this trial. I retrieve my phone from my purse and check the time. I still have a full half-hour, and it's a five-minute walk back. Deciding this call is private, I round the food trucks again and sit down on the bench. I don't actually have Royce's number, so I call Lauren.

"Hi, Cat. Wow. What a morning Reese had. He destroyed the prosecution."

"Yes. He did. Kelli Ward confronted him about me and said it was malpractice."

She laughs. "That's ridiculous."

"It is," I say. "But Reese wanted to let Royce know that she is acting erratic, scared even. She might do something rash."

"I'll tell Royce right now."

"Thanks. I'll call you later."

"Cat," she says when I would hang up.

"Yes?"

"Be careful. If she is as crazy as she seems, I don't want you becoming a target."

"I'll be careful," I say. "Thanks, Lauren."

The call ends with another one beeping. I glance at the screen to find Liz calling. Wanting this over with, I take the call. "I'm the agent on record for this deal," she says.

"Yes. I know. I wouldn't cheat you out of the money. I'm just not sure I want to stay with a publisher that pushed me into a deal with Dan. And frankly, I'd like an agent who is invested in me long term to co-agent and shop this project. You can split the deal."

"I don't want to split. I want to represent you."

Of course she does. Now I'm worth money to her. "You told me I was dead in the water, Liz, because I was dating Reese."

"Dan has a relative at your publishing house," she says. "I didn't want to tell you that because I didn't want to tarnish your relationship with your editorial team. I went off on them, though. I told them they were playing games with my author over a personal connection."

"They offered me half a million dollars."

"I know. They told me. And considering how pissed one of the executives was about your meeting with Dan, I didn't expect it. I wasn't trying to undermine you. Just the opposite. I'm on your team, Cat. We're good together."

"You weren't upfront with me."

"I was protecting you."

I feel like I just had this conversation. "You talk about my business with me before you make decisions."

"Fair enough. We tell them you want seven hundred and fifty thousand or we go wide. But if they say yes, you have to forgive them their shittiness, and take the deal."

"You just assumed I rehired you."

"Did you?"

"Yes," I say. "If I go wide, will I get more?"

"Maybe, maybe not. If you go wide and decline an option, you look hard to work with to the publishers."

"Fine. Seven hundred and fifty thousand and take it. I'm going back to court."

"I'll be in touch," she says, then disconnects.

I stare at my phone and consider texting Reese but this isn't the time to distract him. I'm about to put my phone away when suddenly someone is standing above me. I look up and my lips part at the sight of a stunningly beautiful woman with hate in the depths of her green eyes. It's Kelli Ward.

"If you slander us, if you lie about us," she says, "if you repeat anything you shouldn't repeat, we will sue you and your family for all you and they are worth."

Kara appears beside me. "I think it would be a good idea if me and my gun walked you back to the courthouse." She walks away.

My cellphone rings and I glance down to find an unknown number. I have too much going on to ignore it, and I hit accept.

"Cat, it's Royce."

"Lauren called you."

"Yes, but I'm actually on the bench right across from you."

I look up to find him sitting there. "You're following Kelli," I say.

"Yes. And I wanted you to know that if she gets close to you, we're close to you. I sent you a warning text you ignored."

I glance at my phone, and sure enough, there's a message that reads: *This is Royce. Kelli Ward is heading your way, but I'm here with you.*

"If she approaches you again, Kara is going to immediately join you. We're here."

"She's not going to touch me," I say. "That would be stupid, and that woman isn't stupid."

"We're here, Cat." He hangs up.

He didn't agree with me, but I've been around people like her. I've helped convict them. And I'm going to help convict her, too. I text Reese: *Kelli got in my face. Royce was watching. But she's your girl, Reese. Get her.*

He calls me immediately. "Are you okay?"

"Of course. I worked for the DA's office. This is not new to me. I just wanted you to know that her loose cannon is getting looser."

"Text me when you get to the courthouse. I won't answer, but I need to know you're here. Be careful."

We disconnect and I get up and start walking, the words "be careful" now burned into my mind.

Reese

I disconnect with Cat and glance around the conference table where my two co-counsels sit, along with Nelson Ward, who is directly in front of me. "Your wife not only had that confrontation with me today, she just confronted Cat and threatened her as well. *Control* her."

Nelson's lips thin. "I'll handle her," he says.

"Like you handled her when you got on that plane Saturday night?"

"We've covered that to the point that it's a baseball bat hitting me over the head. It was a mistake."

"If you don't handle your woman better than you did then," I say, "I'll have her banned from the courtroom, and I'll get a protective order for Cat. Actually, that works for us. We need suspicion cast elsewhere. If your wife is volatile, that does the trick."

"What the hell are you talking about?" he demands, leaning forward.

"Are you protecting her?" I press.

"Why would I be protecting her? From what?"

"Did she kill that woman and her unborn child?" I ask.

"I'm not protecting her," he says.

"That's not an answer," Elsa chimes in, sounding appalled. "Did she kill her?"

"No," he says, cutting her a sharp look, and then eyeing me. "Kelli didn't kill her."

"What if she was jealous of Jennifer?" Elsa pushes, while I listen with interest.

"I met Jennifer at a coffee shop," Nelson snaps back. "You know this story but since you've forgotten and you're one of my attorneys, let's repeat. She was crying. She wanted to leave her boyfriend. She said she needed a job. I saw her there several times. She was never without tears. I told my wife about Jennifer. Kelli generously decided to help Jennifer get a job. And the baby wasn't mine. DNA confirms that fact."

"But Kelli didn't have DNA testing when she found out Jennifer was pregnant," Elsa argues.

"There was nothing sexual between myself and Jennifer Wright," Nelson breathes out. "It hurts my heart to know that she is dead. I still can't believe someone pushed her down the stairs. It seems more of an accident than murder."

"The evidence says it's murder," Richard says. "The good news is that the evidence against you being the one who committed that murder is circumstantial."

"And yet I'm on trial," Nelson states.

"Have you not once considered your wife as the killer?" Elsa says, apparently not ready to let this go.

"No I have not," Nelson bites out, irritation in his voice. "She's devastated by all of this."

"And so she ran off to Vermont and left you to be devastated alone," Elsa rebuttals. "Such love."

"She was having a panic attack when she left for Vermont," he claps back. "How could I not go after her?"

"Exactly," Elsa says. "And she knew that. She knew that would get you arrested."

"Kelli is going to take the stand, at the appropriate moment." I interject. "I hope you're certain that she will protect you as you're protecting her. If not, we both lose this trial. Only I get to take the hit and move on. And you get to be thankful the death penalty no longer exists in New York."

Nelson stands up. "I'm paying you to defend me, not destroy her."

"You're right," I say, standing up as well, pressing my fingers to the conference table and leaning forward. "You're paying me to defend you," I say. "That means I find the killer or we put this decision in the hands of a jury that likely hates your guts."

"I know the press hates me but that's about selling papers. They have heard the evidence. I didn't do this. They need to hear from me."

Richard chimes in without standing up. "If you go on the stand, the prosecutor will highlight everything there is to hate about you. And in case you don't see that clearly let me spell it out. You're rich, good looking, and did I say rich? Oh, and your wife is hot and they think you still banged another chick, got her pregnant, and killed her."

Nelson scowls at him. "The DNA links the baby to the boyfriend. What part of this do you people not understand?"

"I didn't forget," Richard says. "But as you're being called a baby killer who fucked this woman, how likely is it that the jury forgets?"

"Then remind them," he snaps, looking at me, a wild animal quality to his eyes. "Remind them."

I arch a brow. "Anything you want to tell us?" I ask.

"Do your job."

"Even if I get you off," I say, "you still have to shut your eyes and sleep every night next to her."

A guard pokes his head in the door. "Five-minute warning."

"It's time for court," I say, heading for the door.

I exit the room and start walking down the hallway when Elsa joins me. "He's covering for her."

"I know," I say.

"Why would anyone cover for someone who did such a hideous thing? What makes a man willing to do anything for a woman?"

I don't answer, but I know firsthand, there's no explaining what makes a woman a man's everything. I'm living that experience. I just obviously chose my woman a hell of a lot better than Nelson Ward.

Which means I'd better keep her. Which means I'd better get out my running shoes, because Cat isn't done running.

Chapter Twenty-Six

Cat

The afternoon is a win for Reese. Every witness he calls plays his tune, and every witness the prosecution crosses fails to turn on Reese. When the courtroom adjourns, Reese sends me a text message: *Meet me at the coffee shop in an hour.*

I text back: *I'll work at the coffee shop and wait on you.*

Right about that time, the crowd breaks and he's staring at me. We both smile, and I swear my cheeks heat, as if the man just whispered naughty things in my ear. I give him a tiny nod and turn away before the cameras catch us. I melt into the hordes of people trying to get out of here, and it takes me ten minutes to get out of the courtroom. Once I'm outside, I hurry through the busy crowds swarming the New York streets, the chilly evening warmed by the pure volume of people.

I order coffee and quickly claim my favorite table in the corner, eager to work on my column and finish it if I can before Reese is done. With plenty of notes for the day, I'm fast. Forty-five minutes later, my coffee is gone, my column is sent to my editor, and I ask one of my neighbors to guard my things while I run to the bathroom. I'm just washing up when my phone buzzes in my pocket. I pull it out and read a message from Reese: *I'm here.*

My heart starts racing just at the idea of seeing him. It's crazy how intensely this man affects me. I open the door, and he's standing right in front of me. "Reese."

He answers in a quick wave of action. He walks me backward, into the bathroom, his hand under my sweater, hot on my skin. "We can't do this," I say, but he's already locking the door and maneuverers me against it. "I missed you."

"You didn't have time to—"

His mouth closes down on mine again, and I forget what I was going to say. He's drugging me. That has to be it. I can't think until his lips leave mine and in the meantime, he manages to tug my shirt up to my waist. "We can't do this here," I say firmly this time, pushing on his chest.

"Why?"

"People—"

He kisses me again, and oh God. His hand is under my panties, sliding along the now wet seam of my body, and I'm arching into his touch. "Come for me and we will wait to fuck until we get home."

I grab his arms. "This is wrong, Reese."

He lifts me and sets me on top of the sink, spreads my legs, and goes down on one knee, wasting no time once there. Already his tongue is on my clit, sending a shockwave of sensation through my body. I lean against the mirror and my hands grip the sink. I have never experienced anything like this with any other man. This total inability to feel anything but him. He's licking me. Touching me. His fingers are inside me. My leg is on his shoulder and I don't remember him lifting it. And then it happens. Right here in the bathroom of my favorite coffee shop. That rise of bliss that renders me incapable of moving right before I quake. Oh, and how I quake and tremble and how perfectly he licks me through it all. Fast. Slow. Perfect.

I'm a limp noodle when it's over, and Reese lifts me to the ground, pulls down my skirt, and kisses me, with my taste on his tongue. He follows that kiss with the declaration of, "That's how I want to taste for the rest of my life."

I take that in with a jolt and possibly another sway. Maybe it was one of those after-sex statements, but those words, "for the rest of my life," affect me, but he doesn't back away from them. He strokes my cheek in that gentle way he does with his knuckles and says, "Don't say I didn't warn you. Let's go get you some extra things at your apartment."

I don't argue. I want to be with him. How can I not want to be with this man?

A few minutes later, I've packed up my briefcase up at my table. In the process, I try not to look at anyone, for fear they will see "girl who just had an orgasm compliments of Mr. Hotness standing right by her" written all over me. Once my bag is loaded, Reese throws away my cup and then, to my surprise, shrugs out of his coat and slips it around my shoulders. "It dropped about ten degrees outside. You'll need this."

"What about you?"

Those blue eyes of his smolder. "You can warm me up when we get home."

Home.

There is that word again. "Your home or my home?" I say before I can stop myself.

"The one we're sharing right now, Cat," he says, lacing his fingers with mine. "Come on, sweetheart."

He leads me forward and we step outside, and he's right. It's chilly and we walk the short walk quickly, and as we do, I can't help but feel this man's presence next to me. I'm aware of him on every level: his smell, his coat, his energy. The world, my world, is simply warmer, no, richer, is the better word, with him in it.

Once we're in my apartment, I pack up, and Reese calls us a car to make carrying my bags easier and traveling to his place warmer. I've finished packing, including enough items to get me by for a week, if necessary. Once I've zipped up my bags, I pull on my favorite Chanel trench coat and exit to my bedroom. Reese is sitting on my bed, looking at a photo from my nightstand of me and my mother about six months before she died. My heart squeezes just thinking about that night. "Your mother," he says, looking up at me.

"Yes. My mother."

"You look like her," he says, setting the photo back on the nightstand.

"I hear that a lot."

"How old was she when she died?"

"Fifty-five. Too young."

"When, Cat?"

"Two years ago. Christmas week. She gave me this coat for Christmas three days before she died."

"Right when you—"

"Broke up with Mitch and left my legal career. Yes."

He stands up, his hands sliding to my shoulders. "I admire you for what you did. You left everything, lost your mother, and re-created yourself."

"Thank you. It was hard to make changes in my life, but my mother was miserable and that inspired me to not be miserable.

And I know this, because she left me a letter. She told me that she used this apartment to get away from my father. She said for me not to live my life for my father like she had."

"And you bravely listened to her."

"Bravely? No. I was terrified. Sometimes, and I don't know why I'm telling you this, but sometimes, I still am. I think—my father pretty much disowned me. I haven't spoken to him in six months. It messes with my head sometimes."

"But you talk to your brothers."

"I do speak to Daniel, the one who lives in Texas, pretty regularly. Gabe, the one that stopped by my place, sometimes. Reid, he's the oldest, and the closest, to my father. Hardly ever." I let out a breath. "Let's leave. I suddenly like the way I feel at your house more than here." I twist away from him, and he catches my arm, and the next thing I know, he's cupping my face and kissing me.

"I just needed to kiss you," he says, his voice low and rough. "You're beautiful and strong and I'm crazy about you."

"Yeah?"

"Yeah. This is where you say you're crazy about me, too."

"I am," I whisper. "You know I am. But as much as this place is about happiness to me, it sometimes suffocates me with her absence. I know that sounds silly, but it's what I feel and I really want to leave now."

"It doesn't sound silly. It sounds like it's time to leave." He kisses my forehead and releases me.

We gather my things, including one big roller bag I grab. Reese takes it over, and heads for the door when my cellphone rings in my pocket. I dig it out to find Liz's number on caller ID. "Hi Liz," I answer, as Reese and I step into the hallway.

"The publisher is going back to the board for more money," she says. "More soon."

"How soon?" I ask as we walk toward the elevator.

"A few days at most," she says. "When will the trial be over?"

I don't like this question. It feels like prodding for Dan, and I hate that I feel this with Liz, of all people. "The only person who knows that answer is Reese Summer, and you'll have to ask him yourself."

"That was an innocent question for our negotiations," she says. "It had nothing to do with Dan and I know that's what you're thinking. He is not my client. You are. You matter."

I breathe out. "I know. I'm sorry."

"Apology accepted. I'll be in touch." She hangs up.

Reese and I step in the elevator. "That was Liz, of course. She wanted to know when the trial was ending. You heard my answer. And in case you're confused. I rehired her because she explained the situation."

"Which was what?"

"She was trying to protect me from Dan's relative that works for my publisher. Now she's trying to get me more money."

"Dan has a relative at your publisher," he says. "That explains a lot." His eyes narrow on me. "You still seem bothered."

"I don't like that Liz wasn't straightforward with me. It feels like a lie, and I've had too many of those in my life."

"But you rehired her."

"Despite the fact that she tried to get me to do something for money that compromised my morals, because Dan has none, this is her job. It's to make money. She's also smart and savvy. I genuinely like her and I'm a loyal person. She got me my first deal and it wasn't small. She's otherwise been good to me. I also don't like the whole "the grass is always greener" mentality. In my experience, the grass is usually not greener. It's just different."

"Are you trying to convince me or yourself?" he asks. "Because that was a long pitch for Liz."

"I'm convinced. Are you?"

"I'll let you know based on how she handles this book deal."

The elevator arrives on our floor, and we're soon on the ground floor. We are crossing the lobby, when I have another one of those revelations I've been having: I talk to Reese about things I would never talk to anyone else about. No one. Lauren and I are good friends but there is a reason Julie is her best friend, not me. Since the whole Mitch nightmare, I tend to withdraw. I shut people out. I don't call her for weeks at a time. I embrace alone so it can't sneak up on me. But I talk to Reese. Once we're in the car, my feelings for this man are begging to be named and swelling inside me. The minute the car starts moving, I turn to Reese, and this time I cup his face, and press my lips to his. "I just wanted to kiss you," I say, repeating what he said to me.

He kisses me again, a long, deep slide of tongue that I feel inside and out, that swell of my emotions expanding between us is now ours. He feels it, too. I don't know what it is, but I don't want it to end. Our drive, however, is short, and it's not long before we are out of the car and walking into the lobby of his building with my bags in tow, to find Blake waiting on us at the security desk.

"I'll make this quick," he says, glancing at my bags, a hint of a smile on his lips, before he refocuses on Reese. "The secretary had some interesting information."

"I'm listening," Reese says.

"Fits of jealousy from Kelli. She also says that she heard the Wards arguing over Jennifer's call the night she died. Nelson didn't take that call. His wife did."

"She's on my witness list," Reese says. "Will she say all of this on the stand?"

"Only if you make it looked forced and spontaneous," Blake says. "She wants to protect Ward, but he's protective of Kelli. She doesn't want to end up fired. And she doesn't want to communicate with you directly and risk upsetting Ward."

"And you feel good about her?"

"Fuck yes," Blake says. "I wouldn't be standing here if I didn't."

"The spontaneous thing is a piece of cake," Reese says. "I'll make it happen. I'll make her feel attacked even though she expects my questions."

"When should she expect to be called?" Blake asks.

"Friday. And Friday, this ends. I'll call her and then the wife right before I rest my case."

Blake hands him an envelope. "She doesn't know it, but I recorded her. Just to make you feel good about her testimony. If you have questions, pick up the fucking phone." He leaves, and Reese and I head onward to the elevator.

A few minutes later, we step in the elevator, and it's not long before we are sitting in front of that view in the chair in Reese's bedroom, listening to the tape with takeout containers on the floor. "She's going to be a huge asset," I say, after the tape ends. "She's loyal to Ward. She really thinks he's a good man and she's got a sweet voice, which helps."

"If she goes right before Kelli, it's a brutal set up."

"With Kelli outside the courtroom, I assume?"

"Oh yeah. She can't hear Geneva's testimony."

"Do you want me to publish my column asking 'Who Killed Jennifer Wright?' or does that alert Kelli, that she's a target? I think it does and I have something else in mind for tomorrow that I'm kind of loving anyway."

"If you love it, then let's go with the something else. Let's keep her feeling protected by her husband. That way when I come at her on the stand, she's taken off guard."

"Something else it is," I say. "What about timing? Why Friday for closing and not tomorrow? You wanted to wrap this trial up without diluting Dan's poor performance."

"Everyone wants to go home on a Friday. It's my way of discouraging long deliberation."

"Which is why you said it ends Friday."

"Yes. And then we know the end of the story."

The end of the story.

Because every story ends.

Chapter Twenty-Seven

Reese

I kill it in court Tuesday and Wednesday. The medical professionals I call tear down the prosecution. The prosecution tears down the prosecution. It's hard to believe they were this unprepared, but what's fucked up is that they could still win. People want justice, even if it's bad justice. It's these thoughts that I wake up to Thursday with only one day left before my closing, if all goes as planned. If I were perfect, I could be sure it would.

Cat rolls over toward me and blinks awake, her eyes a perfect summer green. *Perfect.* That's what she called me last night, and that word hits ten kinds of triggers for me, of which I normally only have a few. "Perfect is a really hard fucking thing to live up to," I say. "You know that, right?" I don't give her time to answer. I roll out of the bed, walk to the bathroom, open the shower, and turn on the water. I step inside and under the hot spray, pressing my hands on the glass wall. *Fuck.* I hate when I get like this. I hate that she called me perfect. I hate that it reminds me of my father. Of my many confrontations with that man when I was a teen and he was sneaking in the door at three a.m. instead of me.

"You have a wife," I'd remind him.

"You think you're fucking perfect, don't you?" he'd growl back at me.

Even then, at such a young age, I was a hell of a lot more perfect than him. He just couldn't stop fucking around on my mother—which is one of those perfect secrets I haven't told Cat. How can I? My father is a cheater. Her past is all about cheaters and overbearing assholes. He was that, too. I'd rather Cat call me an asshole than perfect. That way, I never disappoint her the way my dad disappointed my mother.

The shower door opens and Cat is suddenly between me and the wall, in front of me, and I swear the woman read my mind.

"Asshole," she says, and I'm instantly hard as fuck and ready to fuck. I cup her head and kiss the hell out of her, rolling one of those pretty pink nipples of hers in my fingers, but she pushes away from me, and holy hell, she's on her knees and my cock is in her mouth.

She sucks me like she's on life support and she needs this, when I'm the one who needs it. I need her. I've never needed like this, but I don't fight it. That's the thing. I have always known what I want, and I've never let any obstacle stop me from getting it. I've needed. I've taken. I've wanted but I don't remember, out of any of my desires, dreams, and goals, wanting like I want this woman. She completes a circle that was always incomplete.

I watch her taking me in her mouth, licking me, and oh yeah, I feel her. I tell myself that if I were perfect, I wouldn't come in her mouth. But I'm not perfect, and I do. I come the fuck in her mouth and she doesn't care. I decide she's the one who's perfect. The kind of perfect a man marries and feels damn lucky he's the guy who got her. Because he's not perfect at all.

Flash forward, and I'm not in that shower anymore. I'm walking into the courthouse in my lucky suit, intent on ending this trial today, and I can still feel her mouth on my cock. I'm pretty sure that's the luckiest feeling a man takes with him anywhere he goes. With that luck on my side, my first order of business is to confiscate a room and hold a short meeting with Elsa and Richard, where we recap our plan for court. "As we've discussed," I say, "I'm going to call Geneva Marks first. Elsa will keep Kelli out of the courtroom on the pretense of prepping for her time on the stand." I look at Richard. "You'll bring Kelli in when I finish with Geneva."

"Got it," he says.

I glance between them both. "Let's do this."

I exit the room and cross the hall to the conference room where my client awaits, only to find Kelli sitting with her husband. Kelli is the star today though. She just doesn't know it. She's wearing a low-cut turquoise top, her fake but impressive breasts exposed. It's a good choice for the day I put her on the stand. Of course, she thinks that she will be on the stand next week.

Nelson, on the other hand, looks reserved, and I set my briefcase on the table. Elsa and Richard join us and remain standing. I press my hands to the table.

"You're up today, Kelli," I say.

She sits up straight. "What? No. You said next week."

"What's going on, Reese?" Nelson asks, sounding concerned, and looking professional as always in a navy-blue suit and tie.

"To end this story," I say, "I'm closing today."

Nelson stands up. "Today?"

"Yes," I say. "Today."

"What about the character witnesses?" he asks.

"The prosecution has a bombshell waiting on us," I say. "Let's not keep hunting for it. Let's get your wife on the stand and let's get you back to your normal life."

"You think we're going to get an acquittal?" he asks.

"A jury is never a sure thing," I say. "But in theory, we've proven reasonable doubt. Kelli can help seal the deal."

"What are you going to ask me?" Kelli asks, standing now as well.

"Elsa is going to spend some time prepping you this morning," I say, knowing very well that my questions won't resemble Elsa's, but that's the plan. "You'll be called midmorning, after which I'll rest my case, and we'll close this afternoon. Unless the judge decides closing will be Monday, which I doubt he will. He wants the jurors to go home, if they can go home." I turn and exit the room, and yes, I'm nervous. I'm always nervous for closing, my adrenaline pumping, and that's a dangerous feeling that can be distracting if not reeled in.

Fifteen minutes later, I walk into the courtroom and, as always, my attention gravitates to Cat. I find her in her normal spot, her notebook in hand, her beautiful blonde hair pinned primly at her nape. And there is nothing hotter than a schoolteacher image in public who saves her wild side for me. Fuck. I'm crazy about this woman, and rather than distracting me, there is something about her being here that helps me center that adrenaline. It's the damnedest thing.

I take my spot at the table, and it's not long until Richard joins me and Dan appears at his table. Soon, the judge and jury are in place and the day is set to begin. I call Geneva Marks, Nelson's secretary, a pretty thirty-something brunette dressed in a blue suit dress. She's sworn in and states her name, and I start with softball questions.

"How long have your worked for Nelson Ward?"

"Five years."

"How well do you know him?"

"I know more about him than probably even his wife."

"Based on that statement, is he a man of honor?"

"Objection," Dan shouts. "Leading."

I rephrase. "What is your assessment of his character?"

"One of the best men I've ever known. Honest, kind, generous. Smart."

"Have you ever witnessed him and his wife fighting?"

She inhales and lets it out. "Yes."

"What about?"

"Me. She was jealous of me."

"Does she have reason to be?"

"No. My relationship with Mr. Ward is completely professional, which is one of the things about him I respect. He would never, ever dream of cheating on his wife, or making a woman feel uncomfortable."

"Did you hear them fight about Jennifer Wright?"

"Yes."

"What was the context?"

"There was a call to Mr. Ward's cellphone from Jennifer Wright the night she was murdered. He wanted his wife to admit to the police that she took the call, not him."

There is a rumbling of voices in the courtroom that fades quickly, and you can almost feel the courtroom waiting for what comes next.

"What was Mrs. Ward's response?" I ask.

"She said it would make her a suspect. She—"

"Objection!" Dan shouts, jumping to his feet. "Hearsay."

"This is not hearsay," I argue. "She was sitting outside the office and heard the conversation."

"Overruled. Continue."

I look at Geneva. "You were saying. She what?"

"She cried and accused Mr. Ward of not loving her if he wouldn't protect her."

"And how did Mr. Ward respond?"

"He proclaimed his love and promised to protect her."

"Did either admit to murdering the victim?"

"No. I did not hear any admission of guilt."

"At any time has Mr. Ward admitted to killing Jennifer Wright?"

"Not when I was present."

"I'm done with the witness," I say, walking back to my table and sitting down, while Dan stands.

Nelson leans into me and whispers, "What the hell are you doing?"

"My job," I say, as Dan asks, "Ms. Marks, was the door open when you heard this conversation about the phone call between Nelson and Kelli Ward?"

"No," she says.

"In other words, the conversation was muffled?"

"The walls are thin," Geneva states. "I hear everything."

"Is there any chance you might have overheard a portion of the conversation?" Dan presses.

"Unlikely."

"Yes or no?"

"Ah—yes."

"I'm done with the witness," Dan states, walking back to his table.

Nelson grabs my arm and leans into me. "Leave it."

I stand back up, forcing his hand from my arm. "Redirect, your honor?" Seeing the judge's agreement, I press forward, "Ms. Marks, have you ever heard something through the walls and found it to be untrue later?"

"No, I have not."

She's dismissed, and I motion for Richard to retrieve Kelli. "Judge, we're retrieving Kelli Ward, who will be our next witness."

"Ask for a break," Nelson orders.

I clench my teeth. I'm on a timeline I don't want disrupted. I lean into him. "If we break and I don't close today, we risk a long deliberation next week that's not in your best interest."

"I'm going to fire you if you continue on this path."

"You won't get that approved, but you'll make yourself look guilty or make Kelli look guilty along with you. Do you really want to do that?"

He inhales sharply and settles back in his seat. I am smiling inside, though. That interaction was witnessed. He looked afraid, and not for himself. For his wife. He looks like a man protecting a guilty woman. I didn't understand this kind of connection between two people before Cat. I do now. After only a few weeks, I'd do anything to protect Cat. The difference between me and Nelson is that, unlike Kelli, Cat is worth the battle.

Chapter Twenty-Eight

Reese

Kelli takes the stand and is sworn in, completely unaware of the conversation I had with Geneva in this courtroom.

"Do you love your husband?" is my first question.

"Yes," she says. "Of course."

"Why?"

"He's everything. Good looking, generous, kind," she says. "He's everything," she repeats.

"How long have you been married?"

"Five years," she states.

"The same amount of time Geneva Marks has been his secretary."

"Objection," Dan growls. "Is there a question?"

"How long has Geneva Marks been his secretary?"

"Since the week before we were married," she says. "Five years."

"Did you ever work for your husband's companies?"

"Yes. I was a secretary to one of his partners in another building."

"What do you do now?" I ask.

She frowns. "Why is this relevant?"

The prosecutor interjects, "Objection. She's right. Why is this relevant?"

I look to Judge Moore, who is sixty, with a lifetime in the court, but he's tough, and not always fair. "I'm on a path, judge. I'm getting there."

"Get there quickly," he states, looking at Kelli. "Answer the question."

I nod. "What do you do now, Mrs. Ward?"

"I run our household," she states. "My husband is a busy man. I look out for him."

"In other words, your life is about your husband. You live for him."

"Objection," Dan shouts. "Leading, and again, where is this going?"

"I'll move on," I say. "As a secretary, would you say that a secretary knows the innermost workings of a busy man?"

"Yes. I would."

"Including Geneva Marks, your husband's secretary?"

"Yes. Including her."

"Did you know Jennifer Wright?"

"Yes."

"How?"

"My husband saw her crying at a coffee shop he frequents. She worked there. He started talking to her daily for a few weeks. When she finally opened up about her situation, he talked to me, and asked my input. That's when I suggested a better-paying job would work wonders for her, and I just happened to know about a friend looking for a nanny."

"And that friend can confirm the interview was set up?"

"She can, yes."

"Please state her name for the courtroom records."

"Carrie Matthews."

I look at the judge as Richard moves forward. "Entering into the record a statement from Carrie Matthews confirming this information."

Once that is complete, I move on and return to the prior topic. "Have you ever fought with your husband in his office?"

"Yes. Couples fight."

"Have you ever fought over Jennifer?"

"No. Of course not."

"Did you ever fight about this investigation in his office?"

"Yes."

"What about it?"

"Random things. I don't remember."

"Did Jennifer Wright call your husband's phone the night she's believed to have been murdered?"

"Yes," she states.

"Did you have an argument about that call in your husband's office, within hearing range of his secretary?"

She stares at me. "I think we might have."

"Was Geneva Marks at her desk at the time?"

"Yes. I believe she was."

"Why did you argue?"

She shifts in her chair. "Does it matter?"

"Answer the question, Mrs. Ward," the judge orders.

"I wanted to tell the police that I took that call, but he didn't want me to," she says, contradicting what Geneva told us.

There is rumbling in the courtroom, and, of course, assumed guilt placed on my client. But I'm not done. "But you did not."

"No."

"Why?" I press.

"He felt it would drag me into this," she says. "More so than I already have been."

"Based on that argument that was witnessed by your husband's secretary, who took the call?"

"Me. I took the call."

There is another rumbling of voices in the courtroom and the judge calls the court to order, and then looks at me. "Continue."

"How did you go about answering your husband's phone?"

"I was reading in bed and he was asleep and I didn't want to wake him up," she says. "I grabbed the call and went to the other room."

"How long was the call?"

"An hour or so. It was a lengthy conversation," she confirms. "But she needed to talk."

"Did your husband talk to her?"

"No."

"Was your husband aware that *you* were talking to her?" I ask.

"Not until I'd been on the call with her for a while."

"Why did you take the call at all?"

"I knew Jennifer wanted to know about a job interview I mentioned and how it went. She was working late that night."

"Why did she call your husband and not you?"

"Her mother was very judgmental of her pregnancy. I think that made her more comfortable with men than women. But we were working on that."

"In that conversation with Jennifer, what else did you talk about?"

"She had a lot of problems with the father of her child. We talked about him."

"Were you jealous of Jennifer?"

"Of course not! I loved her. She was so sweet. And I loved that my husband wanted to help her."

"Did you believe he was having an affair with her?"

"Not at all."

"Were you ever jealous about other women?"

"No, never."

"Not even Geneva Marks?"

"No. Of course not."

"You never fought with your husband over Geneva in his office."

"I—I don't remember."

"But you were never jealous."

"I don't remember!"

"Did you kill Jennifer Wright and her unborn child?"

"No. No, I did not."

"Did you agree to meet her that night?"

"No."

"And yet you were the last person to talk to her that night."

"Objection," Dan shouts. "Badgering the witness."

"I'm done with this witness." I walk to my table, and Dan walks toward the stand.

"Did you kill the victim and her unborn child?" Dan asks, echoing my question.

"No," Kelli says.

"Did your husband?" he asks.

"No."

"That's your opinion, not a fact, correct?" Dan presses.

"It's a fact," she says. "I'd bet my life on it."

"Do you make a point of claiming opinions as facts?" he asks.

"I do not."

"But you needed to bet on this one because there were no facts," the prosecutor states.

"Objection," I say, but Dan moves on before I finish.

"Were you with your husband at the time of the murder?" Dan asks.

"Yes, according to the timeline I've been given."

"Are you being truthful with us today?" Dan asks.

"Of course," she states.

"Did you tell your husband that you wanted to confess your conversation with Ms. Wright, or did he tell you to confess?"

"As I stated, I wanted to confess."

They go back and forth for an hour until the prosecution takes his seat. I stand up. "Judge, permission to redirect requested"

"I'll allow," the judge states and Dan remains silent.

I immediately focus on Kelli. "Where was your husband at the time of the murder, as stated by law enforcement?"

"Asleep in bed."

"Where were you?'

"Also asleep."

I sit down. Dan stands up. "Judge permission to recross."

"Objection," I say. "He had his time."

"The jury needs the facts," the judge replies. "Recross allowed."

Dan moves quickly to questioning Kelli. "Could your husband have left the house while you slept, without you knowing?"

"Yes, but—"

"That's all," Dan says, and he sits back down.

I stand. "Judge permission-"

"Last time counselor. This is it. Make it good."

"Objection," Dan shouts.

"You're late," the judge says. "I've granted his request. Make it quick, Mr. Summer."

I nod and look at Kelli. "Have you ever left the house while your husband was asleep without him knowing?"

"Well, I—"

"Yes or no."

"I— Yes."

I look at the judge. "The witness is dismissed."

The judge looks at Dan, and he approves. I stand now and make my declaration: "The defense rests its case."

The judge looks at his watch. "It's now ten-thirty a.m. In the interest of time and the weekend, we'll break for a thirty-minute lunch and proceed with closing statements." He hits the gavel on the block.

The courtroom erupts in voices and movement, and I, along with my team and client, head toward the door, while I prepare for the war I'm about to fight. Nelson and Kelli are guided into the conference room first, and as soon as I step inside, Kelli slaps me in the face. "You bastard."

She tries to slap me again, and I catch her arm. "What are you mad about? You just ensured your husband's freedom."

"And turned the police attention to me."

She tries to slap me again, but one of my co-counsels obviously got guards, because they grab her. "Do you want to press charges, Mr. Summer?"

"No charges," I say. "Just get her out of here."

They drag her out of the room. "You're fired," Nelson growls.

I arch a brow. "You want to deliver your own closing statement? Are you sure about that? Because this trial is ending with or without me." I don't tell him the judge won't let him fire me this far into this thing. I want him to fear being lost and lonely in that courtroom.

"You're fired."

I smile. "Well. Good luck." I turn and walk toward the door.

"Wait. Fuck."

I face him. "Did you want pointers?"

"Since when does an attorney ignore his client's wishes?"

"You told me to get you off at all costs. The cost was what just happened in that courtroom."

"If they come after her, will you defend her?"

"No. Because I don't defend killers unless they had a justified reason for their actions, namely survival. Is she worth becoming a play toy in jail?" I ask. "Because you will be. The pretty boy who gets everyone off. Literally. And I'm not sure the guards will provide Vaseline."

He covers his face with his hands, and he's trembling. "I love her."

I walk to the conference table and press my hands to it, angry now. "A woman and her unborn child are dead. Do you really love a woman who would kill them?"

He opens his eyes. "I don't know that she did it."

"Don't you? And you know what? If you let her get away with it, you are just as evil as she is. In fact, I'm not sure I can even do the closing. Maybe I should hand it to my co-counsel."

"What do you want me to do?"

"Do you have proof that she killed Jennifer?" I press.

"No. Yes. Maybe. I found something last week."

"What?"

"In her purse. There was a necklace that Jennifer always wore. I saw it in her purse, but it doesn't mean she killed her."

"Tell the police."

"I will," he assures me and he sounds like he means it.

"And get the fuck away from her before you end up dead, too." I push off the desk and exit the room, entering the one across the hall. I don't rehearse my closing that I've beaten to death. I call Cat.

Chapter Twenty-Nine

Cat

The short break is over at eleven, and I swear I'm so nervous for Reese that I feel like I'm the one about to deliver a closing. I have to force myself to sit, and when Reese finds his way to his table and his eyes meet mine, that connection between us is more powerful than ever. He lets me see the nerves that no one else in this room can see, and I watch them transform into hard determination. Somehow, in that brief moment, a million words pass between us without one spoken.

The court is called to order, and Dan takes center stage. His closing is a short twenty minutes, but despite this conciseness, at its conclusion, I can say that it is far better than I expected. He uses words like "dead baby" and "young woman kept from motherhood." He talks about the brutal hit to her head as she was pushed to her death. And the real kicker that he plays on over and over: A rich, powerful man who didn't want his business and his life destroyed by a pregnant mistress. A rich, powerful man that didn't know the baby wasn't his.

I'm feeling pretty worried until Reese stands up. He speaks for forty minutes exactly in what is a powerful, intelligent delivery of the critical points. He recaps the key points about no evidence and details the only evidence in the crime: Fingerprints on a door that could have been left at any time.

"If I," Reese says, "visited the victim two days before her death, should it be assumed I killed her? Is that the way you would want our justice system to work if you or your loved one was innocent and sitting on the stand? Let's talk about reasonable doubt. Did the prosecutor prove to you that my client put his fingerprint on that door the day the victim died? If not, if you aren't sure he was there that day, that's reasonable doubt. If you have reasonable doubt, you must acquit."

He ends his statement with a list of suspects. "If you have any inclination to believe one of these people I've presented as suspects killed the victims, then you also have reasonable doubt about my client. Reasonable doubt equals acquittal. Guilty until proven innocent is another country. This is America. Here we are innocent until proven guilty."

The jury is attuned to him, listening, nodding, scribbling notes. I didn't see them doing that with Dan. By twelve, all eyes are on the judge. "The jury foreman has spoken on behalf of the jury and asked that they begin deliberations this afternoon rather than Monday morning, in hopes they can end their sequestration. We will reconvene at four thirty, at which time we will either read a verdict or adjourn for Monday morning." He bangs the gavel.

When I would exit the courtroom with the rest of the crowd, a bailiff catches me. "This way, miss." I follow him to a private hallway, and it's not long before I'm in a private office with Reese, who immediately kisses me.

"Well?" he asks.

"It was as brilliant as I knew it would be."

His hands settle on his waist under his jacket. "Did you watch the jury?"

"You had them."

"Dan?"

"Not like you. And you ended the trial. You have this. What do Elsa and Richard think?"

"I don't debrief with my team. I don't want opinions when I can't change history."

But he asked for mine. "Where is Nelson Ward?"

"With my team. He forbade me from entering. He has his panties in a wad over Kelli."

"After all you've done for him, he forbade your entry?"

"Fuck him. I defended the hell out of his ass." He puffs out a breath. "Let me go check with my team and let's get some air. I need air."

Fifteen minutes later, we are at a coffee shop around the corner with an outdoor area and heaters, talking nonstop about everything but the trial while Reese's phone blows up with text messages and calls, most of which he ignores. "Anything on the publishing deal?"

"No, but when a board has to approve money, it takes time."

He glances at his watch. "It's been almost an hour."

"Do you think they will even call us back until four thirty?"

"I was hoping they'd walk into a room, cast a vote, and be done."

"One and done," I tease.

"That's right, sweetheart. This time, I wanted a one and done."

"What's next after this trial?"

"I actually have a case that I have a junior partner working on, but it's my client and someone I went to school with."

"So it's personal."

"Not personal but he's a casual friend and like I said a good guy in a bad situation that hit him right as I went to trial. I actually need to go to the office tomorrow and catch up on the case, so I can hit the ground running Monday."

"Tomorrow? You are a beast, aren't you?"

He laughs and nuzzles my neck. "You ain't seen nothing yet, sweetheart. After I have that meetup with him, though, I'm decompressing. No anything."

I have this sudden realization that after this trial, I don't know what comes next for him or me. Or us. I'm only staying with him until the trial is over, and it's basically over. His phone rings and he glances at the number, a strange look on his face. "I need to take this," he says. "I'll be right back."

He stands up and leaves me here alone to take the call in private.

I'm dumbfounded. I don't even know what to think. He's never acted like something was too private for me to be privy to it. I feel odd. I feel out of place. I feel like I have never felt with Reese. Maybe the ride is over. Maybe I just got too serious. He's gone for almost fifteen minutes. I watch the news on a television nearby after ruling out working. I can't write. I'm too off right now.

Suddenly, Reese is rushing back. "The jury is back."

"Oh God," I say. "That was fast."

"The Friday night cure for a long deliberation," he says. "Let's go see if we're drinking to celebrate or wallowing."

I grab my coat and he helps me slip it on, and it's not long before we're running toward the courthouse. Fifteen minutes later, I'm holding my breath as the judge reads the jury's ruling. "We the jury find the defendant not guilty on the charge of first-degree murder."

Reese, his team, and Nelson Ward all slump forward in relief.

The formality of the jurors verbally confirming their vote begins, and then I'm led to the back room again with Reese, who grabs me, picks me up, and spins me around. I'm laughing with his team in the hallway when Nelson comes up to Reese and holds out his hand. "Thank you. *Thank you.*"

Reese shakes his hand. "Do what's right now. Justice is in your hands."

"I'm going to," he assures Reese. "But I need an attorney to protect me while I do."

"You're untouchable now," Reese says. "But if you want to hand over a killer, I'll proudly represent you through that process. Where is she now?"

"I don't know, and I have concerns she might flee."

Reese grabs his phone and dials. "Royce. Yes. Thanks. Make sure Kelli doesn't get out of your sight." He gives Nelson a pointed look and adds, "Nelson Ward needs a detective we can trust to talk to about Kelli. Can you make that happen? Right. Got it." He ends the call. "Royce Walker will be here with law enforcement when the press conference ends. Let's go do this."

His team heads for the door, and he stops beside me. "I'm going to have to deal with the police and Kelli."

"I know."

He pulls me close. "Meet me at my place. Okay?"

"Yes. Okay."

He kisses me and presses his cheek to mine to whisper, "I can't wait to get you alone again." And with that he walks away.

I don't. I stand there feeling awkward, like the kind of awkward I never felt after the first night, the one and done that is yet to be one and done. I don't like how this feels.

Chapter Thirty

Cat

I watch the press conference, and when it's all said and done, I can't seem to get myself to go to Reese's apartment. I don't seem to want to go to mine, either. I end up at the coffee shop, with my coat on a chair, and a coffee and my MacBook as my company. I'm also in my pink dress, which I wore today because I like pink and I can. No other reason.

I exhale, really, really hating this nagging feeling inside me, but I power through my work. I've just reached my closing statement when Lauren calls. "Royce said Nelson Ward is turning on his wife?"

"Yes. I was there when he asked Reese to help him do what was right."

"Wow," she says. "Just wow. I hope they get her."

"Me too. I really do."

We talk for a good half-hour, and right when we're about to hang up, she says, "What's wrong?"

"I'm exhausted. I'm writing my column and just mentally drained."

"Is something up with you and Reese?"

"No. Nothing."

"You're sure?"

"Yes. I'm sure and you sound better, by the way."

"I am," she says. "It's crazy and sudden. I was sick all the time. Now I'm not."

We hang up five minutes later, and I ask myself the same question she asked me. *Is* something wrong with me and Reese? Maybe it's just dysfunctional me, looking for a problem. I shake off that thought and go back to my closing statement but I end up staring at the page. Nothing comes to me. I force myself to start typing:

The system worked today. You are innocent until proven guilty. Nelson Ward was not proven guilty. But justice is not done until the crime is solved. It's time that we the people demand that the crime be solved. Demand justice for Jennifer Wright and her unborn child. Until then, —Cat.

There. Done. Marked off my list.

From there, I plan out next week's columns, and I've just finished up when my cellphone rings again. I look down to find Liz's number on caller ID. "Hi Liz."

"I just heard from your publisher," she says.

I glance at the time. "At eight o'clock on a Friday night?"

"Yes. The trial ended. They're in a panic to sign you. They raised the offer to seven hundred thousand. Five hundred for the trial book as long as Reese Summer signs on as a consultant. His compensation is on you. The second option book, will be two hundred thousand, which is double your last book."

As long as Reese signs a consulting form. That knots my stomach for no good reason. He will. I know he will. "Okay."

"Okay? I just said seven hundred thousand dollars and you said okay? I know we said seven-fifty but this is close."

"I know. I'm exhausted. It's been a crazy week."

"You and Reese have issues."

"No."

"No?" she presses.

"No."

"That's it? That's all you're going to say?"

"Yes," I say. "Is this better than taking a proposal out to the masses? I don't like their connection to Dan."

"I believe it is for this reason: If you walk away from your option publisher and don't get more, your option publisher won't take you back at this price. This is a lot of money to gamble with."

"Right. I'll let you know Monday."

"Sunday night," she insists.

"Okay."

"I don't like 'okay,' Cat."

"Okay."

She makes a frustrated sound. "I'll call you Sunday." She hangs up. I send my column to my editor that appears to be hanging in my browser and consider starting on Monday's, but Kelli's arrest would change it completely. Instead, I research what I'm going to write about post-Nelson Ward. Maybe post-Reese Summer. I pinpoint a few interesting cases and start doing research, two of which I'd like to sit in on the trials when they begin.

It's nine, and the coffee shop is empty and closing in half an hour when my phone rings with Reese's number, and I breathe out, nervous to answer when that is not what I feel with Reese. "Hello."

"Hey, beautiful. Are you at home?"

Home. Which home? His home? My home? "I'm at the coffee shop."

"I'm in an Uber. Hold on." I can hear him giving the driver this address. "Okay. On my way. Nelson gave a statement about Kelli before getting on a plane and out of town."

"Out of the country?"

"No. He agreed to be within reach if needed. Kelli was taken in for questioning."

"How do you think that will play out?"

"I think she'll lawyer up and be tough to break, but Nelson is going to file for divorce and pile it on her all at once." His phone beeps. "Hold on." He is gone a moment and returns. "That's Royce. I'll see you in ten."

"Okay."

We disconnect and I sigh. I seem to be the queen of "okay" tonight, when I'm not sure I've said that word this many times in my life. I'm simply not that agreeable. I yank at the tight knot at the back of my head and free my hair before I start to pack up, and suddenly Dan is sitting in front of me. "You're writing a book with Reese, I hear."

"You heard wrong. I'm writing a book. Reese agreed to be interviewed. Would you like to be interviewed?"

"I'll tell my story my own way."

"Of course you will. Because you are so very predictable."

"What does that mean?"

"It means an asshole never lets someone else tell their story because they don't want to be called an asshole. Hopefully your writing is better than your ability to present evidence."

"There's more to my story than you know, little girl."

"Little girl?" I laugh. "You really do speak great asshole."

"You have a smart mouth."

"Thank you. My mama taught me. She'd be proud."

"You were hell on me in your write-ups."

"And now we get to the reason you're standing here. Do better. I'll do better. I'm fair."

"You were hell in a courtroom, weren't you?"

"Yep, but I hated every minute of it. I think you do, too." I lean forward. "And you will never do better if you hate what you do."

"Maybe I'll retire and write books."

"If that's what you want, then you should do it. Don't keep losing cases when the result is no one going to jail. Because like you said, no one went to jail. And Jennifer deserved better than that."

"Bitch."

"Asshole."

He turns and walks away.

I watch him exit, and Reese walks in the door, his dark hair a rumpled, sexy mess, his tie loose. Dan grunts at him and disappears. Reese frowns and walks toward me, all loose-legged swagger and hotness and just seeing him still makes me warm all over. He stops at the table and pulls me to my feet, and he doesn't seem to care that we're in public. The fingers of one of his hands tangle in my hair and he's kissing me—no, drugging me is the only way to describe how this man's tongue makes every nerve ending in my body tingle.

"Hi," he says, stroking hair from my face.

"Hi."

"You having an affair with Dan?"

I laugh. "No. Believe it or not, I'm not attracted to assholes."

"Good thing I'm not an asshole. How do you feel about pizza, champagne, me, and bed?"

He assumes I'm going home with him, when I'd assumed—nothing. I didn't know what we were doing, but now, with him, I think I was living in the past again. Seeing the ghost of Mitch who is long gone. "Yes to all," I say. "Please."

We both start smiling when I say please.

I decide that call he took in private was nothing, while he's becoming everything.

Chapter Thirty-One

Reese

I wake Saturday morning to Cat curled next to me, that sweet floral scent of her clinging to me and the sheets, pretty much sealing the deal on morning wood. Unfortunately, my phone is also buzzing on the nightstand, and appears to be the reason I woke up. I grab it and note the seven a.m. hour and my sister's number on the display. My cell stops ringing and she immediately sends me a text. *Answer your phone, superhero. Glad you won your case, but the rest of your life calls.* She means my parents' marital problems, and that isn't a situation I'm prepared to deal with in front of Cat, at least not until Cat and I have the "my fucked-up family" conversation. Which, to be fair, I need to have this weekend.

Knowing Stacey, she'll call back another ten times. I ease away from Cat, careful not to wake her. I snag my pajama bottoms and T-shirt from the floor and pull them on but I don't walk away. I stand beside the bed, staring down at Cat, fully aware that my invitation for her stay through the end of the trial has ended.

No. My excuse to have her stay. Only, I still want her here, and it's time to have that straight up conversation. She needs to know that I don't want to wake up or go to sleep without her next to me. I'm not letting her leave.

I round the bed and walk into the bathroom, brush my teeth, and splash water on my face. Since the meetings I set up for today when I was on my way to pick up Cat last night aren't until after lunch, I decide coffee and Cat are on the menu. I exit to the bedroom again, and find Cat has snuggled deeper into the blankets, completely content and sound asleep. Coffee first, I decide. Cat later. I smile and head downstairs, flipping on the fireplace in the den, which is off the kitchen, before I brew a cup of coffee and set up my computer on the island. I grab a barstool at the end cap of the island, with a good view of the stairs, where Cat will eventually travel.

After keying my MacBook to life, I scan the headlines about the case and pull up Cat's column with the intent of reading it. I also plan to make this my new morning ritual now that the trial is over and the millions of cameras are off. Now, I can admit that was a hell of a lot of pressure.

My phone rings, which I expected. I glance at caller ID and answer the call. "Hello, sunshine."

"Answer your phone when I call," my sister snaps.

"I was asleep. I do that occasionally."

"Mom and Dad had a huge fight."

"You said that yesterday when you called me on the final day of the trial of my career."

"Yes, but now she left him. She won't answer our calls. No one can find her. Dad's freaking out."

"Maybe she finally got smart and found another man," I suggest, one of my few statements anyone could call hopeful.

"That's your reply?" Stacey snaps. "Really, Reese?"

"I spent years battling this war with them and got the fuck out. You should too."

"She won't return our calls. What if something happened to her?"

"How long has it been?" I ask.

"Twelve hours."

"She's fine," I say, comforting my sister, though I'm secretly worried. She doesn't cut off her kids. Or her ass of a husband, for that matter. "She's a fifty-five-year-old woman who's beautiful, smart, and capable. Give her some space."

Her phone beeps. "That's her. I've gotta go." She hangs up.

I dial my brother Dylan. "He's got another girlfriend," Dylan says as his greeting.

"Of course he does," I say, weary of this topic.

"She's thirty-two. Blonde. Beautiful. I'd fuck her. Dad's fucking her. It's fucked up."

"I knew he wouldn't change," I say. "I don't know why she stays. We're all grown up now. We don't need stability, and there was never stability in the first place."

"Apparently, she's not this time," he says. "She disappeared."

"She just called Stacey."

"Thank God," he says. "I had this image in my head of one of Dad's women killing her. I've told him that. He's going to pick a crazy one, one day, and there will be no turning back."

"And now you get why I left."

"I'm taking that to mean you won't be home for Christmas again," he says.

"Hell the fuck no."

His line beeps. "I don't have to look at the caller ID. Stacey is calling me."

"Text me an update. I'm going to be in meetings today."

"Always working and winning. Congrats, man, on the win. I hope he didn't do it."

"He didn't."

"Fuck," Dylan growls. "Stacey hung up."

My line starts beeping. "She's calling me," I say.

"I'll call her. Consider Christmas. You have about three months to decide. I can't do another one alone."

"Come here to me," I suggest. "Get away from the hell there."

"I might. I really might. Ciao." He hangs up.

I start reading Cat's column, lost in the mind of this woman who has taken over my world. She's sharp, witty, and intelligent. She's also tough as nails, with a big attitude that shows in her writing. My fingers thrum on the table. My mother is all of those things, and yet she stays with my father when I am certain Cat would kick me to the curb if I acted like him. Why does my mother stay?

Footsteps sound, and I look up to find Cat entering the kitchen in a fluffy pink robe, the top gaping widely and offering me a glimpse of her left breast. Her long blonde hair a tangled, sexy mess that just makes me want to fuck her ten times to Sunday and forget work. She crosses to the island to stand on the edge right beside me, her green eyes bright as she reaches for my coffee and takes a sip. She crinkles her nose. "You drink your coffee like stout whiskey," she says, setting the cup down. "It gets the job done, but it's no fun in the process."

I laugh and swivel my chair around, pulling her to me. "Like I get the job done?"

"Yes, but sometimes you're fun."

"Sometimes? Is that right?"

"Yes," she says. "Sometimes. Sometimes you're very intense, like in the shower yesterday."

"Right. About that—"

"You don't need to explain," she says, flattening her hand on my chest. "You had cameras and the world watching. I know how trial days are, remember? And I wasn't at your level of public exposure." She kisses my cheek. "I'm going to leave you with your stout coffee and make something more palatable." She skirts around me, and I swivel my chair to follow her, watching as she navigates my kitchen like she's lived here more than a week. And she is basically living here.

"What time are you going to work?" she asks, sticking a pod in the coffee maker and setting a cup underneath the spout.

"Noonish," I say. "But my meeting isn't until four. I'm reviewing pretty much everything going on in the firm that I've missed up to today."

"I'm sure that is a load," she says. "I'll head home after I shower." She turns away, giving me her back as she doctors her coffee, while I'm focused on that word: *Home.*

Fuck. She has one of those that isn't here. We can both forget that anytime now.

"Cat."

She turns to face me, crossing her arms in front of her. She never crosses her arms in front of her. "I have work to do too, and laundry, along with what is probably piles of mail. I can't believe I haven't even thought about my mail."

I stand up and step in front of her. "Do you really want to be there instead of here?"

"I have my own apartment, Reese," she says, those arms uncurling, her hands settling on my chest.

"Okay. Would you rather be there than here? We can stay there."

"We?"

"Yes, Cat. We. That's what we're doing, right?"

"We have been, but—"

"But? I can tell you that you don't have to finish that sentence and I already don't like it. Either we are or we aren't."

"Okay."

"Okay? That's passive for you."

"It's my new word. I do agreeable, and then when I'm not agreeable, you remember how agreeable I've been. Because when I'm not agreeable, I'm *really* not agreeable."

My hands settle on the counter on either side of her. "You referenced how intense I was yesterday. You do know that I was not in normal form, right?"

"Of course I do. Like I said, you had the cameras on you. The pressure was intense."

"Talk to me, Cat."

"I—It's stupid and I feel ridiculous."

"Please tell me."

"You took a call and just left me sitting there in the coffee shop, and I don't know why, but it felt weird. Like you were hiding something. And no, I don't know why. Because you've never been secretive before, but it felt secretive, though you have a right, and—"

"You're right," I say. "I got up because I didn't want you to hear that conversation. It was my sister and it was family drama."

"You think I can't handle your family drama? You do remember mine, right?"

"Look," I say, pushing off the counter and scrubbing the stubble on my jaw, "my parents are one big war zone. They always have been. They are the reason I've had no interest in relationships."

"And yet I'm here."

"Yes. You're here. You're different. You made me break my own rules, but I need you to know that I'm not going to be my father, and yes, I'll elaborate on what I mean. I would just prefer to do it when I'm not about to leave for work."

"Okay," she says, "but know this: Nothing you tell me about your parents affects who you are to me."

I cup her face and kiss her. "I hope not, because I'm not letting you go. One way or the other, we're together this weekend. We can stay here or at your place."

"We can stay here, but I do need to go home and check on things and get some things handled."

"Why don't we meet back here right before dinner and I'll take you someplace nice? Or I can pick you up and bring your things here, if you have a bag."

"Why don't you just call me when you're wrapping up?"

"That works. Do reservations at eight work for you?"

"Yes. Great."

"In the meantime, breakfast." I scoop her up and start walking, with the bedroom our destination breakfast location. I climb the steps and lay her on my bed then join her, settling on top of her.

That's when my phone starts ringing in my pocket again. I ignore it and lean in to kiss Cat, but she presses her fingers to my lips. "Shouldn't you get that?"

"No." I remove her hand from my mouth and kiss her. She tasted like toothpaste earlier. Now she tastes like toothpaste and coffee, which is apparently exactly what I needed to have that morning wood return. My phone starts ringing again. Cat pushes me back. "What if it's your family?"

"It is my family."

"Then you take it. You deal with it. I'll go take a shower."

I roll off of her and onto my back. "Fuck." I grab my phone and look at the number. "My sister."

Cat leans over and kisses me. "I'm not going anywhere. Take care of them."

She climbs off the bed, and I roll to watch her leave, not giving two shits that my phone stops ringing again. Right now, my mind has gone to a place it has never gone with any other woman: I'm falling in love with Cat. Hell, I probably already am in love with her. Either way, there's no turning back. I wasn't lying when I said she had me at "asshole."

Cat

The moment I walk back into my apartment, I have knots in my belly. I love this apartment. It represents freedom and my decision to live my life, not the one my father designed for me. But it's also a place where my mother forced seclusion on herself. It's a place where I have forced seclusion on myself. Where alone felt better than being with anyone else.

No. Alone felt safer. At that time in my life, I think it was actually safer. I wasn't in a place to have a relationship. I wasn't sure that I would be ever again. But then came Reese. And oddly, his place feels more like freedom, while this place feels like a prison. It was my mother's prison, the place she went to hide from my father, rather than just leaving him. It kills me to think of what she felt when she came here.

I walk to the kitchen, drop the pile of mail in my arms onto the counter, and start going through it. I consider dusting and cleaning, but instead I just call a maid service and arrange to have it handled through security. I left my laundry at Reese's house, and I have no court visit to dress for next week. Really, I'm pretty set. With hours left before dinner, I'm already in my comfy VS boyfriend sweats, and my writing chair is calling me. I settle down in my favorite chair in the living area. I have missed this chair, which is a soft navy felt, my contrast piece to all the grays of the living room's decor.

I go back to working on next week's features for my column, but I keep pulling up the book outline I started. I have to decide about that book deal, but that means I need to talk to Reese. I need to pay him. That way he never feels taken advantage of, and I don't want to hide my pay from him. Even if I give him two hundred thousand, I'll make three times what I made on my last book. I'm going to talk to him.

I get to work and write three more columns about the Nelson Ward trial, and then pick a new case, which I email to my editor as a proposed feature. Right at three, my phone buzzes with a text message and I look at the screen to find a text from Reese: *I got us a reservation at nine at Eleven Madison Park. That was the earliest I could get us in.*

I smile because that's a place I mentioned to him today, as a favorite, which I never indulge in visiting. I text back: *It's perfect.*

He replies back with: *I will need to shower and change. My place—eight o'clock? I'm going to stay here and get all my work knocked out.*

I answer with: *That works.*

He replies with: *Make it seven. You can shower with me.*

I smile and type: *Six forty-five. We'll need the extra time.*

Six-thirty it is, he replies.

I laugh, but it fades quickly. I think I might love this man. I'm pretty sure *I do* love this man, but I'll stick with pretty sure for now, since I don't know what he and I are doing. Am I sleeping here or there, or what beyond this weekend? Has a one night stand become a one month fling or more? Talking to him about the overstep of calling my publisher, and about that phone call, worked. I just need to talk to him about this and the publishing deal, too. Talk to him. I like that he's made that feel like the answer.

I get back to work, and ideas start flowing and I lose myself. That's the release I love about writing, and investigating a case I want to attack from a view no one else is highlighting. I'm blurry-eyed when my phone rings, and I glance down to find Gabe's number. Gabe again? This is odd. Frowning, I answer the call. "What's wrong?"

"Can you meet me for dinner tonight?"

"Actually, no. I have plans."

"How about drinks, then?"

My brow furrows. "Why?"

"I want to see you."

"Why?" I press.

"Dad has some business situation going on. In case it hits the press, I want to talk it through with you."

"What kind of issues?"

"I don't want to talk about this on the phone. I'm bringing that other guy you call your brother, too."

"Reid is coming. Okay. Now I'm worried."

"It's nothing we can't handle, but like I said. If it gets out, I want you to have a heads-up."

"What time and where?"

"Boulevard Two on Fifty-eighth at eight."

"Too far. I have reservations at nine. Make it six and pick someplace closer to me."

"We'll just come there at seven thirty. This won't take long. I'll bring booze."

"Booze? *What* is going on?"

"See you then, little sis." He hangs up.

I glance at the clock. It's three thirty. Reese's meeting is at four, and he must be preparing for it.

I opt to text, not call. *I need to meet you at the restaurant. I've had something come up.*

He calls me. "Is something wrong?"

"I don't know. Two of my brothers want to stop by tonight. Gabe says it's something to do with my father's business, which is their business, too. It might make the press."

"What are you thinking?"

"A buyout or merger, but I'm not sure why they think I need to know in advance. They won't tell me anything else."

"Sounds odd. Why don't I just pick you up there?"

"Being honest here—I don't want you to come face to face with my brothers right now."

"Why, Cat?"

"Again being honest: They want me paired with a powerful attorney. That's what they loved about Mitch. They want someone they can align with and who they see pulling me back into that family circle. They will lean on us, and I'd rather do us as us, not us and them. At least until we know how we define us."

"I want to have a conversation about defining us anyway, but I agree. We need to have that conversation before we step into the mix of our families. I've got to go. I'll see you tonight, sweetheart." He hangs up.

He wants to define us before family is involved.

I'm not going to read into that in a good or bad way.

But between my brothers and Reese, this afternoon is going to be slow, and tonight eventful.

Chapter Thirty-Two

Reese

My office is off Central Park with a view to kill for. I glance out the window, taking in the view and wonder how many times I am here and actually see it even when I look at it. I wonder what Cat would think of the view. That's what she does for me. She makes me see things with fresh eyes.

Someone clears their throat, and I turn to find my junior partner, Nate Douglas, in the doorway. He's young, in jeans today like myself, and looking ten shades of hung over. "You're late," I say. "You were supposed to be here at two thirty. It's three thirty."

"Sorry, boss," he says, crossing to sit in front of my desk in a high-backed leather chair, the wood finish is a mahogany that matches my desk. "I have the flu."

"So you thought you'd tell me that now as you sit across from me, making *me* fucking sick. That seems like a good lie to you?"

He pales. "I'm hung over."

"You're a junior partner. You don't get hung over and come in late."

"You're right. It won't happen again."

"Do you have my file?"

He hands me the file I saw in his hand upon entry. "Here you go."

I glance at it and then him. His dark hair is newly buzzed and his expression is awkward, and it should be. "What am I looking at?"

"We notified the Feds that you represented the client."

"And?"

"The client doesn't want anyone else to talk to them," he says.

"The response, per this memo, is due Wednesday, and there is no case research at all."

"The client wants no one but you handling this."

"What if I was still in trial?"

"I understand, but—"

"Prep a letter asking for two weeks," I say, dropping the file in front of him. "Get me a number and an agent name that I can call now."

"It's in the file. Top page."

"Get me some research on the guts of this case, and who is involved now. I'll let you know what else I need after my meeting."

"Right," he says, heading for the door, and I want to kick his young ass. But he's not that young. He's twenty-eight. At twenty-eight, I was already impressing people, not burying them which is what he's about to do to my client. At some point, he obviously *did* impress my team here or he wouldn't be a junior partner in a firm of eight attorneys.

"Nate," I call out.

He turns to face me.

"What the fuck is going on?" I ask.

"Nothing."

"Answer again."

He covers his face and drops his head. "My wife left me. I work too much."

"Then you have the wrong wife or the wrong job. Make a decision and do one or the other right. I don't do in between. Now. Not later."

"Yes. I will. You're right." He turns and leaves.

I stare after him, aware that I was an asshole, as Cat would call me, but you don't take a partner role and fuck around with your work. You don't take a wife and fuck around on her by way of time or other women.

I dig for the agent's information, a guy named Joseph Downs, and call him. He actually answers. "I took this case as I was going to trial because I know this guy. He's as honest as they come."

"He shouldn't be playing with people who aren't, then."

"I need time to research what happened. Three weeks."

"One week."

"Two."

"Fine, but not a day longer, and I want an in-person interview on the fifteenth day. You get fourteen free days. And you know why you get those days?"

"Tell me."

"My buddy aided the Jennifer Wright case. He said the wife did it, and I hear you got the husband to turn on her."

"I did, but it's too bad that wasn't the direction law enforcement went in the first place. I wouldn't have defended her. Someone who sucks would have."

"I hear the DA made that decision. But like I said, you get a favor. One. This doesn't protect your client." He hangs up.

The elevator dings and footsteps sound. My client, Casey Allen, appears in the doorway. "Hey, man. You ready for me?"

"Yeah. And fuck, I forget how tall you are. I guess there's a reason you played basketball."

He laughs. "Because I could walk it to the hoop." He shuts the door and joins me. "I wish I was still living the NBA life right now."

"I scanned the file," I say. "Nothing more yet."

"I get it. That was a big case you just won. Congrats, by the way."

"Thanks," I say. "He was innocent. He deserved that ruling."

"So am I."

"Tell me the story."

"I invested in this company that basically does investing. It seemed brilliant at the time, as do all stupid moves. Now they're being investigated for securities fraud. The principal is a guy named Larry Kurt. Good guy, I thought. Law degree from Yale. How could I go wrong, right? Next thing I know, the Feds are knocking on my door."

I believe him. "I bought you two weeks for me to research and prep a response," I say. "My team is going to research and prove you should be removed from this investigation."

"Two weeks?" he asks. "That's forever. I want this over."

"I get it, but it's better to respond right, not quickly."

We talk through a few important details and then I send him on his way. I buzz Nate's office. "I need to know everything about every principal in that company, down to what time they go to the bathroom. Take the files home. Get to work." He agrees, and I dial a partner who is damn good at corporate law, chat through the case, and form a game plan. He'll take over a portion of the case.

By the time I've gone back and forth with him and called my client to update him, it's already five. I'm meeting Cat in only a few hours. I decide to haul my stack of random case files home and work from there.

Thirty minutes later, I walk into my house, and holy fuck. It's empty. It's really damn empty without Cat. I walk to my home office and sit down, trying to work. I do work, but I'm aware of her not being here every moment. I glance at my watch, and it's time for me to go shower, and it has to be time for her to meet her brothers, which means she's likely stressed. I have half a mind to go over there, but I overstepped with the book deal. I won't do that again.

Cat

I dress in a burgundy pencil dress with long sleeves and a V-neck that I pair with black heels with sexy silk wraparound straps at my ankles. I then change into a simple black dress with a flared skirt and snug waist. I am, after all, seeing my brothers before Reese, and they will ask a million questions about my plans. I leave my hair loose and flat-iron it. My makeup is a bit more dramatic for evening, but still soft. I exit the bathroom for the bedroom door and turn back around. What am I doing? I see my brothers and I'm going to change clothes to avoid their questions? No. I just won't answer their questions. Period. I put the burgundy dress back on.

At seven forty-five, I've finished a glass of wine. I don't drink well, but I have to survive my brothers. My doorbell rings, and I consider another drink but decide to forgo it. I head to the door and open it. Sure enough, there stand my two big, blond, gorgeous, arrogant brothers. Reid, as the oldest, has a few age lines and a few extra inches on Gabe, but otherwise, they are twinkies, and both twinkies are looking me up and down. "Who is he?" Reid asks.

"You haven't spoken to me in months," I say. "And that is the first thing you say to me? The answer is none of your business. To the kitchen," I add, and turn and walk away.

I get there and pour that wine, of course. I need it. The two of them are in jeans and T-shirts which always seems off for them. Sometimes I think they sleep in three thousand dollar suit-pajamas. I consider saying that. I don't think they will be amused but I am. Gabe sets a bottle of some whiskey on the counter I won't drink. I don't look at it, but rather just stand on the opposite side of the island from them. The whole me-against-them thing.

"You look too good," Gabe says. "I don't like it."

"You both really need to not speak," I say.

"Your column's good, Cat," Reid says. "The kind of good it wouldn't be if you weren't a damn good Harvard graduate attorney. You should be practicing."

"Do you know, Reid, where you are standing? You are standing in the house that Mom came to get away from men who tried to rule her life. And our father, who fucked around on her all of the time."

"Mom didn't want to get away from Dad," Reid snaps.

"No? Stay right there." I walk to my office and return with the letter Mom wrote to me, which I've never let them read. I set it in front of them.

"What is that?" Gabe asks.

"The letter Mom wrote me before she died."

"I'm not reading that," Reid says sharply.

Gabe picks it up and starts reading, and it's not long before he's walking to the living room to be alone. Reid focuses on me. "We need a criminal attorney in the firm."

"Then hire one."

"We need someone we trust."

I narrow my eyes on him. "What's going on?"

"Dad wants to make peace."

"So he sends you, who hasn't made peace."

"I'm here."

"Because he sent you."

"No."

"Yes," I say.

"I think you're wasting your skills."

"I think you're a jerk who doesn't care about anything but your own agenda," I say. "Why do I matter?"

"It's a family business. You're my sister."

"What is really going on here?" I demand.

"Dad might have had a mini-stroke."

"What?" I shout, feeling as if I've been punched. "When?"

"Two weeks ago."

"Two weeks ago?!"

Gabe comes walking back in the room. "Reid, you have to read this."

"Dad had a stroke?" I demand of Gabe.

"Fuck, man," he says to Reid. "You couldn't wait on me?"

"You weren't here," Reid says.

"You didn't have a friend with a tragedy," I accuse of Gabe. "It was Dad."

"Both," Gabe says. "I had both happen."

"Why didn't both or one of you call me?"

"He wouldn't let us," Reid says. "And he's fine. He's back at work."

"He doesn't want me back in his life, does he? You two just think you can use this to get me back into the circle."

"This should be a wake-up call," Reid says.

"You asshole!" I yell. "Mom died of a stroke. You don't use this as leverage."

"I told him that," Gabe says. "I think you should keep doing what you're doing." He looks at Reid. "Read the fucking letter."

Reid snatches it up and starts reading while Gabe looks at me. "Dad's been stressed, on edge more than usual. We don't know why, but maybe it was the stroke coming on. He's fine though. He's going to take a trip with some woman he's seeing for the holidays and take time off work."

"If you don't agree with Reid, then why are you here?"

"To tell you that I don't agree with Reid, but he was coming at you anyway."

"Have you told Daniel?" I ask of my younger brother. "I assume he's shut out too, since you guys don't speak to us outsiders?"

"We wanted to tell you first. I'm going to call him when we leave, unless you want to call him."

"No. You call him. He deserves to find out and ask questions I can't answer."

Reid lowers the letter, scowls, and starts walking. Gabe grabs me and kisses my cheek. "I'll call you tomorrow."

He takes off too, and when the door shuts, I realize they took the letter. Damn it. I grab my purse and keys, and then my jacket off the coat rack, and go after them, but it's too late. I reach the elevator and the lobby and they are gone. I flag a cab and head to the restaurant. I'm early, but I don't care. I'm going to drink more wine, and one thing I know with certainty: Reese will carry me home if I need him to. He's the one man in my life I know really will catch me if I fall. I don't need a man to catch me—I can catch myself—but it's nice to know that he would right about now.

❦

Reese

I've just finished dressing in a black button-down and black slacks, and have pulled on a jacket, when my phone rings with a call from security. "Sir, you have a visitor at the front desk."

"Who?"

"She says it's a surprise and asked if I can send her up or if you could come down. I can escort her up if you like."

It has to be Cat. "Just send her up."

I end the call, and as much as I want to see Cat, it hits me then that she's cleared with security. I walk downstairs and pour a drink, downing the rich stout whiskey, while remembering Cat's stout coffee comment. I laugh and there is a knock on the door. Cat has a key. I set my glass down, and walk to the door, pulling it open. And the woman standing there is not Cat. She's the last person I expected to be here right now.

Chapter Thirty-Three

Cat

I sit in the restaurant waiting on Reese. And waiting. He's late, but I know how this goes. You get with a client and can't get out. He must still be at work. This night sucks. I'm not mad. Not at him. I don't have that capacity right now. I'm too focused on my father's stroke. I have a glass of wine. That makes three. My limit is really one. But I eat a bunch of bread and I'm remarkably okay. Funny how anger can sober you right up. Reese is still not here. At nine thirty, I decide maybe I'm angry. He can't be at work. I'm not going to make excuses for him. Then I get worried. My dad had a stroke. What if Reese had an accident? I call him. It goes to voice mail. I hang up.

I feel sick.

I hate men.

I will never have anyone in my life that is more than a fuck buddy. Fuck. Buddy. Fuck all day and all night to please me, and then get the fucking fuck buddy out of my life.

I throw money on the table and leave. I don't have a car. I call an Uber and sit on a bench at a corner I'm lucky to find. And then I just dial my father. I don't think. The wine does. He answers. "Cat?"

"You had a stroke?"

"It was nothing."

"And you didn't tell me?"

"It was nothing."

"It was a stroke. I don't like you, but I love you. You tell me when things matter, and just in case your hard head doesn't get it. This *matters*."

"It doesn't matter."

I hang up on him. And then I call him back. "It matters."

"I love you, too, Cat. And your book was good."

"You read my book?"

"Gabe nagged me until I did, and I'm glad I did. And your coverage of the trial was brilliant."

"Brilliant? Did my father just say brilliant?"

"Yes. Which is why you should—"

"Do not say it, or any ground we just made will be lost."

"Then we should hang up or I'm going to say it. We'll try this again soon."

"Okay."

"Goodnight, Cat."

I hang up and I really hate that I want to cry. I hate tears. They are born of weakness, and I don't like weakness at all. A stroke. He had a stroke and Reese still hasn't called. My Uber pulls up, and I stand up and get in. I'm alone again. I hate Reese Summer. Before him, alone felt good.

I turn my phone off.

I'm done.

Really, really done for the night.

Reese

My mother is melting down, crying hysterically, clinging to me. "I hate him. I hate that I stayed with him. I don't even know how to start over. I just—I don't know."

Every time I try to move, she clings tighter and cries harder. Finally, she calms down enough that she wants to freshen her face. I'm pointing her toward the bathroom, since she's never been here, when my phone rings. She stops walking and looks at me. "Is it your father?"

"Does he know you're here?"

"Yes. I told him I was leaving him and you would help me divorce him."

I don't tell her I don't handle divorces, despite believing she needs one. I'll get her an attorney. I pull out my phone, and yes, it's my father. "Dad," I say.

"Your mother isn't answering her phone. Is she there?"

"Yes. She's here."

"Put her on."

"I don't think—"

"Put her on."

My mother is already in front of me and grabbing my phone. "John," she says, and a sob follows.

Fuck. Cat. I glance at my watch. It's nine forty-five and I've fucked the hell up with a woman I really care about. I walk to my mother's purse and look for her phone. I can't find it. I follow my mother to the other room. "Where's your phone?" I call out. "I need a phone."

"I don't know. I can't find it."

"Holy fuck," I murmur. "I'm going to find a phone." I don't wait for an answer. I head for the door and the elevator. The minute I'm in the lobby, I make my way to the security desk. "I need a phone," I tell the guard.

He hands me the landline under the desk and I dial Cat. She doesn't answer. Of course she doesn't. No one answers numbers they don't know, but I leave a message. "Cat. My mom showed up in a hysterical fit. She's now on my phone and I can't find hers. Please, sweetheart. Call me back. I'm sorry. I feel like shit." I hang up and realize I didn't give her the number, and I can't just stand here.

I charge through the lobby, and when I hit the street, I grab a cab to the restaurant. In the meantime, I use the cabby's phone and dial Cat. Once we're at the restaurant, I pay for him to wait. Cat's gone. Damn it. I should have just gone to her place. Thirty minutes, and a shit-ton of traffic later, I'm at her apartment. The guard knows me—it's the same older, dark-haired guy—and I play it off. I walk past him. He stops me. "She's expecting me."

"She didn't tell us that."

"I will pay you five hundred dollars to walk me up there and let me check on her. I can't reach her."

"Maybe she doesn't want to talk to you."

"Come on, man."

"I'll go check on her," he says.

"A thousand." I hand him my card. "I'm good for it."

He studies me. "I could get in trouble."

"I'll sue whoever comes at you."

"I'll go get her." He waves at the lady behind the desk and points to the elevator. He starts walking, and the minute the elevator opens, I'm in it with him.

"Oh, come on, Mr. Summer."

"I'll pay you the money."

"I don't want your money. Just don't cause a scene up there."

"I have only good intentions."

He grimaces and faces forward. The elevator opens, and he doesn't get the chance to exit first. I am out and down the hall at Cat's door, knocking, before he is halfway here. She flings the door open, and she's in a burgundy dress, and mascara has smudged the skin under her eyes. "I made you cry," I say.

"Why are you here? How are you up here?"

She tries to shut the door, and I catch it. "My mother has my phone. She showed up at my place melting down and hysterical. I left her there to go get you at the restaurant. And now I'm here. I left her to come to you. I need to go back. I need you to go with me."

"Your mother?"

"Yes. My mother."

"Oh."

"Oh."

"Ma'am, I can remove him," the guard says.

"No," she says, and I pull her to me.

"I'm sorry. I hate that I made you feel this." I cup her head. "I wouldn't do this to you. I'm not that guy." I kiss her, a long, deep, tell-her-I-love-her kind of kiss, when I can't tell her yet. It's too soon and the wrong time and place. "Come home with me."

"I shouldn't because—"

"You should for about a hundred reasons I can't list now. Come with me. I need you, Cat."

"I actually need you, too."

Relief washes over me. "Grab your things. What can I carry?"

"I just need my purse," she says, rushing inside and grabbing it before returning.

We exit to the absence of the security guard and hurry to the elevator. Once we're inside, I turn to her, my hands on her waist. "Cat—"

She pushes to her toes and kisses me. "It's okay. How are you and how is your mother?"

"How am I? I don't know if anyone has asked me that in years."

"I am."

"And I'm more than fine because you're here. My mother is a wreck."

"I might embarrass her."

"Maybe you can help. She won't leave him. He called, and she jumped all over that call. Cat, this is what I was going to talk about tonight. He cheats. A serial cheater, actually. And I don't want you to think that's in our blood. I'm not—"

"Him. Or my father. Or Mitch, or anyone else I've ever known. I know. And you're right. Maybe I can help. I know my mother's regrets. If she gives me the opening, I will talk to her."

I kiss her. "I'm crazy about you, woman. Another something we need to talk about, because this isn't going away." I lean back to look at her. "What happened with your brothers?"

"One family at a time," she says. "Yours first."

"Speaking of family. Can I use your phone to call my sister?"

"Of course."

She hands it to me, and I've finally calmed Stacey down when we reach the lobby of my building and end the call. "She wants to talk to you. We don't have time, but beware. You're now on my sister's radar."

Cat laughs, this sweet, bubbly sound that brings me down about ten notches. We step onto and back off the elevator on my floor when she stops me. "I drank three glasses of wine. Am I talking normally?"

I smile. "Yes, actually, you are."

"Huh. I don't get it, but good."

We stop at my door. "Let's hope I didn't save my drunk talk for your mother."

"At this point. I'd rather you use that frank talk you do with me with my mother." I open the door and take her hand, leading her down the hall.

"Mother?" I call out.

"In the kitchen."

We follow her direction and when we walk into the kitchen, she's standing at the island with a glass of wine in her hand, mascara down her cheeks. Her hair is a mess. "Who's this?" my mother asks.

"Cat. Someone who matters to me."

"Hi," Cat says. "You're really beautiful."

"Thank you," my mother says. "You're dating my son."

"Yes," Cat says. "I am. I like him when he's not being an asshole."

"He's very arrogant," she says. "But not like his father."

"He told me that," Cat says.

"Cat, why do you have mascara under your eyes? Did my son make you cry?"

And then Cat does the most incredible thing. "Because I thought Reese stood me up, but of course he wouldn't, and I would have known that, but it was bad timing. I talked to my father, who I haven't talked to in months because, you see—I hope it's okay that I know this—he's like your husband. He cheated on my mom, and she died of a stroke, unhappy because she never left him. But two weeks ago, he had a stroke and no one told me. And he's still an asshole, but I don't want him to die."

Cat starts crying and my mom starts crying, and two of the most important people in my life are hugging and they barely know each other. But then, Cat apparently has a way of making the Summers fall instantly in love.

Hours later, my mother is in the bed in my spare bedroom, and I am finally able to sit with Cat in the chair in my bedroom, her by my side, her hand on my leg and mine on hers. For a good hour, we sit there and talk about her father and her brothers. "Bottom line," she says. "Nothing has really changed."

"You talked to your father. That's big."

"We talked. That's all that changed. But for your mother I think a change really is going to happen for her."

"She says she's leaving him," I say. "She's never said that before, but it's hard to know where this leads when she goes back home Monday. My father always wins her over."

"I predict that won't happen this time," Cat says. "She's stronger than you realize. I read some books on the psychological factors of people staying in these situations because of my mother and my father. Basically what I learned is that, we as humans, radiate towards the familiar. The familiar is safe in our minds, even if it's really destructive to our lives. We're creatures of habit. But your mother came here, outside her safety zone with your father. To me, that says that she was testing the waters, seeing if she could leap to the next dock and still settle her feet firmly on the ground."

"Maybe. We'll see." I pull her legs to my lap. "Moving to a completely different subject. Anything on your book deal?"

"Yes, actually. I have to make a decision by tomorrow night. They offered me five hundred thousand for the Jennifer Wright book and two hundred for an option book which is double what I got last book."

"But the last book hit the Times."

"Yes, for four weeks and it sold very well."

"Are you happy with the offer?"

"Of course," she says. "That's a huge figure but you have to sign on as a consultant on the Wright book. That's part of the deal."

"Done."

"Which means I need you to sign an agreement and take at least two hundred thousand of the money for yourself."

"I don't need that money, Cat."

"If we break up—"

"We're not breaking up," I say. "That's not part of the equation. But here's my *counter* offer. I'll sign the agreement and if you want me to take the money, I'll put it in savings account for us to use on whatever. Together. Agreed?"

"I don't think—"

"Take it or leave it, Cat."

"Okay. Deal."

"Good. Now. Next item on the agenda. Move in with me."

"I—You want me to officially move in with you?"

"Yes. I know you love your apartment, but—"

"No. Yes. I like it here. The apartment isn't the issue."

"Then what is it?"

"We've only known each other a short while."

"We've lived together almost the whole time. I've never even considered living with someone."

"Why me? What makes me different?"

I slide my hand to her face. "Because you're everything, Cat."

"I repeat. We're new."

"And that means what?"

"I can't be everything."

"And yet you are. That's the only explanation I have to any objection you give me. *Move in* with me. We'll do a trial. Keep your apartment. If you end up unhappy, you know you have it." I roll her to her back and settle over her. "Say *yes, Cat.*"

She rests her hand on my face in that way she does that undoes me and I have no clue why. It just does. She does. "Reese," she whispers.

"You're killing me here. Say—"

"Yes. Yes I'll move in with you."

And there it is. Her undoing me all over again.

Chapter Thirty-Four

Reese

Sunday starts with Cat and I standing at the island in the kitchen, drinking coffee, when my mother joins us and announces that she's leaving my father, as if she didn't announce the same thing last night. "But I'm not leaving my job at the university, or my home. I called him and told him to be gone when I get back."

There's the part she didn't give us last night. She told him to leave. She just seemed to need to say it all out loud again. And she never wavers. She is strong about her decision, and there are no more tears. I make a few phone calls and line her up an attorney, and by evening, my siblings have talked to all of us, Cat included, about ten times. Cat and I cut them off when we take my mother out for a nice dinner. The night ends with Cat accepting the book deal and with her in my arms, in *our* bed.

Come Monday, since I have to be to work, Cat sees my mother off to the airport and then heads to her place to pack up some things, to bring what she needs. I arrive at work, and my secretary, Maria, a forty-something and a smart mouth, is mumbling in Spanish, which she still, after four years, doesn't know I understand. I enter my office and sit down, and she appears in my doorway, her dress bright red and blinding. Everything about Maria is bright and bold. "You won. You're a badass. All that stuff. Moving on. The press is calling constantly. Are you doing interviews at all?"

"No. Decline all."

"I need a recording that says decline all," she says. "Just so you know. It's that many calls."

"And?"

"Just letting you know how hard I'm working." She turns and leaves, but she'll be back.

My line buzzes, and I have about ten calls, all from clients and partners trying to catch up, congratulate me, or ask for something. Around ten, Royce Walker calls. "We have a problem."

"Of course we do," I say. "Why wouldn't we have a problem?"

"Let's start with the good news," he says. "My insider says Kelli Ward is about ten seconds from confessing. The bad news is that they think your client knew all along and covered the murder up."

"And they're going after him for accessory this time."

"Bingo."

"Fuck. Thanks for the heads-up." I end the call and dial Ward. "Where are you?"

"Vermont," he says.

"Get on a plane and get back here."

"Why?"

"Kelli will likely be charged today."

"Holy shit. She confessed?"

"Yes," I say. "She confessed."

"I can't believe it," he says, sounding dumbfounded. "I didn't want to believe it was true."

"I know, but you knew she did it," I say, testing him.

"On some level, yes," he says, "I think I did, but I wouldn't have admitted that to even myself."

"They're going to try to say you did."

"I was acquitted," he argues.

"Knowledge of a crime even if you did not commit it is a crime. We'll make this go away, but it looks better if you're here, but not with her. Get a hotel room and stay away from her."

"I don't know if I have another round in me."

"If I do, you do. No interviews. Don't talk to anyone but me. Call me when you get back."

"Understood." We disconnect, and I call Cat.

"Hey," she says. "Your mom's plane just took off."

"Kelli Ward is about to confess."

"Why do you sound so unhappy about this?"

"They're going to come at Nelson for covering it up. Or so Royce's insider tells me."

"Did he?"

"No. I don't believe he did. I believe he was in love and oblivious, much like my mother for all of these years. Now you know what you're writing about for tomorrow."

"And what will be consuming you. Don't you have that old friend that needs attention?"

"The corporate division is going after the people who got him into the mess he's in. I need to go. I'll call you later." I start to hang up but stop. "Cat."

"Yes?"

"I talk to you about my work."

"What about it?"

"I talk to you about my work. I don't want to stop. I need to have you sign a more extensive consulting agreement than the one you signed for the Ward case. More all-inclusive. Do you have a problem with that?"

"No. Of course not. I was actually going to suggest we do that. To protect everyone involved."

"I'll bring it home."

"Home." She laughs. "Yes. Bring it *home*, Reese."

I smile. "Bye, sweetheart." I hang up and stand, crossing my office, and passing Maria's desk. "I'll be upstairs in corporate."

I take the stairs, not the elevator, and walk upstairs into the office of the senior partner who heads up that division. I don't ask his secretary to enter. I just pass her by and enter his office. Kent, who is as good a friend as two workaholics can be, the same age as me, and just as aggressive as me, looks up from his desk. "What's up, man?"

"That Allen case I have you working. How's it looking?"

"Just digging in. You said I had two weeks to get your answer. Why?"

"Ward's wife is confessing and they are going to try to get him for covering it up. I'm going to be buried again."

"I've got this," he says, running a hand through his dark hair. "I'm going to unbury everyone involved in this firm, and their illegal operations, use it to get your guy an out, and hand that to you to voodoo it away with the Feds."

"This guy is a good guy," I say. "I don't want him fucked. I'm trusting you."

"This is me you're talking to," Kent says. "I'll get them. I'm a master at digging up dirt that others think can't be dug up."

"My guy doesn't sign a release. Bluff them and sue the fuck out of them for putting him through this. And while you do that, I'm going to hand every dirty secret you find over to the Feds."

"Now we're talking. I love when we throw down."

I exit his office and head back down to mine, passing Maria as she mumbles in Spanish again. I re-enter my office, with another spurt of phone calls driven my way, and it's not long until I get the one I expect. The police want to question Nelson Ward again. I set the meeting and text Cat, giving her the heads-up. Because Cat has become a part of every inch of my life. I really don't remember a few weeks ago before she was with me, and I don't want to try.

Chapter Thirty-Five

Reese

One month later...

I've just gotten back to my office from a court appearance and I sat down at my desk when my cellphone rings. I dig it from my pocket and glance at the number to find Cat calling. "Hey, sweetheart," I say, answering the line. "How'd your interview with Detective Newman go?"

"It was one of the better ones of the dozens I've had for this book," she says. "He had some interesting information he said to pass along to you."

"Really. What would that be?"

"He says that the only reason Nelson Ward has been questioned three times in the past month about his wife, is that Dan has it out for him and you. He's still living the disgrace of that trial and even the decision to charge Nelson Ward. If he gets Nelson as an accessory, he saves face."

"Of course Dan's behind this. I'm at the point now where I'm going to file harassment charges against them and ask for damages. They're hurting the man's livelihood. He has a multi-billion-dollar conglomerate to run and he's smeared all over the news again."

"Dan needs to be pushed out of his job. He's motivated by all the wrong things. Oh and a side note, a big jump in subject here: Your mother called. Your father proposed to his mistress and your mother is just fine with it because she's now dating another professor at the college who she calls brilliant and sexy."

"Hold on a minute. My father proposed to his mistress and my mother is dating again? Okay. I don't know how you know this and I don't."

"Actually you do know because I told you."

"You knew before I knew."

"Your mother likes to talk."

"Obviously and for the record I could do without any sentence that includes my mother calling a man 'sexy.'"

She laughs. "Duly noted."

"For clarification," I say. "Are they divorced and I don't know it?"

"Your father has been acting like he was divorced for years. Your mother just decided to join the party. And they will be soon, anyway."

"Or they could just date other people."

She laughs. "Right. Or that. I need to go though. I'm having a champagne brunch with Liz. She wants to celebrate the press release that went out this morning. For the book that I haven't even finished writing."

"Champagne and you. Should I send a car?"

She laughs. "I'm perfectly capable of calling my own Uber, even after champagne. I just might not find it. If that proves to be the situation, I have you on auto-dial. Though I might go to my brother's office, while drinking of course, and demand that he give me back my mother's letter."

"Still won't call you back, huh?"

"No. He's such an Asshole."

"Now I know just how much you hated me when you called me an asshole that first day. Did you tell your father he took the letter and you want it back?"

"The entire two times I called to check on that man and he actually took my call, no. The calls were short and he won't care. He tolerates my check-in calls and when I bring the letter up to Gabe who gave it to him, Gabe just tells me he'll tell him. But you don't have time for this and I'm about to be drunk anyway."

I laugh and we hang up, only to have Maria buzz my intercom. "Casey Allen is on the line."

I grab the phone. "Casey," I say. "I have news."

"I hope it's good because I thought this would be over by now."

"It would have been if we could have strong-armed the investment firm into certifying your lack of knowledge of the transactions, but they won't do it. But that's going to change. Kent filed a lawsuit on your behalf today against everyone with any interest in the firm and all the cloaked investors, of which he says there were four."

"And how does this help me with the Feds?"

"It shows that you aren't one of them and it provides financial damage for your legal defense. I know this hasn't gone as quickly as we'd hoped, but we'll get you through this with money to ease the pain of the stress."

"I just want this thing over with. It's haunting me. I can't sleep. I was going to propose to my girlfriend, but I can't have her engaged to a felon."

"You are not going to be a felon. I'll end this and soon. They haven't charged you. They're stringing you along, planning to use you wherever they can use you. It's a sad truth, but a real one. I've got your back. I'll call you soon."

We disconnect and Maria pops her head in the door, speaking in rapid Spanish as she walks toward me. "Why did you just have a Tiffany's bag delivered and please tell me it's for me."

"No," I say. "It is not for you but stop cursing me in Spanish and you might get something nice for Christmas."

"I don't curse you in Spanish."

I arch a brow.

"How do you know I curse you in Spanish?"

"You just admitted it."

She smirks. "You do know that Christmas is only two months away, right?"

"Yes. So I suggest you have restraint."

"I always have restraint," she claims, setting the bag in front of me. "You're proposing to Cat," she says, knowing Cat well now since she's been to my office any number of times.

"That's between me and Cat."

Her eyes light. "You *are*." She claps. "Can I see?"

"No. You cannot see. Leave and shut the door."

She grimaces but does as I ordered. I open the bag and pull out the blue box inside. I inhale and think about Cat opening it as I open it, staring down at the ring that I had sized after sneaking one of her rings. It's stunning like Cat and I pull out a card from the store clerk that reads: *The Tiffany Nova Princess Cut ring was a perfect choice. She will love it. Congratulations.* It was perfect and expensive, but Cat is worth every dime and a million more.

This is my Christmas gift to her and her gift to me will be agreeing to marry me.

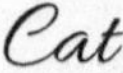

Cat

Liz and I sit at a fancy restaurant she'd insisted on taking me to, giggling over champagne. "I don't know why I let you talk me into this," I say. "I can't drink. It's doesn't make for a good me."

"You signed a huge book deal, fell in love with a gorgeous man and—"

"Wow. I never told you I love him."

"Oh please. You love him and you're so much more relaxed with this man. Look at you. You're in a pink fluffy sweater."

"It's just a pink sweater and I paired it with a very conservative pink shirt," I say. "And what does pink have to do with anything anyway?"

"You lived in black before Reese. You're different. I can't explain it. Softer maybe."

"I lived in black in the courtroom," I say. "And why are we talking about sweaters? *Pink* sweaters."

She downs her champagne. "Because, bitch, we're too drunk to talk about anything else."

I laugh. "Okay, bitch."

We both laugh and I'm reminded how well we connect. I can't believe I fired her. I can't believe she made me. "Seriously, though," Liz says. "You know I love you right?"

"Most of the time. Except that time you tried to get me to work with Dan."

"I told you. That was a complicated political mess. And you just sobered me up. Thank you for that. I was protecting you."

"Yeah yeah. I don't want details. Just don't try to get me to do something you know breaks my moral codes again."

"When it's half a million dollars, I'm obligated to present the option."

"But not obligated to push me or leave out details."

"You would have freaked if you knew Dan had a relative at the publishing house. And you would have thought that you couldn't decline. You had to take the meeting. You didn't have to accept. That was the freedom I gave you."

"You pushed me."

"It was a lot of money. Hell yeah I pushed you. I can't apologize for that. I won't. That amount of money is kind to me but you get most of it. After one big deal like that you start having freedoms and opportunities you didn't otherwise have open to you."

"Okay. Yeah. I get it. Stop being sober. I don't like it." My cellphone rings and I glance at the number. "My brother." I down my champagne. "I have to yell at him over something personal. Pretend you're not here." I answer the call. "Finally, you call?"

"What the hell, Cat?" Reid demands.

"What the hell yourself. What does that mean?"

"I saw the press release," he says. "You're writing a book with Reese Summer. The man is suing me, Dad, and Uncle Rudolf and he set the Feds' sights on us."

"What?"

"You don't know. Well at least there is that. That man is trying to destroy us."

"Reese is a criminal attorney," I say. "He wouldn't be suing you."

"His firm is, and he's damn sure involved in this. He's representing the man they sued on behalf of."

And now I know why Gabe asked about Reese. "What's the client's name?"

"Casey Allen."

I know the name. I know all of Reese's cases. "What did you do, Reid?" I demand, despite knowing more than I want him to know I know.

"I have to be in the wrong? Is that it?"

"What are you accused of doing?"

"Securities fraud," he says.

"Please tell me you didn't do it."

"Fuck you, Cat." He hangs up.

I look at Liz. "I have to go."

"You've been drinking. I'll get you where you need to go."

"Believe me," I say. "I've never been so sober in my life."

I grab my coat and pull it on, and then snap up my briefcase and purse and rush for the door. Reese is now involved in a lawsuit against my family that could ruin them. It doesn't matter that he didn't do it intentionally which he didn't. I know he didn't but it's a problem both personally and legally for both of us. It might even be the end of us.

Chapter Thirty-Six

Reese

I'm sitting at my desk with Maria standing next to it when Cat comes charging in without warning, her coat half off one shoulder, and her briefcase and purse on the other. "I need to talk to you now. Alone."

Cat's intensity is impossible to miss and for once Maria has nothing smart to say. "I'm leaving," she says, hurrying around Cat and shutting the door.

Cat sets her things on the guest chair. "Casey Allen."

That's the last thing I expect her to say at this very moment. "What about him?"

"You filed a lawsuit on his behalf."

"My firm did, yes."

"My family. You filed against them."

I stand up. "What? No. That firm is Blue Banks Investment."

"My family is apparently involved. Reid called me."

"That can't be right." I punch in Kent's extension on my phone and put him on speaker.

"What's up, man?" he answers.

"Name the parties on that lawsuit against Blue Banks. It's important. I need it now."

"Sure. I know them by heart" He lists four names that are non-issues, and then he adds, "Reid Maxwell, Mike Maxwell, Rudolf Elway."

I restrain a curse word that will set Kent off and say simply, "That's what I needed," before I disconnect.

"Rudolf is my uncle," Cat says, "but not by blood. I don't know how he became Uncle but he's a long-time family connection and friend of my father's." She presses fingers to her temples. "Now I know why my father was stressed enough to have a stroke."

"Fuck," I murmur, running fingers through my hair, my hands settling under my jacket on my hips. "You know I didn't know."

"Of course I know you didn't know. My mind never went there." We both lean on the desk, facing each other. "But that changes nothing," she adds. "This is a problem: Morally, ethically, and legally."

"I'll fix this. I'll represent your family and get them out of this."

"No." She pushes off the desk. "You *will not* change your moral code for my family and if you do that, Casey could sue you for split interests."

"I'll remove myself from Casey's case."

"Again, no. This is not who you are and I like who you are. I don't like what happens to us if I change your moral code for me. That's not an option."

"If I remove myself—"

"Then the firm has to remove itself. If you do that, Casey, who is your *friend*, casual or not, could end up in jail. You can't walk away from him and I won't let you for my family. And my family will use me against you. If you think they won't, you're wrong. We can't—"

"Do not go where you're about to go," I warn.

"I have to go there. We have to go there. We can't be together while this is going on. You know it. I know it. You will not lose your license over me. I have to move out."

"No. I will fix this. We're both in the heat of the moment right now."

"We're both attorneys too who know the law and the ethical confines of the job. I'm a consultant on this case with you. That's ten kinds of wrong. I have to be removed immediately."

"That's an easy fix."

"Look. Reese."

"Cat damn it, stop going there, to us—"

"You need to do the right thing. That's the man you are and the man I—that's the man you are."

"I'll be honest with Casey."

"He could still come after you. If he goes to another firm and they fail he can say your malpractice led him there. And my family—"

"Will not want this in the press," I supply.

"No but they will go to Casey and he might. You do have to talk to him and give him the option to move or stick it out with you. Don't let my family get to him first."

"Understood. I'll talk to him. I'll get him to sign a release saying he won't sue me. We'll be apart a few days at most."

"He might not sign it."

"I'm convincing."

"What about the press? My family won't go there but what about Dan or any other enemy you have to have made over your legal career? He hates you. A law suit is a public filing. He knows we're together. He could leak this. We are dangerous right now to your long-term career. And you are not losing your career over me." She grabs her bags. "We can't talk. We can't communicate. Not until this is over."

She's right. I know she's right and at this moment, I can't think us out of this.

"I have to back out of the book deal," she adds.

"No," I say, rejecting that idea immediately. "You do not. I'll call the publisher and handle this with them. You have a contract. This conflict will not last and it will not be repeated. You will not lose this over me. This is a two-sided coin. We protect each other. Say it, Cat"

She starts backing toward the door and I'm around the desk in front of her by the time she's there. I press her against the door, my hand at her hip, under her coat. "Say it. We protect each other."

"We protect each other."

"Do not back out of the book deal. Promise me."

"Yes. I promise."

"Keep working on the book. You know my side of the story. I'll have Liz call you with the update on the contract, but *I will* handle it. I'll fix all of this."

"Do it right, not fast," she says.

"I have no choice if I'm going to fix this. Cat, I'm going to have to fix this with your family or it will affect us."

"It won't," she says. "You didn't make them commit a crime and they did. I heard it in Reid's voice."

"It will affect us, if I don't fully fix this. I'm going to and I'm telling you this so you know I may be communicating with your family. I'll come to you the minute it's done." She nods and my hands find her face. "I love you. This isn't how I wanted to tell you, but I need you to know."

"I love you, too."

I kiss her, lingering inside that kiss, for what I wish could be eternal moments, before I press my forehead to hers. "I'll find a way to get us out of this," I promise.

She grabs my tie. "I hate this but I'd better go. I'll be gone when you get home." She twists away from me and it kills me to let her. I back up and she exits the office and I shut the door, walking to my desk and calling Lauren, who answers on the first ring.

"I need you to listen because Cat is going to come to you and I need you to be armed with facts when she gets there. And then I need to set that aside and talk as legal peers."

"I'm listening."

I tell her everything and end with, "Now that you've heard the story. What do you think?"

She follows with every conclusion Cat and I have already made with one cutting addition. "Her family is vicious and they have no loyalty to you. But she's personal to them and you've made it personal by that connection to her. They won't go to the press but they will find nasty ways to come at you, now and later."

"In other words, I need to find some semblance of peace with them."

"That's my thought, but how do you even feel about that?"

"I will do anything for Cat." I laugh without humor. "But she's afraid I'll compromise my morals and it will ultimately affect us."

"She could be right."

"No. She didn't do this. Her family did and I love her enough to know that."

"You love her."

"Holy fuck yes. I bought a ring to propose at Christmas."

"It's not even Thanksgiving, Reese. You have time. This will work out. You're good at what you do. You'll find a way and I'll help."

"You're connected to Cat and the Maxwell's too. You can't help but the fact that you want to, is appreciated. Just take care of my woman. That's what I need you to do."

"If you love each other, and I know you do, this won't be the end. You know that, right?"

"This is Cat, Lauren. The queen of putting up walls and I won't be able to do anything to pull them back down."

"If she puts a wall up she was never yours. If she doesn't, you know it's real. And in a way this a gift. We all need to know it's real."

Her line beeps. "That's probably her. You two will get through this." She disconnects and I wish like hell I had something to hit.

Chapter Thirty-Seven

Cat

The minute Lauren opens the door, I know she knows. "He called you."

"Yes." She backs up and I enter the house, and walk to the giant chair by the couch and sit down on the ottoman.

She joins me as she sits on the couch. "How are you?"

"How *am I*?" I laugh without humor. "I drank champagne to celebrate my press release, after which my brother called and told me Reese was suing my family. This was right before Reid told me to fuck off. Next up. Reese told me he loves me right before we said goodbye forever, for all I know. So how am I? I'm doing just peachy."

"You and Reese will get through this. This mess sucks, but you will get through it."

"You know the facts, I assume. Are we overreacting?"

"No you aren't overreacting. This is a monstrous problem."

"We can't be together right now, can we?"

"That's a potential challenge. Do you think your family will use you against Reese at Reese's expense?"

"Yes. In some dark, underground, dirty way, they will lash out at him and I don't know how to stop that from happening."

"I talked this through with Reese, but let's you and I try, too."

For two full hours, we talk and talk, and talk some more, until there is nowhere else to go. "I think this will end us," I say, voicing my biggest fear.

"Not if you love each other."

"You don't know how brutal my family is. They will make Reese hate me and I won't be able to stop it."

"You don't give Reese credit if you believe that."

"He's brilliant. You're right. I know. But so is my father."

"Reese is younger, more agile in every way, and he's in love. And love is powerful. While you are worrying about Reese, do you know what Reese is worried about?"

"What?"

"Your walls. That while you two are apart, you'll find a way to shut him out."

"I won't. Not Reese. I want him to know that. Tell him I said that."

"I can't, Cat. Because for two years, all you have done is shut everyone out, even me. Julie is my best friend. You are as close to that as someone can be without being that because you go months without even calling me."

"I know. I just—sometimes I deal with being alone by being alone."

"But you're not alone unless you make yourself alone," Lauren says.

"My family shuts me out. I don't shut them out."

"Right. And you shut me out. Don't do that to Reese. Don't do that to me anymore."

"I won't," I say. "I don't want to. I might need you to shake me here or there. Old habits and all."

"Do I have permission to shake you up if needed?"

"Yes, times one thousand."

"Good. I will."

I stand up. "I need to go get my things from his apartment. I have to deal with this and get home before I melt down."

"Buy a stock of Ben and Jerry's. I'll be by to see you, and it helps anyway. Eat it. And I'll bring Julie with me. She's a good friend, Cat, and good friends get us through bad times."

I hug her and I leave.

Thirty minutes later, I stand in my apartment—no, Reese's apartment. I start packing up my things, but I decide, no. I'll take only what I have to take. I'll be back and soon, I hope. I fill a bag and then sit down on the chair where we often watch the sunset, and where we often just sit and talk. I'm going to miss this spot with him so much. My eyes prickle and I stand up before I melt down.

My gaze goes to my nightstand where I have a pad and a pen. I walk to it and sit down, and on a blank page I write: *I wish I was right HERE right NOW* in huge letters. I tear off the page and set it on my pillow.

I then write him a note:

Reese,

There is no wall that could survive the force of how much I have fallen in love with you. My family is vicious. They will find a way to strip your license if they can. Don't risk it. Don't call. Phone records can be traced.

I left most of my things because I am coming back.

Love, Cat

Chapter Thirty-Eight

Reese

The first night apart...

I walk into my apartment and it is silent, empty, cold. Cat is gone. My phone rings and it's my mother. Cat and I didn't even talk about what to tell her. I answer the line and walk to the bar, and pour a stout drink, as I begin telling her everything.

"I don't even know what to say," she breathes out. "Yes, I do. She really loves you or she'd still be there, as backwards as that sounds. She's worried about protecting you. She should be and you're worried about—"

"Losing her."

"You won't. She loves you. That is so obvious. The kind of love a mother wants for all of her children." She laughs bitterly. "And herself. Go solve this. You can. Focus. Do. Get your woman back."

When we end that call, I'm reminded of how strong my mother is apart from my father, just not with him. Cat is strong with or without me. I need her to be strong without me now, and keep that damn wall down. I refill my glass before heading up the stairs. I walk into the bedroom and spot the note on her pillow. Adrenaline surges through me and I down the whiskey before I pick up it up to read: *I wish I was right HERE right NOW.* "Me too, sweetheart," I murmur, before lifting the second piece of paper. I sit down and read it, emotions punching through me.

She's coming back. I hope like fuck she still says that when this is over.

I consider buying disposable phones and sending her one. We could talk, but she will ask questions and worry about every move

I make. I have to do what I have to do to ensure her family doesn't ruin me and us. I need a level head, not an emotional one.

Cat

With my MacBook in my lap, I sit on my bed among the pink pillows, under the pink comforter that used to feel like my bed. It doesn't anymore. I consider going to my family but if I do, I risk exposing my personal feelings for Reese. I could put a target on his back or at least paint it a little larger.

No.

I can't go to my family. I can't go to Reese. I just have to lay here in pink frilly everything and do nothing. An idea hits me. I don't have to stop talking to Reese. I can send him a message in every column I write. One line. Something small. I stare at the column I've just completed, which is a piece about a recent police shooting. I look at the final few lines of my closing and rework them.

In a world where the lines between peace and war seem to have fallen, I suggest that we don't seek to widen those lines. We look to erase all that divides us. And we can't do that by blaming each other. We can't do that by letting the press tell our story. We the people must come together and let no one else tell our story. We must tell our own story. Until then —Cat

It's not perfect, but hopefully he reads between the lines. I'm not going to put a wall between us. Not now. Not ever.

Reese

Day two apart...

I start my day reading Cat's column and the message inside it for me: *We tell our own story.* In other words, her family doesn't get to control us. She's right. And the Maxwells will soon find that out.

I call Cat's publisher as my first order of business. The agreement to release and promote this book after this conflict ends, is easy to resolve, especially when I agree to consult on a second book on Kelli Ward. Knowing they offered Cat a smaller fee for a second book, I negotiate Kelli's book outside that contract and call Liz.

"You're better at this than me," she says. "I'll call Cat."

"Tell her to tell her family the book is on hold indefinitely. That's important."

"Understood."

Next, I call Kent to my office and tell him everything. "How serious are you about this woman?"

I open my desk and set the Tiffany's bag on the desk. "You? Married?" he gapes.

"Me. Married."

"Okay then. I don't know you anymore, but I'm going to help you help us."

Hours later, Kent and I put our plan into action. I sit with Casey and Maria at the conference table. "I'm recording this for all of our protection," I state. "Maria will read the legal disclosures."

"Understood," Casey states.

Maria proceeds and when she's done, Kent begins. "When I filed the lawsuit on your behalf, I did not disclose the names of the parties I filed that lawsuit against to Reese."

"In other words," I say. "I had no idea that there was a conflict of interest between me and your case."

Casey sits up straighter. "What conflict?"

"I was dating a woman who is the daughter, sister, and niece of three parties named."

"Holy shit," he says. "So you're dropping me."

"No," I say. "I'm giving you the option to stay or go, but before you make that decision, I need to make you aware of all the facts. Cat Maxwell and I have stopped seeing each other until this is over. However, there was a press release yesterday that made a book deal public. I'm consulting on her true crime about the Ward case. Those interviews are complete and the release and press will be put off until after this conflict is resolved. The book is on hold. Additionally, Cat is estranged from her family anyway, and as far as

I'm concerned, they treat Cat like shit. They deserve to be fucked to hell and back again.

"Then why stop seeing her?" Casey asks. "If you hate them, that's in my best interest. I mean, if I was an excuse—"

"No. Cat is not going away. I need you to know that too. This break is to get us through this case. I've already gone after her family. They will come after me no matter what. I have to deal with them. What you need to know is that I'm the best at what I do."

"I already know that, man," Casey says. "I'm lucky as hell to have you as a friend on this case."

"You can go elsewhere, but here's the bottom line. If they screw up and don't get you off, I'm recording you right now being told that this is your decision. The outcome of going elsewhere is your decision. I'm also telling you that I will work one hundred percent for you. I can't promise you I will get you off, but nothing I've told you will be a factor, and to stay on this case, I need you to sign an agreement that you will not sue me or this firm over the outcome. The language will be lengthy and it will include full disclosure of everything I just told you."

"Done," he says. "I trust you. How can I not trust you? You left your woman for me."

"I didn't leave Cat. She left me because she's that ethical."

An hour later, he's shaking my hand. "Don't lose her over this."

"I won't," I say and I mean it.

Cat

Since my family won't take my calls, I march into the lobby of their offices, and I don't bother to ask for entry. I walk right past the receptionist and down the hall.

"Cat," my father's secretary, Nancy, says. Nancy is blonde and gorgeous, of course. She's probably fucking my father. That's his thing. He, like Mitch, likes his secretaries. I walk right past her too and enter the office, opening the door to find my brothers present.

"Oh good. A Maxwell family reunion." I shut the door. "Well, except for the youngest, who was smart enough to leave the city. I'd call him, but why bring him into this hell. Let him lead a happy life."

My father, who I haven't seen in months, looks good, not sick at all. His grey hair is thick, his complexion warm. His weight healthy as always. My brothers just look like assholes, one on either side of his desk. Twin assholes. "I told Reese Summer that we had a conflict. He immediately called my publisher and asked to back out of the consulting agreement thanks to that conflict of interest. For those of you who think my career sucks, that's half a million dollars. Yes. More than my asshole brothers are probably making in a year with their fucking Harvard law degrees. Thank you. I love you all, too."

"He's suing us, Cat," Reid says.

"His partner is suing you."

"Semantics," my father says.

"Well, now you can duke it out with him. He's done with me and my book. I watched him in court. I hope you will all call me before you zip up those orange suits and at least say goodbye."

I turn and walk out of the office and when I reach the elevator and punch the button, it's with relief that it opens. I put on a show in there, but I felt every angry word. I step into the elevator and Gabe joins me just before we're shut inside.

"A half million dollars."

"Yes. I sold a lot of books with the last release and this time I had Reese on board. But it's done now. I move on."

"Put it off until this is over."

"Why?" I demand, and then grind through harsh words I don't want to speak. "We both know if you can ruin Reese Summer, you will. He'll be worth nothing to me."

"It might not end that way."

And there it is. The confirmation. They are going after him, but at least I've been assured I'm not leverage.

"But it might and it doesn't matter. I'm already talking to my publisher about another option with the prosecutor, though I hate that prick almost as much as I hate you right now."

He reaches into his jacket and hands me the letter from our mother. "I've been carrying it around. I was going to bring it by, but I keep reading the damn thing. I'm on team Cat just like Mom.

And I'm not being sued. I didn't fuck up and get involved. For the record, I don't think Dad knew what was going on either."

"Reid?"

"He says he didn't. I'm not sure. Uncle Rudolf. He knew. He's the root of all of this." The elevator dings and he adds, "Team Cat."

I don't reply. Gabe and I have a big wall to climb. The one my family put between me and Reese. I exit the car and I try to figure out how to tell Reese what is going on. I don't want to put anyone in the middle. That means my column.

Hours later, I'm back in my pink-covered bed without Reese, writing my column. I find a case that fits perfectly. A woman accused of murder, but ultimately the uncle is now being questioned. I walk my audience through how the woman became the accused. In the end, I close simply: *The uncle has yet to be charged, but I predict that that tide will turn, and he will soon be the defendant in a court case we will follow here with interest. Until then —Cat.*

The message is there. Look at my uncle, who isn't my uncle at all, and who my mother never liked. Now I know why. He's trouble.

***

Reese

Day three apart...

I start my morning at my coffee pot reading Cat's column and I understand the message. Her uncle is trouble.

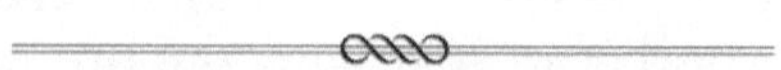

Cat

Day fourteen apart...

I am miserable, sitting in my overstuffed chair by my fireplace, with Ben and Jerry's ice cream next to me after eating two last night while Lauren and Julie hung out here. I'm going to be buying new clothes if I keep this up and I don't seem to care. Cherry Garcia, and my MacBook, are my friends. I love them. I need them. I worship them. Not really, but ice cream is a known substitute for sex per me, the expert, who is not having sex right now after having had the best sex of her life.

My cellphone rings and I grab it, hopeful that it's Reese and this is over, but it's not. It's his mother. I answer with a reprimand. "I told you that you can't call. It connects me to Reese."

"I know," she says. "But Reese told me he can't talk to me right now. He has shut himself off. He's completely focused on whatever he is doing."

"He's got a lot of plates in the air to juggle."

"I know. Are you okay?"

"No, but I will be when this is over. You can't call again."

"I know, but he needs you. I feel it."

"Thanks. I needed to hear that."

"We will never have family get-togethers with your family. Just so we're clear. Take care, honey." She hangs up and I grab the remote to my fireplace and turn it on high. It's cold and I'm chilled to the bone, which could be the ice cream, or maybe it's all about my shitty family.

I start typing my column, which features a married couple, and a man who died saving his wife's life only to have the family file a lawsuit against her for wrongful death. It's an unheard of insane, first of its kind, case. My closing statement reads: *What would you do for the one you love? What would you give up? This man sacrificed everything for his woman and not only did she lose the love of her life, she was tortured by his family, and this is torture. I hope they read this. I hope they can reach inside themselves and see that the pain they cause this woman doesn't bring their family member back. It drives him deeper into his grave while the woman he loves, bleeds.*

That closing wasn't for Reese. It was for my fucked up family, who won't even read it and doesn't even know how much Reese means to me. If they did, they'd make him bleed.

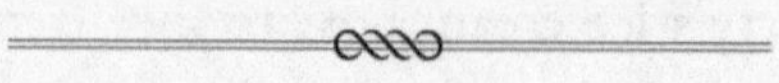

Cat

Day twenty-four apart—Thanksgiving Day...

I retreat to the kitchen of Lauren's busy house, leaving her and Julie, a Marilyn Monroe look-a-like who I am coming to really like, and a cluster of Walker brothers and staff that overwhelm the place. I grab a bottle of water from the fridge and find the table empty. I claim a seat and set my phone on the table. It rings with my youngest brother, Daniel's, number.

"Hey, Cat."

"Hey," I say. "Happy Turkey Day."

"Happy Turkey Day. How are you?"

Considering I called him three weeks ago and told him everything about Reese, and the Maxwell family drama, we both know he's not asking a generic question. "The same," I say.

"No news at all?"

"Nothing. Are you with your girlfriend?"

"Yes. Heading to her family outing."

My line beeps and the caller ID shows Gabe. "Go have fun. Gabe is calling, believe it or not."

"Hell froze over and on Thanksgiving. We need to mark this on the calendar. Call me if you hear anything about anything and I will you, too. Take care, sis."

He hangs up and I reluctantly answer Gabe's call. "Hi Gabe."

"Happy Thanksgiving."

"Yeah thanks. Happy Thanksgiving to you, too."

"I just wanted to tell you that you are missed today. You can still come over."

"I'm at a friend's house."

"Right," he says. "Okay. For the record, I love you."

I blanch. "You love me?"

"This is where you say: 'I love you, too, Gabe.'"

"I love you, too Gabe."

"Good. Next time you say it first. I'm the macho guy remember?"

"Who likes to take bubble baths."

"Hey. That's a family secret. Don't go spreading that around."

We laugh and I actually enjoy talking to him. We disconnect and I'm about to go back to the party when Royce appears at the table and sets a phone in front of me. "It can't be traced. Answer it when it rings." He nods and backs away.

The phone rings and my heart flutters. "Hello."

"Cat."

Just hearing Reese's voice, punches me with relief. "Is it over?"

"No. It's not over, but it's close."

"How close?"

"Soon is all I can say, and I don't want to talk about this. I want to just talk to you."

"Where are you?"

"Home."

"Home," I repeat. "That place we used to share?" I don't let him answer. "Who are you with?"

"I'm alone by choice. Cat, I need to know that you haven't found ten reasons we aren't good for each other."

"Why would you even think that? I write to you in my column every day."

"I know. I read it the minute I wake up."

"Then how can you think that I'm not still with you?"

"Because I know you and you don't know how I'm solving this and you can't right now. I need to keep you away from it."

"I don't care what you do to end this as long as you don't compromise who you are."

"I'm doing what I need to do," he says.

"You're doing something you don't want to do."

"I'm doing what I hope we both still want. Making sure we end up together."

"You're worried that something you're doing will push me away."

"Yes. I am. Only time will tell."

"You can't push me away."

"Challenge accepted."

"Don't say that."

"Actually, I have to say it because if I can push you away, we weren't real."

Lauren's words, which she has repeated every time she feels like I'm shutting down, come back to me. *"Everyone wants to know love is real. I told Reese the same thing."*

"Reese—"

"I love you," he says. "I'll talk to you soon."

He hangs up.

Chapter Thirty-Nine

Cat

Four weeks apart...

My Tuesday includes me sitting at the island of my kitchen writing a chapter of the book on Nelson Ward, while drinking insane amounts of coffee. The book is slow going as I type a few paragraphs here and start replaying that call with Reese on Thanksgiving, and how much he doubted me and us. He needs to know that we're real. Me too, but I caution myself every time I start going down a rabbit hole of doubt, and decide he's the one bailing. Distance creates insecurity.

This cycle continues until nearly two o'clock when the doorman buzzes my phone. "Your brother Gabe is here."

Fabulous, I think. "Send him up," I say ending the connection.

I then consider a drink and decide against it.

I might have ice cream.

I pace and I don't know why. Oh yes. I do. He is probably going to tell me some news about the legal action against our family, which means, he will hint at what is happening with Reese. I walk to the front door and Gabe knocks. I yank it open and walk away. He follows me to the kitchen and we both sit down. "Why are you here?"

"We settled with Casey Allen. We made peace with Reese Summer. Get your book deal back."

"When did you settle?"

"Yesterday."

Yesterday and Reese didn't call me. He was strange on the phone. "What does peace mean?" I ask, trying not to sound as anxious as I am right now.

"Reese got Casey Allen off with the Feds and then approached us about a truce."

"Did he say why he would do that?"

"Because the publisher threatened to sue you and him," Gabe says.

"Oh. Yes. I know." It's a lie, of course. It's not true. I'd know if it were true.

"Why didn't you tell us?"

"Would you care?"

"I care Cat," he says. "Dad cares, too. Even Reid cares. I had to pry mom's letter from his hands. He's slow coming around but he will. And for the record, I read it to Dad when he wouldn't read it."

I lose patience. "What does truce mean? Damn it, just tell me."

"Uncle Rudolf was behind everything. Reese helped him plea out a deal with a massive fucking fine of seven hundred million dollars, but it's done and no one goes to jail."

"The Reese Summer thing. Are you sure I can work with him without a conflict?"

"Oh yeah. Reese made sure."

"What does sure mean? You're killing me here."

"The two law firms, ours and his, signed an agreement to work together."

I blanch. "Your firm and Reese's firm?"

"Yes. It's not a merger but our criminal division is weak which is why Dad pushed to get you on board. But now, on a case-by-case basis Reese will represent our clients." His phone buzzes. "Shit. I have a client freaking out over a merger. I gotta go. Go get that book deal." He heads out of the kitchen and I puff out a breath.

Reese aligned with my family. I don't know what to think. Is he one of them now? No. That's silly but he didn't come to me last night. The ink must not be dry. That's it. I run after Gabe and catch him at the elevator. "Have you signed the contract with Reese yet? Is it safe to contact him?"

"Not yet. We're meeting Friday but it's done. We all agree."

"Right. Thanks."

He steps into the elevator and I head back to my apartment. It's not done. I have to talk to him. I don't want him to do something bad for his firm and career, for me. I run up the stairs to my bedroom, and grab my purse when it hits me that I'm wearing sweats. I rush into my closet and do a quick change into that pink dress that I deemed "lucky" and thigh-highs with black high heels. I fluff my hair, and actually put on make-up.

Once I've inspected myself in the mirror, I figure this will do. A few minutes later I'm in an Uber and pulling up to Reese's building. I have a momentary second thought. Is my family setting me up, looking for a relationship between me and Reese? No. I rule that out. I have a book deal with Reese worth a lot of money. Of course, I'd rush here to save it. I exit the car and walk inside the building. I have never been so nervous in my life.

Once I'm inside the elevator, I stand close to the doors, eager to get to Reese, for about a hundred reasons. Mostly, because every time I think of our phone call I think of his doubt. He has done so much to clear our path. I need to run down it and to him. I arrive on his floor and I don't check with the receptionist. She tries to stop me when Maria appears in the lobby.

"Oh thank God," she says. "He's a bear without you."

"Is he here?"

"Yes," she says walking with me toward her desk and motioning to his closed door. "Go in. He's alone."

"Thanks Maria."

I hurry to the door and pause with my hand on the knob.

"Don't doubt that he loves you," Maria says. "I promise. He does."

I look over my shoulder at her. "Thank you."

I face forward again and open the door, stepping inside and shutting it to lean against it. Reese is sitting at his desk, and he's still gorgeous. He still consumes a room and me with it. He stands up. "Cat."

"Hi."

"Hi."

Neither of us take a step. "You can't sign with my family."

"I already did, about fifteen minutes ago."

"Gabe said Friday."

"Gabe was wrong."

"You don't do things like they do."

"They're reputable, Cat. They weren't involved in this mess. Just your uncle as you told me in your column."

"What does this do for you or to you?"

"I'm only offering aid and consultation. That's all. But I've ensured your family will not lash out at me to get to you."

"You sure you're okay with this?"

"Yes. Are you okay with it? That's the question and you're not moving. You're way over there and I'm way over here."

"I know."

"Why?"

"I need to know this doesn't mean you're going to align with them not me."

"I still don't like them. I'm tolerating them because that's what a man does for his woman. Are you still my woman?"

"Yes. Is all of this still in play in some way? Because you're still over there and I'm over here. Do I have to leave?"

"Why the hell would you leave? I was about to go get you." He starts to move and I do, too, and we all but collide in the center of the room in an embrace. "I missed you," I say. "I—"

"I missed you, too, sweetheart." His mouth crashes down on mine and that's all it takes. We are all over each other, so hungry for us, that we can't get enough. I barely remember how the skirt of my dress ends up at my waist or how his pants get unzipped. Suddenly it just is and he's sitting on the couch in the corner, with me on top of him, him pressing inside me, filling me. I sink down on his cock, and when I have all of him, we just sit there, connected. Together.

"Let's make a pact," Reese says, tangling fingers into my hair, and dragging my mouth to his. "We don't ever separate again. Ever, Cat."

"Never again," I agree, and he kisses me and we're wild all over again, and slow again, watching each other, just savoring each other. Neither of us wants it to end but it does. Another burning need to just feel more and more of each other, sends us over the edge, until we peak and crash into one other. We lay there a full minute before I realize where we are. "We're half naked in your office."

He laughs and says, "Best day I've had in this office."

I press on his shoulders and sit up. "I should get off now."

"Yes. You should. So that I can take you home. Our home, Cat."

"I want to come home. It is home. *You* are home."

Thirty minutes later, we walk into his apartment and I swear I can breathe again but just when I think I might run through the whole damn place, Reese scoops me up. "I can walk," I say. "And I promise only to run to the bedroom."

"It's more romantic if I do it."

"Romantic," I say. "I taught you manners and romance. I love it."

"I hope you do."

"Now you're talking in secret code."

He enters the bedroom and walks to the chair, our chair, and sets me down. "I missed this chair," I say. "Good. Don't move and don't look." He walks away and I'm dying. I almost turn. I might have to turn. Okay I won't turn because he's now covering my eyes.

"Is that one of your ties?"

"It is. I have a surprise." He knots the cloth at the back of my head and places my arms on the sides of the chair. "Leave them here."

I do as he says and he adds, "Don't move them, Cat."

Heat rushes through me and my heart starts to race. "I've actually never let anyone cover my eyes."

I feel him settle in front of me. "I plan to be the first of many things," he says, his hands sliding up my legs, inching my skirt up my hips. "I'd undress you but I'm too impatient. Remember. Don't move your hands."

"I know," I say, but he's moving his. He catches my panties at each side and drags them down my legs, kissing random spots on my leg as he does. He untangles them from my feet and they are gone now, but his mouth is not. His lips press tiny kisses all over me: My thigh, my calf, and my knees. His tongue travels up my inner thigh and I am panting when it finds my clit. I almost come that easily.

I grip the chair and arch upward and he gives me what I want. He suckles me, licks me, touches me and release hits me with a sudden jolt. I stiffen and then tremble all over until it's over. I melt into the chair, and I feel Reese tug my skirt down. He then sets something in my lap. "Come here, Cat."

I lean up and he kisses me, pulling away the tie and whispering, "Marry me, Cat. I need you in my life...Look down."

He eases back and there is a stunning diamond ring, sitting on my lap. "A ring. I mean, I know it's a ring. I just—"

"Say yes, Cat. You're killing me here."

"Yes. Yes. Yes. Of course. And just so you know. That was the best way of proposing any man has ever come up with. Of course, I'll leave certain parts out of the story but—"

He kisses me and I'm home to stay.

Chapter Forty

Cat

One year later...

Still reeling from our wedding a month ago at the Summer ranch, Reese and I are now sitting at a table in the center of a ballroom at the Ritz Carlton Battery Park as part of a launch party for our book we're told is already set for the *New York Times* just with pre-orders. I'd worn a pink dress to get married in and Reese a tuxedo. And today, I'm wearing my pink suit for the signing and he has on his lucky blue suit. Or it will be lucky after today. Everyone we know, and many we don't know, are here with the exception of my baby brother Daniel who had to go back to work after the wedding. Even my father, Gabe, and Reid, are here, who of course, are thrilled I married an attorney. Reid is still one big cranky ass but he's slowly easing up. Reese has saved two of Reid's clients from certain hell in jail, and since they were innocent, Reese and I, were both just fine with him helping.

I sign a book for a man who raves about my column and Reese's skill in the courtroom. He watched "every moment of the trial on TV." I smile and sign his book "Cat Summer" which is pretty darn surreal. The next person in line is quick to attack Dan. "He was horrid in court," the sixty-something woman says. "Horrid. Don't you think so, Mr. Summer?"

"He put Kelli Ward in prison for life," Reese says. "I forgive him for being a jerk for that reason."

"I hope Nelson Ward has found peace."

"He has," Reese says. "And with this book, we hope his story gets heard."

I hand a signed book to her, and she leaves us with a break from the long line we'd managed the past hour. I reach for my bottle of water, when Reese nudges me. "Look," he says, motioning to his mother, who looks stunning in a knee length emerald dress. "She's flirting with a guy twenty years younger than her."

"And he's flirting back. I love it."

"I do not love it," Reese says. "I'm supposed to go help her install a new television tomorrow. I don't want to show up to her apartment and find a guy my own age, or any age, running around naked."

I laugh. "I doubt he will be running around. I still can't get used to her apartment being my old apartment but I love it. My mom wanted to start fresh there, I did start fresh there, and now she's teaching here, and starting fresh in that same apartment."

"And flirting with young kids."

"He's not a kid," I laugh again.

"Holy fuck," he says.

"What now?"

I follow his lead and find his sister, who is an absolute brunette goddess, in conversation with Gabe who has actually become friends with Reese. Flirty conversation. "Oh my," I say. "They are cuddly."

"I have to stop this." He tries to stand.

"You will not. Let them have fun."

He looks over at me. "Isn't that like saying one and done? It never works."

"Right. Someone either gets hurt or gets married. She lives here now, too. Maybe we should go break them up." We both stand and start walking in that direction, Mr. and Mrs. Summer to rescue one dirty rich one night stand at a time.

Cat Does Crime: Christmas Day

In closing: Contrary to popular talking heads in the media Santa did not steal Christmas, or any other holiday. I did. At least where Christmas is concerned since that is what I celebrate. Christmas is right here in my house, with a tree decorated in silver, in case you wondered. I hope whatever it is that you celebrate is alive and well in your house, too, because this time of year is about family, friendship, and a whole lot of eating. We need more family and friends in this world. We need more pumpkin pie, actually, but that's for another day. For those of you who have written in asking how becoming Cat Summer changes me or this column, I hope you have had a few months to see that it changes nothing. For the record, if Reese Summer missteps in a trial I will not only tell him, I will tell you. Merry Christmas, happy holidays, and until then, —Cat

Part Two

PART TWO

Two Years Later...

Chapter Forty-One

Cat

Day one: The day before the second biggest trial of the century...

No matter how many times I wake in my husband's arms as I do now, it never gets old. Reese is mine. Yeah. Never gets old. Today though there will be no lingering and making love as we do so many mornings. He's starting what could be the second biggest trial of his career, on edge, and overworked, and the minute the alarm goes off, I expect him to jump out of bed. He doesn't. He wraps his arm around me right along with all those sinewy muscles, and his lips press to my ear. "How about a morning fuck for luck?" he murmurs, his hands sliding over my belly, cupping my breast, and teasing my nipple.

"Your luck or mine?" I murmur, covering his hand where it's pressed to my breast. "Because it feels like mine."

He slips his cock along my now slick sex and presses inside me. "Mine," he says. "The luck and you."

I bite my lip at that possessive, sexy comment that I would have pushed back on long ago, but not now. Now *I am* his and I like it. He presses into me again and I arch against his hand squeezing my breast, and the hard length of him buried inside me. There is this raw burn between us, his raw need, that edge in him he gets right before a case, and even before it happens, I know it's coming. I'm flat on my stomach and he's driving into me, hard and fast, intense. *He's intense.* It consumes me. He consumes me and I lose myself in every drive, pump, and touch. I don't know where he begins and I end, and somehow we're in that shuddering, over the edge, sweet spot together, his low guttural moan so hot, I'm clenching tighter. He stills on top of me and then rolls to his side, taking me with him.

"I will never start a trial without doing that, ever again," he murmurs near my ear.

"Today is not your trial day."

"Today is practice for tomorrow." He kisses my neck. "I love the hell out of you, woman. You know that, right?" He doesn't give me time to respond. He moves and in a blink he's carrying me to the shower with him.

Half an hour later, Reese is dressed in a gray suit with a blue pinstripe and a blue shirt to match, looking all tall, dark, and handsome, while my hair is still wet and I'm just finishing my make up. He approaches from behind and I turn to face him. "I hate to tell you this," I say, "but you're living up to the Mr. Hotness blogs right now."

He groans and pulls me to him. "I'm going to pretend you didn't just taunt me with that. Every fucking time I go to trial it starts again."

"It's the burden of being so hot."

"Stop, woman, or I will find a way to punish you."

I laugh, but he's moved on, focused on his case. I see it in his eyes even before his jaw clenches and his fingers flex on my hips. "Come to the office today. I need you to work with me on my opening statement."

"It's brilliant. You know that."

"It'll be better with practice. Write your 'Cat Does Crime' column and come to the office when you're done."

My hand settles on his chest. "I will," I promise. "Of course I will, but not because you really need practice. My column is going to take a while though. Everyone will be watching it for shades of you and this trial. A young, beautiful woman accused of killing her wealthy father to inherit his money plays like a movie and you're the leading man."

"And my client is the innocent victim made out to be a villain. Are you going to go for it and write about her?"

"Yes. I am. Though I can't tell you what will end up on the paper. I'm just going to wing it."

"That makes for some of your most compelling work." His cellphone rings and he snakes it from his pocket, and answers it, without letting go of me completely.

"Yeah Royce," he says, Royce being the owner of the security firm he uses often for his cases and for the firm's activities. "Right. Thanks for the head's up." He disconnects and sticks his phone back in his pocket. "Picketers at the office and I don't want you to have to deal with that mess. I'll bring the team here to you late this afternoon."

"I don't mind. You know that."

"I know, but I want to be home." He kisses me. "I'm going to take off. I'll see you back here as soon as possible." He heads for the door, all loose-legged swagger and perfection and I sigh. He's mine. "I'm going to keep you!" I call out.

He leans back inside the doorway. "Did you just decide this now, or almost two years ago when you married me?"

"Just re-affirming my vows."

"Well then, I'm going to keep you, too, and naked as often as possible" He winks and disappears.

I'm still smiling when I've finished dressing in dark jeans and a pink sweater worthy of the later October season. I head downstairs to the kitchen, power my computer up on the island where it sits, and start a cup of coffee brewing. As usual, I grab a bottle of water and open the drawer by the coffee pot to pull out my birth control pill. That's when I realize that I'm on day three of the blank sugar pills and I haven't started my period. And my breasts are sore. I grab the cabinet. Oh God. The flu. I had the flu and nothing stayed down for days and yet Reese and I managed to have sex the morning I got sick and on the heels of me getting better, because well, he's Reese, and sex with him, always feels good.

I'm pregnant. This isn't like when my friend Lori thought she was pregnant. I am. I feel it. Thinking back to the last few days, I felt different. *I feel different.* I inhale and let it out. This is okay. We have talked about this. We want kids. We said next year, but now is fine. I just don't want to freak Reese out during this trial. I'm not going to do that to him. Pregnant. A baby. Reese's baby. *Our* baby. I feel so many things that I don't even know how to name those emotions. I want to take a test. I press my hand to my head.

I have to write my column first in case Reese shows up earlier than expected and needs help prepping for his case.

I grab my coffee, doctor it up and sit down at the island. I can do this. I'll get the test afterward. I pull up a blank document and start typing. Two hours later, I'm finally at the end and I read my conclusion: *Tomorrow Dana Warren's trial will begin, but as you follow it on the television and in the news, I ask you to play a game with me. Pretend you are a juror like I do with every case I cover. Wipe the slate clean and assume Dana's innocence the way you would want to be assumed innocent. Then pull out a pad of paper or your computer and take notes right along with me. In the end, the prosecution must prove guilt without reasonable doubt. At the end of the trial when the jury deliberates, write down on a sheet of paper what your verdict is. I'll share mine, even if it's not the one my husband wants to hear. I'm calling this the Honest Jury Challenge. So—challenge on. Who's taking it with me? I'll be in court tomorrow, and back here every day to share my views. You can email me with yours, and I plan to share random tidbits from my readers. Until then, —Cat.*

Happy with the final product, I email it to my editor and rush upstairs. I grab my purse and I'm out of the door and headed to the store in about three minutes. Fifteen minutes later, I'm in the bathroom, peeing on a stick which I sit on a towel on the sink and watch. And watch for what feels forever but is really only about two minutes. I suck in air at the results. I'm right. I have to sit down on the tub to process the words and then say them in my mind. *I'm pregnant.* I'm pregnant right before Reese's trial. I don't know if he can hear this now.

I need to go to the doctor. I need confirmation first and what if I miscarry in the middle of his trial? My God. Why am I thinking about miscarriages? I'm not going to miscarry. I just don't want to worry or rattle Reese during his trial and he has a responsibility to his client as well. I pull up the address book on my phone. I'll talk to the doctor and decide when to tell Reese. I make the appointment and I'm dying. I want to call Reese. We tell each other everything and this is huge. I *want* to tell him that we're having a baby, but this isn't like other times. I can't be selfish. I can't do this now. Not the night before his opening statements. Doctor first. Reese later.

Chapter Forty-Two

Cat

My doctor appointment is not for a week. The more I think about my doctor putting me off that long, the more uneasy I am. I call the office back and beg for an earlier appointment but it appears my doctor is on vacation. The nurse, however, can do a test. I schedule that appointment for two days from now but keep my doctor's appointment with the real doctor, too.

Next, I call my close friend Lauren, who's the mother of a toddler, and the wife of Royce Walker, who heads Walker Security. I choose Lauren because she's a trial attorney like Reese and a good friend. Also because Royce doesn't just do a lot of investigative work for Reese's firm, he's ex-FBI and his team is compiled of FBI, CIA, SEALs, Special Forces and more, meaning they have stressful jobs. They have been on and continue to take dangerous missions. It's not the same as a court case, but it's high pressure. Lauren will know how those men deal with baby news in the middle of something big.

I get her voicemail. "Lauren, I have a crisis. Or not a crisis. But I need someone to talk to. Call me." I hang up and text her the same message.

My cellphone rings and when it's Reese's number nerves overcome me. Why am I nervous? This is my husband. This is my soul mate. This is the man who is the father of my child. I answer the call. "Hey," I say.

"Hey, sweetheart. How's your column coming?"

"Done. Already sent to my editor. How are things there?"

"We're going to head to the apartment around three. Does that work for you?"

"Works great. How are you feeling about everything?"

"Like hell."

"You always say that right before trial and it's never hell."

"Keep reminding me," he says. "I need to hear it right now. I'll see you soon."

We disconnect and I press my hand to my belly. *Is there a baby growing in my belly?* Reese's baby. I walk back into the bathroom and check the stick and then read the box just to make sure I'm not confused. The test still reads pregnant. I bag up the test and stuff it at the bottom of the trash. Lauren still hasn't called me back so I just decide to go to her office which is in the same building where she lives. I need advice. I need to tell someone I trust. I need to tell my husband but no matter what, before his opening statement is not the time. But when is?

Thirty minutes later, I find Lauren's office dark but Walker Security, just next door is open. After being told by the receptionist that Lauren is having lunch in the conference room, I invite myself to go on back. I poke my head in the door to be suffocated by testosterone, as not one but six men, all about as big and intimidating as Royce—who is a bear of a man—sit around the pretty, petite brunette Lauren.

"Cat," she says, her eyes going wide. "What's wrong?"

"I've been calling and texting you. I need you."

"Oh God. Sorry. The little one dropped my phone in the toilet this morning." She stands up and I step into the hallway.

She joins me, pulling on a suit jacket over her pale pink dress, and motioning me to an open office door. We step inside and I whirl around to face her. "I think I'm pregnant."

Her eyes light and then she holds up her hands. "Okay I know you two want kids but I sense panic in you so before I respond, tell me what you're feeling."

"We talked about next year."

"It's a little early but is that a big deal?" Lauren asks.

"He's starting a massive trial tomorrow, Lauren. You know that. This is big news. It's life-changing news. It's not the kind of news you give someone before a trial."

"I admit that the timing is delicate so let's take a step back. Are you certain you're pregnant?"

"The test says I am and I feel different but, I'm not sick. I googled that on my way to the subway. They say when you're sick it's a sign of a healthy baby. Those who miscarry often aren't sick."

"Wow." She holds up her hands. "Wait. Why are we going there? You're *not* going to miscarry."

"You did."

"I know," she says grimly. "So I guess we know why you're going there. You lived that with me."

"And Royce. I saw what it did to you both. I'm a calm, rational person, Lauren. You know that. I'm thinking about all the ways this could affect Reese. I'm worried about my husband."

The door opens behind Lauren and Royce steps inside. He towers above us and consumes the room. "Is there a problem?" he asks.

"I need to ask you something," I answer.

"I'm listening," he says, folding his arms over his broad chest.

"If you were leaving for a dangerous job, you couldn't change, would you want to hear Lauren was pregnant before you left?"

Lauren holds up her hands again. "I'm not pregnant."

He looks at me again. "I'd want to know," he says.

"But would you be better off knowing? Reese starts a trial tomorrow. He has someone's future in his hands. He's a protector. He'll worry about me. He'll worry about the baby. If you were on that big job, and Lauren miscarried during it, how would it affect you?"

His lips thin. "I wouldn't know if Lauren was pregnant in the scenario you're suggesting. I'd be on radio silence."

"But Reese won't be. He'll worry about a miscarriage just like me. A trial could take months or he could do his magic, corner someone into a confession, and end the trial." Royce opens his mouth to speak. "Wait, please. Before you say anything else. There are already picketers, and it could get worse—"

"It will with this case," he interjects. "Reese hired us to handle that for him."

"See," I say. "And if he's worried that they are stressing me and the baby so he rushes something with the trial, even if it's not conscious, what if he makes a mistake?" I look at Lauren. "You know the pressure. You're a criminal attorney just like him."

"It's extreme pressure," she agrees. "Your client's depending on you."

"But he's also the father," Royce says. "And your husband. He wants and needs to protect you." He scrubs his jaw. "But I concede that you make good points."

"But we're best friends, too," I say. "We tell each other everything and this is special." I press the back of my hand to my forehead. "I don't want to keep this from him. I feel like I'm selfish to keep it a secret and selfish not to have the willpower to wait and tell him."

"When do you go to the doctor?" Lauren asks.

"I see the nurse in two days. My doctor is out until next week."

"My suggestion," she says, "is for you to let Reese get past his opening statement. See the nurse. Confirm the pregnancy. Think. Breathe. Then decide what to do."

"I'd let him get through opening statements," Royce agrees.

"Okay then. I wait at least two days." I press my hand to my belly and start to tear up. "He's going to be an amazing father."

Lauren smiles and hugs me. "And you're going to be an amazing mother."

I stop by my favorite salad spot and grab lunch. I don't feel sick. I don't crave anything. By two I'm sitting at the island in the kitchen eating and googling pregnancy articles. It's making me crazy to think of all the things that could go wrong which most would say are really statistically not a big deal. But Reese will read them just like me now and they will feel big when he's in a high-profile trial like this. I don't know what to do. I'm still hyper-focused on pregnancy articles when the door opens. I quickly clear my browser and hold my breath, waiting for Reese to appear. In a few beats, he's entering the kitchen, and he's stealing that very breath I was holding, just by being him.

He rounds the counter and comes to me, cupping my face. "I need you. You know that right?"

"Good. You're stuck with me for life but why are you saying that?"

"Because I do." He smiles and brushes hair from my eyes. "Which is why I'm going to keep you."

I laugh at his mimic of my declaration from this morning. "When did you decide this?"

"Just reaffirming my vows, sweetheart."

I have to tell him. I need to tell him. I have to *tell* him. "Reese—"

His cellphone buzzes and he glances at the screen. "The team is headed upstairs. Lori and Cole are coming too but you're the one I need input from. My opening is a mess. I need you to listen to it."

"I've read your opening. It's brilliant. *You* even said it's brilliant."

"And then audio of my client fighting with her father, she's accused of killing, leaked."

I blanch. "What?"

"You heard me. An audio was leaked to the press."

"Oh no. How bad is it?"

"Bad. The kind of bad that might have kept me from taking this case."

"You think she's guilty?" I ask, knowing how much he hates defending people who are guilty.

"I still don't, but this is going to make it tough to win."

"Strike it out of evidence," I suggest.

"This judge is tough."

"And you're the best of the best."

His lips curve. "And to think I started out as the asshole who cut in front of you in the coffee line."

"Thankfully now you have manners."

The doorbell rings and he laughs before pressing his cheek to mine, and whispering, "I love you, Cat." And then he's walking away and I can barely breathe again. I don't know what to do. I don't know how to be a good wife right now but that's what I want. I want to do the right thing. I have to do the right thing.

Chapter Forty-Three

Cat

Reese heads to the door to greet his team, our team really because this is our life. We do everything together. We deal with all things together. I'm a part of his work and he is a part of mine. I barely breathe without this man and yet I'm having his child and I can't tell him. I know I can't. Not yet.

"Hi, Cat."

I blink to find Elsa standing in the doorway, looking blonde and beautiful as usual in a blue suit. She *is* beautiful and also with my husband all the time, but never once have I worried about them together. How many women would feel that confident with a man as successful and gorgeous as my husband? But I do.

"Hey, Elsa," I greet. "I hear there are some bumps."

"Have you heard the recording?"

"No. Bad?"

"Yeah. It's bad. Your husband is going to have to work magic in his opening statement because of course, the jurors heard the tape. It's everywhere." She heads to the coffee pot, comfortable here, and why wouldn't she be? Reese loves to hold game planning sessions here. I love that he loves to come home to find his magic with his cases.

I twist around to face her. "That doesn't seem like the opposing counsel. Reese could move to delay the trial to allow a fair jury to be selected."

"Cat."

I turn to find Reese in the archway between the kitchen and the hallway. He motions me forward. Richard, another attorney on Reese's team, walks in and heads to the coffee pot. "Hey, Cat," he says, shoving his longish brown hair from his eyes, his red tie at half mast.

"Hey, Richard."

I join Reese in the hallway and we walk to the office down the hallway. He sets a tape recorder on the mahogany desk and leans on the edge next to it. "I want to play the leaked phone call. Ready?"

"Hit me with it," I say, sitting down in one of the wing back chairs as he punches play.

Dana Warren, my husband's client and heiress to the Warren Empire, starts to speak: *"He's mean. He's so mean. He says horrible things. He does horrible things. The world would be better without that man."*

"I understand wanting someone dead," a male voice says. "You know I do. You know what I've been through."

"Only you escaped. I can't escape."

"You can always walk away," the man says.

"Not until the day he's dead and he might even have provisions to enslave me after that. The money will be my prison. I don't think I want it anymore. I don't want it."

"No one walks away from that kind of money. When he's gone, you'll have control."

"He'll find a way to make sure I don't. I need to just—"

The tape cuts off. "Where's the rest of it?"

"I don't have it and Dana swears that's when she said she loved her father. She says she said she couldn't hurt him but it hurts that he could hurt her."

"Who was the man?"

"Reginald Hicks, her boyfriend, and he says that he didn't leak the call. He doesn't know how anyone got it. He's willing to testify to the rest of the content of the call."

"Do you believe him?"

"I do."

"Delay the trial. You have to get a new jury, maybe a new location outside the city."

He gives a shake of his head. "She won't let me."

I blanch. "What? Why?"

"She wants it over. She says she's considered suicide from the stress of it all."

"Please tell me you got her help."

He scrubs his jaw. "I'm trying. I want you to talk to her."

"Of course," I say. "I'll do what I can. You believe her right? The suicide thing isn't guilt?"

"I'm sure there is guilt there but not for the murder. There's no evidence but her inheritance to convict her. The man was evil, which I'm going to show in court. He destroyed people and hurt people just because he could. I don't think her feelings were abnormal."

"I need to see if I can rework my column for tomorrow and include this." I grab his phone. "I have to call my editor and you need one hell of an opening statement."

"Now you know why I say my opening sucks."

"Yeah. It's obsolete now." I punch in Melanie, my editor's, number.

"Cat," Melanie greets. "Why did I know I'd be getting this call? Yes, you can have time to rework tomorrow's column."

"How long?"

"I need it now."

"I need two hours."

"You can have one."

"Two it is."

"Cat—"

"You know you want that voicemail covered and you know readers are going to look to me to see what I say. My husband is the defense counsel."

"Fine. Two."

We disconnect and I look at Reese. "I have to work on my column and you have to work on your opening but for both, I told Elsa, this wasn't the opposing counsel. They'd—"

"—wait until, mid-trial when we couldn't move the trial. Agreed. So who the hell did this?"

"The boyfriend. It has to be him."

"It's too obvious," he argues.

"Right. It is. And yet sometimes that's what makes things less obvious."

"Don't point a finger at him," he says. "I need him on the stand, on our side."

"No one walks away from that kind of money, he said. He's the boyfriend. Were they engaged? Because maybe he was afraid she would walk away and he'd get screwed."

"And I plan to go there with him on the stand, but I need him to say the right things, to help my client, first. But if he killed the father, why release the voicemail?"

"He got spooked," I suggest. "He's afraid he's on the radar. He wants his freedom more than the money, which ironically is what your client said on that call."

"Maybe. And I do have Walker Security investigating him. The good news though is that I can show dozens of people who wanted that man dead and at least three who threatened to kill him."

"I need to write."

He gives a nod. "You know the drill. Don't give away my position."

"I'm just going to make sure your client isn't convicted before the trial over that call." I stand up and Reese shoves off the desk, and the next thing I know, I'm pressed against it instead of him.

"Do you know what I want right now?"

I arch a brow. "Coffee?"

"*You.*"

"You can't have me the way you're talking about right now. We have people in our house."

"Who will have no idea that I'm fucking my wife."

"Reese."

He kisses me, a deep, drugging, hungry kiss. "Reese."

"I'm on edge, sweetheart. Like I haven't been for a trial in a very long time."

My hand goes to his jaw. "You're going to kill it. You always do."

"Tell me that when I'm inside you and I might believe you." His mouth closes down on mine again, and there's this dark need in him, this possessive hunger, and I wonder if some part of him senses I'm holding something back. I don't want him to feel this.

I sink into the kiss and I forget about our guest, my column, and his trial prep. There is just me and my husband, the father of our child that he doesn't even know about yet. He doesn't know, but in some way, here, now, I want him to feel how much I want this, how much I want to tell him how much I want him. He turns me and presses my hands to the desk. "Toe off your sneakers," he orders.

I do it and I don't even know how my pants are unzipped and unbuttoned, but he's tugging my jeans down my hips and in a flash I'm naked from the waist down. He turns me to face him, his fingers tangling in my hair, and then he's kissing me again, drinking me in, drugging me with his need, and God, I know he senses I'm holding back. I know. I'm sure of it. I have to fix this, but in this moment there's only one way to communicate and that means fucking him the way he needs to be fucked.

Chapter Forty-Four

Cat

Reese shrugs out of his jacket, his starched white button down still managing to stretch across his broad chest, and even as I watch him, I know what he wants and needs. I know this man. I know those moments when he's on edge and fucking is all there is to him, and that works just fine for me. He makes love to me. He fucks me. He does everything just right. Right now, he needs to fuck me. He needs to know that I'm all in, that I'm right here with him. He needs to know that whatever he thinks he senses right now, it's not a division between us. It's a secret, yes, but it's a special secret. It's a gift I want to share with him so very much and I can't. Not now. Not yet. Not before his trial.

I reach for his pants and stroke a line down the thick ridge of his erection and his mouth comes down on mine, a possessive, devouring kiss, and I meet every lick and stroke he gives me, until he's lifting me to the desk, shoving down his pants, and without any preamble, pressing inside me. "God, woman," he murmurs against my lips before he cups my now naked backside and lifts me, one of his hands settling between my shoulder blades.

It's a wild frenzy from there. Us kissing. Us moving. Him thrusting into me, pulling me down onto his thick erection, sending a ripple of sensation spiraling through me. I lose myself in his touch, in the feel of his hands on my body; the sound of our breathing, our moans. We are wild, in need of more, and more, and Reese shackles my waist, urging me backward, forcing me to trust him to hold me up, and I do not believe this is an accident. Reese and I are too connected. He knows when something is off between us. He doesn't just need to fuck and feel close to me. He's testing our trust, and I don't even hesitate to give it to him. I'm one hundred percent into the passion between us and the play of our bodies. I push into every pump of his hips, holding onto his wrists and nothing else while he holds onto me, driving into me. The urgency between us becoming hard and fast, and he sits me on the desk, leaning into me to the point that I'm forced to settle on my elbows. His mouth comes down on mine and after a deep, consuming kiss, he's thrusting into me again, his head buried in my neck.

I tangle my fingers into his hair, wrap my leg around his hip and I'm right there in that sweet spot that this man takes me to all too easily. "Reese," I breathe out at the same moment that he lets out a deep, guttural moan and shudders against me. I tumble with him and the room spirals into nothing but this man, his delicious, earthy scent, and the feel of him all around me. We collapse into reality and he drags me to a sitting a position.

"You okay?" he asks, brushing hair from my temple.

"My husband just fucked me on a desk. How can I not be okay?"

There are voices outside the door—Lori and Cole's voices—and my heart leaps. "Reese," I plea urgently and he hands me a tissue, fixes his pants and then sets me on the ground.

We don't speak again until I'm dressed but the voices fade. "I can't believe we just did that with guests in the house."

"It's our house," he says, fitting me between him and the desk again. "Why do we feel off?"

And there it is. Proof of how connected we are. Proof that he reads me like no other human being ever has. "We're not off. Not even a little off."

"Then what do I feel?"

I don't want to lie to him. I won't lie to him. "You feel me fretting with you over this case," I say, which is true. It's why I can't tell him about the baby now. I stroke his jaw. "I know how much pressure you put on yourself but you always win."

"Always winning becomes expected," he says, "and I want to live up to that expectation, but that, too, becomes more pressure." It's a confession I know that he would share with no one but me. "I feel that pressure," he adds.

"Added to by the fact that you and Cole are now partners and neither of you have ever lost a case. You don't want to blow that track record for the firm."

He presses his hands to the desk on either side of me and looks skyward before fixing me in a turbulent stare. "It shouldn't be about my record. It should be about my client."

"It is," I say, pressing my hand to his chest, his heart thundering beneath my palm. "It is about your client. Your perfect record staying perfect is about your client. It means you win this one, for her and you. And the firm. You pick your cases well, but if they aren't a challenge, anyone could win. They can't, but you can."

He cups my head and kisses me. "I love you for believing that, sweetheart, especially since I know you'd call me on a poor performance."

"There will be no poor performance," I say. "That's not you."

He settles his hands on his hips. "You're right. I'm going to win. I'm going to go make sure the team knows that. Do you want me to bring you your computer before I get started with them?"

"No. I'll grab it and say hello to Lori and Cole."

He heads for the door and I grab his arm, laughing as I wipe lipstick from his cheek. "You just love wearing my lipstick."

"I love wearing you," he teases, winking at me before he opens the office door.

We head into the kitchen where Lori and Cole are talking in hushed voices. "Hey you guys," I greet, joining them at the island to scoop up my computer. "I can't stay. In light of the leaked phone call, I'm off to rework my column for tomorrow."

Lori's eyes go wide and she shoves her brown hair out of her eyes, pressing her hands on the counter. "What are you going to write? What's the angle?"

Cole motions to Reese and the two of them step out of the room. "You know I never know until I write it. Any thoughts?"

"You know that I don't like to mess with your creative process, not unless you need me."

Do I need her? Yes. I need to talk, but not about my work, about the baby, only I can't. I've already told Lauren and Royce about the baby. I adore Lori. She's such a good friend, but it feels like a betrayal to Reese to tell yet another person about the baby. And Lori and Cole are like me and Reese. They tell each other everything. I'm not having Cole know about this and Reese be in the dark.

"I'm good," I say, and the truth is, I am. I'm in love. I'm married to my best friend and we're having a baby. "I'll join you guys to strategize in a few."

I hurry away and return to the office, another smile playing on my lips as I think about me on that desk, and Reese on top of me. I sit behind that very desk and begin to edit my column. My new beginning reads: *By now, most of you have heard or read the transcript of the leaked phone call between Dana Warren and her boyfriend. The interesting part of this call to me wasn't that*

Dana wanted her father dead. It's that she was willing to walk away from the money. The question becomes, who was afraid she really would?

I frown and delete everything I just wrote. I can't put the boyfriend on edge and risk turning him against Dana. Reese already told me that he needs him on his side. I start again: *By now, most of you have heard or read the transcript of the leaked phone call between Dana Warren and her boyfriend. I've dissected this conversation, and I don't believe any of us can put it into context until we learn more but I was struck by one detail: She was willing to walk away from the money and yet we're to believe she killed for the money? Those two things contradict each other to such a point that I've written them down, as hot points I want addressed in the trial.*

I read that passage again and decide I like it. I leave my closing statement as it was, along with my challenge issued to my readers to follow the trial objectively and with me. I send my updated version of my column to my editor and then I sit there and replay Reese's question: *Why do we feel off?*

I decide this question is a big problem. Once I tell him about the pregnancy, what if he thinks back to today, and worries that I was feeling regret of some sort? An idea strikes me. I know how to wipe out any worries he might have later and I put that plan in place. I pull up a new document and I type: *Our parenthood journey begins—a journal and gift for my husband and our unborn child.*

The first few lines read: *Today, I woke up to the man I love. It was only moments after he left the house, the day before a major trial, that I realized I didn't start my period. Even before I went to the store and bought a test, I knew I was pregnant. I also knew that I had a decision to make. Do I tell my husband, my protective, amazing husband, that I was pregnant right away, as I wanted to, or wait until after opening statements or even the trial itself?*

I go on to detail everything I can think of and then some. The calls to the doctor, the visit to see Lauren and Royce, my fear about not being sick, my fear of how he'd worry, the moment he'd come into the kitchen a few minutes ago, and made me want to tell him right then, only to share the trial challenges. When I'm done, I close the document and my MacBook. I'm going to document every day and every thought I have right up until the moment I tell him about the pregnancy. He's going to know I wanted to tell him. He's going to know how much I love him. I won't let this go any other way.

Chapter Forty-Five

Reese

Two hours after fucking my wife on the desk in our apartment, I'm standing in the living room with Elsa and Richard both sitting on the couch, all of us frustrated. Running fingers through my hair, I crumple up a sheet of paper with yet another version of my opening on it, letting it pile up with the other ten versions.

Cat enters the room, and I know she's what I need, and not just because she's become my confidant and my best friend. Something is wrong with her and us. I have no idea what is going on with my wife, but I know her. She internalizes and frets but she talks to me and yet whatever this is, she doesn't want to tell me and I know why. Tomorrow is my opening statement and she doesn't want to distract me, but not knowing what's bothering her is driving me crazy.

"What's this?" Cat asks, rounding the couch to stand in the middle of the crumpled paper pile I've created.

"Behold," Elsa says. "Ten excellent opening statements that he hates."

"Three of them were shit," Richard says, loosening his tie. "Is it time for pizza yet? Because we're going to need fuel."

Cat drops to her knees, right there in the middle of the floor, sits cross-legged, and after shoving her long blonde hair behind her ears, starts reading one of the openings. She's only about halfway through and she crumples it and tosses it over her shoulder. God, I love this woman. She grabs another and Elsa and Richard start debating new ideas I tune out. This isn't working for me and in ten minutes Cat obviously agrees as she's tossed all ten openings back into the pile of tossed paper balls.

"Let's appeal to the child in everyone," Richard says.

Cat starts to stand and I catch her arm, helping her to her feet, her eyes meeting mine. "Can we step into the kitchen?" she asks.

I give her a nod, and we leave Richard and Elsa in heavy debate. Once we're in the kitchen, we do as we always do when we debate, her on one side of the island and me on the other, both with our hands on the counter. "Tell me," I say.

"You know what your problem is?"

"Like I said, tell me."

"You prepare brilliant opening statements. You. Alone. I don't even help you beyond listening to the final product and offering a tweak here or there."

"Well in advance, and I don't have that luxury now."

"You don't have the luxury of doing it any other way. Nothing I just read was you. Unless you need to work on additional prep, I think you should send them home and do this your way." She glances at the clock on the stove. "It's only six, Reese. You could spend the next four hours, working on this, and still get a good night's sleep to be fresh tomorrow."

I thrum my fingers on the counter. She's right. I push off the island and walk into the living room. "You two, go home or somewhere else. I need to do the opening statement on my own."

A few minutes later, they're gone and my wife points up the stairs. "Bedroom. That's where you pace, while I write, and magic is made."

I grab her and pull her to me. "You're the magic."

"You were magic in the courtroom when I met you, Reese. I watched you work your magic on a jury while you worked it on me right along with them." She takes my hand. "Come on. You start to work and I'll order dinner."

Three hours later, we've both changed into sweats and we're now sitting in our favorite spot, the couch in front of the window in our bedroom, eating pizza, and I'm feeling so much relief. Thanks to Cat centering me, I have one hell of an opening statement all but a few tweaks from ready for tomorrow's trial. "When can I hear it?" Cat asks for the third time.

"Soon," I say, taking a bite of my pizza.

"I can't wait," she says, picking a green olive off her pizza and setting it aside. "I love reading your openings. I love watching you deliver them even more."

I frown. "You aren't eating the olives? You love olives."

"They taste funny." She motions to the pizza. "Taste one."

I laugh. "They taste funny so you want me to eat it?"

She crinkles her nose. "Probably not a good idea the night before your trial."

I shut the pizza box and set it on the floor, pulling her leg across my lap. "This is where I proposed to you."

"Yes. It was. I remember being naked when you set the ring on my stomach. I love that part of the story even though I can't exactly tell it."

I caress her cheek. "Two years, Cat."

"Going on three."

"And in those years, we've been inseparable."

"I like that about us." She frowns. "You like that about us, too, right?"

"How can you even ask that? You know I do."

"Then why do I feel this is leading somewhere?"

"Because it is. I know you, Cat. What's going on with you?"

"Nothing bad," she says. "In fact, something good now. I have a secret project that I'm working on and it wasn't going well. I had a breakthrough."

"What secret project that I don't know about?"

"It's a surprise and something I want us to finish together. I don't want you distracted right now. The minute your trial is over, I'm going to hand it to you to read."

"I can read it now."

"No," she says. "Not with the hell you have going on."

"Cat—"

She presses her lips to mine. "It's not a big deal. I was just in between projects and needing a purpose. The trial and this new project I'm working on will do that. You need to work on your opening statement."

I roll her to her back and settle on top of her. "I can't imagine a trial without you in the audience, writing about the case."

"Me either." She slides her hand to my face. "You know what would turn me on right now? And I mean like really turn me on?"

"Tell me," I say, sliding my hand under her perfect backside.

"For you to read me your opening."

I groan and press my forehead to hers. "You're a slave driver."

"Yep. Up. Read. Work."

I kiss her and sit up, but I'm more than a little curious about the secret project that my wife won't share with me. Something still doesn't feel right.

It's a feeling that doesn't go away. It's near midnight when I'm holding Cat next to me, inhaling the sweet scent of her body lotion that she favors at bedtime, and I make a decision: Tomorrow night I'm reading her special project.

Cat

I wake to my husband's hand on my belly, and I smile sleepily for a moment. Then my eyes pop open and I wonder if my belly feels bigger. It's not a thought that lasts though. How can it? His hands are now all over my body, his mouth on my nipple, and his fingers pressing into my sex. I moan and then he drags me to my back, and the next thing I know, he's between my legs, licking my clit. I have another of those strange moments when I actually wonder if I taste differently now that I'm pregnant. It's a silly thought that fades into his tongue on my clit, his fingers pressing inside me again, and my orgasm that is perhaps world record fast. I can't help it. There is just something so sexy about the fact that I'm having this perfect man's baby.

Reese kisses my belly, right there where our unborn child rests and gives me one of his blue-eyed stares. "Are you awake now?"

"Oh yes," I say. "I'm very awake."

"Good. Because we're just getting started." He rolls to his back and takes me with him, with me, and my newly pregnant body on top of his hard, perfect, everything. And that's what I want this pregnancy to be: perfect. I need it to be perfect. Nothing can go wrong. It won't. I won't let it.

Chapter Forty-Six

Cat

I'm flat on top of Reese, his erection pressed between my legs, and he's kissing me, but there is something in this kiss. Something off. I tear my lips from his. "What's wrong?"

"You tell me"

"Nothing. There is nothing wrong between us Reese. We are so far from wrong. I love you, husband. I want to die your wife. Well, a long, long, time from now. I want—"

He cups my head and pulls my mouth to his again and there is a demand in his kiss, a possessive demand that guts me. He's going into his trial worried about us. How have I let this happen? And I can't go back now. Not hours before his opening statement. "Stop kissing me like something's wrong. There's nothing wrong." I press my lips to his again, and this time I kiss him, and I try to tell a story. I love you. I need you. You are everything to me. I feel the moment he relaxes. The moment we become us, as I know us, again. Reese's hands slide over my back, and he molds me closer, my naked breasts to his naked chest. He deepens our kiss, takes control in that way he does, and in the midst of a drugging lick of his tongue he presses inside me, and I slide down the hard length of him.

He sits up with me, kissing me, his hand on my breasts, and I am so lost in this man. I want to just blurt out "we're pregnant," but I store that thought for later, for the journal. I just—sometimes I don't know where he begins and I end, and vice versa. We are that connected, and when that would have scared me with anyone before him, it makes me feel safe, and I didn't even know I needed to feel safe. He nips my lips and lies backward, his eyes are hot, watching me, devouring me, and I'm again thinking too much—do I look different? Can he tell I'm pregnant?

I don't want to have these thoughts. He'll know I'm outside of the moment. He'll know. I drag my hands over his chest, and rock against him, his hand finding my breast, my nipple, and I swear my sex squeezes in reaction. He pumps into me and I push against him, and from there it's all about need, want, lust. I am free with this man. I want. I need. I have no inhibitions and that is a gift only love can give you. As Reese once told me: love is the freedom to fuck each other senseless. And we do. Crazy, wild, frenzied, and when it's over, I collapse on top of him.

He rolls me to my back and whispers in my ear. "Every time I want to throttle someone today I'm going to think about you on top of me and smile."

I laugh and he kisses me. "Come take a shower with me."

Before I can reply, he's literally maneuvered me off the bed and is carrying me to the shower.

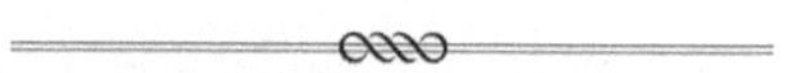

Forty minutes later, Reese is in a blue suit that I picked out with a blue pinstriped tie and is headed downstairs to make coffee and read over his opening statement. I'm in my robe doing my makeup. I'm about to get dressed when a wave of sickness hits me. It comes hard and fast and I rush to the toilet, fall to my knees and hug the bowl. I heave and it's horrible. My stomach is empty and the clenching of my belly muscles is torture.

"Cat!"

I cringe at the sound of Reese's voice and in another instant, he's on a knee beside. "Sweetheart. What's happening?" He hands me a washcloth.

"Stupid olives," I say wiping my mouth. "I told you they tasted off."

"What can I get you?"

I twist around to face him. "A kickass opening statement. I'm fine. It's passing. I just need to get dressed." I cup his face. "I'm ready to go to court."

"Cat, sweetheart. If you need to miss—"

"I will never miss one of your openings, ever. *Ever.*" I try to stand and he helps me up. "I'm good, but I should probably brush my teeth again. Go get ready. I'll be dressed and ready myself in fifteen minutes."

"You're sure? Maybe we should have someone come be with you in court today, in case you get sick again."

"Reese," I say, grabbing his arms. "It's nothing. I'm better now. I promise."

He hesitates and backs out of the small room, guiding me with him, but he doesn't leave. He hovers until I brush my teeth and prove I'm fine again. Once I'm minty fresh, I kiss him. "I'm great. I'll be right down."

His cellphone rings, and he grabs it to eye the caller ID. "Royce." His lips thin. "I'll meet you downstairs." He disappears out of the bathroom and I suspect that Royce calling means that we already have picketers though I'm not sure what they will picket and not even because of the case, as much as the company the family owns. They're like a Wal-Mart, so big that the public has high expectations and no matter what they do, they never meet those expectations. But the bottom line is the picketers make the trials nuts and I know they would make Reese worry about me if he knew I was pregnant. I'm making the right decision to wait.

Eager to find out what's going on with Royce's call, I head into the closet, pull on a pale pink sleeveless suit dress with a jacket. That way I'm prepared for a hot or cold courtroom, and the ever-changing October weather. I give myself a once-over in the mirror, my hand settling on my belly. I got sick and that feels like a normal thing for a pregnant woman. I smile. I'm pregnant and I think we're having a girl. It's just a gut feeling I'll have to write about in the journal. I hurry to the sink, gloss my lips pink and then grab my purse.

My cellphone buzzes with a text and I glance down to find a message from my editor: *Have I told you how much I love the way you tease readers? They know you know more than you're telling and it's making them crazy. The hits to your article this morning are insane. Now, off the record, did she do it?*

I grimace and type a reply: *Reese doesn't defend guilty people.*

Her reply is instant: *But that recorded phone call had to have taken him off guard.*

I'm irritated and concerned. My editor is smart and wide in her thinking, and yet she is focused on the scandal of that call. She didn't really hear it and that worries me. I think of Reese's opening statement and type: *If anything that call proves innocence.*

Once I'm downstairs, I find Reese in the kitchen, staring at his MacBook. The minute I walk in, he glances up, giving me a critical eye. "How are you?"

"I'm good." I step to the island opposite him. "What was up with Royce?"

"The courthouse is a madhouse. His team will be here in a few to escort us." He motions to my computer. "I read your column. Brilliant as always."

"Thank you." I consider a moment and then say, "I want you to read this exchange with my editor because I think you need to know what you're up against." I offer him my phone with the messages pulled up. He accepts it and reads the messages before handing it back to me. "In other words," he says, "my client is guilty until proven innocent."

"Can you convince your client to push the trial back?"

"No. She won't do that. I've tried."

"Then what are you going to do, Reese?"

"Win by making that call, and the assumption of guilt, work for me and my client. I tweaked my opening statement." The doorbell rings and he stands up. "I'm ready. I feel in the game now." He heads for the door and my stomach churns again. He's in the game now. I cannot let him see me get sick again. I rush to the pantry, grab some crackers and stuff them in a baggy, before tucking them inside my purse.

I've just finished packing up my MacBook when Reese joins me to do the same of his. That's when Royce appears in the archway, and his eyes meet mine, a question in their depths. Reese glances at a text message and I answer Royce's unspoken question by giving a tiny shake of my head. His eyes darken with what I think is disapproval. He thinks I should have told Reese, even though he himself said to wait until after opening. I want to throttle him and worse, I share a secret with Royce that I should be sharing with my husband. The wrong man knows I'm pregnant.

I suddenly can't wait to get to a place where I can start writing in my journal. Putting down my feelings there is clearly going to be the only way I survive the guilt of keeping this from Reese.

Chapter Forty-Seven

Cat

The minute we're in the back of the black SUV with Royce and his look-a-like brother Luke, in the front seat, Reese grabs my leg and pulls me close. He says nothing, but his actions are words. He's nervous, but nerves are good. Nerves force you to be one hundred percent present and I've watched enough of his trials now that I know he settles into his zone. When he steps behind his table in the courtroom, he owns the room. And he needs to be in that courtroom fully, not worried about his pregnant wife. I made the right decision to stay silent, but I hate that Royce knows and Reese doesn't. How do I justify that part of my silence?

The drive to the courthouse would be short, as we live only two blocks away, but we're picking up Dana, Reese's client. "Have you talked to her today?"

"Not yet," Reese says, "but I'm about to call her now and let her know we're on the way."

"Tell her one of our men is about to be at her door," Luke orders.

He pulls out his phone and makes the call. I listen to the short exchange and Reese disconnects. "Done," he tells Luke before he glances at me. "She's cold and removed. I'd rather her cry."

"Because cold and removed comes off as rich, arrogant, and indifferent."

"Exactly," he says.

"It's an expectation," I reply.

He glances over at me. "Meaning what?"

"Meaning address that head-on. She lived under an iron fist of expectations that meant no emotions. That call was an explosion of everything bottled inside."

He studies me a few beats and kisses me. "You really need to be practicing law, Cat."

I warm with the compliment he gives freely. That's the thing about Reese. He's the only person in my life that has lifted me up, not torn me down, my brothers included. That's how he will be with our child.

"I do." I say, lacing my fingers with his. "With you and then I write about it which is the definition of an inside source."

"I love your column, Cat," Luke says. "My wife is an attorney and she gobbles it up. She got me hooked."

"Thank you," I say. "It's very flattering to have people enjoy my random thoughts about cases." My phone buzzes with a text.

I grab it and glance at the number to find a message from Lauren: *Any change?*

Sick this morning, I type.

Oh good, she replies.

I laugh and Reese glances over at me. "Lauren. Girl talk." My phone buzzes again with another message from Lauren: *How are you going to the doctor with the trial going on?*

I reply back with: *I got a seven am appointment. I'll call you later.*

We pull past Dana's high-rise apartment and the press is everywhere. "We're picking her up two blocks down," Luke says, glancing over at us.

A few minutes later, Dana, who I've met once before, is in the backseat next to me, her navy blue dress prim and proper, her blonde hair tied at her nape. "Hi," she says to me and then in general to everyone. And that's it. She says nothing else. Reese was right. She's cold and removed.

"How are you?" I ask.

"Sick," she replies, suddenly showing her human side. "I threw up three times this morning."

"Have you eaten?"

"I can't eat," she says. "How can I eat? I'm being accused of killing my father."

I reach in my purse and offer her crackers. "They might help."

"Do you carry crackers for all of his clients?"

I can feel Reese's attention and I quickly add, "I have food poisoning. I thought they might help me, so maybe that was lucky and they can help you. Try one. You need to be strong in court."

She grabs a cracker and munches and Royce offers her a bottle of water that she takes. I settle back into my seat and Reese squeezes my leg, willing me to look at him. I inhale and glance over at him, meeting his penetrating blue stare and while he says nothing, there's a question in his eyes. Maybe he's even wondering if I could be pregnant. Or I'm paranoid. I'm paranoid. How can I not be?

We pull up to a side door of the courthouse where the police have blocked off an entrance. Dana inhales. "This is it."

Luke leans around the seat. "I'm coming to get you, Dana."

Reese leans forward and looks at Dana across my lap. "This *is* it. This is where we end this. There's no evidence to convict you. You shouldn't have been charged. We will win."

I squeeze her arm. "Deep breath. He's the best of the best. You *will* win."

"I didn't do it," she whispers. "I swear to you. I didn't do it." She tears up and the door opens.

She swipes at her eyes and exits the vehicle. I start to follow and Reese catches my arm, turning me around to face him. "How sick are you?"

"I'm presently thinking about how good you look naked and about the benefits of waking up to you between my legs," I say. "I'm pretty sure that means not very sick." I kiss him. "Time to win. I'll see you at the food truck for your lucky hot dog."

His eyes warm and he kisses me before thankfully releasing me.

I scoot out of the backseat and we're rushed inside the courthouse where Richard and Elsa are waiting. Reese, his client, and his team are ushered forward with Royce and Luke on their heels. I am now alone, only I'm really not alone. My hand presses to my belly. I'm *not alone*. And I love it. A security guard motions me forward, and I'm given a badge that I'd normally have to get in another area of the courthouse. Ready for the courtroom, I hurry forward when suddenly my new little passenger decides to stir up the sickness again. I can't do this now. Reese needs to see me in that courtroom. I glance at the time on my phone and I have about ten minutes to spare. I cut right to a bathroom that is usually missed by all but me, and enter.

The sickness seems to have passed and I look in the mirror. Do I look different? Apparently, my baby doesn't like this question. My stomach rolls and I hurry into a stall, shut the door, and heave up nothing. My stomach is empty and maybe that's the problem. Whatever the case, it's over and I walk out of the stall to find Lori, standing in front of me. Lori, who knows about the secret bathroom because of me.

"What's wrong?" she asks and as silly as it sounds, the floral pattern of the blouse under her jacket seems to make me sick again.

"Bad olives, I think," I manage to explain, "but I need to be in that courtroom now. Reese will look for me. He'll worry if he doesn't find me there."

"Do you have anything with you to take?"

"Nothing," I say darting for the door.

She follows and catches me in the hallway. "I'll grab you something."

"No," I say quickly, not sure what is safe. "No. Reese will be distracted if you come in late. Let's just go sit. I have crackers."

She looks like she wants to argue but she doesn't. We enter the courtroom and we're escorted to a row right behind the defense table. I sit down and stuff a cracker down that I'm not supposed to eat in here and do so as quickly as possible. "Is it helping?"

"I think so," I say, "except I'm about to choke with no water."

She opens her purse and points to a bottle of water. I discreetly grab it, take a drink and stuff it back in her purse, deciding that for now, I'm stable. The doors to our left open and the courtroom goes nuts as Dana, Richard, and Elsa walk in and take their seats. Dana is back to stone. She's cold. She's hard on the surface when I know she's falling apart inside. Next comes Reese and he's barely stepped to the table before he finds me. I love how he does this at the start of every trial. I love that we're this connected. I had to be here today. I will always be here when he starts a trial.

The prosecution enters the courtroom and a few minutes later, we're standing for the judge. We sit and that's when Lori leans close and whispers, "Are you pregnant?"

Chapter Forty-Eight

Cat

I love Lori to pieces, but I really want to throttle her for asking if I'm pregnant when a) I'm not telling her before Reese, therefore I now have to try to make her forget this topic without lying to her and b) Reese is about to begin one of the biggest cases of his career in a few seconds.

"Forget I asked that," she whispers, pulling out a notepad as I ready my own. "That was silly," she adds. "You two have a plan and it doesn't include getting pregnant right now during this trial." Reese walks to the center of the courtroom and she squeezes my arm. "I can't wait to watch Reese in action. I'm so glad I'm between cases."

Relief washes over me at her backtrack, but we're also working on a book together that I think I need to push back our efforts until after I tell Reese. Lori knows me too well. If we spend time together, she'll figure out what's going on. For now though, I focus on the prosecutor, a man named Milton Wicker, who Reese has gone head-to-head with before and beat. Milton, like everyone, wanted to dethrone Reese and break his winning record, and save his pride from losing once before, and lost. So we can all bet he has vengeance in his sight this time around. Tall and good looking enough, I guess, he's mid-thirties, with dark-rimmed glasses and sandy brown hair. He begins his opening statement:

"Today we are here because, in the defendant's own words, she wished her father was dead and she followed through to make that wish come true. The defense will tell you that dreams don't always come true, but for the defendant they did. Facts are facts. Dana Warren wished her father dead and now he's dead. Do you know what that means for her? Five hundred million dollars. She is set to inherit five hundred million dollars. That's an astounding sum of money, isn't it? And what did it take for Dana Warren to inherit that money? One bullet. Who else benefited from Nelson Warren's murder? No one. No one else inherits. No wife, girlfriend, non-existent sibling. No one. Not even a charity. I'm not going to feed you a laundry list of reasons she did this when you already have five hundred million reasons and a phone call where she wished her father dead."

His opening is that fast and over, leaving me certain that he doesn't have evidence to prove his case that we don't yet know about. He's grandstanding. "He's putting on a show," Lori whispers, as if reading my thoughts, "and not a good one."

We hope, I think, despite my more confident thought a moment before. We never know how a jury will respond in a trial, but then Reese stands up, and my nerves fade. This is Reese's wheelhouse. He's a master. He will win over the jury and I can't wait to watch him work. I poise my pen over my notepad, ready to take notes, irritated that I haven't yet evaluated the jury. In all cases I follow, I like to see them in all phases of the trial from beginning to end. I like to read their state of minds before and after each opening. I quickly take as many notes as possible and then Reese begins:

"First I want to thank each and every member of the jury, and of course our honorable judge, for taking the journey to justice with me. I'm proud of being a part of a court system that ensures innocence until you are proven guilty. I, for one, find comfort in knowing that I'm protected. No one, not even the press, can convict me of a crime. They can demonize me. They can humiliate me. But they cannot take my freedom. Or can they? Those things in today's media outlets become prisons in ways that you cannot escape. No matter what your ruling, the press will say it's wrong. No matter what your ruling, the press will assume they know what you do not even though you are right here in this courtroom. No matter what your ruling, my client is already guilty because the press says so and the prosecution has made it clear by charging that they believe she is guilty. It's a scary thing to sit in a chair and hear a guilty plea be read with no evidence. It makes you fear that you could be next. It makes you fear that if the wrong people were against you, you could go down for something you didn't do. That's where a jury comes in, where *you* come in. No matter how much you like or dislike the person being charged, you rule based on facts. If you have any doubt that the person is guilty you legally must rule them not guilty. That's reasonable doubt. If I give you reason to doubt guilt, the ruling is not guilty. If the prosecutor tells you the defendant is guilty, they must prove that guilt with evidence, not words."

"That comes back to me. I don't defend guilty people. Ever. We've all heard the phone call that was leaked. My client sounded angry and that anger had people asking me if I regretted my choice to represent her. My answer was and is no. Her father was a brutal man with many enemies. She was angry, hurt, scared. She was human. She wanted to walk away from everything just to escape. This is not an escape. My client didn't think she could shoot her father and inherit. Her father was vicious to her and everyone around him. He destroyed people and laughed about it. She might have wished him dead but you'll learn during this trial, that so did a long list of other people."

"I'm asking you today to remember your responsibility to assume innocence and make the prosecution prove guilt. My client inheriting her father's fortune does not make her his killer. The list of suspects, of those people I just mentioned that wanted her father, the victim, dead, is excessively long and completely ignored by the prosecutor. The prosecutor's office wanted an easy win, not justice. Therefore, they decided you, the jury, would be so small minded, so ignorant, that you would put someone in jail for no reason other than she inherited money. They picked the person the public would prosecute rather than doing their job, finding the real killer, and coming to court with evidence. Why? Because if the press and public prosecute my client, then it puts pressure on you to follow. But the press and the public won't see the facts and evidence. That's your honor and responsibility. To see the evidence and rule on the evidence. Your responsibility is to rule not guilty if you have reasonable doubt. Your responsibility is to rule guilty if the prosecution proves without a shadow of a doubt that my client killed her father. That means they must provide evidence, not assumption. None of us want to live in a country where we can be accused and convicted without proof. Make the prosecution live in America with us. I have confidence in you to make the right decision. The prosecutor brought this case because he has confidence that you don't care about our country, our laws, and real evidence."

Reese closes his opening statement, and I breathe out. He did well. The jury responded well. They didn't like the idea that they were being looked at as stupid by the prosecutor. "That was brilliant," Lori whispers.

Reese walks back to his table and his eyes find mine the way they always do, and I give him a tiny nod of approval. I let him know that he was received well. He sits down, and the prosecutor calls for a recess. At this point, it manages to get to eleven o'clock and court is adjourned until one o'clock. "I need to go to the office," Lori says. "I have a case I may end up taking that just had activity." She turns to face me as the crowd begins to disperse. "How are you feeling? Do you need anything?"

"I'm good," I say. "It's passing."

She hugs me. "Love you. I'll be back this afternoon if I can. Tell Reese, aside from Cole, he's my idol."

"Says the brilliant attorney herself," I comment.

"Not as brilliant as your husband, or mine, but I'll get there. Walk out with me?"

I nod and the two of us make our way out of the courtroom, and the crush of the crowd that normally doesn't bother me, bothers me now. I feel like I'm suffocating. It's with relief that I exit the courthouse, through the safe side door, and Lori hurries away. With my computer in my backpack and the crowd focused on the front of the courthouse, I dart down the sidewalk that leads to the park where Reese always escapes for his lucky hot dog during trials. I assume he will decompress with his team for a few minutes before joining me, so I decide to write in today's baby journal.

I pass the food truck that provides those lucky hot dogs, and sit on a park bench, powering up my MacBook to begin typing, this time to Reese: *Every moment I'm with you, I want to tell you that I'm pregnant. I wonder if I look different, if I feel different, and yes, I even wondered if I tasted different this morning. I know that is silly, but I really did have that thought and I'll let you use your imagination to determine when I had that thought. When I was throwing up, I smiled. I know that sounds crazy, but I read that sickness means the baby is healthy. My God, Reese, this is killing me. I want to tell you so badly, but you have so much on you and what if you were worried about me when you had to give that opening statement today? I don't know when to tell you. I love you so much and I want to support you and I see how much pressure you feel to win. I see how much your client needs you to win. What if you worry about picketers, and press, and a million other things that might make me miscarry and it changes how you try this case? I don't know what to do but to keep writing what I feel and praying that you feel I made these decisions for the right reasons: love.*

I love you.

It's right then that a wave of sickness overtakes me. I shut my computer and my eyes, and will it away. "Cat."

I blink and Reese is on his knee in front of me. I lean forward and press my hands to his cheeks. "You were brilliant."

"What's wrong, sweetheart?"

"I'm good. I've been good since the minute some asshole cut in line in a coffee shop and changed my life."

"What aren't you telling me?"

Chapter Forty-Nine

Cat

What aren't you telling me?

I hate this question from Reese and with him on his knee in front of me, those blue eyes looking at me with concern, I decide to be as honest as possible. I also decide when to spill the news. "I have a birthday surprise I'm working on for you. I hate I'm telling you this because that makes it less of a surprise, but you're obviously sensing something." I kiss him. "So you were right. There's something I'm not telling you."

His brow furrows and he moves to sit on the bench next to me. "Now you have me curious."

"Good. Be curious. And as for what's wrong? I'm just not good at secrets, even good ones. You know that."

"Yes, sweetheart, I do," he says, taking my hand. "But we aren't your parents or even mine. We don't lie and cheat. A surprise isn't those things."

"You just know me so well that the minute this surprise came into the picture, you knew."

"That's not a bad thing."

"No. No, it's not and I know you, too. Go get your 'must have' lucky hot dog, and then tell me everything."

He stands and pulls me to my feet. "Come with me."

I smile and motion to my computer. "I need to guard it."

"It'll be fine."

"It's New York City." I grab it and stuff it into my briefcase. "You're a criminal lawyer. You know it wouldn't be safe."

He laughs and laces his fingers with mine, dragging me along with him. "You were brilliant," I say. "And your opposing counsel was not."

"Less is more sometimes," he says, as we stop in front of the food truck. "We both know that was the idea and it wasn't a bad strategy." He orders his hot dog, and without even asking, my bag of nuts, which is all a part of our lucky lunch during trials.

Once we're headed back to the bench, I pick up the conversation again. "You made it look like less is more, translated to the prosecution thinking the jury was stupid. They responded well and that's why we're on recess. The prosecutor is scrambling."

"I'll reserve judgment until I feel out the courtroom and their case this afternoon."

We sit down and he takes a bite of his hot dog. I set my nuts aside. "You aren't going to eat?" he asks.

"I'm still feeling really crappy. I think olives are ruined for me for life."

"You love olives, so I bet that statement won't last more than a month."

Or nine, I think, the idea of telling him on his birthday really taking root. "How did Richard and Elsa feel about the openings?"

"The same as you."

"And Dana?"

"She didn't say much and she asked for a private place to eat lunch alone."

"I can't say I blame her," I reply. "All those eyes on you are pretty intense when you're the attorney. When you're the one on trial it has to be ten times more intense."

He finishes off his hot dog with his normal ridiculous speed and somehow still looks sexy doing it.

"Have you asked her who she thinks leaked that call?"

"She dropped that bombshell on me right before we opened this morning. She believes her father had her calls recorded, which means that someone close to him could have done it, at least, per her. I still think it was the boyfriend."

"Wait," I say, alarmed. "There could be more calls?"

"Yes, and while that's concerning, as I sit here with you, with some space, I ask myself, why, if she knew she was being recorded, would she make those statements to her boyfriend?"

"Anger? Frustration?"

"And the prosecution will say those same emotions made her pull the trigger. I hope like hell she has a better answer than that when I ask her in a few minutes."

"Maybe she wanted her father to hear? I mean I know that my father is such a bastard, but I can't stop hungering for his love. Sometimes people act out to get attention."

"I'm not sure that makes her look any better."

"It makes her look like a victim," I say.

"Pushed to the brink," he counters, scrubbing his jaw and pressing his hands to his legs. "You've made me eager to get back and ask her about ten questions." He leans over and kisses me. "I need to go find some new magic."

"You will. You always do."

He reaches around and cups my head, kissing me deeply, passionately, before saying, "Yes. I do. You." His cellphone rings and he grabs it, "Richard," he says, answering the call. "When?" he asks. "Is he still there?" He disconnects and sticks his phone back in his pocket. "The boyfriend is at the courthouse making a scene because Dana won't see him."

"Interesting," I say. "She must believe he released the audio of that call."

"I still think that's a big possibility," Reese says. "I keep going back to the premise of him killing the father, marrying Dana, and becoming a rich man."

"I get him getting cold feet," I say. "I get him being afraid he'll be convicted but hurting her defeats the entire idea of inheriting her money. It just doesn't feel right."

"Jail scares people. You know that." He kisses me. "I need to go. Maybe he'll talk to me, especially in his current state of mind." He stands. "I'll call you if I can before I go back into court." He takes off and I open my computer and start typing in the baby journal, detailing the "birthday promise" and I end with: *When I watch you in that courtroom, I am certain our child will be both beautiful and intelligent.* I smile, and add, *Until next time, Cat,* as a play on how I sign my column.

A sudden sense of being watched has me scanning for the press but all I find is a pregnant woman with long brunette hair in a pink dress, sitting on a bench to my right and eating of all things, a hot dog. Something about her bothers me but she's not looking at me. I don't know why I feel odd about her presence. It must be hormones. For now, I focus on the hot dog she is eating and it reminds me of Reese's lucky lunch, which has me smiling, while the size of the women's belly, quite round and full, has me wondering how big I will be soon. It's a little scary and intimidating to think about being responsible for a living being's development. What if I do it wrong? *Reese won't*, I think. He won't get it wrong.

I refocus on the journal and add an entry about seeing the pregnant woman and all of my thoughts. I'm about to start working on my column for tomorrow, to the best that I can this early in the day's events, but I find myself glancing toward the woman to find her gone and for some reason, this bothers me as much as when she was here. I'm losing my mind.

Reese

A secret.

I walk into the courthouse again, with those two words on my mind. I'd known there was something going on with Cat, but hearing she has a birthday surprise she considers a secret makes sense. She's huge on trust. Thanks to her father, she's nursing betrayal issues that I don't know if we will ever fully defeat, but I'm damn sure going to spend every day of the rest of my life trying.

The minute I enter the building, Royce Walker greets me. "The boyfriend is in a private room. He wants to talk to you."

"Me?" I query, but I don't expect an answer. "Interesting."

"I thought so," he says, motioning me forward, and as we walk he adds, "We're looking for a way to connect him to the gun."

"I'll take anyone you can connect that is not my client," I say.

"Understood," he says, and we turn down a hallway to find a guard by a door.

"He's all yours," Royce says, but as I'm about to enter the room, my phone buzzes with a message. I grab my phone to check the message to find a text from Richard: *Dana is flipping out. We need you NOW.*

I grimace and glance at the guard. "I need ten minutes." I look at Royce. "Don't let him leave."

He nods, and I head down the hallway. I'm just about to turn down the hallway that leads to our private rooms when something pulls my attention toward the doors of the courthouse. A pregnant woman in a pink dress catches my eye. She glances in my direction, and I grimace with the sight of a familiar face I really never wanted to see again. What the hell is she doing here?

I dismiss her out of desire and necessity and head down the hallway toward my client, and the current crisis, on hand. Dana's freak out.

Chapter Fifty

Reese

I change my mind about dismissing Debbie Miller on the walk toward the conference room where my team waits. She's crazy and she's here. I don't believe that's a coincidence which means I need to talk to Cat, and quickly. Richard steps into the hallway and pulls the door shut, starting to walk toward me. "Dana is losing her shit. Big time."

I grab my phone. "I'll be right there. I need two minutes."

"We don't have—"

"I need two minutes. Alone."

His lips purse but he nods and heads back to the room. I dial Cat. "How are things?" Cat asks, obviously referencing my rush here to solve what feels like a dozen problems.

"I need to see you in between talking to Dana and her boyfriend. Can you come to me?"

"Yes. Of course. I'm almost back to the courthouse now."

"I'll meet you in the hallway." I disconnect and walk toward Richard, who's lurking by the conference room door.

"What do I need to know?" I ask, stopping in front of him.

"Apparently the boyfriend, Reginald, has been trying to call her and she won't talk to him. She freaked out that he was here, and started screaming and crying. Now she's sitting on the floor, in a corner with her knees to her chest."

I inhale sharply. "On the floor," I repeat.

"Yes. On the floor."

"I need the doctor who did her mental health evaluation here now."

"Elsa just talked to her. She's testifying in another case today, in Chicago. She recommended another doctor. Elsa wants to know if you want to get her in here."

"Yes, but after hours. I can't risk a new name and face making this worse while I'm about to walk into court."

I step around him and enter the conference room to find Dana now on her feet on the opposite side of the rectangular shaped conference table, hugging herself, her black dress making her look like she's at her own funeral; her mascara staining her cheeks adding to the effect. "My team is concerned," I say. "They wanted to call in a doctor."

"I don't need a doctor," she says tightly. "I'm fine. I melted down, but it's over."

"Why did you freak out?" I ask, moving to stand across from her, my fingers pressed to the cheap wood of the desk.

"Come on, Reese. Who else but Reginald could have released that audio? He was the one on the call. He must have recorded me."

"You said your father recorded you."

"I said I suspected it, but I just didn't want to believe Reginald would do that. Why would he do that?"

"You tell me."

"I don't know. I just—I don't know. But it hurts. I thought he was the man I would spend the rest of my life with."

"How did he feel about you walking away from the money?"

"You've asked me that," she says. "I told you. He didn't want me to walk away from the money."

"Could he have killed your father to ensure you inherited?"

Her lips curl, pressed together like she's biting back a sob before she pants out a breath. "I don't want to believe that."

"But you've considered it."

"After that call was released, yes, but then I thought that makes no sense. If he wanted the money, he wouldn't help them send me to prison, and that call does."

"Unless," I prod, wanting her to go where I already have.

"Unless he got spooked and was afraid they'd look at him. Unless he wants freedom more than the money. I sure do."

"Our team is looking into his activity but we need him to testify for you."

"So you need me to play nice with him."

"Yes. I do. Record your conversations and once he testifies for you, expect me to destroy him. If he did it, I *will* make him confess."

"If he did it, and then released that call to make it look like I did it, I hope you burn him in hell."

"Good, because I will. Now, he's here. Call him. Tell him I'm coming to talk to him but that you'll talk to him tonight."

She nods. "It's going to be hard to be civil."

"You need to be more than civil. Make him believe you two will live a happily ever after with loads of cash. Motivate him to testify for you, not against you."

"Okay," she agrees hoarsely.

"I've asked this, but I'll ask again: What else does he have on you?"

"Nothing. That call was me giving up. I went to my father the next day. I told him I was giving up my inheritance."

"That was the day after the call?" I confirm, already aware that she'd tried to disinherit herself.

"Yes, but he, of course, told me I'd be back and groveling."

All facts I'm aware of and not pleased with either. It makes it look like she had a reason to kill him that wasn't money. And that reason might resonate with a jury as guilt. "Call Reginald. I'm going to a brief meeting and then I'll talk to him."

"What are you going to say?"

"The truth. That you're emotional and you need him." I walk to the door and exit into the hallway where Richard, Elsa, and Royce now wait on me.

"She's fine," I say. "She just believes that Reginald betrayed her and she's hurting. I'm going to talk to him." I glance between Richard and Elsa. "She needs to fix her makeup and wear something other than black tomorrow. Funeral attire is all the wrong notes for this case." My attention moves to Royce. "Anything on Reginald?"

"Nothing yet, but I wanted to let you know that we have men following him when he leaves."

I nod and step around them all, heading toward the end of the hallway as Cat steps into view. I motion her forward and into a private office. "What's going on?" she asks as I shut us inside.

"There's a woman here today, that could be a problem."

Her brows furrow. "What woman?"

"Five years ago a woman I showed fleeting interest in turned into a stalker situation. She was everywhere I went. I slept with the woman twice and she was obsessed with me. It looked to turn nasty and I was about to take further action when she just stopped. She went away."

"And she's here?"

"Yes. Which probably means nothing because she looks like she's about six months pregnant. She could be here for something else, but since this was a problem in the past, I wanted you to know and to be careful."

"Pregnant," she breathes out. "In a pink dress?"

"Yes," I say, alarmed now. "Why?"

"She was in the park. She was watching me. I think she was there when we were there together. Or maybe not. I noticed her after you left."

"Fuck. Let me grab Royce." I open the door and step outside to thankfully find Royce walking by. "We need you."

He joins us in the office and I update him. "I'm concerned for Cat."

"She didn't try and approach me," Cat says, "and I really hate that this is happening now, during the trial."

"What better time to gain attention," Royce comments.

"Where's the guy the baby belongs to?" Reese says. "I mean she should be focused the hell on him."

"If they broke up," Royce says, "she could be reverting back to a prior obsession. I need a name and all the details you can tell me about her. We'll do a background check and find out everything about her we can while you're in court."

"She's an interior designer that remodeled our offices five years ago," Reese says. "Miller Designs. Her name is Debbie Miller."

"How bad did the stalking get?" Royce asks.

"Gifts on my desk she shouldn't have been able to get to. Showing up at restaurants where I had meetings. Infesting my favorite coffee shop to the point that I stopped going. I could go on."

"Behavior that indicates this isn't a coincidence or to be dismissed," Royce says, then turns his attention to Cat. "The fact that she was watching you bothers me the most. You need to wait for me, or one of my men, to escort you everywhere right now. Even to the bathroom."

Cat nods. "Yes. Okay. What about protecting Reese?"

"We'll be with him at all times as well," Royce assures her before running down a few other safety measures with us and then leaves us alone. I step to Cat and settle my hands on her shoulders. "It's probably nothing."

"It's not nothing," she says, her hands settling on my chest. "I'm worried about her trying to shoot you or something."

"She's not going to shoot me."

"That stuff happens," she says. "It happens." She presses her hands to her stomach. "I'm sick." She twists away from me and sits down, pressing her hands to her face.

I kneel beside her. "Sweetheart."

She looks up at me, tears in her eyes that are very out of character. "Talk to me."

"I'm just—I'm sick and it's bad timing to be this kind of sick. This isn't how I wanted this to go for us."

"How you wanted what to go?"

She presses her hand to my cheek. "Go win this case, but damn it, stay alive. I can't live without you."

I kiss her hand. "I'm not going anywhere. Do you need a doctor?"

"I'm going in the morning."

"I'm worried about you, Cat."

"Which is exactly what I didn't want." She grabs my lapels. "Go win, damn it."

I hesitate, but I cup her head and kiss her. "I love you."

"I love you, too," she says, and I force myself to walk to the door, but exiting the room and leaving her behind about kills me.

Chapter Fifty-One

Reese

C at is rattled and my wife *doesn't* get rattled often, but something still isn't right with her. Not that I would expect her to be anything but rattled. I just told her I had a crazy person in my life, that is now potentially in our lives. Which I won't let happen. Life is too damn good with Cat for me to let anyone ruin that and no one will ever hurt her. I will hurt them first.

I return to the room where Dana's boyfriend Reginald is waiting and stop beside the guard. "Anything I need to know?"

"He's calm and quiet."

"Reese."

I look up to find Savage, a big bear of a man with a goatee, who works for Royce coming my way. "I'm your back up, man." He stops beside me. "I can go in or stay out."

"You're intimidating as hell, Savage," I say. "The idea isn't to scare the man."

"If you say so," he murmurs, grinning. "If you change your mind, I'm right here." He steps to the side of the door.

I knock and enter to find Reginald sitting behind a basic wooden desk. He stands up, his tall, but lanky build, bending over the desk, as he presses his fingers to the surface. "She has to know I wouldn't release that call. I love her."

He looks older than his forty years in this moment, the lines of his face, around his eyes, exaggerated. "Who else could have?" I ask.

"I didn't record that call. Unless Dana did, someone tapped our phones."

I have no idea why the suggestion that Dana released her own call bothers me, but it does.

"I'd say it was her father, but obviously that's not possible." He scrubs a hand through his hair. "I can't believe she thinks I did this. *Fuck*. I didn't do it. Why would I do that to her?"

I could go at him. I could tell him he benefits from inheriting the money, too, if he marries Dana, but I don't. I can't turn him on her. I can't warn him. "Whoever killed her father obviously wanted to set her up. They most likely had that recording before they killed him and released it before trial to ensure the jury heard it."

"What can I do to help?"

"Understand that she's scared and her placing blame right now is just a product of a million emotions she's fighting. She melted down when she heard you were here. Obviously, the idea of you betraying her rocked her."

"And me. The idea that she believes that guts me."

"Just—try to put yourself in her shoes, sitting on trial, and having the world cover it, on top of losing her father. Even when you hate a parent, having them die, shakes your world."

He nods and swallows. "I know. I lost my asshole of a father two years ago."

He says "asshole" so fiercely that I make a mental note to find out what happened to his father. "I need to get back. We're headed into court in half an hour, but give her some space. I'm sure she'll talk to you tonight."

"She called me. Right before you walked in."

"And?"

"She said she'd talk tonight. Did you tell her to talk to me?"

"I told her to pull herself together before court. Obviously to her, that translated to calling you."

He breathes out as if my words are a relief. "I hope so. Okay. Go win. I need her back."

He needs her back.

Or he needs her money?

I nod and exit the office, shutting the door behind me. I cut right and start walking, and as expected, Savage falls into place with me. "I take it I don't need to intimidate the fuck out of him for you?"

"Not yet," I say.

"*Not yet.* Interesting response."

"His asshole father, as he called him, died two years ago. I need you to find out the details."

"On it," he says. "I'll intimidate the fuck out of whoever I have to to get the facts."

I cut him a look. "That doesn't sound ethical and I *am* ethical."

"Pretend you didn't hear and murder isn't exactly ethical though I must say, sometimes it's necessary."

Royce appears at the end of the hallway as we're about to exit. "Who's with Cat?" I ask.

"She's in the courtroom and I have a man at the door. Debbie is nowhere to be found. We checked the cameras and she left right after you spotted her."

"I'd like to say that means she didn't expect me and headed out when she saw me, but this trial is big news, and she's crazy, not stupid. I don't feel good about it."

"I would agree," Royce says. "I did run her record and she's had no activity to be concerned about. Additionally, we pulled her medical records, and there's no indication of a psychological issue."

I don't even want to know how he got her medical records.

"But," he adds, "that doesn't mean much. Often people aren't diagnosed with a mental health issue when they should be."

"What now?" I ask.

"You go back to work and win your case," Royce says. "We insulate you, protect you, and get you answers."

It's not the answer I want to hear, though aside from arresting Debbie, for basically nothing at this point, it's the only one that works right now. I nod and step around Royce to head back toward my client and team. I need focus and the one thing that allows me to shift gears is knowing that Cat will be in the courtroom with me. She'll be safe.

Cat

I sit in the courtroom, waiting for Reese to return and there is no question that I'm shaken. I need to talk to Lauren. I *want* to talk to Reese, but everything I've feared has happened. A pregnant woman is distracting him during his trial and she's not me. It not only hurts him and his client, by way of the distraction, it shadows our baby news. This isn't how I wanted us to be pregnant and for the first time since taking that test, I might regret it. I want a baby. I want to be a mother to Reese's child but I want it to be a joy we celebrate. The action in the courtroom begins to kicks off again and I set aside the personal, to focus on the case. Besides, maybe Debbie Miller was here by coincidence. It could happen. It probably didn't happen but Reese walks into the courtroom and I set that aside. I swear my stomach still flutters when that man claims a room.

The minute he's behind his table he turns and looks for me, his eyes finding mine, the connection delivering a punch of awareness, that is so many things—attraction, friendship, love, a bond no one can break—and in Reese, I sense relief. He needed to know that I'm okay. He seemed to need to feel the connection between us that we're in this together. I don't know why he would doubt this and I won't let him doubt it again. I can deal with whatever is thrown at me, as long as we're in it together. I nod, letting him know that I'm fine, that I'm here for him. Whatever this Debbie Miller thing is, we'll deal with it. I just wish it wasn't happening now. *Not now.*

Reluctantly it seems, Reese turns back to the courtroom, and I hate the distraction that his actions spell. His distraction expands into concern in me and I find myself scanning the room, ensuring Debbie isn't here and she's not. She's not here. I want to feel relief, but I don't. She's not gone. She's going to stick around and muddy up my baby news. I don't know why I know this, but I do. Debbie Miller is a problem that isn't going to go away, but she doesn't get to ruin our baby news. I'll find a way to make it special and I'll find the right time to tell him, that protects him and his client. I can ensure this part of the equation, but it's up to Reese to find a way to focus on his case, to win, even when he's mentally and emotionally split in different places.

The judge enters through the right far doorway and we all stand, but I know that my husband can and will own this courtroom. He is the one everyone will be watching. He is the one that will win this case. He has to. Dana's life is on the line.

Chapter Fifty-Two

Cat

Milton Wicker, the prosecutor, begins his case by calling Martina Hernandez, the housekeeper who found the body, to the stand. Martina is short, a bit plump, with dark hair streaked with gray. She's in a plum-colored dress and sensible shoes. She claims the seat before us all and even from here I can see her visibly shaking. Considering she found her employer dead, and the world is now watching, this reaction shouldn't feel off to me, but it does. There is something off and I don't know what.

The prosecutor steps in front of her. "Please state your name for the court."

"Martina Anna Hernandez."

He presses his hands on the wood in front of her. "How are you doing, Martina?" he asks.

She brushes hair from her heavily wrinkled eyes. I guess her to be a haggard fifty, a hard living under her belt. "I'm not good. Mr. Warren is dead. How can I be good?"

"I know," he says. "But we need to get him justice. We need to tell your story, okay?"

"Yes. I told you I will tell my story."

"Tell us about finding Mr. Warren."

"I'd gone to get groceries and returned to cook dinner. His favorite stew. He'd requested it for that night. He was locked in his study and when it was ready I knocked, but he didn't answer. An hour passed and then two and I became worried. I returned and knocked again. Still no answer. I decided to risk him yelling at me and I opened the door. That's when I found him sprawled on his desk—" She sobs and presses a fist to her lips. "He—his head was blown—hole—there was a hole and blood. A pool of thick blood. It looked thick. Like a horror movie." She drops her hand. "I'm sorry. I just—I have nightmares."

"Of course you do. The man you saw every day, your boss, was murdered brutally."

"Objection," Reese says. "Commentary leading the witness."

"Sustained," the judge, a stout man in his late forties, says, before eyeing the prosecutor. "Move on, counselor."

"Apologies, judge," he says and refocuses on Martina. "How long did you work for Mr. Warren?"

"Twenty years."

"How well did you know him?"

"As well as anyone," she replies.

That's a loaded reply I'm certain Reese will jump all over. The prosecutor doesn't. He moves on. "How well do you know Dana Warren?"

"I watched her grow up since she was five years old. I know her very well. She was good to me."

Another comment Reese can use.

"And to her father?" Wicker asks.

"He was a difficult man," Martina replies. "Mean. He was mean."

"That's not an answer."

"She gave what she got. She had to survive that man."

"Did you give what you got?" the prosecutor asks.

"Well no, but—"

"That was a yes or no question," the prosecutor says, cutting her off. "Did you survive?"

"Well yes, but—"

"That was again a yes or no question," he says. "You survived and you didn't have to give what you got. Did you ever consider killing Mr. Warren?"

"No, but—"

"Yes or no."

"No," she says tartly.

"How did Dana and her father get along?"

"Fine."

"Fine as in good, bad, indifferent?"

"The way he got along with everyone."

"Which is how?" the prosecutor presses.

"Badly. He got along with everyone badly."

"Including his daughter?"

"Yes," she confirms.

"Did you see Dana the day of the murder?"

"Yes," she says.

"She saw her father that day?"

"Yes."

"Did they fight?"

"They always fought."

"Do you know what they were fighting about that day?"

"He wanted her to go meet with someone she didn't want to meet," she says.

"Who?"

"Some Prince from another country. He wanted them to date. Something about a business deal it would help make go through. That's all I heard."

And there it is, I think. Another reason for the boyfriend to kill the father.

The questioning goes on for another fifteen minutes before the prosecutor rests with the reserved right to recall the witness. Reese stands up and approaches Martina. "Hi, Martina."

"Hi," she says, softening with his greeting. God, he's good. He's so charming and she's melting under the force of his attention.

"How many people did you hear fight with Mr. Warren over the years?"

"Hundreds."

"How many in the past year?" Reese asks.

"At least twenty," she says.

"In person?"

"A few. Often by way of the phone."

"How many have you heard threaten to kill him or wish him dead?"

She considers a moment. "Six or seven."

"How many in the last year?"

"Two."

"Was Dana one of the two?"

"No."

"Please tell us who those two people were."

"Gerome Nichols and Sara Newton."

"Who are they?"

"Gerome is a business acquaintance and Sara was seeing Mr. Warren up until a month ago."

"You said Dana got along with her father about as well as he got along with anyone. Explain, please."

"Mr. Warren was mean. He was really mean. He hated people."

"And yet you stayed why?"

"He paid me three times what anyone else would."

"So he was mean but generous?"

"I never considered him generous," she says. "He used money to bribe us all. It was a tool for control."

"Did he use his money against Dana?"

"He tried and she's done well at the real estate firm she opened. She's selling to the rich and famous."

Which makes Dana look obsessed with money, I think.

"She's making pennies to her father's billions," Reese points out.

"But she's making it on her own. She told him that. I heard her many times."

"Objection," Wicker shouts out. "Hearsay."

"Mr. Warren isn't here to tell his story," Reese says.

"Then save it for your client," Wicker snaps. "Put her on the stand."

Reese moves on. "Did you see Dana at the house the evening of the murder?"

"No. She left around eleven am."

"And you found the body when?"

"Seven pm."

Reese considers her a moment. "You practically raised Dana?"

"I did. I was there for her."

"You protected her."

"I did."

"Do you think Dana killed her father?"

I blanch. This could go so wrong. I can't believe he went there.

"No," Martina replies. "Dana didn't do this. I would bet my life on it."

"Thank you," Reese says, dismissing her.

Wicker stands up. "Do you have a job right now?"

"Yes. I still manage the house."

"Who pays you?" he asks.

"Dana."

"So you really can't call your boss a killer. That's all," he says and sits down.

Reese stands up. "Judge—"

"One question counselor."

"Two. I need two."

"*Two.* Not three."

"Have you lied under oath today, Martina?"

"No. Of course not."

"Then I ask again, do you believe Dana killed her father?"

"No, I do not."

I breathe out in relief and Reese sits down. The prosecutor calls the first of five police officers, who were on the scene and have little to offer but gruesome bloody details of a dead man, meant to refocus the jury on blood and murder.

When finally, the court is adjourned, I believe it's a good day for Reese and all the other drama feels secondary. The room hasn't even cleared when Reese calls me, "I know you have to write your column. We're coming to the apartment to recap the day. I'll meet you at the apartment after I debrief with Dana."

"Perfect," I say. "It was a good day. You wiped the floor with Wicker."

"It was—acceptable. No better. I'll see you soon."

I reach the exit to the courtroom and Royce is waiting on me right along with Lauren. "He was good," she says. "Really good."

I glance at Royce. "You told her I needed her."

"You do," Royce says, all stoically.

Lauren wraps her arm around me. "Of course you do. Friends need friends when weird stuff happens."

She's right, but the fact that she's here because of that pregnant woman brings back every bad feeling I'd suppressed this afternoon. In turn, my stomach churns, which seems to indicate stress is impacting me in my current condition.

We start walking and I'm sandwiched between the two of them. "I thought I'd go to the doctor with you in the morning," Lauren says. "What time is it at?"

"Seven."

"Seven it is. Why wasn't Martina Reese's witness?"

"I asked that when I sat in on a prep session," I say. "Dana was confident in her and Reese wanted Wicker overly confident with her."

"Interesting strategy."

"Reese has a lot of interesting strategies," I say proudly.

We reach the exit and one of Royce's men, Savage, opens the door for us, giving me a wink. "Cat Summer. The one that got away."

I laugh. "We only met once before."

"Which is why you got away," he jokes.

"I wouldn't let Reese hear you say that," Lauren warns. "You might be big, but he'll beat your ass."

I step outside with Royce and Lauren still by my side. We cut right toward the sidewalk that leads to the sedan waiting on us, when suddenly I hear, "Cat Summer."

I look toward my name to find Debbie standing in the grassy area to the left. "It's his baby you know. Tell him to call me or I'm going to the press." She turns and starts walking away.

I have not one second of doubt in Reese. Not one. Anger surges through me and I launch toward her. Royce grabs my arm and so does Lauren. "Debbie!" I shout.

"Cat, damn it, "Royce bites out.

She whirls around.

"You're lying, and I'll write about it in my column. You will not scam us. You will not extort us."

"Be careful what you say," she says. "Or my payday may be by way of slander."

She turns and leaves. I double over with nausea. Royce scoops me up and starts carrying me. "Reese," I say. "I need Reese."

Chapter Fifty-Three

Cat

I barely remember Royce placing me in the backseat of the SUV. I'm just sitting there, my hands on my face, beside Lauren.

"We're moving," Savage calls out from the front as if warning me and my stomach.

"Are you okay?" Lauren asks, her hand settling on my back.

"Lauren?" I whisper, her presence really hitting me.

"I'm right here."

"She's ruined everything," I whisper, turning to face her, and then it hits me that *Savage* is here. I can't talk about this. But I *need* to talk about this.

"She hasn't ruined anything," Lauren says. "I know you. You won't let her. Neither will Reese."

"But it will always cloud this moment in our lives."

"It won't," Lauren says beside me. "He didn't do this. You know that, right? I've been around this man often. He is madly in love with you."

"I don't question Reese or who we are together, but it's still happening," I say. "Everything I try to make perfect is getting crushed. I wonder if he knows yet. He can't know. He hasn't called me."

"Royce went to him," she says. "Royce will handle this. How are you feeling?"

I glance toward the front of the car and back at her. "I'm fine."

"Right. We'll talk at your place."

I rotate and settle against the seat. "I just need to rest my eyes." I lower my lashes.

"We're about to be at your door," Savage says, because of course this time we aren't going by Dana's place so the drive is much quicker.

I sit back up, grab my briefcase and purse that are somehow next to me and prepare to get out of the vehicle. As soon as we are at the door, Savage calls out. "Stay where you are. I'm coming to get you."

He's acting like I'm about to be murdered when the crazy woman is back at the courthouse. That idea jolts me. "Do we have eyes on Debbie? She can't get to Reese and hurt him, right?"

"Royce is with him," Lauren reminds me. "He's safe."

"Bullets have a long reach," I say and my door opens as Savage appears, all big and intimidating, which makes me want him to be with Reese. "Why are you here and not with my husband?"

"Your husband is just fine, and bullets have to get through us to get to him." He offers me his hand. "And she can't blackmail him if he's dead."

"Right," I say. "That's comforting, I guess." I accept his hand and let him help me out of the car. "Can you just confirm he's okay?"

"He's fine or I'd know," he says. "I have an earpiece. Royce is with him."

"Does he know yet?"

"No," he says. "He's with Dana and his team in a conference room."

I swallow hard and nod while Savage shuts my door and another man I don't know climbs in the driver's seat of the vehicle. "Is he stealing your ride or does he work with you?"

He laughs. "He works with me. If he tried to steal from me I'd mess him the F up, like I will anyone that tries to hurt you." He motions me forward. "Let's go inside."

"Right," I say again, because it seems I have a limited vocabulary at present, which really doesn't suit a writer on deadline.

Lauren meets me on the other side of the car, and I'm just glad there are no reporters here. For some reason, we have been lucky to be spared that at home during these big trials and it feels like a real blessing right about now. I ride up the elevator with Savage and Lauren and when we reach the apartment, I'm in the door and darting up the stairs to the bedroom immediately.

I end up on the floor in front of the toilet, on my knees, my shoes left somewhere along the way. When the hell is over, I lean against the wall just trying to think. Lauren appears beside me and sits down against the opposite wall, her shoes gone as well. "He didn't do this."

"I know," I say. "That's not my issue. I wanted this to be special. I was going to tell him on his birthday."

"Don't change anything because of this woman."

"I'm keeping a journal of every moment since I found out. Am I supposed to include Debbie? It was supposed to be such a special gift."

"Leave her out and it is special."

"It can't even be true to what I feel without her in it."

"Then leave her in and document the trust you have in him. That matters. I wouldn't question Royce either and that is *not* something every couple could say."

My cellphone rings in the other room and I jolt. "Reese," I say urgently.

"I'll grab it," Lauren says, moving quickly and returning with my phone right as it stops ringing.

She hands it to me and joins me on the floor as the ringing starts all over again. "Cat," Reese says the minute I answer. "I didn't do this. I would never—"

"I know," I whisper, tears springing to my eyes, because as much as I trust him, hearing his voice, hearing the words, apparently matter. "I never doubted you. I just—it's still hard."

"I know, sweetheart. I'm on my way there, but I love you more than life itself. You know that, right?"

"I do," I whisper. "I love you, too, but don't rush here. Take care of business. She doesn't get to screw up your trial. Dana's future depends on you. We're okay."

"Cat—"

"Reese, do *not* rush here. Do what you need to do, but please be safe."

He hesitates. "I won't be long."

"Be as long as you need to be. I'm going to write my column and Lauren is with me. I'm not delicate. You know that."

"I love you, Cat," he says again and hangs up.

I breathe out and let the phone settle on the floor. "I need to write this column so when he does get home, I can be free."

Lauren's hand settles on my legs. "You have to eat. Trust me, I learned that an empty stomach is dry heave hell. How about soup from the place you love down the road? Or ice cream. Remember? That worked for me."

"I don't know what works for me. I don't want to eat."

"Soup and ice cream it is." She stands up again and helps me to my feet. "Where are you going to work?"

"In here. I'm going to change clothes and just settle on the bed where I can rest if I need to."

"That's sound good." She hugs me. "It's going to be okay. I promise." She pulls back to look at me. "I promise." She releases me and leaves me alone.

I change into sweats and a T-shirt and give my belly an inspection. It's still flat and I'm glad. I don't want Reese to know yet. I want Debbie to be dealt with by his birthday and I'll make telling him special. A few minutes later, I walk into the bedroom to write my column, when Reese is suddenly walking into the room. Clearly having ignored my order to take care of business first, and the minute I see him, in all his tall, dark, perfection, tears prickle my eyes.

"Cat," he breathes out, and then I'm in his arms and we're holding onto each other like we're both afraid we're going to lose each other.

Chapter Fifty-Four

Cat

Reese cups my face and stares down at me. "I would never cheat on you, Cat. You're my life, my wife, my best friend."

My hands go to his wrist. "I know. I told you on the phone. I don't doubt you."

"There is no one that can hear a claim like that and not have it cut and create doubt. You're human, Cat."

"I didn't doubt you. I *really* didn't. I don't."

His head rests against mine. "The only person I'm ever going to touch again in this lifetime is you. The only person who will ever be the mother of my children is you."

I swallow hard, feeling like I should tell him now. Yes, now, but no. No. I can't tell him like this. This is about her. I don't want it to be about her. "Reese—"

He kisses me, a soft brush of lips against lips, his mouth lingering against mine, and there is so much in this kiss; love, fear, passion, friendship, more fear. I pull back. "We're good," I promise him. "She didn't break us."

"I didn't break us, Cat."

"I know. Reese, I know. I'd know if you did. I'd feel it, but we need to talk about what to do about her."

He inhales and releases me, turning away to run a hand through his hair. "Right," he says, as I did about three times in the car before he walks to the bedroom window in front of the couch and stares out of the glass.

I cross to join him, stepping to his side. "I know that Royce will have an opinion and it will matter, but what about Cole? He's your partner and this affects him, too. It's going to affect a lot of things."

He turns to face me. "The only thing that it can affect that matters, is us."

"We won't let it."

He steps to me again, his forehead finding mine. "We won't let it," he agrees, kissing my temple and then guiding me to the couch, where I happily, queasily sit down. Did I really wish for morning sickness that is apparently all-day sickness?

"You're right though," he says. "I have to talk to Cole. I called him. He and Lori are on their way over here. You need to call your family."

My family that I barely get along with. "I guess so. I could—I guess ask Gabe to come over. He's the one I'm closest too. Actually, Reid's the real bastard. We might need him. Should I just ask them to come over?"

"Yes. Ask." He pulls his phone from his pocket and hands it to me.

I breathe out. "I hate calling them."

"I know. I'm sorry."

"Don't say that. Just—just don't." I dial Reid and he answers on the first ring.

"Cat?" he asks, sounding surprised.

"I have a problem. I need you and Gabe."

"I don't remember the last time you said that to me. Are you okay?"

"Yes, but I need you. Now. Here at my place, as soon as possible."

He's silent a beat. "I'll cancel my evening meeting. I'll be there. I'll bring Gabe. Whatever it is, it'll be okay."

"Did you, Reid Maxwell, just comfort me?"

"I'm your brother," he says and hangs up.

Tears burn my eyes as I hand the phone back to Reese. "He's coming."

Reese takes the phone and swipes tears from my eyes. "I heard what he said. He loves you."

I nod. "I guess," I say. "And Royce? Is he here?"

"Downstairs waiting on us," he says, angling in my direction. "But I needed to talk to you first. Everything is you first, Cat."

I grab his hand. "Stop, Reese. Stop acting like we're delicate. We're not. She's a bitch and we're going to beat her. Let's figure out how."

He stares at me a few beats and then laughs. "She's a bitch and we're going to beat her?"

"Yes."

He leans in and kisses me. "That's my Cat. And yes, to both."

"Good," I say. "Will she go public?"

"She's crazy. She's capable of anything which is why Royce is having Savage shadow you unless you'd prefer someone else?"

"Savage is funny," I say. "And I get the idea he wouldn't mind killing someone just because it felt good, and he'd consider that loyalty, so right about now, that works for me."

"Savage it is," he says.

"What about you?"

"What about me?"

"Will someone be with you?"

"Yes," he says, "and not because I want protection, but because there are too many people around me at all times who could get caught in the crossfire."

"And with a gun?" I ask urgently.

He pulls me closer. "If I'm dead, she can't extort me, but that's why I'm worried about everyone else."

"What about Dana?" I ask. "If this goes public, she could freak out."

"I'm going to call her this evening after we have a plan. I'd rather talk to her in person, but the press will make that challenging."

"What about the police? Do we talk to the police?" I shake my head. "Never mind. She hasn't broken a law yet. She hasn't asked for anything."

"She did. She told you if I didn't contact her, she'd go to the press. Royce wants me to talk to the police, too, but after we all talk. Him, you, me, Cole and Lori."

"Do we know who the real father of the baby is?" I ask.

"Royce is working on it, but that could take time."

"I go back and forth between the need to keep her quiet, and the need to just beat her to the punch and expose her in my column."

"I don't want you affected," he says. "If I have to pay her off—"

"No," I say, a sharp pang of emotion in my chest jolting me. "No, you will not pay her off." I try to get up and he holds on to me. "Let me up."

"Cat—"

"Paying her off feels like guilt."

"It's not about guilt, you know that."

"Paying her off feels like guilt and admission of owning that child's future for the rest of our lives, and her with it."

"It's about protecting the firm."

"And she knows that. She picked now, while you're in the middle of this trial, for a reason. Not only do you need her silence, you can't demand a DNA test now without endangering the child."

"But I can demand it as part of the settlement and I will, Cat. I shut up her up now with money she can keep even after the test. It's about protecting everyone else, including you, but damn it, Cat, I'm not guilty."

"*I know.*"

"You don't," he says, his voice hard now. "I feel that in you now." He squeezes his eyes shut. "*Damn it.*"

"I trust you, Reese, but the idea that other people might not, feels weird which is probably why I just want to do it myself and write about it. It's about control. I'd have some kind of control I don't have right now but it's not your fault. I don't want her to punish you through me."

"She is. She most definitely is."

"No," I say. "Pay her off. Your career matters."

He lowers me to the couch, and comes down on top of me, like he needs to hold me in place to keep me from running. "You matter. Only you."

"Your career matters," I say. "It matters to you and me. It matters to us and our future. It matters to our future *family*. Pay her off."

"Our family?"

"Yes. Our family, Reese. We want one. Don't we?"

"Yes, sweetheart. *We do.*"

"Then let's go downstairs and end this."

"Not yet," he says. "I'm not ready. We're not ready."

"We are ready. We're strong together. We need to show that strength now."

"You're strong," he says. "So damn strong, Cat, and I swore when you said 'I do' I'd keep you from having to be that strong. I'm supposed to protect you."

"We protect each other."

"I need to feel you right now," he says, his mouth closing down on mine, a deep drugging lick of his tongue stroking against mine, possessiveness, passion, and something I've never felt in Reese in that kiss: desperation and fear. He's afraid of losing me and I feel that same fear, for no reason. We're in love. We're happy. That isn't going to change because of Debbie.

Chapter Fifty-Five

Reese

I kiss my wife, who is my life, and I will let no one take her from me. I want her to know this. I want her to *feel,* not just hear, how much I love her, and yet, there is a rage of anger inside me I need to bury and control. I have to go downstairs and act like I'm king of the fucking world when everything I love is right here in this room, and delicate, too damn delicate. As surely as I think those words, though, Cat bites my lips, and not gently. "Get out of whatever place you are in your head," she demands. "Right now. I know what you need, so use me."

"I never use you, Cat."

"I use you," she says. "Every time I need out of my own head, I drive you to the edge until you fuck me the way I want to be fucked. Until you make me forget and," she grabs the lapels of my jacket, "stop what you're doing right now. Stop acting like we're different because that makes me think things that I didn't think before, that I know aren't true, but you're scaring me. You're making me think this is going to change us."

"It's not," I say roughly. "I'm just angry."

"Then be angry. Angry at her. Deal with it, *with me.* Show me."

I don't need to be pushed any further. I need *her.* My mouth closes down on hers, my tongue licking into her mouth in a deep, hungry kiss, and I let her taste everything I feel. My fear of losing her, and us. The gut-wrenching moment I heard what Debbie claimed. Just thinking about how that must have affected Cat, gutted me. Just thinking about her actually believing it, tore me apart. And some part of her has to doubt. It's human. I don't want her to doubt.

I tear my mouth from hers. "You're all I need. You're what I needed before I even knew I needed it." I kiss her again and then raise up on my knees to shrug out of my jacket, tugging away my tie and tossing them both. I'm back with Cat in all of sixty seconds, kissing her again, my hand caressing her waist, reaching up to cup her breast.

She arches into my touch and while moments ago, I just needed inside her, the anger in me refocuses on the here and now, and Cat. It's all Cat. I want her to moan for me. I want her to come for me. I want and want where she is concerned, and she needs to feel that now. I didn't do what Debbie claims I did, and Cat needs to be reminded how much she completely rocks my world. I skim her T-shirt up her body and tug it up and away, but I don't let her lower her arms. I do what I rarely do with Cat. I pin her hands over her head.

"I need you to trust me, Cat," I whisper, pressing my cheek to her cheek, pulling back to look at her.

"If I didn't you wouldn't be in this apartment right now, let alone pinning down my arms."

I reach down and unhook her bra, my hand caressing the material away to cup her breast; my lips finding that small space on her neck just below her ear, and I laugh, when moments ago I didn't think I could. "I wouldn't, would I?

"No," she whispers. "You wouldn't because I think more of myself than being with a cheater, but you aren't that Reese. You think more of us than that too, which is why you need to stop worrying about me and us."

"It's why I *can't* stop worrying about you and us." I cover her mouth with mine, kissing her even as I pinch her nipples. I rotate her and drag the bra off of her shoulders and then grab my tie from the ground, sitting up on a knee and pulling her wrists together in front of me.

"You have to test the trust, Reese," Cat says when I wrap the silk around her and bind her hands. "It's there," she says. "You can do anything to me because I'm yours. You know that, right?"

I cup her face. "Anything, Cat?"

"Anything," she whispers, no hesitation in her voice.

I drag her to her back again and pull off her sweats and panties. When she's naked, bound, and lying there, I lean over her, my fists on the couch on either side of her but I don't touch her. "Do you know how much—"

"Yes," she says before I can finish. "Yes to anything you can finish that sentence with. Yes, I know how freaked out you were when you heard about Debbie. Yes, I know how angry you are. Yes, I know how worried you are about us and yes, I know you still have to do your job and it's tormenting you right now. Should I go on?"

I don't know how any two people can know each other like we do. I stand up taking her with me, and again my mood shifts. I don't want to press Cat to do more with me than she's ever done. Not now. Now with people downstairs, and time ticking. I don't need to make her prove her trust. That's another mistake. It's unfair. She's not on trial. I untie her hands and toss away the binding. I just want to make love to my wife. I cup her face and her hands go to my hands.

I kiss her and back her up against the glass of the floor-to-ceiling window and I turn her to face it, pressing her hands to the glass. Mine go beside hers, and together, we're right here, above the city, in control of our world, the way we always are when we're here in this place. My hands caress up and down her waist and gently tease her nipples. She moans, and I cup her breasts, molding them to my hands and she leans into me, lifting her face, offering me her mouth.

I kiss her, and this time it's one-part tenderness and one-part burning, barely-contained passion. "Don't move yet," I whisper, a soft command as I stroke her cheek and then release her.

She stands there, hands on the glass, gorgeous as fuck, her skin perfect, her ass even more perfect, and that's trust, too. Letting me look at her. Letting me stand behind her when she has no idea what comes next. I undress and I'm back to her without delay, my hand settling on her belly, my lips finding her shoulder, teeth scraping the delicate skin there. She breathes out, a trembling, delicate breath, and I brush her hair over her shoulder, my lips finding her neck, the way I plan to find every sensitive spot on her body before this night is over. Many now, before we go downstairs, back into the flames of hell. My hands drag down her shoulders and back up over her breasts.

I go down on one knee, settling at her side, my hand on her backside, and the other on her belly. I squeeze her cheek and then slide my fingers lower, teasing her clit, while my teeth scrape her hip. She gives me one of those moans I'm after and I want more. I turn her to face me as I rotate to stand in front of her, but I don't press my lips to that most intimate part of her. Not yet. I press my lips to her belly and when I look at up Cat, I'm almost certain I find tears in her eyes.

Chapter Fifty-Six

Reese

The tears in Cat's eyes undo me. Cat isn't a crier. For her to do so now is significant and it's because of me. I push to my feet and cup her face, stroking tears from her eyes. "God, woman, I do not want to make you cry. Ever. Any emotions that create tears is not what I ever want you to feel."

"I know that," she says, her hands going to my face. "I'm not myself today. If I wasn't in my current condition I'd handle it better."

"You're sick and I'm trying to fuck you. Fuck." I back up and take her with me, lowering her to the couch again on her back and settling at her side.

She rolls to face me. "I want you to fuck me, Reese. I want to feel close to you right now. I need that, too, just like you." She tangles her fingers in my hair. "So can we—"

"You were crying, Cat." I say. "We do not need to do this."

"I need it. Please ignore the tears. I've just never considered not being with you and—"

I roll her to her back, settling on top of her. "You're considering not being with me?"

"No. No. I just had these few random thoughts that amounted to how badly you could hurt me. How badly you *can* hurt me."

"You could hurt *me* just as badly. That's part of love and marriage. We could, but we won't because we love each other. Because we're best friends. Because there is no reality where we aren't us and us is our reality."

"Kiss me, now," she orders. "Kiss me now and—"

My mouth closes down on hers, and I swear she breathes out and into the kiss as if it's a relief. As if for some reason, until this kiss, she still wasn't sure we are okay and I don't know how to make that right. I deepen the kiss trying to let her taste how much I love her, how true every word I've spoken to her is, and as much as I want to kiss her all over, to take my time, I know Cat. The unknown is driving her crazy. She needs me inside her the way I need inside her and then we need to fix this, together. I cup her backside and lift her, the thick ridge of my erection pressing into the wet heat of her body, and this time, I think we both breathe into our kiss. This time, we're connected, our bodies intimately joined, in a way we both need.

For long seconds, our lips part and we just breathe together, a million emotions between us, before we are kissing again and this time we're moving too, a slow sway that becomes urgent. We are touching and kissing, and every pump of my hips is a lift of hers. I can't get deep enough or close enough. I can't kiss her enough. I can't get enough of Cat, but that is nothing new. I need her. I cannot lose her. I will *not* lose her and as if she understands, her leg hooks mine and she drags me tighter against her. I squeeze her breast and thrust hard, she pants, nails digging into my shoulders a moment before she's spasming around me and that is all it takes. I tumble with her, shuddering into release, and it is over in a blink when I want an hour. I roll to my side and take Cat with me again.

"I'm going to tell everyone to leave. We need us this evening. I'll deal with the rest tomorrow."

"No, you're not," she says. "We have us. You have me. We need this dealt with and you know as well as I do, that you can't wait for the bomb to drop. You have to grab it before it does. I'm fine. I needed this, us, this reconnect, but I'm okay now. I was really always okay. Let's go figure out how to stop her from ruining your firm and career."

"Cat," I say, my hand on her hip, fingers flexing possessively.

"Reese," she replies, pressing her palm to my cheek. "Let's go deal with this together. That's what we do. We do it together."

"I love you."

"And you don't have to prove that just because some woman wants to blackmail you, but I love you, too." She twists away from me and we both sit up on the edge of the couch.

She grabs her clothes and starts dressing in her sweats and T-shirt. I walk to the closet and pull on jeans and a T-shirt, along with a pair of boots. I re-enter the bedroom to find Cat back on the couch. I join her and sit down. "Don't tell Dana," she says turning to look at me. "There's no reason to freak her out if you pay off Debbie.

Dana's life is on the line. She doesn't need this now and it shows how selfish Debbie is that she would do this now."

"Try manipulative," I say. "She chose now, with the cameras rolling, to ensure I have to protect Dana and the firm."

"You're at your best under pressure," Cat says. "Dana and Debbie won't know that, but how much money are we talking and how can we be sure she won't just keep asking for more?"

"All we can do is write a tight contract and make her agree."

"And if she won't?"

"She will," I say. "She wants money. That's what this is about. For all we know the real father is in on this and it's one big scam. Ruining my reputation won't get her money. It takes away my reason for giving her money." I stand up and take Cat with me. "Let's go get this over with so we can get back to us."

She nods and we walk to the bedroom door and when I open it, I hear Cat suck in a breath. I pull her to me and kiss her. "We'll make this fast."

"Everyone is going to question if it's true. Everyone but me. I hate that."

"No, they're not Cat. Everyone downstairs knows you rock my world. They know." I kiss her. "You'll feel it." I take her hand and we start walking and soon we're in the living room with Lori, Cole, Royce, and Savage waiting on us.

Lori rushes at Cat and hugs her. "That bitch," she says before pulling back and holding her arms. "She doesn't know this won't work. Everyone knows how devoted Reese is to you. *Everyone.*"

"But we can't let the firm take a hit," Cat says. "We won't. We have to pay her off."

"But then what?" Cole challenges as Lori rejoins him, standing by his side. "She gets pregnant again and says it's mine? We can't cave and accept this."

"I have a client on trial," Reese says. "Her life and the life of every person we represent right now is on the line."

"We'll take the hit and back her the fuck off," Cole argues. "We'll let our clients know we can't be extorted and that's a good thing for them."

I look at Royce. "What do we know?"

"We've talked to her," Royce says. "And the result wasn't surprising. She wants money."

"Then give it to her," I say. "As little as possible. Surely Cat screaming about her willingness to go public will help with that."

"She has a number in mind," Royce says.

"And the bitch is fucked in the head," Savage says. "I say let me make her disappear. We'll save the baby."

There's a small part of me that thinks he's serious, but of course, he's not. "I'll pretend you didn't just say that," he says.

"That's okay," Savage assures me. "Cat heard me."

"Stop, Savage," Cat pleads, her voice soft but crisp. "Please."

"How much?" I ask again.

"One million," Royce replies and the room fills with a combination of gasps and curses.

Chapter Fifty-Seven

Cat

One million dollars.

In the midst of the curses and gasp, Lauren enters the room. "What just happened?" she asks, a cup of steaming coffee in her hand.

"We all just got group fucked," Savage replies dryly, and I'd laugh if the truth wasn't more like Reese and I just got fucked because some woman from his past says he fucked her in the present. I fight the urge to rush out of the room. It's an emotional response my hormones want to create in me. I need to be a grown adult and ask questions. I need to stand by my husband's side and make decisions. He didn't do this. I am not punishing him with my pregnancy-induced emotions.

Reese's hand settles low on my back. "We're not paying her a million dollars," he says. "Talk to us about options."

"You get her on tape extorting you for money and we take that to the police."

"I get her on tape?" Reese asks. "I don't want to go anywhere near that woman. She's liable to scream rape."

"I'll do it," I say. "I'll meet her in public."

"No," Lauren says. "You're too close to this. It will hurt you. She'll hurt you." She looks at Reese. "And no, I do not believe you're guilty and neither does Cat, but it will hurt her to sit with that woman. And if this woman is a stalker, her obsession with you will make her lash out at Cat."

"I can handle it," I say, turning to face Reese. "I can do this. I'll make her go away."

His hands come down on my shoulders. "Lauren is right. I'm not letting you do this."

"I'll do it," Lori offers. "I'm a female, an attorney, and I have a vested interest in protecting the firm."

Reese and Cole look at each other and I can't tell what passes between them but I suspect Cole isn't interested in putting his wife in danger, and I understand. I love Lori. I don't want her in the line of fire. "No," I say. "I don't want you to wade into this quicksand."

"We're in this," Cole says. "It's not a matter of us staying out of the quicksand. We're partners and friends." Cole looks at Royce. "Where is your head on this?"

"I think I should do it," Lauren suggests, before he answers. "Because I don't have a vested interest and I'm married to a man who is surrounded by the kind of people that will put her in jail." She steps in front of Royce now. "I can do this and you know I'm the best choice for all kinds of reasons."

She means my pregnancy and while part of me wants to blurt that out to the room, the other wants this problem to go away so I can just enjoy this time in our lives with my husband and keep his birthday surprise.

Royce stares down at his wife and then looks at Reese. "She can do it. It makes sense."

Lauren rotates to stand by his side. "Reese? Cat?"

Reese looks at me and I nod. "Yes. She's a criminal attorney and it works. I think it works."

"When?" Lauren asks, looking at Royce. "The sooner the better. I can do it anytime tomorrow. I have to be in court at random times on Wednesday and Thursday. I'm more limited on all those days and I think we all just want this over."

"I'll make a call," Royce says, but he motions to Reese and Cole. "I need to talk to you both."

"You talk right here," Reese says. "There's nothing you can't say in front of Cat and Lori."

"I need to see you both alone," Royce repeats.

I turn to Reese and press my hand to his chest. "I need some air. I'm going to the patio. It's okay."

He cups my head and kisses me. "We're going to make this go away."

"I know," I say. "I do." I turn away and hurry toward the hallway that leads to the second living area and the kitchen, bypassing both rooms to head to the patio where I exit and shut the door. I can't get to the balcony rail soon enough. I grab it, holding on to my emotions with it.

The door opens behind me and I turn to find Lauren shutting it again. "Lori wanted to check on you but I asked her to give me a minute."

I burst into tears, all the emotions I've held in to be strong for Reese overcoming me. "Oh honey," Lauren says, rushing forward and wrapping me in her arms. "It's going to be okay."

"I never cry."

"Or throw up," she says, leaning back to look at me. "Welcome to pregnancy. This is a lot to deal with when your hormones are all out of whack."

I cry for a good two minutes before I swipe at my eyes and ease away from her, "I don't like this part of pregnancy."

"It'll get better once you get past the first few months."

"Months? How many months?"

"After I get rid of Debbie for you, I'm sure it will be better."

"How many months?" I ask again.

She purses her lips, reluctantly admitting, "I was bad for about three months which is another reason you need to tell Reese. He needs to understand why you aren't yourself."

"I want to tell him on his birthday. I'll wrap the journal and have him open it that morning. I want to do it that way. It will be special and perfect, but I need Debbie gone by then."

"We have three weeks. We can do it but can you wait that long to tell Reese?"

"It's the perfect time. He'll be well into the trial. He'll have a grip on what is happening. It'll be a special birthday gift. Debbie will be gone. I love the idea of doing it then."

"I think it sounds special," she says. "I'll handle Debbie. I promise. You know he didn't do this, right?"

"Of course I know. I don't doubt him. I don't even doubt him one little bit. We're too in love. Our sex life is amazing. We're amazing which is why our baby will be amazing. But that's why the way I tell him has to be amazing, and without Debbie."

The doors open and Reese appears, his handsome face etched in worry, his eyes dark, troubled. "I need to see my wife."

"Of course," Lauren says as he steps outside.

She's walking past him when he says, "Thank you, Lauren."

"I'm with you both. Anything you need."

He nods and she disappears, shutting the doors behind her. Reese crosses to stand in front of me, backing me against the railing, his hands coming down on the steel, his legs caging mine. His eyes probing. "You've been crying."

"Reese—"

"Cat. Talk to me."

"I had a small meltdown."

"You don't meltdown. You're afraid it's true. I told Royce I want a DNA test no matter what it costs me."

"No," I say. "No. That isn't the problem and if you think that, then it will affect us as much as if I really distrusted you. You aren't even thinking about your case. You have to be in court in the morning. Make everyone leave. We have to talk. You and me."

"Cat—"

"Make them leave. We need to talk now."

Chapter Fifty-Eight

Cat

"Reese, send them away," I say, and try to push away from the balcony railing and step around him.

He holds me steady. "We need to finish working out the details of what comes next, Cat."

"A DNA test is not what we need. We need it over and that delays this and she's not giving it to you if she's lying."

"If? Now it's if."

"No," I breathe out. "That's not what I meant." I press my hand to my face and then drag it through my hair. "I don't need the test."

"I need it for us."

"You can't end this while asking for the test. Walk away now if we can walk away now. The plan to get her arrested is a good one and if they do arrest her, they'll take her baby. She's crazy. They need to take her baby. I think. God, I don't know what is right. I'm emotional."

"And you're never emotional."

My hands come down on his shoulders. "Make them go away and get ready for court tomorrow."

"No," he says. "We're planning a way to end this and get the DNA test. Royce is waiting for me. I came after you because my gut said you needed me and I was right."

"What did Royce say about the DNA test?"

"It could complicate things, but if it were him, he'd do it, too. He'd want Lauren to know—"

"I *know*, Reese. Focus on your trial."

"You don't know, Cat. I know you. I know you like I know myself. You're not yourself."

"You said that before the Debbie thing happened. Remember?" I flatten my hand on his chest. "I have a very special gift for you on your birthday. I have it all planned out and the special project

I'm working on isn't a book. It's something for you. I'm so freaked out because it's special and I don't want this to be hanging over our heads when I give it to you. So I beg of you. End this, Reese. To the best of our ability, let's end this."

"What gift, Cat?"

"It's a gift for a reason. It's a surprise. It's very special. Please, Reese. End this. I promise you with all that I am that I believe in you and us. I do not believe that you would or have cheated on me. I wouldn't want to give you this gift if I did and you'll understand that when I do. Have enough faith in us to wait until then. To know that this gift is about how much love we share."

He cups my face and presses his forehead to mine, his thumb stroking my cheek. "You know you're killing me with this gift stuff. I want to know what it is."

My hand covers his where it rests on my face. "I can't wait to give it to you. You have no idea how much waiting is killing me, but it will make your birthday really special."

He pulls back to look at me, his blue eyes soft and warm. "I love you so much, woman."

"I love you, too. And I love watching you in court. Let's get rid of Royce and everyone else and get your team over here. And I have to write my column, but I'll sit in on the game planning. I love that, too."

"Me too," he says. "Let's go get rid of everyone together." He starts to turn and I catch his arm.

"Let the DNA test go, Reese. The police will handle that if they arrest her and if they don't, she won't take a payout if that's a condition."

"We aren't paying her a million dollars."

"Thank God," I murmur.

"We aren't paying her anything if we can play our cards right."

"Let's hope," I say letting him pull me behind him, and together we walk back to the front living area where we find everyone huddled around the coffee table in some way, shape or form.

That is, except for Royce and Lauren who are standing at the window, him towering over her petite frame in deep conversation that ends abruptly upon our return. "Okay," Reese says. "Just make this go away. Let's set her up and shut her down. No DNA test or money."

I'm watching Cole and Lori when he makes this announcement, the two people who have the most to lose with us, as they are partners in the firm, but they don't look relieved. They just look worried, and I love them because I think they're more worried about us than themselves. "All right then," Savage says, rubbing his hands together from where he sits at the edge of a chair. "If we can't kill the bitch, let's get her arrested." He eyes Royce. "I'm still working on my enjoyment of the more means to an end, boss, but you know. I'm getting there."

Again, I think, *he's joking*. Mostly. Maybe? Royce doesn't look amused and ignores him. "I have the number. I'll make the call and set the meeting. We'll record the entire conversation, but I'll see if I can get an active detective to sit in."

"No," I say. "Too often they leak to the press. We can't risk that."

"No one we trust," Savage says, "would leak or they would end up dead." He glances at Royce and amends. "More like they'd wish they were dead."

"We have a reputation of taking down dirty cops," Royce says. "They'd regret it. I won't call in anyone I don't personally trust." He motions to Savage. "We'll get this under way and check-in in a few hours."

"When are you going to make contact?" Reese asks.

"Once we have recording devices in place," Royce replies. "And we have men following her now. We're looking for an accomplice which brings me to a suggestion. I know we want to end this but we need to know who we are dealing with. Savage and I, as well as our team, have chatted in the past fifteen minutes, and the consensus is we need a few days to play this right."

"What if she goes to the press?" I ask.

"Then she gets no payday," Reese says. "She won't. Take the time. End this right."

Royce nods and Savage does the same. They head for the door and Lauren stops beside me. "You want a ride in the morning? I'll come to court unless I'm taking down Debbie."

"Yes, please," I say, certain she can update me in the morning.

She nods and leaves but not before she squeezes my arm.

Cole and Lori step in front of us and Cole is the first to speak. "We're in this all the way, no matter what that means."

"Of course we are," Lori assures us as well.

Cole motions to Reese. "Walk me out," he says, and the two of them head toward the door.

Lori stays with me. "Do you need to talk?"

"Not yet," I say, hating the way I've shut her out. I love her. We are so very close, but if I talk to her, I'll want to tell her about the baby, and I just can't. It's not fair to Reese. "But soon," I add.

"I can't be in court tomorrow. I wish I could, but I'll call you." She hugs me and soon she is gone.

I stand there, waiting on Reese, and when he returns, he stops in front of me, the two of us just staring at each other. I expect him to lay something heavy on me, but instead, he pulls me close. "How many orgasms is it going to take to find out what the surprise is early?"

I laugh, the way only he can make me laugh, under this much stress. "Two hundred," I say, giving him an unreachable number.

He arches a brow. "That's a big number and since you have to write your column I'll have to make this one fast." He picks me up and starts walking toward the bedroom and for now, Debbie doesn't exist. I love that about us. We can make everything else disappear. *He* makes everything else disappear and for the first time since Debbie appeared, I realize I'm certain this is all going to work out. Of course, Debbie thinks the same thing. She thinks it's going to work out for her.

Chapter Fifty-Nine

Cat

Reese carries me up the stairs and lays me down on our bed, his big body coming down on top of mine. "I love you, woman."

"I know you do," I promise. "You have nothing to prove to me. I told you. My reactions are about this surprise."

He leans up on his elbows. "Tell me what it is."

My hand goes to his face, tenderness overcoming me when I think of what I have to share, but I haven't even gone to the doctor yet. I'm not telling him now. "You have to wait until your birthday. I promise. It's worth the wait."

"You're killing me, Cat. I can normally take your teasing, but now—"

"You can take it," I tease. "You're 'Mr. Hotness' and by the way, the blogs about you have already started again."

"Fuck," he growls. "Not more of the Mr. Hotness craziness."

"I like it more now," I say.

"And why is that?"

I scrape my teeth over my lip and then kiss him. "I'm the girl who got Mr. Hotness."

"You do have me, Cat. *All of me.* You have from the moment you called me an asshole."

I laugh and it feels good, all the emotions I've been feeling seem to be fading in a wave of calmer hormones that might not last but I'll take it while I can get it. My hands slide under his shirt. "You weren't the asshole I thought you were."

"Glad to hear that since you married me," he says, lips brushing mine. "I'm going to fuck you now. I have to. You know that, right?"

"Have to," I agree, as his hand slides under my shirt and over my breast, his fingers tugging down my bra to tease my nipple. "Definitely." He drags my shirt up and over my head or he tries.

The doorbell rings and I catch it at my neck. "Oh God. I called my brothers. Why did I call my brothers? If you pay her off they don't even need to know about Debbie."

He rolls us to our sides, facing each other. "Relax, sweetheart." He cups my face. "I know your relationship with your brothers is tense, especially Reid, but the very fact that they rushed over here says they care. And Reid's a beast. If anyone is going to represent us legally on this, unless you're against it, he's a good choice in my book."

"Let's not tell them. Let's say it's something else."

"Cat—"

"I don't want to tell them."

"You're embarrassed," he says, sitting up as the bell rings again. "Fuck. Of course, you are."

"No." I scoot to the edge of the mattress beside him. "I'm not. I'm not—I don't want anyone to assume we're broken."

He glances over at me. "No one, your brothers included, who I work with frequently, who knows me, and us, believes we're broken or that I cheated. Reid is a good choice, Cat."

I swallow hard. "You're right. It's just so awkward with him."

"I say him being here shows he's trying to change that."

"If he's here. It might be just Gabe. He's the one on the approved list at security."

"I put Reid on a long time ago."

"You did?"

"Yes. I hoped you two would mend your relationship." He kisses me. "Let's go find out."

Mend. That's a hard thing when Reid disapproves of my career and pretty much all of my decisions, but I nod. Reese stands and takes me with him, and when he would turn away, I grab his arm. "I'm sorry."

His eyes narrow on me. "For what, Cat?"

"Me being emotional and embarrassed isn't me showing you how much I believe in us, but I do. I swear, I do."

He pulls me to him and kisses me. "I know you do. Don't apologize for anything. You've handled this far better than I might have." His cellphone rings and he snakes it from his pocket. "Reid," he says, glancing at his caller ID. He releases me and motions to the door as he answers the call. "Yes, Reid. We're on our way to the door right now." He motions me through the doorway and when

I would pass, he catches me and kisses me. "Reid will help. This is a good thing."

"I know," I say. "He's a bastard. You want the resident bastard in your corner and for once, maybe he's my bastard." I walk down the stairs but I don't even think about getting the door and Reese knows I won't. He knows me. I head away from the door and he catches my hand. "I'll feel them out before letting them get to you."

I nod and rush toward the kitchen where I brew a cup of coffee, not even sure how that works with pregnancy. Can I drink coffee? I google it. I get "moderation" as my answer, and that's good enough for me. I need something warm to burn away the chill Reid always delivers. My cup is full and piping hot when Reid, in all his arrogant good looking asshole glory, walks into the kitchen alone. "Where's Gabe?" I ask.

"Talking about a case he's on with your husband."

"I see." I hug myself.

"Stop acting like I bite, Cat." He steps to the opposite side of the counter. "I'll bite for you, but not you."

"You've done plenty of biting where I'm concerned."

"I'm proud of you, Cat."

I blanch. "What?"

"I *am* proud of you. I am."

I should revel in this. Instead, I feel angry. "Says the man who shut me out because I didn't join the family firm."

"I had reasons for what I did and felt."

"Yeah—dad. He made you think there was no other life but the one he chose for us."

"That's not true," he says.

"I can't do this now. I have—I have way too much on me now." My stomach rolls and I swallow hard. "Not now."

"Cat—"

"Everything okay?" Reese asks from the door.

My gaze jerks to the archway to find him and Gabe standing there, and both look concerned. Gabe and I have had our issues, along the same lines as those I've had with Reid, but they were never as bad as with Reid, and Gabe and I have come a long way, while Reid and I are nowhere close to that in my book. He's just hurt me too much.

"It's fine," I say tightly, and Reese is quick to join me on this side of the island, while Gabe steps directly across from him. I'm still directly in front of Reid.

Reese's hand settles on my back and he looks down at me. "What do you want to do, sweetheart?"

"You tell them," I say. "Please."

"You're sure?" Reese asks.

"Holy hell," Gabe says. "Tell me now. Is someone sick?" He looks at me. "Cat?"

"No," I say. "No, that's not it."

"What is it then?" Gabe says.

"First," Reese says, "I'm innocent and need legal help."

"What does that mean?" Reid interjects tightly.

"I had a stalker before I met Cat," Reese explains. "It was pretty crazy. I slept with her twice, and she became obsessed. She showed up everywhere I went and then she was just gone."

"She's back?" Gabe assumes. "Is she after Cat?"

"She's back," Reese confirms. "Pregnant and claiming it's mine. I haven't seen this woman in years and she confronted Cat to deliver this news."

Reid looks at me, his blue eyes fierce before they shift to Reese. The two men stare each other down, and I hate Reid in this moment. I hate the accusation in him that would call my husband a cheater. I hate that this is how my brother finally decides to protect me. It's wrong. He's wrong. "This was a mistake," I say, turning to Reese. "This was a mistake." I turn to my brothers. "Please leave. No, not please. Just leave."

Chapter Sixty

Cat

"Leave," I repeat, looking at Reid but speaking to him and Gabe. I don't need them working against Reese. I don't need them judging me or us at all.

"Cat—" Reid starts, but I cut him off.

"Say nothing, Reid. I don't need this right now."

His jaw sets hard. "I do not think he's guilty. That's not the look I gave him. You're looking for what isn't there."

Reese's hand comes down on my back. "Cat," he says softly. "Sweetheart. He doesn't believe I'm guilty."

"I damn sure don't," Gabe interjects.

I twist around to face Reese. "But he—"

"No," he says, his hands coming down on my arms. "He didn't look at me with accusation, but rather anger that this is happening."

"But I—"

He kisses me hard and fast. "He's on our side."

My lashes lower but I don't turn back to my brothers.

"Cat," Reid says. "Let's talk alone."

I rotate to face him. "No. Now is not the time for you to—"

"Please," he says softly.

I blanch. "Did Reid Maxwell just say please to me?"

"Yes, little sister, I did. Let's talk alone."

"I—well, you said please so yes, but do not accuse my husband—"

"Reese didn't cheat on you, Cat," Reid says. "I know that."

I swallow hard and Reese leans in close. "Gabe and I will go to the front living area." He kisses my temple and then rounds the island. In another thirty seconds, I'm alone with my brother who I've had a tenuous relationship with my entire adult life.

"I know that we're broken," he says, using the same words Reese and I have today, as well, only with Reese and I it's not true. With Reid and I, it is.

"That's an understatement, don't you think?"

"Yes, and I had reasons for everything I did, namely to protect you."

"Rejecting my goals and dreams was protecting me?" I challenge.

He looks skyward before casting me in a turbulent stare. "Right now, you have a big problem I can help you fix so I am not going to make this about me. It's about you and Reese but that said, I read mom's letter she left you when she died, and Reese is not dad."

"The letter where mom told me to chase my own dreams and to never be with a man who cheated like our father did on her. And?"

"I didn't know dad cheated on her like that. I thought—fuck, Cat—I thought she was the one thing that kept him human. If I'd known, I'd have done something. Just like if I thought Reese was cheating, I'd drag you out of here, but he's not. Let me help. I'm good at ending bad situations. I'll represent you both if you'll let me. And I'll protect you both."

I swallow hard. "I hate this," I whisper.

"Of course you do, but you're strong—proven by the fact that you keep all the Maxwell's in line—and anyone who does something like this is weak. You called me, Cat. I'm here. Let me really be here."

"I didn't want you to get sideswiped if she went public."

He arches a brow. "You didn't want my help or support?"

"You aren't really one to dish those things out."

"I am always here for you, Cat. The fact that you don't know that needs to change, but right now, let's go talk to Reese and Gabe and end this woman."

"I'd agree about ending her but what kind of person does this? She must be mentally ill."

"Or just greedy, Cat. I see it all the time in ways that I'm glad you're naive too. Thank you, mom, for urging you to chase your dreams, because I wanted you to come inside our world where you wouldn't be naïve to this kind of stuff."

"Or you're just so jaded that all you see is greed."

"I wish that were true. I wish what I've seen could be undone, but it can't." He motions to the door. "Shall we?"

"Yes," I breathe out. "We shall."

I round the island and he catches my arm, turning me to look at him. "Why do you look different?"

My God. My brother is going to guess. "Because you're actually looking at me."

"I always actually look at you. More than you know. What's different?"

"I'm not myself right now. I'm rattled when contrary to what you seem to believe, I'm a Maxwell by blood. I don't get rattled."

"He didn't cheat, Cat. I've looked in that man's eyes for years now, and all I see is intelligence, skill, and a man who loves his wife. I watch for changes. They aren't there. I'd tell you. As painful as it would be after reading that letter from mom, I'd tell you."

"I know he didn't cheat. I never once doubted him. I just hate that he's distracted during his trial and that he thinks I might doubt him. That hurts our relationship, too. I don't want what is perfect to get hurt."

"We *are* perfect, Cat."

At the sound of Reese's voice, Reid releases me and I turn to find my husband in the doorway. "You're perfect," he adds when my eyes meet his.

I rush toward him and he pulls me against him, hugging me, becoming my sanctuary as always. I love this man so very much. "You okay?" he whispers, his lips at my ear.

"Yes," I say, looking at him. "Reid wants to represent you and us if we need it."

"You do need it," Reid says firmly.

"Agreed," Reese replies.

Gabe steps into the doorway. "I guess we're back in here."

"Yes," I say, pushing out of Reese's arms. "We're here."

Gabe grabs me and hugs me. "We'll beat this together," he promises in my ear.

"Thank you," I whisper, so very confused by both of my brothers right now, but not in a bad way. In a bit of a sad way. There have been so many lost years between me and them with a lot of built up baggage from that divide.

He releases me and Reese links our arms, leading me around the island again. Reid steps to the spot in front of me again, and Gabe steps in front of Reese. "We should file a restraining order," Reid states.

"Not yet," Reese says. "We're going to try to trap her into blackmailing me on tape." He goes on to explain the plan Royce and Lauren came up with earlier.

"A restraining order could keep her from going public," Gabe interjects. "I've seen an order intimidate people."

"I'm the criminal attorney here," Reese says. "And the person who's dealt with Debbie. She's unstable. We will need protection and we have it. I hired helped. But what I'm telling you all right now, is that I need us to have multiple plans, and they all need to consider that as I just said, she's unstable. I don't want to set her off, if we can get her on tape, and get the police to get involved on a broader scale, than an order, that might trigger some rash action on her part."

"She won't go public," I say. "If she does, she won't get the money."

"Not true," Gabe says. "I had a big wig I represented that was getting blackmailed over a pregnancy. The baby wasn't his which is exactly why she went public. She wanted my client to pay her off to retract the story and say she lied. And he did."

My stomach knots. "In other words. She might go public to force Reese into protecting his reputation."

"That's the worst-case scenario," Gabe confirms.

Reid disagrees. "The worst case scenario is her coming after Cat because she's a crazy fucking bitch who's obsessed with Reese." He looks at Reese. "She needs protection."

"Arranged," Reese confirms. "And I agree. Protecting Cat is everything."

In other words, I'm pregnant with his child, and a crazy pregnant woman might well come after me. Which is believable, since I'm the one she came to at the courthouse.

Chapter Sixty-One

Cat

Protecting Reese is what's important. Protecting my baby is what's important, I think. Protecting his or her father is what's important. "Crazy stalkers kill the people they get obsessed about, too," I say, turning to Reese. "You will have someone with you tomorrow, right?"

"Royce has it all taken care of. I'm fine. You're the one I'm worried about"

"Lauren's going with me to the doctor in the morning. I have a feeling Royce will be tagging along."

"Why are you going to the doctor?" Gabe asks.

I glance in his direction. "Nothing that's going to kill me," I say and needing an escape from all these watchful eyes, I quickly refocus on Reese and add, "I have to write my column and you need to get your team here working."

"You're my team tonight," he says.

"Reese—"

His hands come down on my arms. "There's nothing that happened today in court that changes my strategy. You were there. You know that. I'm going to win. We're going to win. Write your column. I'll finish up here and you can help me prep for tomorrow the way you always help me prep." He kisses me. "Go. Write. I'll find you when we're done."

He's decided he's not having his team over. He's affected by this Debbie thing and worrying about me to the point that it's affecting his case. "Just to be sure we're on the same page. You're not telling your client yet, right?"

"No," he says. "I'm not telling Dana until we find out where this trap we're setting for Debbie leads us and I hope like hell that's a good decision."

"It's a good decision," Reid says. "We'll end this one way or the other. You have my word."

I am suddenly glad Reid's involved because he's intelligent and hard in every way, brutal even. When Reid makes a statement like that, he doesn't fail. I know. I've felt his wrath.

I kiss Reese and head out of the kitchen. I'm two steps down the hallway when Gabe catches my arm. "You okay?"

"I'm not used to you and Reid acting like you care."

"Come on now. The past two years you and I have come a long way. That's not fair."

He's right. "You're right. I'm sorry. It's Reid that I'm not used to, but I'm fine." I hug him. "Thank you, Gabe."

"Call me after the doctor tomorrow, okay?" He pulls back to look at me. "Reese will be in court. I'm free tomorrow, so I'm going to come watch Reese with you after your appointment."

"You want to sit with me in court?"

"Yeah. I might learn something from that husband of yours."

"You don't even practice the same kind of law and you're a master at your job."

His eyes light with what is apparently a naughty private joke of some sort. "I won't even go where that comment could take me. Call me when you leave the doctor." He kisses my cheek and heads back to the kitchen, leaving me with a smile that I appreciate today more than usual.

I turn away and a few minutes later I'm on the bed in the master bedroom, my laptop in my hands. I think of the day in court that ended with Debbie confronting me and one word comes in mind: Lies. This DA is all about lies which is why I've been working on a book with Lori to expose him. We've also decided to release it after he leaves the office for one reason: Protecting the firm and its clients. I don't like it and this trial is stirring the pot for me. I start typing and that one word is back on my mind: Lies. Debbie's lies. The DA's lies. The prosecutor's lies. And so I start my Cat Does Crime column now with that word: *Lies.*

When a person is charged without evidence to satisfy an elected official's need to appear active in an investigation, to, of course, support reelection, is that a lie? Are they lying to the public they want to elect them? Lying to the judge? Lying to the jurors? Like many of you, I followed a case recently here in our very city where the district attorney charged a man with serial murders. Even after the jury acquitted, he did not reopen the case. The real killer then killed again.

As I sat in the Dana Warren trial today, I thought of that case. Someone killed her father. In my legal opinion, Dana was charged prematurely without evidence. The opening statements today read to me as fluff and drama, meant to downplay the lack of evidence. In opening statements, the prosecutor seemed to prosecute Dana Warren based on her inheriting money, not for killing her father, which would make sense since thus far, I've seen no evidence that supported charging her, let alone convicting her. Am I biased because of my husband? No. He won't take a case if he believes the person to be guilty. Nothing he has seen, nor I have seen, supports guilt. So unless I'm presented with evidence that says otherwise, I am not convinced she killed her father. If the prosecutor charged Dana, not on evidence, but a need to charge someone, where is the real killer? And if they killed once, can they kill again? When do we hold law enforcement criminally liable? When does political position become lies? When does it become criminal?

I don't like lies. To those of you who lie with no concern about who you hurt, I am not your friend. I will write about it. I will expose the lies. I will tell the truth. That's who I am and I hope that you, my readers, embrace my words as truth. And so, I'll be in court tomorrow, and look for the truth to share with you, my readers. Until next time —Cat

I'm done and in that column is a message for the DA, yes, but also to Debbie. I send it to my editor and shut my computer. Reese appears in the doorway in that moment, looking deliciously male and perfect. He narrows his eyes on me. "What did you do?"

"What does that mean?" I ask, a hint of a smile on my lips. I feel empowered through my writing. I needed that outlet.

"I know you, Cat." He crosses to join me on the bed, and before I can blink I'm beneath him and he's leaning over me. "You're different. You're not tears and fear. You're fierce and in control. What did you write?"

"Fuck you to the DA and Debbie, though I didn't mention Debbie. Just liars that I will go after."

He drags my shirt over my head and tosses it. "You said fuck you, to the DA and Debbie."

"Yes," I say, sliding my hands under his shirt. "I did."

"What happened to not poking the beast until we finish setting her up?"

"I'm not rewriting my column. I sent it to my editor."

"I didn't ask you to, but if you're fucking everyone else," he pulls his shirt over his head, "why aren't you fucking me?"

And suddenly his hard, hot body is my reward for everything I've been through today. "Get naked, Reese Summer."

Chapter Sixty-Two

Cat

Reese does get naked and so do I but when he comes back down on top of me, with all his hard perfection, we are not edgy and intense as we were right before we met with my brothers. Not yet. Not in this moment. We are softer, our lips coming together in a breath, our bodies pressed close, but we don't move. This is us, alone, the rest of the world gone. Feeling each other. Loving each other. Needing each other. I can feel this man in every part of me, inside and out, and that is nothing I knew or understood before Reese. That is why he is the man I want to have a family with, share my life with. The man I love so very much.

His fingers stroke my cheek, a tender touch that sends a shiver down my spine. His hand then closes down on the side of my neck, his mouth over mine, his tongue licking past my lips, and I moan with the touch, with the thousands of sensations this man creates in me. My nipples ache, my sex clenches, my fingers dig into his shoulders. He pulls back, breathing with me again, and it is everything to just be here like this with him, savoring every moment. He kisses me again, this time a deeper stroke of tongue, a deeper connection and then his mouth is gone again and he's kissing a path down my neck, over my shoulder.

His hands cup my breasts and he shifts lower until he's licking my nipples, one at a time, then sucking, teasing, driving me wild. I want him inside me. I want so much right now, but his mouth is on my belly now, and his fingers are stroking a line along the wet seam of my body. "I want you, Reese," I whisper. "Please."

He licks my clit and looks up at me. "This is me," he says, suckling me and I moan and arch into him, but God, I just want him inside me.

"Not like this," I insist. "Not this—time." The last word comes out as a pant, as he runs his tongue in all the right directions and places and I melt into the mattress, no longer fighting what comes next. He's too good at this. He knows my body too well. And I'm too aroused to do anything but tumble right over into orgasm in another few licks of his skilled tongue.

He doesn't linger or slowly take me to completion. He knows exactly what I need. He's on top of me, pressing inside me, letting those last spasms of my sex happen with him buried inside me. It's perfection and I am arching into him, even as he pumps into me, his mouth now on my mouth, the salty taste of me on his lips. Lips that travel my jaw, my breast, my shoulder. Lips that are back on my lips as we sway together and time stands still. There is just us and there is nothing between us, but us. I don't want this to end, and I can feel that in him, too. We go slow and savor each other but at some point we snap. At some point we become urgent and there is no more holding back. We ride the high of need together and shudder and quake into orgasm. The next thing I remember, I'm pressed to Reese's side, my head on his chest, and the heaviness of sleep overtakes me.

I wake to darkness and the roll of my stomach, which has me scooting away from Reese and glancing at the clock to read two am. I hurry into the bathroom, and without turning on the light, kneel in front of the toilet, and heave up nothing. When the wave of yuck passes, I grab a gown from a hook on the back of the door, push it shut, and then brush my teeth.

I've just finished when Reese opens the door, now in pajama bottoms, his hair a sexy rumpled mess. "You okay?" *Am I okay?* I'm having his baby. I'm perfect, and Debbie doesn't get to change that fact.

I walk to him, hug him and say just that. "Perfect," I say. "Let's go back to bed."

He strokes my hair, kisses my temple, and a few minutes later, my alarm is set and my husband is wrapped around me. I smile into the darkness. A few hours from now, I'll officially confirm the pregnancy I know is real. Yes. I am indeed, perfect. And I decide this moment, these very thoughts, with him holding me, must be a part of my journal.

I wake at six in the morning and thankfully I'm feeling better, because Reese carries me to the shower and makes a vow to fuck me every day before trial, not just on day one of new trials. I am not going to complain about the lofty goal, not one bit. Mr. Hotness is all mine. I dress in a pink dress that I decide means I want a girl, though a little boy who could grow up to be just like his father has just as much appeal. Reese dresses to impress, as he always does, in a blue pinstriped suit with a striking royal blue tie that brings out his blue eyes. The jury doesn't have a chance with this man. He's already in the kitchen on his laptop when I join him to wait on Lauren who will arrive any minute.

"Well?" I ask, stopping across from him, aware that he reads my column every morning.

"It's you, Cat. A fighter all the way in every way. I like it."

"I poked the bear. Bear meaning Debbie, by telling her I'd out a liar and in hindsight, Gabe seems to think she might come forward just to get us to pay her to later say she lied."

"We don't fight any war scared. That's not who we are. I'm glad you did this. If she comes at us, we'll come at her. *We,* Cat."

The doorbell rings. "That will be Lauren," I say.

"I hate I can't take you to the doctor."

I sigh. "I hate I'll miss the beginning of the court proceedings."

"I'll update you at the food truck." He says as we meet at the end of the island.

"It's a date," I say, smiling and pushing to my toes to kiss him.

"I'll walk you down," he says, grabbing his briefcase. "I want to get an update from Royce.

A few minutes later, we're standing on the sidewalk with Lauren, Royce, and Savage. "One of our men is following Debbie," Royce says. "She hasn't returned my calls, which means we'll approach her today in person."

It's not grand news, but Reese and I both accept it, and he departs in a vehicle with Savage as I leave with Lauren and Royce. "How are you holding up?" Lauren asks, sitting in the backseat with me. "I read your article."

"What did you think?"

"That you're a badass pregnant princess who takes no shit from anyone."

I laugh. "Pregnant Princess. I'll take that description and right now, I'm perfect. I'm excited about confirming the pregnancy. I'm excited about telling Reese on his birthday. I'm going to set Debbie aside and embrace that feeling."

We chat and Royce parks in front of the building where my doctor has his office. He leaves the black SUV he's driving idling and walks us to the door. "I'll park and be right up."

"You don't have to do the waiting room thing with me," I say. "In fact, please don't. I feel like Reese would feel weird knowing that and I'd tell him. I'd have to tell him."

His jaw clenches but he nods. "I'll wait in the lobby."

"Better, I guess," I say. "Thank you."

"Good luck," he replies.

Lauren and I step into the elevator and she links her arm with mine. "This is it. You're about to get the pregnancy stamp."

I laugh. "Yes. I suppose I am."

I'm smiling as we walk into the office, and it's not long before I'm peeing in a cup and giving blood. I sit on the table and I wait and wait, to the point that I stand up in my gown and pace, despite the gap in the back where my ass is hanging out. The door opens, and I fold my arms in front of me. "Well?"

"You are indeed pregnant," Anna, the nurse practitioner says. "Congratulations."

I tear up. "Oh my God. Thank you. How far along?"

"Let's do an exam and we'll estimate a due date."

Thirty minutes later, I find out that I'm five weeks pregnant, have samples of prenatal vitamins and set an appointment to come back again. I exit to the lobby and the minute Lauren sees me she squees and hugs me. "YAY! You are going to be such a good mom."

"Thank you, but now, I just want to get to court and watch my baby's father kick butt."

"Agreed," she says, and we exit to the hallway to find Royce standing there.

And while Royce always looks gruff and rough and hard, there's an edge about him. "What?" I breathe out. "What is wrong?"

"Everyone is safe," he says. "But Debbie showed up at the building."

"What building?" Lauren asks before I can.

"This one," he says, and the message is clear. She came here for me. And coming for me means coming for me and my baby now, and that is not acceptable, nor is it something I will take without fighting.

Chapter Sixty-Three

Cat

I take just a moment to digest Royce standing in front of me telling me that Debbie followed me to my doctor's office but only for a minute, if that. I'm done with emotions. I'm ready to fight. "Where is she now?" I ask.

"The man I had following her stopped her from entering the building. He's presently working on setting up a meeting with her."

"I want to talk to her," I say.

"You are not talking to her," Lauren states. "She's crazy. She's stalking you now."

"Or she's trying to freak me out and get a fast payout," I say. "I'm not letting her think it's working. It's not." I look at Royce. "Do not tell Reese until after court tonight."

Royce's jaw sets hard. "He needs to know."

"A woman is on trial to go to jail for the rest of her life," I remind him. "Reese needs to focus on her. He knows you'll protect me. You did protect me."

"Negotiation time," he says. "You do exactly what I say, and I'll wait to tell Reese."

"What is that you want me to do?"

"Stay away from her. Savage is at the courthouse. Once I drop you there, you go nowhere without him, not even to pee."

"I'm fine with that," I say. "My brother Gabe is supposed to be in court today, too. What else?"

"Reid called me," he announces.

"My brother called you?"

"He wants to deal with Debbie instead of Lauren." He pulls his wife to him. "Don't argue. Debbie's crazy. She proved that this morning. I don't want you in this."

"He's right," I quickly agree. "*He's right,* Lauren. She is crazy. And Reid's good looking, intelligent, and brutal. He'll grab her attention and lure her into a trap that'll let the police take over."

"Then I'm coming to court with you today as well," Lauren says. "I have time today. I want you well-insulated."

"Good," I say. "I'd like to have you there." I look at Royce. "I really want to get to court and watch my husband work his magic, please."

He nods and we head to the elevator. By the time we enter the lobby, he's gotten a call. "Debbie agreed to a meeting," he says. "Reid's meeting her at his office."

"If I know my brother, this could end today," I say, as we cross the lobby. "Any idea who the father of her baby is?"

"No obvious candidate at this point," he says, ushering us out to his SUV.

I'm just settling into the backseat when my cellphone rings. I dig it from my purse to find Reid's number. "Cat," he says urgently. "Are you okay?"

He sounds genuinely concerned in a way I'd forgotten Reid capable of being concerned. "Royce is taking good care of me. I don't want Reece to know about this until after court is adjourned today. Promise me you won't tell him."

"I'm not going to tell him," he says. "I'm going to end this. I got this and you. Understand?"

"I believe you," I say. "Thank you, Reid."

He's silent a beat before he says, "Whatever was between us, I was always protecting you. I'm going to protect you now." He hangs up and before I can even begin to deal with the knot of emotion in my chest, my phone rings again, this time with Reese's number.

"Reese?" I answer, surprised he called. "How are you calling me?"

"We got into court and the prosecution called for an immediate fifteen-minute recess."

"Waiting on a witness?"

"That's what they said. A medical examiner. What did the doctor say?"

"I have a prescription for anti-nausea medication I need to fill. I want to get to court before I miss something."

"I can fill it for you," Lauren says and leans forward to talk to Royce who's behind the wheel of the car and pulling us into traffic. "Drop me at the pharmacy by the courthouse."

"Lauren's going to get my meds," I say, mouthing, "thank you" to her.

"But what did the doctor say?" he presses. "Is this something serious?"

"Serious?" I ask, glancing at Lauren who gives me a big grin and mouths "yes," before I continue with Reese by adding, "More like *lingering*," I reply to Reese. "It could take a while for the nausea to pass." I quickly change the subject because I'm not going to lie to Reese. That's not who we are and talking in circles is becoming uncomfortable. "How's Dana?"

"She spent the night simmering. She's angry this morning about being in this position. She said she read your column this morning and it just drove home how much she needs to fight back."

"Is that good or bad? I'd say good but you're the one in the heat of battle."

"It's good, Cat. I'm glad you wrote it. I gotta go. I'll see you at lunch."

"Yes. See you at lunch."

His voice softens, "About that birthday surprise."

"I'm not telling you what it is," I say, smiling.

"I'm telling you that it can't be ruined. Nothing ruins us. I love you, sweetheart." He disconnects and I sigh, that smile lingering on my lips.

I glance at Lauren and she smiles. "I don't know what he said," she says. "But I'm glad he said it."

"Me, too," I whisper. "Me, too." I grab my MacBook from my briefcase I'd left in the SUV when we were in the doctor's office. "I want to write in my baby journal for Reese. There's so much about this morning I want Reese to know."

Lauren squeezes my arm. "Do that. Focus on him, not Debbie."

"I am," I say, but mentally I'm prepared to do whatever I have to do to end this. I want to just go public, I do, but that could hurt the firm. "But really, what power does she have?" I ask.

"What does that mean?" Lauren asks.

I grab my phone and dial Reid. He answers on the first ring. "She's here. What do I need to know?"

"I just want to make sure you know where I stand on Debbie," I say. "If she goes public, if Reese and Cole agree, I'll embrace it and turn it into columns and a book with a big payout, probably a million dollars, that I'll invest right back into the firm to offset the damage. Use that to strip her power."

"Did Reese and Cole agree to this?"

"No, and this doesn't mean I'll do it. It just means I could. Use it. Take her power."

"We'll see. Call me at recess. We both know if you get up and call me Reese will know and be distracted."

"Yes. It would, but waiting is going to kill me. Can you just text me everything you can?"

"I will. I'm going to make her sit in the conference room to stew which means it will be a while."

A voice sounds in the background. "Reid. She just threw something at the receptionist."

"Fuck," he murmurs. "I need to go."

"She threw something at the receptionist?"

"I need to go, Cat." He hangs up.

"Royce, Debbie is—"

"One of my men is there," he says. "He'll handle it and update me."

Everyone is handling my problem but me. "I want to go to Reid's office. I need to go to his office *now.*"

"You need to let Reid handle this," Royce says, eyeing me in the rearview mirror. "You need to be in court where your husband knows you're safe."

"I know," I say. "But there's a crazy woman raising hell in my brother's office because of me."

"Trust your brother to handle this."

Trust my brother. He doesn't know what a loaded statement that is but he's right again. I have to trust Reid, the way Reid has never trusted me. The way I trust Reese and Reese trusts me. I'm back to Royce being right. I need to be with my husband and since the SUV is currently pulling up to the side door of the courthouse that's exactly what I'm going to do. Be with my husband.

I grab my bags and I'm about to exit when Lauren catches my arm. "Prescription?"

"Yes. Thanks." I pull it from my purse and hand it to her. "I really appreciate this and everything."

"Of course. I'll bring it to you so you can at least take it at the lunch break."

I nod and my phone rings with Gabe's number. "Savage told me you're about to be here. I'm waiting outside the courtroom for you. We have five minutes until they reconvene."

"I'll be right there." I disconnect, truly living in an alternative universe when both of my brothers are a part of my day and both are trying to protect me. I really don't know what to do with that information but I'm not rejecting the help. I have a husband and a child to protect.

Savage, looking as big and barbaric as ever, meets me at the door. "Before we go into the courtroom, I need you to come with me."

"Where?" I ask, falling into step with him.

"Woman," he says. "You always have to ask questions."

"Where are we going, Savage?"

It's in that moment that someone grabs me and pulls me into a hallway.

Chapter Sixty-Four

Cat

I yelp with the tug on my arm that pulls me into a deserted hallway, only to be whirled around, and pressed to a wall with Reese's big body molded to mine. "Reese," I breathe out. "Why aren't you—"

He kisses me, a deep, drugging, make-me-moan-right-here-in-the-courthouse kiss that has me pushing on his shoulders and panting out, "What's wrong?"

"Tell me again what the doctor said," he orders softly.

He must suspect I'm pregnant. Does he? "You need to be focused on court. Why aren't you with your client?"

"Cat."

"I told you. She gave me medicine. I'm fine. Lauren went to get it so I can take a dose at lunch. This isn't like you. When you're in court, you're *in* court. What is going on?"

He presses his hands on the wall on either side of me and he looks skyward, torment radiating off of him as he fixes me in a turbulent stare. "I asked the judge for an extra fifteen minutes."

"Why? I know it wasn't to ask about my doctor's appointment."

"There was an envelope delivered to me a few minutes ago. The envelope was marked 'important, read before you go into court.'"

"It was from Debbie," I assume.

"I will assume that to be accurate. It was pictures of you Cat, taken over the course of weeks."

"She's been watching me," I say flatly.

"That's another safe assumption. Cat, there's more."

"More? What more could there be?"

"The note in the envelope said, 'I'm going to tell her everything.'"

I have just a moment that those words punch me in the chest, but it's a moment and it's gone. "We're good," I say. "That means nothing to me."

"I could have hidden it from you, Cat."

"But you didn't. You wouldn't. She's at Reid's office now. I was going to wait and tell you until tonight but she showed up at my doctor's office. Royce's team cornered her, and that's how she ended up with Reid."

"At your doctor's office."

"Yes," I breathe out.

"At seven in the morning."

"Yes," I say, and only now do I realize how crazy that really is. "How could she know where I would be when Royce was watching her? She couldn't have been at her apartment, but rather ours."

"Exactly," he says. "Fuck. I need to call Reid." He pushes off the wall and grabs his phone, dialing my brother on auto-dial, since they talk often for work reasons. The two firms partner on crossover cases and have for years. It's how I know Reid isn't as much of a bastard that I used to think he was, but he can be when he so chooses, and I want him to so choose now.

I listen to Reese and Reid talk for a full minute, with a conversation about the police, among the many fast-moving topics, before Reese disconnects. "He's handling things. Trust him. I do." His hands come down on my shoulders. "I wish I could get out of court, but Dana and the jury and—"

"Go in there and do your job."

"I need you to stay in the building. Come to the back room with the team for lunch. We'll skip the truck."

"She's with Reid. We need that lucky hot dog and she doesn't get to make us hide."

"We're being cautious. We'll order in hot dogs. Don't leave. I need to know—"

"I won't. If it will make you focus, I won't go anywhere without you."

He presses his forehead to mine. "If she touches you, Cole will be defending me. Fuck. Now I know how he felt when that man attacked Lori."

"She was literally attacked. I haven't been and I won't be." I cup his face. "Go win and give me juicy stuff to write about."

His fingers tangle in my hair and he stares down at me. "Do not leave the courthouse."

"I promise."

He kisses me, another deep, drugging, curl my toes kiss, before he releases me, and says, "Don't move." He steps to the edge of the hall, leans around it and then Savage is joining us. "Stay with Savage," he orders, kissing me once more, hard and fast on the lips, and then he's gone.

Savage steps in front of me. "Ready to go to court?"

I stare at this big, hard man, a scar running down his face, and right now, I need a distraction to calm my mind. "How did you get the scar down your face?"

"Enemy combatant overseas."

"What happened to the other guy?" I ask.

"He died. Painfully. Ready to go to court?" he asks again.

"Yes, but just so you know, that story is very comforting right about now."

"Yeah. I should have been a doctor. Great bedside manner and all."

"Then I should tell you something. I'm sick right now. I may have to get up suddenly and go to the bathroom. How do you want to handle that?"

"Gabe's here, but text me and wait for me at the door. If you don't see me, throw up on Gabe or the floor, I really don't care which, but do not leave without me."

"So much for your bedside manner."

"The only good bedside manner is the kind that keeps you safe. Let's go before the crowd makes me pull a running back move to get you into your seat."

I don't laugh but I do start walking. I just want in that courtroom with my husband in the same room. We head down the hallway, and the minute we hit the bustle of people, Savage's hand is on my arm. A few more steps and I spot Gabe waiting by the courtroom door, looking as handsome as ever in a grayish blue suit, his blonde hair rumpled as if he's been running his fingers through his hair anxiously. That's not like my brother and that tells me he knows what happened this morning.

The minute we're in front of him, he pulls me close and hugs me. "Way to make me regret every asshole moment I've ever had with you, little sis." He pulls back to look at me. "I'm repenting. I'm sorry."

"You've already said that to me. Stop saying it. We're okay Gabe."

"We're not, but we're gonna get there." He eyes Savage. "I'm with her. I know the rules. I won't let her leave without you, even to pee."

"Or throw up," Savage says. "You both wait for me."

"Throw up?" Gabe asks, eyeing me. "What does he mean?"

"I'm fine. Lauren is bringing me medicine and it's nothing you'll catch."

"That means pregnancy or food poisoning. Which is it?"

I don't want to lie to my brother, but I have to protect this secret and—I have to protect this secret. "Food poisoning," I say, nearly choking on the lie that I hate. "And I need to get into court." I walk past the doors and Gabe is instantly by my side.

We speak to the guard and he ushers us to the front, near Reese, which is exactly where I need to be right now. I claim my seat and Gabe is instantly beside me and just in time. The jury is returning. In another two minutes, Reese walks into the courtroom and he seeks me out. The minute his eyes meet mine, I feel relief wash over him, and there is a transformation in him. He relaxes into his job and then, in turn, claims the courtroom. He's magnetic, all eyes on him, and for now, I'm forgetting about Debbie. I'm ready for my husband to show us all what he's got.

Reid

About sixty seconds after I disconnect with Reese, with the news that Debbie stalked my sister, for God knows how long, I'm on the phone with Royce Walker to coordinate my plan. I've just hung up when my assistant, Connie, who is attractive, forty, and single, the latter of which she blames on me, appears in my office doorway. "She's throwing another fit. You have to get her out of here. Debbie isn't about to do Dallas, she's about to do our receptionist."

"Do our receptionist?" I repeat dryly.

"As in Freddy Krueger-style, Reid. Wait her out once she's behind bars or in a rubber room."

"That's exactly where she's going."

"To jail or a rubber room?"

"Jail," I say, because I've been watching Debbie on our cameras and she's putting on a show that I'm about to end. No one threatens my sister.

Chapter Sixty-Five

Reid

I walk into the conference room where Debbie is standing at the window. She turns and her lips part as if she expected some fifty-something man with a pot belly and a weak attitude. I shut the door and walk to the table, pressing my fingers to the desk. "What do you want?" I ask, sizing her up. She's pretty, brunette, and all belly.

"What I deserve," she says. "What my baby deserves. To be taken care of."

"How many men have you fucked in the past nine months?"

"It's his baby," she snarls, leaning on the table to face off with me.

My lips twitch. She's easily agitated. That works for me. "How many men have you fucked in the past two years?"

"Why? You want to join the list?" she challenges.

"There's a list," I say. "Interesting."

"He's the father!" she shouts at me, her cheeks flushing.

"How many times did you fuck Reese Summer?"

"Many."

"When and where?" I ask.

"My place," she says. "Often."

"There are security cameras in your building. I checked. So you'll be able to prove that. Make a call and get the videos."

"I have no rights to that footage."

"Offer the landlord a few perks and I'm sure you can work it out."

"You're such a prick."

My lips twitch. "I love it when you talk dirty, sweetheart. It tells me all about you. I'll be back in fifteen minutes." I head for the door.

"Come back here, asshole!"

I exit the office and leave her there to simmer and panic. She doesn't have control. She won't ever have control. I do. I have control. I will end this for my sister.

Cat

Court is delayed, and we aren't told why. We just wait and wait and I start to worry the threats from Debbie escalated in some way, perhaps by way of an accomplice, and Reese had to delay the return. Thirty minutes into the wait, my phone buzzes with a text and I discretely check it to read a message from Reese: *The judge is the delay. We don't know why. I didn't want you to think it was something else.*

I'm touched and relieved that he's thought of me, but I don't want to feed his need to worry about me either which is why I refrain from asking what he knows about Reid and Debbie. He'd tell me if he knew anything. *Thank you for telling me. That's weird with the judge,* I type instead. *Is he with the prosecutor?*

I'm told no, Reese replies. *I'll let you know if I get an update on anything.*

I show the messages to Gabe and his brow furrows. "Maybe he has a woman in his chamber," he jokes.

I scowl. "Did you really just say that?"

He nudges me. "Laugh, little sis."

I laugh. "Okay. There. Happy?"

Finally, Reese and his team enter the courtroom and my nerves about what was happening before he entered, linger on the personal. Did Debbie do something else?

"He'll be fine," Gabe says, from beside me, as Reese settles at his table in the courtroom. "He's a pro and he knows you're safe. He'll step into his zone."

"I know," I say, but Gabe and I both know there's no way Reese isn't affected by Debbie's threats. He's human. I look at Gabe and lower my voice. "Thank you. I need you and you're here."

He squeezes it. "From now on, Cat."

I believe him when there was a time not that long ago I would not have. I still hurt over the way he and Reid treated me when I decided to go my own way, outside of the family business, but showing Gabe the letter mom left me, changed him. Maybe it changed Reid more than I realized, too.

The judge enters the courtroom and we all stand which has me wishing I was sitting. This baby wants me hanging over a toilet and I really can't wait to get my meds. We sit and the judge wastes no time getting us started. The prosecutor takes the floor and I grab my notebook and a pen. He calls the medical examiner, a fifty-something, heavy-set man with gray hair and glasses, to the stand. The questions are basic but avoid all the damning topics. I write down what I expect Reese to ask and Gabe grabs the pad and reads my list.

He smiles and winks at me as if telling me how on target I am. I shouldn't need his approval but he's my older brother and for so long he and Reid were driven by my father's anger at my independence and they didn't even read my books. I hit the *New York Times* bestseller list for my first true crime novel, and if they had known, they didn't act like it. It hurt. It stills does.

Reese stands up and walks to the stand, confidence radiating off of him. The prosecutor left holes that a lesser attorney would potentially miss. Reese will nail them all. "Mr. Monts," he says. "How tall do the forensics indicate the shooter to be?"

I check off one of the items on my list.

"That's inconclusive," Mr. Monts states. "The shooter was eye level with the victim who was sitting at the time of the bullet's impact."

"In other words, the shooter was sitting in front of the victim who was sitting on the couch in his den?"

"That's my conclusion, yes," Mr. Monts agrees.

"Objection," the prosecutor shouts. "Leading the witness."

Reese looks at the prosecutor and laughs, "I'll rephrase." He looks at Mr. Monts. "Were you made aware of the location of the body when it was found?"

"Yes."

"Where was the body found, Mr. Monts?"

"On the couch in the den of his home," he replies.

"And you know this how?" Reese asks.

"I was at the crime scene," he supplies.

"You were at the crime scene. Forgive me for asking the obvious, but did you see the body?"

"Yes," Mr. Monts states. "I did an extensive inspection."

"Was there any indication of the sex of the shooter?" Reese asks.

I check off another one of my points.

"Nothing discernible."

"I see," Reese says. "And why is that?"

"Because the shooter was at eye level when they fired."

"And you know this how?" Reese asks.

"The projection, entry and exit points of the bullet, as well as blood splatter."

"Under what situation can you suggest the sex and height of a shooter?" Reese asks.

"That goes back to blood splatter, entry and exit points, and to that end, even the size of the weapon in a female's versus male's hand can impact entry point."

"And with this weapon and the location of entry," Reese says, "is there anything that indicates the shooter was male or female?"

"There was not."

Reese continues to question him for another half hour before taking his seat. The prosecutor stands. "Mr. Monts, is there anything in your findings that rules out Dana Warren as the shooter?"

"There is not."

Gabe reaches for my pen and writes, "Weak."

And of course, I know he means the prosecutor. I take the pen and write, "The entire case is weak. The DA has a history of charging just to charge."

Gabe nods as if he's well aware of the problem. Of course he is. Reid has just finished suing the DA, and winning, over charging the wrong person, among a variety of other sins. A case that I'm writing a book about with Lori, and plan to release as soon as I know the DA can't lash out at Reese, which means after the DA leaves office.

The rest of the morning continues on with Reese ruling the courtroom, but if Dana sees this as good news, and it is, she doesn't show it. She's thrumming her fingers on the table often and even thumping her foot. I write this down to ensure I warn Reese that it's happening. Right about that time, Reese leans in toward Dana, and whispers to her, and her foot stops moving. I scratch out the note. He knew. He saw. Of course, he did. It makes her look uneasy in ways that she certainly has a right, but could also be read as a sign she's guilty.

Finally, it's lunchtime and the courtroom is adjourned. Reese turns and seeks me out, the look in his eyes warning me to be careful. The fact that this is where his head is now, tells me somehow, he's performed like a master when he never really let go of his fears for my safety. I nod and he turns to follow his team out of the room. Once we're at the door of the courtroom, Savage meets us.

"Any news from Reid on Debbie?" I ask.

"Nothing," Savage says. "But I need you to come with me, Cat." He looks at Gabe. "Alone. Reese wants to see her alone."

"I'm going to the office to see what I can find out about Debbie anyway," Gabe says, turning to me. "I'll call you the minute I know what's happening but I suspect Reid is behind closed doors with Debbie." He pulls me to him and whispers, "Be safe. I'll call you later." He kisses my temple and leaves. *He kissed my temple.* I'm in the twilight zone.

Savage clears his throat. "Ready?"

"Yes. I'm ready." We start walking and I grab my phone from my purse, quickly punching the auto-dial for Reid. When he doesn't answer I dial his secretary.

"Hey, Cat," Connie says and without me asking she adds, "He's in the conference room with Debbie. He keeps leaving her in there and then going back."

I puff out a breath. "He's told you nothing?

"No, but he's working some strategy. And his strategies work."

"Okay. Thanks. If you hear anything—"

"I'll call." We disconnect, and I realize that we've walked to the side exit door. "I thought I was staying here and eating with Reese?"

"He's asked me to escort you to another location."

"The park," I say.

He glances over at me. "Yes. The park."

That Reese wants to meet out in the open seems like good news and I quicken my pace, hoping that I'm about to arrive at the park and find out that our problems with Debbie are over. We take the walk briskly and the minute I see Reese standing at the food trucks, I rush toward him and into his arms. He grabs me and drags me out of the walkway, behind the truck. "What's happened?" I ask.

He answers by tangling fingers in my hair and kissing me, leaving me just as desperate for more of the kiss as I am the answer to my question.

Chapter Sixty-Six

Cat

Reese thoroughly kisses me, a passionate, deep kiss, behind a food truck in the park, where we first started to get to know each other. "I cannot stand the idea that she was following you," he says, tearing his mouth from mine, "that she came to your doctor's office. It scares the shit out of me and you know I don't get rattled."

"You can't be rattled. You have court."

"I'm just fine in the courtroom with you there, but Debbie clearly has someone working with her. She didn't follow you, Cat. She knew where you were and went to you." His hands settle on my shoulders. "That's a problem."

"A private investigator maybe?"

"Or an accomplice as crazy or crazier than her. Royce is working on it. We have a team around us working on this. Savage is staying with you everywhere you go."

"Under the circumstances, I'm not going to complain."

He cups my face. "But even with all of this going on, I came here for a reason. This place is part of our good luck ritual, it's a part of us. We're not giving that up. No one takes anything that is us from us."

Our ritual. Our good luck. It's his trial, but since we met he treats everything like it's ours. And so do I. My hand presses to his chest. "No. No, we're not. Let's get your hot dog."

He cups my face. "You really haven't doubted me once, have you?"

"No, I haven't. I'd know if you were cheating. We wouldn't be us anymore."

"You would and so would I, not many couples can say that."

"Debbie picked the wrong couple," I say.

"Yes," he agrees, lacing his hand with mine. "She did." His blue eyes are warm and the bond between us rich with history and the friendship that has made our relationship everything and more.

We round the truck and Reese orders his hot dog and my ritual bag of nuts. I don't spy Savage anywhere, but I know he's here, watching us, protecting us. "I'm going to try to call Reid," I say.

"I talked to him on the way over here," Reese says, handing me my nuts and a bottle of water.

"And?"

"Not much to tell," he says, accepting his hot dog and facing me, he motions me forward. "Let's go sit."

I nod and we move to our favorite bench behind the truck, far away from the courthouse and press craziness. "Debbie told Reid I visited her apartment regularly. He told her he wanted the security footage. She refused. Reid called Royce to see if his team can retrieve it."

"Can they?" I ask.

"Royce said he'd already pulled the footage to look for an accomplice. As far as proving I was never there," he looks at me, "and I wasn't, never, not even the two times I was with her, he's working on it, but he needs to narrow the timeline. He's guessing based on her pregnancy timeline. And even that's a guess. Reid said he'd work on pinning her down."

"She's still at his office?"

"Yes. He basically left her in the conference room simmering. He also said she continues to ask for a million dollars but he hasn't gotten her to say what she'll do if she doesn't get it, yet."

I know what there is to know now and I decide it's time to refocus my husband. "How'd you feel about this morning?"

"I'd feel unchallenged if not for the audio release. This case is a joke. There's no evidence, but that audio hitting right before court, when the jury could hear it, lingers in my mind, as it will in theirs. They'll want to convict her."

"When you look at it like that, then maybe the DA did release the tape. He'd have gambled that you wouldn't postpone the trial. And why wouldn't he gamble with such a weak case?"

Reese finishes off a bite of his hot dog. "Regardless, and as it always is, the only way to one hundred percent get a client set free is to force a confession from someone else or at least prove guilt. We won't prove guilt so we need to force the confession."

"The boyfriend?"

"Yes." He tosses his trash in the can next to him. "He's all I've got right now. I've been working to keep him in her favor until he testifies on her behalf, but she's angry with him over that leaked call." He tilts his head. "Unless she and the boyfriend think we assume the DA did it. Then they'll both hold steady and let me do my thing. Yes. That works." He kisses me. "These talks with you always help." He breathes out and pulls me close. "No one takes this, or anything, from us, and no one takes you from me, which means that tonight we make some decisions."

"What does that mean?"

"Someone is helping Debbie, Cat. We may need to consider having Savage take you to the family ranch in Texas. Just to get you out of here until I end this."

"No. No, you need me here. I'm in the courtroom. You can see me. We need to be together and I have Savage."

His phone buzzes with a text. "I need you with me the rest of our lives. That means protecting you."

"No one takes our rituals. Remember?"

"Cat—"

"I'm not leaving you. I'll stay with Savage but, Reese, she could come after you, too. You can't leave. I can't take being at a distance with you as the only target. And look at your text message. You have to."

He grimaces and grabs his phone, only for his grimace to deepen. "Dana is fighting with her boyfriend who was allowed to visit her for lunch. I have to go. We'll talk tonight." He stands and pulls me to my feet.

"What if I talk to Dana? Girl to girl stuff? Maybe have her over for dinner?"

He scrubs his jaw. "Maybe. She likes you. She reads your column. Right now, let's get Savage and get back to the courthouse." He sends a text and turns to me, his hand on my shoulder. "I do need you here, Cat. I do. You're always in this with me, but I can't lose you. I won't. And lord help that woman and anyone helping her if anyone comes near you again."

He says those words so fiercely, that it's clear he means them. He pulls me close, under his arm, and sets us in motion and I can feel his torment radiating off of him. Am I helping him by staying or hurting him? I don't know the right answer. Stay or go?

Reid

I'm behind my desk, and it's forty-five minutes after I left Debbie in the conference room because she has yet to leave, which was exactly why I left her there so long; to find out if she'd stay or go. Someone with a real case walks out because they can. Because they know they are going to win. Someone faking has to stay and work for the payout before they get caught. My cellphone rings and a glance at caller ID tells me it's Royce. "She just made a call to a man named Wilson Moore," he tells me when I answer. "He's an attorney who went to law school with Reese. He now practices at a local firm but he's considered average at best."

"And he hates Reese for his success," I assume. "What do you have on the apartment feed?"

"We're working on it."

"I'll get her to name exact times Reese was there," I say. "That pins her in another lie."

"More soon," Royce says and we disconnect.

I stand and exit my office, making my way to the conference room where our scam artist waits. I enter the room to find her sitting at the long, rectangular table. I walk to her and press my hands on the desk again, leaning in her direction. "Where's my video footage?"

"I'm not giving you that and having you blackmail people I know."

Blackmail is on her mind, I think. "What do you want?"

"A million dollars," she replies. "I've already stated this."

"You aren't getting a million dollars. So I repeat, what do you want?"

"I'll negotiate with Reese himself. I want to talk to Reese."

"That's not happening. Why did you follow Cat this morning?"

"To apologize. I know this hurts her. I shouldn't have gone at her like I did at the courthouse."

"How did you know where she was?" I demand.

"I followed her."

She's lying. Royce's men were following her and she never had eyes on Cat. "I'm going to ask this one more time: What do you want?"

"To talk to Reese," she repeats.

"That's not happening so you think about what you really want and I'll be back later." I start walking toward the door.

"I'll go to the press," she calls after me.

I turn to look at her. "You'll go to the press if what?"

"If I don't get my million dollars."

I could let her think she has me by the balls, but I just don't have that in me. "Cat would welcome that. Her column would become even more popular than it already is and she'd write a book about this entire event, and make millions. To which she'd invest in the firm to offset any damage you did. You aren't talking to Reese and if we're doing the whole press thing I'll call Cat and tell her it's a go."

"We both know they don't want a scandal. That's hard to get by."

I'm done with this woman. I walk to the desk. "Thirty thousand. You sign a gag order. Take it or leave it."

"I'm not taking that ridiculous offer."

"Very well. This is goodbye then." I head for the door and she shouts, "You're such a dirty prick!"

I grab the door handle but don't turn. "I am a dirty prick," I say. "Tell my receptionist if you want to take the deal. Otherwise, leave or I'll call the police and have you removed." I open the door and exit it, shutting it behind me, but not before I hear her sob. That's what happens when scam artists fail. They cry. And if she comes near my sister again. I'll do far more than make her cry, but at least Cat's husband is a damn good criminal attorney.

Chapter Sixty-Seven

Reese

I don't want to let Cat out of my sight, which is why when we arrive at the courthouse again, I keep her close. "Come back to our holding area with me," I say, as we enter the side door.

"No," she says, turning to face me. "I'm reminding you about another problem. You go focus on your case." She motions to Savage. "I have a beast protecting me."

"Indeed she does," Savage assures him.

"And you have some problem to deal with or they wouldn't have called you back early."

I inhale and let it out, dragging her to me, and turning us away from Savage. "I'll make this Debbie thing go away. I promise." I cup her face and kiss her. "I'll see you in court."

"See you in court," she says, and when I would move away, she catches my jacket lapel. "I didn't get to tell you, but you were perfection this morning. You won every witness."

I've never cared about anyone's critique but that of the jury, simply because I can't allow that kind of noise in my head, and still stay focused. But Cat is different. I care what she thinks. I kiss her again. "See you soon." I release her and start walking, dialing Reid again as I do.

He answers on the first ring. "I just gave her the take it or leave it offer we discussed."

"And?"

"She called me a dirty prick." He laughs. "Usually women are naked when they use those particular words, but hey, I'll take it. She was pissed. That's when we get the emotional response that makes her dish out a threat I'll record."

"But she didn't."

"Not yet. But she will. I left her in the conference room and told her to leave. Thus far, she has not. I got this, man. Aren't you supposed to be in court?"

"Soon. I'll call you if we get a break, but Reid, I need this to be over. I don't want this affecting me and Cat."

"Trust me, I have it under control."

Trust him. A man who has caused Cat all kinds of pain.

He seems to read my mind. "She's my sister, Reese. I do love her."

"Tell her that. It won't matter coming from me. Do this for me for all the shit I've done for you." I hang up and round the corner to our team's private hallway. Elsa rushes toward me. "We have a problem. Dana had a fight with Reginald and ten minutes later, Richard saw the DA talking to him."

"I've been gone half an hour. How did she have a fight with that man that pushed him to the DA that quickly?"

"Like you said, quickly," she says. "She called him on her break and then she was shouting at him."

"What did she say?"

"Name calling, but nothing of substance. It was fast."

I rub the tension at the back of my neck. "Where is she?"

"Conference room."

I cut around her and head down the hall, opening the door to find Dana pacing. "I failed miserably at being nice to him. I know he released that audio. I feel it. It's eating at me. He's the only one that gains from my father's death directly if I inherit and he marries me," she runs a hand through her hair. "I hate this money. I will never know if anyone wants me for me."

This makes me think of Cat, and how much it meant to me that my money wasn't a motivation to her. I didn't have to wonder. She had her own money. "Marry a rich man. That's not him."

"I wanted to marry someone I loved but—did he kill my father and let me go through this hell?"

I walk to the conference table across from her but I don't answer her question. "He was just talking to the prosecutor. What does he have on you?"

"He talked to the prosecutor?"

"Right after you fought."

"I have not lied to you. There is nothing. That call was the only time I said anything like what I said and I was at my wit's end. He knew it though. He didn't want me to walk away from the money."

"You think he did it?"

"It's clawing at me," she says. "I think he might have. I don't want that to be true. That means he doesn't love me. I want to take him down."

"Then make nice with him until I get him on the stand and off. I cannot have him turn on you, in front of the jury."

"I'm trying."

"Try harder Dana."

A knock sounds on the door and a guard pokes his head in. "The judge wants to see you in chambers."

"That doesn't sound good," Dana says. "Right?"

It's a problem, I think, but I say, "It happens. It'll happen again after this time. Pull yourself together. Figure out how to reel your man back in." I don't wait for a reply. I turn and head into the hallway while the guard motions me forward.

Elsa quickly catches up. "What's happening?"

"The judge wants to see me."

"Any idea why?"

"None."

"I bet it has to do with that meeting Richard saw."

"Don't speculate," I say. "We'll know in a few minutes and I'd rather know in chambers than in court if we have a problem."

She stops walking and lets me pull ahead. Sixty seconds later, I'm stepping into the judge's chambers. He's behind his desk, not yet in his robes. "Sit, Mr. Summer."

I claim the seat in front of his heavy mahogany desk, bookshelves with law volumes on my left and right. "Your honor," I say.

He tosses an envelope in front of me. I open it and pull out a photo of me that has writing on it in red pen that reads, "Pig. Liar. Bastard. Cheater." I suck in a breath and look up at him. "What is this?"

"You tell me. It was delivered to my office while we were in court this morning."

Debbie, I think, and she most definitely has a partner. I stick the photo back in the envelope. "Is this confidential?"

"Yes. Speak freely."

"A few years ago I had a stalker who faded away. She's back and I've hired private security, but obviously, she's not dissuaded. I don't want to delay the trial, but extra security wouldn't be a bad idea."

"Understood and as long as I feel no one else is in danger, we'll continue. But are you in danger, Mr. Summer?"

"I'm not concerned about me, I'm concerned about my wife."

"What do you need from me?"

"Nothing. Not unless you have a tip as to how I convince her to leave town."

He chuckles. "Been married twenty years, son. Never convinced my wife to do what she's dead set on not doing, but I'll recess the afternoon to give you a chance to try. Go. Do what you can to protect her."

"Thank you, your honor." I stand and head for the door, dialing Royce as I do.

"We're recessing for the afternoon. I need to see you at my place, immediately. There's a development."

"I'll be there."

"Can you tell Savage to get Cat and meet me at the side door?"

"Done."

I disconnect and exit to the hallway and Elsa and Richard are waiting. "Well?" Elsa asks.

"The judge is recessing for the afternoon. Be at my place at seven." I walk past them and enter the conference room, where Dana is once again pacing.

"Afternoon recess. Use it wisely." I turn and exit to find Elsa and Richard standing in front of us.

"Why are we recessing?"

As it stands they know nothing of the extra security for any reason other than Dana's getting a lot of hate. "A personal situation, per the judge." I turn away from them on that statement that isn't a lie. I didn't say who had the personal situation and they'll assume it was the judge.

I'm out of the hallway quickly cutting left and when I arrive at the door, Cat's not there yet. I turn and wait, watching her appear in the corridor with Savage, the sway of her hips mesmerizing. I watch her every step, and when she's in front of me, I kiss her and lead her to the vehicle. Once we're in the backseat with Savage behind the wheel he claimed from one of his co-workers, I drag Cat to me and kiss her. "What's wrong?"

"Nothing you can't solve," I assure her, before pressing my lips to her ear. "Once I'm inside you, and I will be soon."

Chapter Sixty-Eight

Cat

The minute Reese and I are in the back of the SUV with Savage in the front seat, I ask the question, "Why did court dismiss? What's going on?"

"There was a delivery to the judge, meant for me," he says and holds up a finger. "Hold on, sweetheart." He looks to the front seat. "Savage, before you drive, you need to see this." He pulls an envelope with the photo from his briefcase and hands it to Savage before turning to me. "A photo of me with words written over the top of it. It's an obvious threat."

"Debbie," I say. "She's telling you she'll go public. Gabe was right. She'll do it just to get us to pay her off and make her go away."

"Reid's made her a small offer," Reese says. "I'm counting on him ending this."

Savage hands the photo back to Reese. "In a rare move for me, I'll hold my thoughts until we're in the company of Royce."

Reese takes the photo and hands it to me. I suck in a breath and open it, reading the words written across the surface. I hate the word "cheater," scrawled over his image, not because I don't trust Reese, but because it just feels bad, like our perfect relationship, and it is perfect, is being questioned by the world. It shouldn't matter what others think, and it really doesn't, but it still twists me in knots.

I shove the photo back in the envelope. "I want this to end." I look at Reese. "But I do not want to reward someone for this behavior with money. Part of me really just wants to write about this, Reese. It ends this. We take control. We handle the blow. I go back to the money I could make. I'll go to my publisher, pitch a book about it and we can take the payout to invest in the firm, to offset any damage."

"There's no guarantee she goes away," he says. "We don't know her mental health."

"Someone else is helping her," I say, rejecting that idea. "There's no other way she found me today. It has to be about money. We take away the payout, and they move on."

"Let's wait and see what Royce and Reid have to offer."

"I'm here you know," Savage reminds us.

"You and Royce are one," Reese says, to which Savage murmurs something incomprehensible.

Reese tunes him out, rotating to face me. "I'm going to make this go away. I promise."

I cover his hand with mine. "*We're* going to make it go away. You and me."

He brushes his lips over mine, but there is a shift in him, an edginess, that defies the delicateness of the kiss. I know this man. When he's on edge, he needs certain things, he needs *me*. As if reading my mind, he presses his lips to my ear. "I need you alone," he whispers. "Really damn badly."

"Soon," I promise as my cellphone rings.

Reese presses his forehead to mine and then breathes out as if the interruption is an unwelcome reminder of the here and now, but he kisses my temple and says, "Take your call."

I grab my phone to find Lauren's number. "Hey," I say.

"I'm meeting you at your apartment. I have your meds. I'm sorry it took me so long. I had a client with a crisis. What's happening?"

"We're pulling up to the apartment now. I'll explain upstairs. And thank you on the meds."

"Okay. I'll see you in a few."

We disconnect and as soon as we pull up to the door Savage says, "Don't move. My man is taking the car and I'm coming around to get you."

Reese takes my hand, and we are quickly ushered inside where Royce is waiting by the elevator. "The judge on my case received this," Reese says, handing him the envelope. We step into the elevator and Royce glances at the contents once we're there, but says nothing. Despite my urgency to hear his opinion, I like this about Royce. He's discreet. He won't say anything in a place that could have a camera.

And so I endure the elevator ride and walk to the apartment. We're just heading inside when Lauren comes running down the hall. "I'm here." She holds up a bag. "I have the meds."

Reese opens the door and lets Royce, Lauren, and Savage, inside, but holds me back just inside the hallway. "How *do* you feel?"

"Right now, I'm okay," I say, "and I hope that means it's over."

He presses me against the wall. "Cat, we need to make an agreement right now. If Royce believes you're in danger, I need you to go to the ranch, and take Savage along for the ride."

"My job is to cover this trial and even if it wasn't, I'm not leaving you with a crazy woman stalking you."

"Sweetheart, we're going to fight over this and I'm going to win. That's just how it is."

"You don't get to say that's how it is. I'm going through this, too. And we don't even know what's happening with her and Reid or even what Royce's assessment is."

His hands go to the wall beside my head. "I'm going to win on this, Cat. I don't do this to you often. I don't want or need to win with you, ever, until now. Because I love you, you will do this if Royce thinks it's best. Because you love me, you will do it."

His voice is hard, and yet it radiates with emotion. He's coming out of his skin, I realize now. He's really worried, beyond just trying to be cautious. I press my hands to his face. "Let's go talk to Royce, then you and I will talk."

He covers my hands. "You understand that I—"

"I don't need you to finish that sentence. I understand. I just—can we talk about this alone?"

He takes my hand and kisses it. "The sooner the better." He laces his fingers with mine and we walk into the kitchen where everyone has gathered around the island. Lauren has set a bottle of pills on the counter with water. "Thank you," I say, stepping to the spot across from her, while Reese stands across from Royce. Savage is at the endcap between Reese and Royce.

"What's the assessment?" Reese asks.

Royce replies, "We have footage of Debbie with an attorney named Wilson Moore, who I believe is your competitor."

"Hardly," Reese replies. "He's just not that good and I know this because—"

"You went to school with him," Royce supplies. "We're operating on the assumption that he's looking to ruin you, and get a payoff. Is the baby his? Could be. Right now, we're working through all of his electronic data, looking for proof. What we need you and Reid to do is buy time with Debbie. Keep her from going public before we can take them down. Even if Reid gets Debbie to blackmail you, something damning from Moore seals an arrest."

"This is good news then in some ways, right?" I ask. "We know what we're dealing with."

"This doesn't make Debbie any less crazy," Savage says. "This just means that Moore knew how to manipulate that crazy."

"I want Cat to get out of town," Reese says. "Go to my family ranch and stay off the radar."

"While I'd feel the same way," Royce says. "I don't want to make a sudden move that somehow triggers a retreat that would be temporary and keeps us from taking these two down. Give it twenty-four hours. If between us and Reid we have nothing, then yes. We'll get her off the radar with protection."

Reese's jaw clenches and I can tell he's not pleased. "What about the photo?"

"We'll run it for prints," Royce says, "but my gut is that it's simply meant to pressure you into settling. Reid's already told her you'll settle. He just needs to drag this out and make them think they have a chance. That's what I told him, but I also said that I'd confirm once I talked to you."

"When was the last time you talked to Reid?" Reese asks before I can.

"Right before we got on the elevator. She's still in his office." He narrows his eyes on Reese and I have this sense that he gets how on edge Reese is and as a friend, he knows very well how abnormal that is. "Why don't we let you two have some time to deal with this your way? Give me until five. I'll stop back by, but I'll call if we get a big breakthrough."

Lauren rounds the island, hugs me, and Reese walks everyone to the door. I wait for him in the kitchen and when he doesn't return timely, I exit to the living room to find him standing at the window, staring out over the city. I walk to him and squeeze between him and the window. "Talk to me."

His fingers tangle into my hair. "Talking before fucking is overrated." His mouth closes down on mine.

Chapter Sixty-Nine

Cat

We're still in front of the window, and Reese isn't just kissing me. He's devouring me, his tongue licking into my mouth, one hand caressing my breast while the other drags my skirt up my hips. His hand cups my backside, fingers stroking along the seam, dipping low until he's teasing my sex from behind. I moan into his mouth, our lips parting as he cups both cheeks and lifts me. My shoes don't make the ride, and I wrap my legs around his waist.

He carries me to the couch and I lower my legs, sliding down his body, and he drags my dress over my head, tossing it as he shrugs out of his jacket. I reach for his tie and pull it away, my fingers already working his buttons and he impatiently pulls it over his head, tossing it aside. He cups my face. "You know what I need."

"Yes," I whisper because I know this man. I know when he's about to explode when he is at a rare limit and needs me.

He kisses me and my hands slide down his zipper, over the hard ridge of his erection, stroking him even as I unzip him. His cellphone rings. I pull back. "Your phone."

He tangles fingers in my hair. "Ask me if I care right now, Cat."

"But it could be-"

He kisses me, a deep thrust of tongue while managing to unhook my bra and cup my breast. I moan as he pinches my nipple. "I don't care right now," he murmurs, before kneeling and linking his fingers in the silk strings at my hips to drag my panties down. "Step."

I obediently do as he says, and then his hands are on my hips, his breath warm on my belly moments before he licks my clit. I bite my lips and reach for his hair, but his damn phone rings again. "Reese."

He stands up and grabs his phone from his pocket and without looking at it, he tosses it across the room. He shoves his pants and underwear down and then he's pulling me close, rotating us. He sits down and pulls me on top of him. His erection presses to my stomach and my hand covers it. He drags my mouth to his. "This, I care about. This is what I need. You, Cat." He kisses me, a deep drugging kiss, lifting me somewhere in the middle of it until I'm sliding down the hard, so very hard, length of him, and he's stretching me, filling me. I take all of him and there is no lingering or holding back in either of us. It's like a band breaks, and we are wild.

We move together, rocking together, touching each other. His hands are rough in that way I like them rough, his hand cupping my breast, pinching my nipples, plucking at them. Mine are on his arms, his chest. My teeth scrape his shoulder, my lips reaching for his lips again. He catches my hair and holds my mouth a breath from his. "I need you to go to the ranch."

"What? How can you think of that right now?"

"I need you to do this." He kisses me and his fingers slide down my butt and press inside me, filling me from both directions. "Reese," I breathe out, but he's rocking us, and sensations are rocking me. I can't breathe for how much I need him right now. I can't think for the way he's everywhere and yet I want more. He kisses me desperately, drinking me in, and I am just as desperate and I'm not sure if I'm moving or he's moving me but his fingers and his cock, and oh God. I'm right there. I'm so right there and I tumble into orgasm. I quake, trembling and incapable of anything but feeling the ripple of pure pleasure overtake my body. Reese's grip on my back firms and his fingers slip from inside me, setting on my backside and he shudders into release. And then we're both collapsing, him into the cushion, the hard muscles of his body easing while I melt into him.

His phone rings somewhere in the distance and still, he ignores it. He rolls me to my side, and follows, reaching for the tissue, but he doesn't let me go. He pulls out and then wraps his leg around mine, his hand settling on my hip. "I need to know you're safe."

"I need to know *you're* safe. We have men protecting me and I'm a control freak. I will worry constantly, but I – I don't want to affect your trial. I'll go if Royce says that I need to go."

"Promise me."

"Yes. I promise, but—" I look away with a thought I don't even want to vocalize.

He cups my face and pulls my gaze to his. "But what, Cat?"

"If she goes public and I'm gone, everyone will assume you cheated and I left. I don't think that's good for your reputation."

"I'm not worried about my reputation, but I'm worried about you and us. But you're right. It would look bad and you have to endure that when you come back."

My hand goes to his cheek. "We're better together."

"We are better together. You're right, but it's my instinct to get you to shelter."

"You're my shelter. My safe place. Don't take that from me." I kiss him and his phone rings again.

He groans. "I better answer the damn thing." He stands up and in all his naked, hard perfection, he walks across the room and picks up his phone, and eyes the number, his brow furrowing. "Dana. What's happening?" He listens a minute while I pull on my bra and panties. "Yes," he says to something. "I'll have a car bring you here." He disconnects and looks at me. "She wants to talk." He eyes his caller ID. "She called four times total, one of which I don't remember because I was distracted by better things."

"Any idea what it's about?"

He crosses and sets his phone on the table, pulling on his underwear and pants. "No, and as you know, no attorney wants that kind of call in the middle of a trial."

"What does your gut say?"

"It's a problem."

In other words, he's afraid she's going to confess and he doesn't defend guilty people.

Reid

Debbie doesn't leave and I let her simmer while Gabe camps out on my couch, watching the conference room feed with me, on the couch in my office. We've just heard about the photo sent to the judge being the reason court recessed, via Royce Walker, when Connie appears in my doorway and announces, "She's demanding to see you and not nicely. Now?"

"Yes. Now," I say of my plan I've cooked up with Connie. "Tell her I'm in a meeting and offer her coffee. Try to get her to talk."

"It's going to be hard to be nice to that woman, but I get it. Good cop, bad cop, and all that stuff."

"You'll rock her world, Connie," Gabe encourages.

She frowns. "I'd rather the right man rock mine. Hers has apparently been rocked quite well. At least that's the story her belly tells."

She turns and exits the office.

Gabe laughs. "One day a man is going to rock her world and you're going to be fucked. She'll focus on him, not her job and no one else can tolerate you. Not even me."

I ignore him as is my way with Gabe, and I refocus on my computer screen where the feed from the conference room where Debbie waits is being fed. Connie enters. "Where is he?" Debbie demands, still standing, and ready to attack.

"He's in a meeting," she says. "I slipped him a note that you wanted to talk. Can I get you water or coffee?"

"I need to talk to Reese."

"He'll be here. You okay?"

She bristles. "Why wouldn't I be okay?"

"You're obviously upset."

"Your boss is an ass."

"I know," she says and points to a chair. "Let's sit. You'll feel better. Are you sure you don't want water?"

"No. I'm fine. I'll just have to pee again. It's constant." She sits down.

"I hear that," Connie says. "I don't have a man or kids."

"Why not? You're beautiful." Her eyes go wide. "You and Reid?"

"Oh God no," she says just a little too fiercely. "He's pretty to look at, but he's a beast."

"And yet you work for him?"

"He's fair and I get him like most don't. He likes people to be frank. Tell him what you want. When you play games with a man like Reid you piss him off or challenge him to win, and he will win. He's a beast. That wasn't a joke. And this case is for a friend. He's making no money. He wants it over." The receptionist does as we've planned and pokes her head in on schedule. "I need you, Connie."

"I'll be right there," Connie says and lowers her voice. "I gotta go. I'll check on Reid, but be sure to tell him what you want."

"I did. I want a million dollars. No less. I'm not taking less."

Connie grimaces. "Oh. Well, he won't do that. Try lower." She stands and heads for the door.

Debbie's face reddens and anger pinches her face. "She's ready for me," I say.

"That she is," Gabe agrees.

I stand and head that direction, passing Connie as she returns. "She's all yours."

I nod and make my way to the conference room. The minute I'm inside and shut the door, Debbie gives me what I want. "Tell Reese I want a million dollars by Monday morning or the morning news will be about him and his love child he's denied." She rubs her belly. "And sure you can take that threat to the police, but I'll sing like a songbird in jail." She smirks. "Good luck finding a way to cheat me."

She thinks she's smart. She's not. She's bluffing and I don't get bluffed, especially by the woman making my sister's life hell. "Then you must know already that giving birth in jail and giving up your baby won't be that bad," I say. "There will be lots of women in jail with you, who want to comfort you all up close and personal. Take the thirty thousand or go to jail. You have until tomorrow morning or I'll take the video of your threat to the police."

She stares me down, and to her credit she doesn't blink. She laughs. "You underestimate me, pretty boy." And then she rounds the table and heads for the door.

Chapter Seventy

Reese

Despite a preference to return to the couch and remain naked with Cat pressed close, I dress, sans the tie and jacket while calling Royce to pick up Dana. I then call my team and tell them to head over sooner than later. I've barely tied my damn shoes when Reid calls, "Gabe and I are on the way over. I'll send you an electronic file to watch before we get there."

"My client and staff are on their way here, so be warned," I say. "My client is in some kind of freak out."

"Then you better watch fast. I sent it to Royce, too."

I disconnect and Cat is standing in front of me, now dressed in sweats and a tee. "What was that?"

"Reid and Gabe are headed here. They sent us a video of Debbie to watch."

"A video?" she swallows hard. "Okay. I am not looking forward to that."

I pull her to me and kiss her. "They would have warned me if it was going to upset you. Let's hope it's her confession or a bribe."

"Right. Yes. Let's watch."

I grab my MacBook from my briefcase and Cat and I go in the kitchen to set it up on the island. A few minutes later we're watching Debbie dare us to arrest her. When the video ends, both of us stand there a minute. "First thought?" I ask.

"Bitch." She eyes me. "What's yours?"

"Bitch. Second thought?"

"If you pay her off she will never go away. Just get her arrested. I'll write about it and we'll just weather the storm. She only holds us captive if we let her."

I turn to face her. "I'm not ruling that out as an option but let's hear everyone's input then make a decision."

"Agreed."

The doorbell rings and I grab Cat and pull her to me, kissing her soundly on the lips before I release her and walk to the door. I open it to find Gabe and Reid standing there, looking like fire and ice, as I call them, in damn near the same body. Gabe being the fire because he's always chasing women and money, and Reid the ice because he's as cold a bastard as they come.

"We're in the kitchen."

I leave them there and start walking, they follow and end up on the opposite side of the island from me and Cat. "Royce wants me to call her back and tell her we'll make a deal to drag this out and get ammunition on her and this asshole attorney working with her," Reid says. "I think the bitch is ready to blow. I told Royce I can't promise him more than a week."

"Agreed," Gabe says. "She's not going to back down or take the thirty grand and go away. I think you have to wait her and a DNA test out. If she goes public, and you don't care, you get your redemption. Call your agent, Cat, and cash in on this."

"My issue is not the publicity," I say. "I want Cat safe. I want Debbie committed if that's what it takes. You did a damn good job of helping us get there. Drag her along. Get me more. Get us everything we can use to get her behind bars or in a hospital. That makes Cat safe."

"She'll insist on talking to you," Reid says.

Cat's hands go to mine, instead of her pulling away. She doesn't like the idea. That's what she's telling me. "That's a deal breaker," I say. "Tell her that. I've already told you that. It won't change."

The doorbell rings. "That will be my client."

"I'll get it," Cat says, hurrying away.

I lower my voice. "I want to get Cat out of town but she feels like it will make me look guilty if she leaves, and Debbie goes public."

"It will," Reid says. "And then you, your wife, and your marriage have to survive that added speculation. I don't think Cat's in danger, as long as Debbie thinks she might get paid."

"This is getting to Cat. I hate what it's doing to her. She doesn't deserve this, and I love her too damn much to want to hurt her. She's affected by how your father treated your mother."

Reid, who has always been withdrawn and cold, surprises me by saying, "Cat knows the difference between you and our father. We all do or we wouldn't be here helping. We'd be here pulling her out, even if she hated us for it." He presses his hands to the counter. "I know you play things straight and even, but she's playing dirty. Play dirty."

"He's right," Gabe says. "It's time to play dirty."

"What does that mean?" I ask.

"What does she not want to get out of this? What or who does she want to protect?" Reid asks.

"If she had a secret," I reply. "She wouldn't be coming at us this hard."

"In my world," Reid says. "When you have a secret, you come at the other person harder and con them. And she's conning you. Get Royce to find her trigger, the thing that will shut her down because getting her arrested comes with a price and exposure for Cat."

I inhale and Royce joins us. "I heard. I don't think she has a weakness, but her partner in crime, the lawyer does. I already have one of my men working on where you hit him and how. You control him. He controls Debbie. We hope."

We hope. That is not the confident statement I want and worse, it's the only thing I have right now.

Cat

My stomach is queasy again, but I fight through it because the minute I see Dana standing at our door, I know she's shaken, her eyes bloodshot, her cheek flushed. And now, minutes later, she's been standing at a portion of the window that creates a half moon around our front room. I step to her side. "What can I do for you right now?"

"Make this end, but we both know you can't."

"I can help you get to that end."

"I'm here," Reese says entering the room, and I can hear the footsteps and voices of the other men near the front door, apparently leaving.

Dana spins around and looks at Reese. "I was motivated to make Reginald feel secure," she says, of her boyfriend. "I did. I fucked his brains out. I talked dirty to him when I wanted to hit him and scream at him. I made him feel like I was still in this with him."

My lips part in shock at the bold words that feel so unlike Dana, but I sense the desperation in her. Reese and I share a look of relief, that this is obviously not a confession and he joins us, stepping directly in front of Dana. "What happened?" he asks calmly, his tone even, voice comforting, without accusation. He's smooth and sincere, and that's why he wins over juries, and me, for that matter.

"He went to get us coffee and forgot his phone. I listened to his messages. There's one from a Riley Smith at the DA's office. I sent it to myself and I'll send it to you."

"And?" Reese asks.

"He's plotting with them to turn on me on the stand."

"Play the message," Reese says.

She grabs her phone and I don't miss the trembling of her hands. She hits the "play" button. "This is Riley Smith. We're pleased you're on board. We need a list of gotcha questions, things that will make Dana look guilty."

"What does he have on you?" Reese asks.

"I can leave," I offer.

"No," Dana says. "Your column fired me up to fight back. I want you here." She looks at Reese. "He knows I hate my father. He knows I wanted to walk away from the money. He kept me from doing it. He told me that was insane. There's nothing else."

"Then we have to assume he'll make things up," Reese says. "But we'll be ready for that."

"What do you think he'll say?" she asks.

"What do *you* think he'll say?" Reese asks, leading her to reveal something, I'm certain.

"That I killed my father. He'll say I wanted to kill my father."

"Did you?" Reese asks. I don't believe that she's a killer, and yet, I'm holding my breath, anticipating. I wait for her answer, afraid my relief was premature. Afraid Dana killed her father and that Reese will have Debbie and a guilty client on his hands.

Not to mention a baby on the way he doesn't know about yet.

Chapter Seventy-One

Cat

Reese and I are both staring at Dana, the window in our front living area now her backdrop as we wait for her to answer Reese's question: *Did you?* Meaning, of course, did she kill her father. I don't have to hold my breath long for her answer.

"I did not kill my father," she hisses vehemently. "You're doubting me though. You're doubting me or you wouldn't have asked. God." She shoves fingers through her hair. "I can't even believe this. I thought you believed in me. Why are you defending me if you don't believe in me?"

Reese lets her finish her rant. "Dana," he says calmly, "that's the question every jury member is asking over and over during the trial. I need to ask it with them. I need to find the holes that make people believe you're guilty and seal them."

"Reese doesn't defend people he believes are guilty," I interject. "If he did, I wouldn't be with him."

"Do you believe I'm innocent?" she asks me.

"Yes," I say. "I do."

She looks at Reese. "And you?"

"Yes, Dana. I believe you're innocent. But what I need from you, is not for you to convince me that you're innocent. We're past that. I need you to give me not your best, but the worst of you, because that's what I have to defend. What can your boyfriend say that will convince the jury that you're guilty?"

"I've been with him two years and my father and I had so many fights in that time," she says. "I said that I hated him many times. I said that I wish I never had to see him again many times."

Reese takes that in without so much as a blink. "What I need you to do is go home and type up details on any conversation with him about your father that you remember. I need this tonight because

Reginald is flipping, he could end up on the prosecution's witness list, far too easily and quickly. I need to be ready."

"Yes. Okay. What about him? Do I still have to play nice with him?"

"I can't tell you how to run your personal life," Reese says, "but he's already betraying you. Be careful. However, I can say this: I'm going to ask him if he had sex with you on the very day he agreed to turn on you. I'm going to use the way he's treating you to create an impression of a monster protecting himself."

"Then I'll be nice to him," she says. "You know, if you can make him pay for putting me through this, for killing my father, who I might have hated, but was still my father, the only living relative I have, then I'll keep fucking his brains out. Is someone here to take me home?"

"I'll call and get someone up here to escort you down," Reese says, snagging his phone from his pocket.

"Do you want some coffee while we wait?" I ask.

"Yes, actually," Dana says. "Something warm would be nice. I swear I've been chilled to the bone since my father's murder."

"Come with me then," I say, leading her into the kitchen, and thankfully somewhere during our chat, my stomach calmed down.

Once we're in the kitchen, I let Dana choose her flavor of coffee, as we have several, and as we both doctor our cups with cream and sweetener, she looks at me and says, "Reese really loves you."

My heart warms. "I really love him."

"Women flirt with him."

"Well, he *is* Mr. Hotness. There's a fan blog and all."

She laughs. "Yes. I know about that, but my point is that he doesn't flirt back."

She has no idea how much this conversation hits a nerve. Reese is amazing. He's so very good to me and I hate the idea of Debbie making the world think we're broken. We are *not* broken. I shouldn't care what others think, but I can't seem to help it. I do. "I'm a very lucky woman."

"I've never been loved the way Reese loves you, obviously, since I'm now defending myself against the man I thought I might marry. Heck, I wanted my father to love me even when he made me hate him."

"You don't think he loved you?"

"I guess in the only way he could: by throwing money at me. I thought if I walked away from the money, maybe he'd see me instead. Maybe he'd be a real father. I should have." She shakes her head. "I need to not go there. I start tearing up when I do. So tell me. What's it like to have someone who loves you as much as Reese does you?"

"Perfect," I say. "It's perfect like he is. Don't settle. I didn't."

"Nor did I."

At the sound of Reese's voice I look up to find him in the doorway, and when his eyes meet mine they are warm with love. "Dana," he says, seeming to force himself to tear his gaze from mine. "Your ride will be here any minute." The doorbell rings and he says, "Or rather now."

Dana sips her coffee she's barely touched. "I hate wasting this. Thank you, Cat." She sets her cup in the sink.

"I didn't do anything."

"You occupied my mind. And you're a good listener."

She heads toward the door and Reese follows her while she sparks an idea for my column about what is real and what is a façade. I'm playing it out in my head when Reese walks back into the kitchen and steps in front of me, tilting my cup up to take a sip for himself. And as silly as it might be considering all we share, this act of sharing warms me and even goes so far as to heat my skin.

"What do you think?"

"I believe her. You do too, don't you?" My brows furrow. "Or don't you?"

"I do."

"But?"

"There's something the boyfriend can do to damage her and us. If she doesn't tell me what it is and I get sideswiped, I'm not going to be happy."

"Yeah I kind of got that impression, too, but I think having her write out the conversations is good. Sometimes the tough stuff is easier to write down than speak."

He sets my cup aside. "I need to talk to you about something."

"Okay. Why don't I like how that sounds?"

"Because *I* don't like how it sounds. Basically, your brothers believe that no matter what, arrest or no arrest, Debbie will make a stink with the press. And if we pay her off, she'll come back for more if we don't get a DNA test now. She could threaten to go to the press and not give us the test."

My throat tightens and anger starts to burn in my belly. This is already old. I'm ready to end this. "What do they suggest?" I ask.

"That we find dirt on the attorney helping Debbie and use it to blackmail him to get out of this and take her with him."

"I think I'm a Maxwell in this moment, because yes, do it. They're doing it to us. Make it end." That need to end this builds again, taking root. "You're trying to save me the pain of the bad press and don't, you need to know that what I want is to not be held captive. I want this over. Give her the million dollars. I'll write a couple extra books." I try to duck under his arms.

He catches me. "What just happened?"

"I just want us to be us again."

"We never stopped being us."

"We can't have this kind of thing hanging over our heads."

"If we pay her off we *will* have this hanging over our heads until that baby is born."

"Not if we sign an agreement," I argue.

"Give me a week to work with Royce and end this another way."

"What if she goes to the press first?"

"I'll start negotiating a deal to buy time. Okay?"

"Okay," I agree. "A week. Make it end in a week." I think of the baby and wanting this over with before I tell Reese, and most definitely before he or she is born. "And if we can't negotiate or bribe ourselves out of this, I need to out her in my column, and we need to just deal with the press and questions. With this trial, her gossip will be filed away secondary to it, and if you win, no one cares about her claims."

"Cat, what happened? You were okay, but I don't think you are now. Did Dana say something that triggered this?"

"I'm okay. I'm actually good. I was wallowing and feeling sorry for myself but now I'm back to fighting."

"You didn't answer me. Did Dana say something that triggered your change of mood?"

"Just that you're perfect. And basically that we're perfect, in not so many words."

"I don't understand."

"You will. On your birthday that will be very special, if you make this end." I kiss him. "Go get the door."

He snags my waist and pulls me close. "What is this gift?"

"Perfect, like us, but we need Debbie to go away, not me. I'm not leaving. I'm not wilting or running. She doesn't get that power over us. *I will* out her which was my first instinct. We can handle it. We're strong enough. You're well-respected enough. You know it. You're afraid of how it affects me and us. It doesn't. So let's do what we need to and handle it. One week. Let's deal with this and end this."

"All right then. We end this in one week."

Chapter Seventy-Two

Cat

*B*etrayal.

Defined as: someone you trust, stabbing you in the back.
As I sat in the courtroom yesterday that word stayed in my mind. The prosecutor painted a picture that was based on no facts but as a prosecutor the jury automatically trusts him. I watched Reese Summer, cross-examine the medical examiner, and get to the facts and it became clear to me that the prosecutor is going to spend this entire trial betraying the jury's trust, and even that of the public he defends. But then why would the DA do his job and look for the real killer? He has Mr. Summer to do that for him. So I leave you with this: Deception is a lie and a lie is a betrayal. As you watch this trial on television, watch for the deception and you will find the lies. Until next time, Cat.

I finish my column while Reese works with his team and then I sit in on their game planning session over Dana's boyfriend and his betrayal. We go to bed at two in the morning, and I wake up at four in the morning feeling like my stomach has rocks in it that are trying to kill me. Reese is finally knocked out next to me after working with his team on every surprise the DA might offer them with Dana's boyfriend's betrayal, and I cautiously, despite how sick I am, slip out from under his arm and tiptoe to the bathroom, shutting the door behind me. I'm on my knees in front of the toilet the minute I get there and it's horrible. I want it to just be over. Finally, I lay back on the floor and shut my eyes.

"Cat. My God. Cat."

Reese is suddenly on the floor with me and pulling me into his arms. "I'm going to take you to the ER."

"No. No, I went to the doctor. I'm okay. I didn't take my medicine before bed. I didn't think I needed it. I'm better. I guess I just fell asleep."

"*On the floor*, Cat. You're not good."

I cup his face, and in that moment I want to just tell him, but his birthday is so soon, and I want this to be good for him. I want Debbie gone and she will be in a week. We're going to make sure of it. "The doctor said this could linger for a while. I had bloodwork done. We know what this is."

"Olives did this?"

"I'm pretty sure olives didn't do this," I say, almost laughing at the idea that olives got me pregnant because I'm a little giddy right now. "Let's go to bed."

He stands and pulls me to my feet and then scoops me up and carries me to the bed because Reese really is my hero. I didn't think I needed a hero, but he proved me wrong. He pulls the blanket over me. "Where are your pills?"

"Kitchen. That's why I didn't take them."

"I'll get them."

"No. You need to sleep."

He ignores that plea and takes off. A few minutes later, he's kneeling in front of me and hands me a pill. I lean up and he opens a bottle of water for me. "Thank you," I say downing the water and pill. Reese kisses my nose, and then stands up. He climbs into bed, pulls me close, my back to his front. "Next time, you wake me up. I'll wake up anyway. I know when you're gone."

I shut my eyes and smile. He knows when I'm gone. That's a pretty great thing to say and I drift easily into sleep.

The next thing I remember, I'm waking up and Reese is gone. I sit up and look at the clock, freaking out at the time. I should have been up half an hour ago. I race to the bathroom and Reese is already downstairs. He let me sleep, he knew when I wasn't in bed, yet I didn't know when he left. That feels horrible.

I hurry to take a shower, and I'm dressed and done with my routine in half my normal time, thanks to waiting on my coffee until after I'm dressed. I'm about to exit the bathroom and I look down at my belly in the navy blue dress and my belly looks distinctly rounder. I consider it a moment and decide I'm the only one who will notice. Well, me and Reese. I'm not sure I'm going to make it until his birthday without telling him. He'll know I'm not eating, I'm sick, my stomach is rounder. Maybe he'll think it's the illness. Thankfully I'm fine right now, probably because Reese made me take my medicine. With my purse and briefcase in tow, I head down the stairs with a deep need to see my husband that nags at me. I don't want to lose him and I don't even know why I have that thought right now. It's hormones. I'm not going to lose Reese.

I reach the lower level and stop at the bottom of the stairs when I hear male voices I recognize from the kitchen. "One week," Royce says. "That's fast."

"Cat wants this over," Reese says. "I want this over for her."

"The DNA test will have to be on me," Reid says, "but fuck, man, this woman does not deserve your million dollars. Let me tell her a low figure up front and the rest after the DNA test. We know the DNA test won't come back as yours. That cuts your losses. If you and Cat are willing to let it go public, let me try to save you money."

"My brother, Blake," Royce says, "is one of the best hackers in the world, literally. That's why he gets paid the big bucks. He's been out of the country on a job with the military and I couldn't get to him. He's back tonight. If anyone can get dirt on Debbie or her partner in crime to shut this down, he can."

"Then Reid," Reese says, "don't lowball Debbie to the point that she goes public before Blake can work his magic for us."

"The way to drag this out is to have you agree to a meeting, but tell her you can't do it until next Saturday because of the trial," Reid says.

"I'm not meeting Debbie," Reese replies immediately. "My wife is not going to have to go through that."

"I'll show up in your place," Reid offers. "I get it. I don't want Cat to have to go through that either."

"If you're meeting her, do your thing," Reese says. "I promised Cat we'd end it this week and I have a trial. I need to just give you both that perimeter and have you make it happen. And this is a solid deadline. Cat's sick and I'm not positive stress isn't part of it. I need to make this happen."

"Cat's sick?" Reid asks. "How sick?"

"Asleep in the bathroom floor last night sick," he says. "I need to end this for her and us."

I'm sure Royce is cringing right now and that, along with the deep worry in Reese's voice has me hurrying down the hall and stepping into the doorway of the kitchen.

"I heard everything you just said," I say. "I'm not a delicate flower. I'm sick, yes, and sure this upsets me, but I think the longer we drag this out the more empowered Debbie becomes and the more agitated thus likely to go public. So yes, a week is our goal, but if it takes a few more days, I'm fine." I glance at my watch. "I have to get to court. I'm watching a trial today and the defending counsel is standing in my kitchen when he should be on his way there, too."

Royce clears his throat. "I'll be in touch." He walks my direction and gives me a tiny nod before walking on by.

Reid does the same but he stops. "Tough cookie, my sister, but that's no surprise to me. We'll get it done." He steps past me and leaves.

Reese stays at the island, waiting on me, and I battle this feeling of betraying him by not telling him I'm pregnant. He thinks I'm sick. I can't tell him now before court but I need to think long and hard today about my birthday present. I cross to stand in front of him, my hands settling on his chest. "Let's go win the day."

He cups my head and kisses me. "You are a tough cookie."

"Tough enough to kick your ass if you don't get focused."

His cellphone buzzes with a text, he grabs it and glances at it. "Dana sent me a text she copied from the boyfriend's phone this morning and this just got interesting." He grabs his briefcase. "Come on. I'll tell you about it on the way to court."

We hurry downstairs where Savage is waiting and we settle into the back of the SUV when Reese's phone rings. "I don't know this number." He answers. "Reese Summer." His expression goes dark. "How did you get this number, Debbie? Because we both know I changed it a long time ago."

Chapter Seventy-Three

Reese

I am acutely aware of my wife beside me in the car, while I have Debbie on the phone that is presently pressed to my ear, and I have no doubt that Cat knows this is her. Debbie is trying to get to me through Cat and it's pissing me off. "How did you get my number?" I repeat.

"I'm resourceful," she says, "most mothers are for their children."

"I take it the real father doesn't have money, so you thought you'd just take mine."

Cat's hand come down on my arm and she whispers. "Careful. Buy time."

I inhale and say, "Deal with my attorney, not me, but let me be clear: Go near Cat again and I will go to the police, and she'll go to the press. She's not one to be held captive by threats anymore than I am."

"I have video of us fucking. Do you want me to send it to Cat for her journalistic use?"

My jaw flexes. "Send it. It can be dated, in many ways, by a forensic specialist and I won't even have to wait until that baby is born to prove you as the liar you are. I'll tell Cat and Reid to expect it." I disconnect and press two fingers to the bridge of my nose.

"There's a video," Cat says, her breath rasping from her throat, and when I look at her, her fingers are digging into her leg.

"She's probably bluffing," I say. "It's a last-ditch move to intimidate me into paying up. It's blackmail and I think it's time we go to the police."

She looks at me, her skin pale. "Right. We probably need to."

"I'll talk to Royce," Savage says. "If you do that, we'll get our contacts involved, people we trust."

I turn to Cat. "Sweetheart—"

"I'm fine, Reese. I'm fine. I know this was from before my time. It's just a lot right now."

"I know. You know I love you and I want to make this go away."

"I do," she says. "You are not to blame. I don't want to see that recording though if it exists. Never."

"I understand. I wouldn't either."

"She's bluffing," Savage says. "There's no tape. This is the bitch of blackmail we're dealing with. I feel sorry for that kid, and for the rest of us since she's the one raising him." He pulls us to the side of the courthouse.

"Cat—"

"I'm fine. Go give me a court performance to keep my mind off of this."

Savage exits the SUV. I pull Cat to me and kiss her, and I make sure I do it well, and the pain I taste on her tongue guts me. "Come back with me."

"No. You need to focus. When you walk in that door, the job is what matters. I'll be there watching."

Savage opens Cat's door and I follow her out of the vehicle. I pull her close and we walk inside the courthouse only to have Richard waiting for us just inside. "Dana told you about the message she copied between her boyfriend and the prosecution," I assume.

He huddles in with me and Cat. "The boyfriend is here. He came to tell us about it. He says he was trying to find out what they had on Dana."

"Or he knows she busted him," Cat says before I can.

"Exactly," Richard says. "But Dana believes him."

Royce walks in behind us. "I have something for you," he says, handing me a folder. "It's trial related."

I open the envelope to find a shot of the assistant working for Dana's father for the past few years, and she's naked with Mr. Warren. "How the hell did you get this?"

"We work magic. My brother is a hacker, remember? She had it on her hard drive which may or may not have had a nefarious purpose. That's unclear. She's on the prosecution's list."

I file that away for a moment. "Debbie."

"Savage just told me. We're working on solutions. We're keeping Cat close."

"I am," Savage assures me.

"I'm ready to be the only man keeping her close," I say and turn to Cat. "I need to go."

"I can't wait to see what you do with this," she says, her eyes filled with excitement over this new development. I love the way she's so inside my world.

I wrap my arm around her and pull her close, my lips near her ear. "You're everything to me," and with that, I turn and start walking with Richard falling into step behind me.

"What are you thinking?" Richard asks.

"That I need the boyfriend out of my face and Dana alone in a room."

We turn the corner to our private office areas and Elsa is waiting at the conference room door. "She's in there with him."

I open the door and I don't even look at Reginald. I focus on Dana. "I need to see you alone."

She looks at Reginald. "See you later."

He walks over to kiss her, a tall man with dark hair and an appropriately chosen tattoo sleeve featuring a Harley since he owns a chop shop. He gives me a nod that I don't return. I'm not convinced he's innocent. The minute the door shuts, Dana says, "You heard that he setup the prosecutor."

"Tell me about your father's assistant."

"Martha. She's sweet. I like her."

"And tell me why she's on the prosecutor's list."

"I assume because she'll testify about me fighting with my father."

"And what's the worst thing she ever heard you say?"

"'I hate you.' Probably many times."

That's not good, but I'm prepared for it. "Did you know she was fucking your father?"

She blanches. "Martha. No. No way. That didn't happen."

"It did. I have proof."

I toss the envelope on the conference table. She looks inside and shoves the photos out of sight. "Did she do it?"

"If she did, she's going to come at you hard. What is she going to say?"

"I told you. I screamed that I hated him numerous times."

"Do not leave anything out. I need to know."

"I'm not leaving anything out."

I consider her a moment. "Are you sure Reginald didn't figure out that you checked his messages?"

"I don't see how. No. He couldn't have. We can take down the prosecutor now, right?"

"We can, but that means there's a potential trial delay. Is that what you want? It gives us time to prove who really killed your father, but it could give the prosecutor time to strengthen his case and it drags this out for you. More money. More time. More hell."

"They can't prove I did what I didn't do, but I want this over with. I also need to trust your instincts. What do we do?"

"We decide at the end of today."

"Why today?"

"Because Martha's on the stand today."

I turn and exit to the hallway to join Richard and Elsa in the hallway. "Are you going after the prosecutor?"

"We decide after I'm done with Martha today." I look up to find Royce walking in our direction. "Make sure Dana's head is on right for today," I say. "I'll be right back."

I step around them and meet Royce a few feet away. "Is there any connection between the boyfriend and the assistant?"

"Nothing we've found yet, but we always look for connected dots. I suspect the assistant thought she would get some payday, in some way. If the boyfriend wanted the same, they fit together." He moves on. "Wilson Moore, the attorney I told you was involved with Debbie. We pulled camera footage from places Cat frequents and we picked up images of him following her for a good month now. He's also in financial trouble, neck deep in debt he took out with some pretty rough people."

"He's desperate."

"Yes. And that's not the same thing as just scheming for a payday like Debbie. Desperate people worry me. They do desperate things. If there's a recording of you with Debbie, they'll use it, but that's the least of my concerns. They could go after Cat in a bigger way. I think you might want to get Cat out of town."

"Fuck. She's not going to leave without me."

"You're going to have to make her."

"It's time," Richard calls out.

I scrub my jaw. "I'll talk to you at the break."

I turn and meet-up with my client and team, and when I walk into that courtroom and my eyes meet Cat's, I'm not distracted, I'm motivated. Cat in danger is the best thing that ever happened to Dana. I'm after a confession today from the real killer and I'm going to get one, too. I'm going to end this trial. And then, I'm putting my wife on a plane, with me by her side. Once I get her out of harm's way, I'll go after Wilson Moore and Debbie with every ounce of my force.

Chapter Seventy-Four

Cat

The minute Reese's eyes meet mine in the courtroom I know that he's on a mission and everyone that stands in his way is going to feel the pain. The chaos has come together as a perfect storm, and for Reese, that isn't more chaos. He has this incredible way of centering himself and focusing, that I've seen in actions, but never with this much weight on his shoulders. I'm in awe and I prepare for what I know will be a dynamic day in court. I'm actually impatient as the jury and judge take their places, eager to get started and it starts with a bang.

The prosecution is now up, and Milton Wicker, the lead prosecutor, who in a blue suit and looking rather gaunt today, remains in control. His first order of business is to cast Reese's table a dramatic stare before he calls Officer Marks; a tall, fit, fifty-something officer with salt and pepper hair who'd responded to the crime scene to the stand. Milton proceeds to go through a series of useless questions that all center around Dana's behavior when she discovered her father dead. "Did Ms. Warren cry?"

"No, she did not," Officer Marks replies.

"Did she appear to grieve in any other way?"

"No, she did not."

I expect Reese to object but he doesn't, which means he has a plan, and he's letting the prosecutor walk into a trap. This questioning drags out and presents absolutely no evidence that Dana killed her father. It's all about making her look like a spoiled rich daughter who was after her father's money. Finally, it's Reese's turn to question the officer.

He stands up and approaches the stand. "First, thank you for your service, Officer Marks. Our men in blue are underappreciated."

Officer Marks' eyes light with appreciation. "It's my honor to serve the fine citizens of New York City."

"How long have you been on the force?"

"Twenty-one years," the officer states.

"Ask and answered previously," the prosecutor yells out.

"I have a short memory," Reese replies, but he moves on.

"How many death investigations, murder or otherwise, have you investigated?"

"Fifty-one if you include non-criminal acts such as accidents and natural causes."

"That's a large number," Reese comments. "How many loved ones, spouses, daughters, sons, and significant family members and friends of those people did you interact with?"

"Hundreds."

"Of those hundreds, how many were deeply connected to one of the deceased?" Reese asks.

"All of them."

"How many of those people, when told they'd lost someone close to them, cried?" Reese asks.

"Roughly seventy percent," Officer Marks replies.

"In other words, if you talked to three hundred people, at least ninety of them didn't cry."

"Correct," Officer Marks says.

"Did you find this strange?" Reese asks.

"Objection," the prosecutor shouts. "Leading the witness and speculation."

"I'll rephrase," Reese says. "Is it true, officer, that you've been trained to observe and expect certain physiological reactions from individuals involved in death investigations?"

"Yes."

"How many hours?"

"It's ongoing," Officer Marks replies. "Hundreds of hours. Our training is constantly on repeat. It's impossible to log the number of hours."

"Hundreds of hours," Reese repeats. "And based on this training, what is a normal reaction to grief?"

"There's a wide range of normal reactions."

"Is it normal to cry?"

"Yes," Officer Marks replies.

"Is it normal not to cry?" Reese asks.

"Yes," he answers again.

"Why is this a normal reaction?"

"Shock is a key factor," Officer Marks explains. "They aren't fully processing the death to be real. The body often shuts down to protect us from what we can't handle. It's survival."

"How many homicides have you investigated?" Reese asks.

"Twenty."

"During those investigations, did you have close family members demonstrate this type of shock?"

"Yes," Officer Marks replies.

"Of those people who went into shock and shut down, how many of those were guilty of the crimes?"

"Ten percent."

"Ten percent. In other words, another ninety percent of those close to the victims who did not cry were not responsible for the homicide?"

"Correct."

"How many of the people who cried when they were given news of the death were responsible for the homicides?"

"I would say at least forty percent."

"Thank you," Reese says. "I'm done with the witness."

Milton stands up. "Redirect, your honor?"

The judge nods and Milton turns to the officer once more, "Did Ms. Warren give you any other reason, outside of her emotional withdrawal, to suspect her guilt?"

"She was confused about where she'd been during certain hours," Officer Marks states. "We needed a solid alibi and at the time she didn't give me one."

The prosecutor sits down. Reese stands up. "Judge? Two more questions?"

"One, counselor."

Reese doesn't argue. He focuses on the officer. "Is it normal to be confused when you are in shock?" Reese asks.

"Yes," Officer Marks replies.

I let out a breath. Reese nailed that witness and the morning passes with Reese wiping the floor with the prosecutor over and over. Finally, the last witness before the break: Martha. The secretary. She approaches the stand, a pretty brunette not much older than forty, if that. Milton, the prosecutor starts out hard and fast. "How long did you work for the deceased?"

"Three years."

"How many times did you hear Ms. Warren say she hated her father in that time?"

"At least half a dozen."

"When was the last time you heard Ms. Warren say that she hated her father?"

"The day before Mr. Warren died," Martha states.

"Who was she speaking to?"

"Him. She came to the office and shouted it at him."

"How did he react?" Wicker asks.

"He shut his door. He didn't come out for hours. That's how he handled stress."

The softball questions that all aim to make Dana look like a spoiled brat go on for forty minutes. Finally, again, Reese approaches and he wastes no time digging in. "Did you ever sleep with Mr. Warren?"

Her eyes go wide and Milton stands up. "Objection. Relevance?"

Reese looks at him and arches a brow. "You don't know what this witness having a personal relationship with the deceased has to do with this?"

The judge gavels his desk to death. "Enough."

"Judge, I'll get to the point quickly."

"You better," he says.

Reese refocuses on Martha. "Did you have a sexual relationship with the deceased, Mr. Warren?"

"I did not," she lies.

"You do know you're under oath, correct?" Reese asks.

"Yes. Of course."

"Did you ever take intimate photos with the deceased without any clothes on?"

Milton pops to his feet to object and the courtroom erupts in murmurs that has the judge pounding away again. "Recess until one-thirty, and counselors, to my office."

"Judge, I'd like to request the current witness return to the stand after recess."

"Granted."

I smile. She lied. That's not good for the prosecutor. Reese walks back to his table and when his eyes find mine in the crowd, he doesn't wink, but he doesn't have to. I know my husband. He just got exactly what he wanted.

Reese

I walk into the judge's chamber with Milton already up in arms. "What the hell was that, judge?" He looks at me. "What the hell was that?"

"She lied." I hand the judge the envelope Royce gave me. "That won't be admissible into evidence, but she lied."

He opens it and looks inside, his expression tightening as he does. He looks at me. "How did you get this?"

"Walker Security," I say. "They frequently work with law enforcement and are highly respected."

"What is it?" Milton asks, sounding irritated.

The judge settles his glasses on his nose and looks over at him. "Naked pictures of your last witness with the deceased. I won't allow those photos into evidence, but I'll send her to jail. I don't tolerate lies under oath in my courtroom."

He doesn't offer to let Milton see the photos. He hands them back to me and I look at Milton. "Lies is what the entire prosecution is all about."

"Says the man defending a killer," Milton snaps, his face pinched with anger. "Do I get to see the photos, judge?"

"You'll have to trust me," he says. "She's naked. I don't run a girly show here. I assure you I can validate what I saw."

"Seems to me your witness, who was taking naked photos with her boss, the focus of this trial, has something to hide," I say.

"Your client is the one who has something to hide."

I don't even consider outing his text messages with Dana's boyfriend. Not yet, but I will I have to end this trial and get my wife out of town soon. "Did you know about Martha banging Mr. Warren when you charged Dana or did you even do an investigation?"

"Enough," the judge says. "Martha will be taken into custody when the court reconvenes."

"I need an afternoon recess, judge," Milton says. "Please, I need to talk to my team."

The judge gives him a keen look. "I suspect you do and I'm going to grant your recess for one reason: I don't want another lie in my courtroom. We'll reconvene at one-thirty when the witness will stand before me and be arrested for lying. After which, we will recess." He waves us away.

I exit to the exterior of the office and text Cat: *I need you. Have Savage bring you back here.* I exit to the hallway and as soon as I'm in my team's private hallway, Richard and Elsa are on top of me. "The judge is having her arrested at one-thirty. After which, we recess. Go drill Dana about Martha. I need to see my wife."

I walk around them and head for the end of the hallway to wait on Cat and Savage. The minute Cat rounds the corner, I pull her to me and kiss her. "That was incredible," she says.

"We need to talk," I say, lacing my fingers with hers and leading her toward a private office.

Chapter Seventy-Five

Reese

I shut the door to the office and my need to control everything, especially my wife's safety, has me backing Cat against the wall, my hands on her waist, my legs caging hers. "Reese?" she asks. "Why are you so intense right now? You killed it in court."

"That attorney who's working with Debbie."

"What about him?"

"He's been following you for weeks. Royce pulled footage from random cameras around the areas you frequent."

"Oh," she breathes out. "That's creepy. I admit that freaks me out a little. You're going to ask me to leave again, aren't you?"

"Royce thinks you should. I know you don't want to go. And while my first instinct was to send you away, I really don't know if I can focus if you're out of my sight and in danger. I need to see you in the courtroom."

"I want to be there. I love watching you and I feel safe in the courthouse."

"I'm going to end the trial and we're going out of town. Wherever you want to go."

"I want to stay close, in case we need to talk to the police."

"Then we'll go to Cole and Lori's place in the Hamptons. We've wanted to go for a while."

"I'd like that. Thank you for not just sending me away. If Debbie comes forward I need to be by your side."

"You just need to be by my side, period." I kiss her, a slow, deep passionate kiss, and if we were anywhere but here, I'd be inside her right now. I stroke her cheek. "Let's talk about the trial."

"Yes. Let's talk about the trial."

I force myself to let her go, unbuttoning my jacket to pace as I think through everything that just happened in that courtroom. "We're recessing until one-thirty. I showed the judge the photos.

We're going back to court to have Martha arrested, and then we're done for the day."

"How hard did Milton fight her arrest?"

"He didn't. He's just not that good, which is really damn good for Dana. The judge wanted to prove his court was lawful and make this a big event. If it had been me in Milton's shoes, I would have fought to have that done in private. Now the jury will see her punished."

"And a few hours in jail will make her break if she's going to break," Cat assumes.

"If it doesn't, it will prep her so that I can."

"I agree and the fact that she lied and she's getting arrested, creates plenty of reasonable doubt. The jury is going to wonder why she lied. They'll wonder if she's the killer."

"But it won't end this. I want this over."

"I know you do," she says. "But you're winning, Reese. I'm right here with you and I'm not a fool. I'm not going anywhere without Savage by my side. I have every reason to stay smart and alive. And—as much as I don't want to go, if me being here starts worrying you to the point of stress, I'll go. For you. I'll go crazy, but for you, I'm willing."

I cross to stand in front of her, my hands settling under her hair at her neck. "For me."

"Anything for you."

"Even after that call this morning?"

"We both have a past, Reese. I don't think you came to me a virgin and if you did, you were born with some pretty impressive skills."

"Is that right?"

"Yes." She slides her arms around me. "I was shocked and it felt like an invasion of our world, but it didn't feel like a betrayal. And just so you know, watching you in that courtroom really turns me on."

"Watch out, sweetheart, or I'm going to forget where we are and pull your dress up."

"How much more will it take," she teases, "because I'm trying pretty hard to tempt you right now." There's a knock on the door and she sighs, "Of course."

I stroke her hair. "You're just giving me more motivation to end this." I kiss her and release her to walk to the door, and open it. Elsa is standing there.

"Dana said that she's completely sideswiped. She had no idea her father was sleeping with Martha. She's no help, but she wants to talk to you."

"She doesn't need to help. Martha is doing plenty herself. Tell her I'll be right there." She nods and I start to shut the door and stop. "Wait, Elsa. Give me a minute. I have an idea." I shut the door to refocus on my wife. "That idea you had about Dana and dinner. Let's make it lunch. She admires you. I do think she might open up to you. She might tell you something she won't tell me because she's nervous and on edge. Are you in?"

"Of course. Anything that helps. You know that."

I wrap my arm around her and pull her to me. "I do know, sweetheart." I kiss her and let her go, opening the door and inviting Elsa in to explain the plan.

"It's a good plan," Elsa says. "I like it. I can go grab lunch. I'll just pick up a couple large pizzas so we don't lose time with orders. Yes?"

"Yes," I say. "Do it."

She walks away and I motion to Savage who's standing at the end of the hallway.

He quickly joins us. "I need to go into the conference room without Cat but she'll be joining me. Can you stay with her and nearby the room once she enters?"

"They don't call me the 'right now guy' for nothing," he says. "I'm right here, right now, and whenever you need me."

Cat laughs. "If you use that line on a woman, try 'all night guy.'"

"That, too," he assures her, while I tune him out. "I'll be right back, Cat."

I cross the conference room and enter. Dana is sitting with Richard at the table and she pops to her feet. "Did she do it?"

"We don't know," I say. "But we're working on that. Cat is here. How do you feel about her joining us for lunch? She's signed a contract as a part of my legal team. Anything you say to her is protected."

"Yes, please. Bring her in."

I open the door and motion Cat forward. She enters the room and her and Dana are immediately chatting it up. The pizza arrives, and we all eat as Cat asks questions that are pretty damn probing, but Dana doesn't so much as blink. At one point, Dana tears up. "I did hate him, so how does it hurt so badly to know he's gone?"

Cat, who is sitting next to her, grabs her hand. "My father is like your father," she says. "And when he had a stroke a few years back it terrified me. It didn't take him long to return to his normal, horrible self, but at least he's alive. I get it. They're our fathers. They're a parent that brought us into the world."

Cat shares this with Dana, but I don't believe she does so to earn her trust. She does so because she feels what Dana feels, deeply, completely. It guts me every time I hear Cat talk about her father and until recently her brothers weren't much better, but that's changing, and thank God for it.

Unfortunately, by the time lunch is over, I don't think we've achieved much. I meet Cat in the hallway before I head back into court.

"Anything I missed that you picked up in there?"

"Just that I still believe she's innocent. I believe if you put her on the stand a jury will see that, too."

"I'm not letting this trial get that far," I promise her. "I'll see you in court and then we're getting out of here."

Savage steps to Cat's side. "Don't worry. I'm protecting your most precious thing in life. She's right here with me."

While I'm comforted by his declaration, I really am tired of leaving my wife with other men. Just another reason for me to end this trial. I head toward the conference room to gather my team. It's time to watch Martha feel the heat of being arrested.

Then I'm taking my wife home and reminding her that I'm the man by her side. She knows it, I know it, but after that call this morning, and seeing Savage by her side over and over again, I have a deep need to remind her in every possible way.

Chapter Seventy-Six

Reese

Fifteen minutes later, my eyes are on Cat in the courtroom, and I relax into what is about to be a huge success. The judge calls the court to order and asks Martha to report to the stand where she's arrested for contempt of court. Martha stands up in a panic and starts to cry, pleading with the judge. The room is a crazy rumble of sound as observers react.

When she's finally out of the room the judge addresses the jury, "To the jury," he states, "I have proof that Ms. Banks lied under oath, the details of which will not be placed into evidence, but a lie under oath is a crime and will not be tolerated in my courtroom. We're adjourning until eight am tomorrow. Ms. Banks will be back on the stand at that time." He bangs his gavel. Milton glares at me, while I turn and share a look with Cat before heading for the door.

A few minutes later, I've arranged to have my team at the apartment at seven, and I'm in the SUV with my wife, my hand on her leg, pulling her close. "That went well," she says.

"It certainly did," I say. "And as much as I want to celebrate that with you alone, right now, I think we need to make sure Reid knows where we stand."

"Royce is meeting you at your apartment," Savage says. "He wants to talk about the recent developments."

"That works," I say, looking at Cat. "We need to try to get Reid to the house." I pull my phone from my pocket and it rings with Reid's number. "Speak of the devil himself."

"That he is," Cat agrees, as I answer the call.

"I heard what's going on from Royce," Reid says. "I'm coming to your place, and Gabe's with me."

"See you there," I say and disconnect.

"Your brothers are on their way."

"I swear those two haven't been so attentive since I was a child."

I squeeze her leg, aware that talking about her family stirs emotions over her brothers being assholes over her career, following a path they didn't approve of. At least not at the time. I believe they've come around but not without a lot of damage to their relationships with Cat. Her phone rings and she talks with Lauren, and then Lori, just as Cole calls me for an update. Both Lori and Cole are out of the mix, dealing with a crisis with a client, but they want to be here for us. That's what matters.

A few minutes later, we enter the apartment and we've barely had time to set our things down when Royce, Reid, and Gabe, join us, while Savage also sticks around. There are so many of us that we meet in the front living room. "This guy's been following Cat for weeks?" Reid demands. "What the fuck. Where is he now?"

"We have eyes on him," Royce says. "He's hiding from his bookie in a Motel Six in Queens. He's on leave from his job. He's not going anywhere we don't go with him."

"I don't like this," Reid says, showing the most emotion I've seen that man show in all the years I've been around him. "And Debbie hasn't returned my call and yet she called Reese and threatened him this morning."

"This guy needs to be ended," Gabe says, which is a very out of character statement for him, at least where I'm concerned, too. He looks at me. "Are you going to the police?"

"No," Cat says. "That presses Debbie to talk which is fine, but I want us to try to negotiate out of this in the next few days."

"I'm going to give my guy at the Feds a heads up," Royce says. "This is blackmail and it falls under their umbrella and with Wilson's gambling debt to a nasty bookie, with strong ties to a crime organization, that makes them all the more interested. I'll let him know we're concerned about the press. He will likely want to talk to all of you." He looks at me and Cat. "Unless you two object."

I eye Cat. "I think it's smart."

"Me too," she says.

"Who's the bookie?" Gabe asks. "I might have an insider who can give us something on this guy."

"Guy's name is Dimps McCoy," Royce says.

"Negotiate," Reid grumbles. "I'll negotiate all right." He starts walking toward the door and Cat races after him, planting herself in front of him, and Gabe and I both take up either side of them.

"What does that mean, Reid?" Cat demands.

"Don't worry, little sis, I'm at my best when I'm angry and I might have hurt you, but no one else is going to."

"Reid," I say. "Can I see you alone?"

"No," Reid says. "I need air. And for everyone to back up."

Gabe backs away and Reid steps around him, and the interesting part of this is that Gabe says nothing. He just follows him toward the door.

Cat turns to me. "What are they going to do?"

"They?"

"Don't let Gabe fool you. He is just like Reid, just as dangerous, aside from one hiding behind stone and the other behind humor."

"They're your brothers. As your husband, I know how easy it is to react to this, and want to hurt someone. Give them time to calm down and they'll be back."

"I hope you're right. These are my brothers, Reese. They *aren't* you."

"I'll handle it, Cat. I promise." I kiss her. "Let's finish up with Royce and we'll figure it out. Okay?"

"Yes. Okay."

My cellphone rings and it's an insider I use at the jail. "Martha says she has information she'll trade for immunity, but she wants to talk to you."

"I'll be right there." I hang up and talk to the entire room. "Martha wants to make a deal but she'll only talk to me."

"She wants to find out what you know," Cat says.

"Of course she does, but that isn't going to work out for her."

"I'll go with you on this one," Royce says.

"I'll stay with Cat," Savage says and once again I'm leaving my wife with another man.

I settle my hands on her shoulders. "Come with me."

"You want me to come?"

"Yes, I do. You're part of my legal team. I lean in and lower my lips to her ear, "and I really want you close, Cat." I lean back to look at her.

Her eyes warm. "Yes. I'd love to come."

⬥⬥⬥

Reid

Gabe and I step out of the elevator. "Let's walk and talk."

"Agreed," Gabe says.

Once we're on the street, away from anyone who might overhear or record us, I say, "We need to end this."

"Agreed again. Let's divide and conquer. I'll take Wilson. You take Debbie."

"Works for me," Reid says.

"I'll go first," Gabe says, pulling out his phone and calling someone without identifying them. "I need a number for a bookie named Dimps McCoy. Text it to me."

I don't ask what he's going to do. I know. A minute later his text beeps. Gabe motions me right and we walk about four blocks to one of the few payphones around this area. He grabs the phone, punches in the number and makes the call. "Dimps McCoy?" he says. "You don't know me but I have a tip for you. Wilson Moore is hiding in a Motel Six in Queens. I got nothing more." He hangs up and looks at me. "You're up. Deal with Debbie."

Chapter Seventy-Seven

Reid

I arrive back to my office and dial Debbie's number and end up leaving her a message. "It's your lucky payday. Come to my office at six o'clock or the deal is off." I disconnect and review the file I'd been given by Royce that includes Debbie's parent's information. Mary and Marcus own a restaurant in Long Island. I do a tax search and find a lien on their property.

I dial the restaurant. "Mary?"

"Yes. Who's speaking?"

"I'd like to talk to you about your daughter. Are you aware she's pregnant?"

"Who is this?"

"Reid Maxwell. The lawyer for the man she's blackmailing, who is married to my sister. Here's how this plays out, be in my office by five o'clock and there will be a six-figure check now and a six-figure check later. The condition is this: You get your daughter out of the country and yank that damn thorn from my side. You send me the DNA test when the baby is born, you get another check."

"She's blackmailing someone?"

"Yes. A happily married man who she stalked years ago to the point that he got a restraining order, but he's very wealthy and she wants a payday."

"I know who the father is. He's not wealthy."

Obviously, the mother is honorable. "You get a payday and out of financial distress. What's it going to be?"

"I feel bad taking the money."

"Don't. I want this over. Make it end and I'm a happy man."

"What's the address?"

I read her the address and disconnect. This is going to cost me some money, but I owe my sister this and I damn sure am going to pay up and protect her.

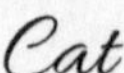

Cat

I stand at a glass window while Reese talks to Martha but not without company. Royce and Milton are both there as well and Milton is not happy. "I know who did it, and it wasn't Dana, but I was afraid to come forward. Nelson, Mr. Warren, and I were having an affair and I was afraid that I'd look guilty. I'm not in the will. He wasn't generous like that. I knew that. I just fucked him. It was kind of my job. He paid me more because I was a fuck buddy. That was all. I had nothing to gain by him dying."

"Then why were you afraid?"

"Because the person who did this came to me. He said that he heard how Nelson talked to me. I deserved better. He offered me money to help get rid of Nelson. He said he'd get a payday and so would I."

Dana's boyfriend, I think. Reginald.

"Who offered you money?" Reese asks.

"Reginald."

Reese doesn't so much as blink. God, how I love how cool and confident he is. "And what did you tell him?"

"What do you say to someone who wants to murder someone? Because you know, they could, then decide to murder you. I just said I'd think about it. Then I told Mr. Warren."

"Did you?"

"Yes. The night before he died. I fear I caused a confrontation."

"Do you have proof?"

"No. And I'm terrified to tell my story. What if he comes after me?"

"I understand the fear. Give me just a minute, okay?"

"Yes. Of course."

Reese stands up and exits the room, joining all of us, but he and Milton square off. "What are you going to do Milton?"

"Not a damn thing. She's got no proof. For all I know she's in this with Dana or you paid her off to speak up."

I gape at the response that shouldn't surprise me. This DA's taught his team to win at all costs including the safety of innocent people. This is, after all, the DA who refused to hunt a serial killer after he charged the wrong man and another victim died. "And if she ends up hurt, then what?" I demand, stepping next to Reese.

"Then I guess you can write about it," he snaps snidely. "I'm done here." He walks away.

Royce joins us. "I'll offer her protection," he says. "We're already watching the boyfriend who has to be nervous right now. It'll be interesting to see what he does next."

"I'll talk to her," Reese says scrubbing his jaw, and walking back to the door. He re-enters the room and sits down across from Martha. "The DA's office isn't going to offer you a deal or protection. They want to win the case they've charged. You're saving an innocent woman by speaking up and potentially stopping Reginald from killing again."

"I'm scared," she says, hugging herself, and I can see her arms trembling.

"Walker Security is going to offer you protection," he says. "I know them well. They're respected. You'll be safe, but we really need your help. I'll post your bail for you and Walker will escort you home and to work until we're sure you're safe. Will you help us?"

"What if he doesn't confess?" she asks. "What if he isn't arrested?"

"He still knows you know," Reese says. "You are just as at risk by doing nothing. No. You're more at risk. Take action with me and we'll do everything in our power together to put him in jail." He leans closer to her. "Please help us."

She presses her hands to her face and then drops them. "Yes. Yes, I'll help."

Reid

Debbie's parents are in their fifties and down to earth nice people who show up right on time. I go over the contract I've drafted with them which requires Debbie leave the state for at least one year. Once the deal is inked I hand them a check for fifty thousand dollars. They get another hundred and fifty thousand once I have proof Debbie is gone and another hundred thousand when I receive the DNA test. It's five-thirty when Connie buzzes my office. "Debbie is early."

I glance at the parents and arch a brow. "We'll handle her," her father says.

They stand up and I escort them to the lobby. They're in the conference room for all of five minutes before they exit with Debbie between them, and leave.

I walk to Gabe's office. "It's done."

Cat

Reese and I end up at his office with his team and game plan for hours. When finally we head home, we both change into sweats and tees and he now sits across from me at the island in the kitchen working, and with him sitting across from me, I should be writing my column, but instead, I write in my baby journal.

Dear husband;

You're sitting across from me right now, focused on your work, preparing to win in court tomorrow. I love these times when we sit across from each other in two work worlds, but in the same space. Today is on my mind. It started with me sick and you finding me on the bathroom floor and scooping me up and carrying me to our bed. I so wanted to tell you our news then. I felt protected and loved, the way I know you will make our child feel.

I had this experience to cling to when we were on our way to court and you got *that* call. You are why I survived this. Because you're giving me no reason to fear we aren't us anymore and every reason to love you and us. Proven again today when you pulled me in that office and told me how much you needed me with you. That meant everything to me. It was a hard day, but a big day. The day you made big waves in court. There were many things that happened today that were challenging but all day I kept thinking about being sick and falling asleep on the bathroom floor, and you scooping me up and carrying me to bed. Any fear you have ever had that anyone could convince me you were less than perfect are misplaced. You show me you are my partner and friend every day.

I remember sitting in court and watching the way you rose to the challenge, despite all this day held, and I know you will rise to the challenge of being that good at parenting. I'm growing impatient for your birthday. I want to tell you *now*, but I want this to be special for you. So very special. For us. I want it to be special for us, so I'm going to keep writing, and anxiously waiting to share our news with you. —Love, Cat

The doorbell rings and I stand up. "I'll get it." I round the island and Reese is already on his feet catching my arm, stepping in front of me. "Cat, you don't need to be answering the door on your own. "

"We have security, Reese. It's fine."

"No. It's not. Not now. I need you to be extra cautious."

He didn't send me away, but I get that he's still worried. "Yes. I'm sorry."

He kisses me. "I'll get the door." He releases me and heads out of the room.

The sound of Reid's and Gabe's voices mingling with Reese's tell me who our visitors are. Another minute and I am surrounded by testosterone and Reese is beside me with my brothers across from me. "It's over," Reid says. "I called Debbie's parents and they're getting her out of town. They're good people who were appalled. They are taking her out of state and sending me proof when she gets there."

"It's over?" I ask, stunned.

"You're sure?" Reese asks.

"Yes," Reid states. "Very sure."

"Reid kicked ass," Gabe interjects. "He was angry when we left and he made that work."

Reid and I have been so broken and he did this for me. He fought for me. I round the island and he turns to face me. I don't give him time to back away. I fling my arms around him and hug him, and to my surprise, he holds me and not gently. He holds on like he was really afraid of losing me and he's been lost to me for so long, that I actually start to cry.

Debbie gave me a gift. She gave me my brother back.

Chapter Seventy-Eight

Cat

We're still in the kitchen and I've just finished hugging Reid and Gabe to thank them for helping us end this Debbie nightmare when the doorbell rings. Reese heads to the door to answer it and when I round the island Reid looks at me. "Why do you look different?" he asks.

"You do look different," Gabe comments. "New hair or something."

Just a baby growing in my belly, I think, shocked that my brothers notice the change. "You two are just actually looking at me for once."

"Ouch," Gabe says. "I don't deserve that, but Reid does."

Reese re-enters the kitchen with Royce on his heels. "Royce has more news," Reese announces, joining me on the opposite side of the island, his hand settling on my lower back.

"Our men were watching the motel Debbie's cohort, Wilson Moore, has been hiding out in," Royce states. "He ordered pizza and got his ass kicked instead. My man probably saved his life. He's in an ambulance on the way to the ER now. He's not going to be a problem in the immediate future."

"Really," Gabe says dryly. "How inconvenient for him."

Royce's gaze narrows on Gabe. "And convenient for us?"

His question reeks of accusations I don't understand and I study the two of them, trying to read their exchange more clearly.

"I'm not sorry the bastard got his ass beat," Reid replies before Gabe can. "He was stalking my sister." He knocks on the island. "And Debbie is handled. Her parents took her out of town and now, I'm going home to drink an expensive bottle of whiskey to celebrate."

"I'll join you," Gabe says, pointing at me and Reese. "You two celebrate the way married couples celebrate, but don't tell us about it."

My brothers then disappear out of the kitchen. "What was that?" Reese asks when the front door opens and shuts, and it's clear Reid and Gabe have left.

"Gabe called me and asked me who the bookie was that was hunting Moore, and an hour later, he's getting his face beat in," Royce says. "I know he did it, and I both dislike and understand it, as contradictory as that sounds."

"My brother did that? *Gabe*? He's the nice one."

Royce is quick to dismiss that idea. "That's like saying Savage is the nice one because what comes out of his mouth is humorous. He's not nice at all and neither is your brother." He eyes Reese. "I won't trust the Debbie situation being resolved until I have eyes on her departure. I recommend keeping security in place."

"Agreed," Reese confirms. "Change nothing."

Royce nods. "Savage will stay in place with Cat." He changes the subject. "Martha. She's home. She's safe. We'll have her in court early tomorrow." He looks between us. "Do you need anything else from me?"

"We're good," Reese says.

"We're good," I agree.

Royce inclines his head. "Then I'll let you know if I have updates." He pushes off the counter and exits the kitchen.

Reese turns me and pulls me between him and the counter. He waits for the door to open and close. "First thought?"

"I hate having Savage follow me around. Your first thought?"

"I hate having Savage follow you around. Second thought?"

"I think Gabe got that man beat up," I say. "He could have gotten him killed. Your second thought?"

"The exact same as yours and I know I should have a problem with that, but, Cat, I don't. He protected you."

My hand flattens on his chest, and I can feel his heart thundering under my palm. "I don't know how I feel right now. My brothers. Debbie. The beating. I just don't know."

He pulls me to him. "Ask me my next thought," he orders softly.

"What's your next thought?" I ask.

"I'm really damn tired of seeing Savage by your side."

"Is that right?"

"Yes." He cups my backside and pulls me to him. "It is."

"You've never been jealous."

"Because I've never had a woman claim I made a baby with her when I didn't. Because I know we're solid and I damn sure know men envy me. I promise you, Savage envies me." His mouth covers mine, his tongue licking into my mouth before he declares, "You're mine."

"And you're mine," I say. "I don't like Debbie saying differently."

"Show me," he orders softly, his mouth closing down and it's as if something snaps between us. Our hands are everywhere, our kisses desperate. I don't even know how my sweats get to the ground, or how his lower, but it happens. He lifts me and presses me against the wall, thrusting into me and my hands are in his hair, my lips seeking his lips. It's wild and hot and consuming. There is just me and him and the way our bodies move together until we shatter into that perfect place together. I have a random thought that I think we might break the baby if we keep having this much sex.

Reese pulls back to look at me. "What are you laughing at?" he asks, brushing hair from my lip.

"Us. Against the wall in the kitchen, minutes before your team gets here."

The doorbell rings. He laughs now and sets me on the ground as we rush to pull ourselves together. I'm tugging my sweats back on when he kisses me. "I'm going to get the door."

He rushes out of the kitchen and I laugh again. This needs to go in the journal. I swipe at my hair and turn toward the door as Reese walks in the door with Savage behind him and I laugh again.

"Why are you laughing now?" he asks.

Savage answers. "Because you have more of her lipstick on your face than she does."

The look that settles on Reese's face is decisively satisfied. I do believe my man just marked his territory. It's not a normal behavior for Reese, but somehow, today, it's perfect. "Just wanted to tell you that attorney asshole that was blackmailing you is in bad enough condition to be placed in ICU. Bad news for him, but good news for you. This just reaffirms the fact that he won't be coming after you anytime soon. One of us will update you if we hear more."

He turns to leave, and Reese and I stare at each other, the lightness of our mood fading. Yes, I'm safe, but at what cost?

❦

Hours after we receive the news about Debbie, Elsa and Richard, are back after a dinner break, and in the living room, preparing for tomorrow, including the possibility that Martha could back out. Every outcome is considered. Every strategy dissected. I'm in the kitchen working on my column and take a break to join them, sinking into a cushy chair as Richard and Elsa have claimed the couch.

Reese is standing, pacing as he often does during these sessions, but he sits down on the ottoman next to me. "Here's the big question," Richard says, speaking to us all. "Do we tell Dana in advance of Martha's testimony?"

"She's sleeping with Reginald," Elsa says. "If Martha backs out, we don't want to have Dana freaking out on Reginald, then him trying to save himself."

"Which could mean throwing Dana under the bus," Richard says scrubbing his jaw, his tie long gone, and his jacket with it.

"We're going to take that risk no matter what," Reese says. "Once Martha outs Reginald, he'll be in survival mode."

"But no matter what," I interject, "the jury will have doubt about Dana's guilt."

"Exactly," Reese says. "But I do think we need to hold back on informing Dana about Martha's testimony until after it happens. Let's let her and Reginald coast through the night."

"Desperate people do desperate things," Elsa replies. "Once Martha testifies, Reginald will panic and Royce's team will be watching."

Desperate people do desperate things. I replay that in my head. Wait.

"What if she lied?" I ask.

The entire room turns to look at me.

Chapter Seventy-Nine

Cat

I stand up and so does Reese, both of us facing each other. "I know we talked about Dana and Reginald working together, but we all believed Martha when we were at the police station."

"But what if she lied?" Reese says. "Yes. That's been on my mind as well. What if she lied?"

"What if she lied *again*," I supply, "since a lie is what got her put in jail in the first place."

"I have to break her on the stand just like I would Reginald."

"Treat her like a hostile witness," I assume.

"Exactly," he agrees, his hands coming down on my arms as he pulls me to him and kisses me. "I need to call Royce and make sure he's still digging around on her." He reaches for his phone and I feel the words in my head forming, with a need to put them on paper.

I slip away again and return to the kitchen, sitting down in front of my computer, considering all that happened today with Martha and even Debbie, before I finish my column and then write my closing.

Too often, we let other people scare us into doing nothing. It's easy to think that if we do nothing, we get nothing in return, which sounds pretty horrible, but it can feel safe. The problem with doing nothing is that the result is not nothing. Something happens because we choose not to act, but we choose to allow the result to be out of our control. By doing nothing, we leave the results to someone else. We accept their outcome. What does this have to do with the day in court? Martha Banks went to jail for lying. Lying is not doing nothing. It's doing something. She chose to lie. A lie is complex, rooted in a truth that doesn't want to be told. What is that lie for Martha Banks and what is the truth that hides behind it?

I'm interested to find out what happens tomorrow when she returns to the stand when she must choose to a) tell the truth, b) lie again, or c) plead the fifth. I certainly hope she chooses to tell the truth, but what is that truth? Her own guilt or perhaps knowledge of someone else's? Until then, —Cat.

I think of Debbie and her lie. The lie hides the truth. Her lie hid the real father of her baby, to in turn deliver her a payoff. Desperate people do desperate things. Tomorrow, Reese is going to make a lot of people a whole lot more desperate, including the prosecutor.

Morning comes with a jagged-edged energy. I'm hanging over the toilet and hiding it. Reese is hyped up on caffeine, and eager to step into the courtroom, where we all believe he'll win the trial by way of reasonable doubt, even if he doesn't end it by way of a confession. I dress in a black dress that fits loosely around the waist, while Reese wears a blue pinstriped suit he has me pick out because he's on the phone with Royce and can't seem to actually get dressed.

"Well?" I ask when we're finally in the kitchen with coffee in hand and he's off a good half dozen calls.

"Royce doesn't have anything else for me," he says. "It's going to be all on me to break her."

"You can't lose," I say. "You'll get your reasonable doubt."

The doorbell rings. "And it's time," he says, finishing off his coffee and setting the mug in the sink.

We both gather our things and head to the door. Reese opens it and Savage stands there. Reese and I look at each other, memories of last night in the kitchen encounter between us and we both laugh. Savage runs his hand over his face. "What? Do I have lipstick on my face?"

We *all* laugh now, and I feel the stress of the last week fading into the past. Even more so, when Royce is waiting for us downstairs. "Wilson was so freaked out about his attack that he confessed to blackmailing you two for money in exchange for police protection. He says the baby's his."

Of course, I knew the baby wasn't Reese's but knowing that we have that closure is still a relief to hear, and when Reese pulls me to him and kisses me, I know he feels the same. "It's going to be a good day in court," I promise him.

We settle into the SUV and Reese pulls me close. "And a good night, too," he murmurs, the sexy promise warming me all over. We're back to us, and the idea that someone tried to take that from us doesn't go away because we won. It just reminds us to hold on and never take each other for granted, which is perhaps the best lesson we could have learned before having this baby.

Lori calls me on the way to the courthouse. "I heard all of the news. My God, we've been in hell with a client. I feel horrible that I haven't been there for you, but I'm so happy it seems to be over."

"Me too," I say. "You and Cole are wonderful to be so supportive."

"Supportive? We haven't been there for you since you heard at all, but Cole's been talking to Reese. He's been keeping me informed and I was afraid if I called too, I might just stir the demons and make you have to keep thinking about them."

We chat until the SUV pulls up to the courthouse. Reese and I head inside and once we're there, he kisses me. "Wish me luck, sweetheart."

"You don't need luck. They do."

He winks and I know he's feeling confident. "Savage," he says. "Protect what's mine."

"Like she is mine," he says.

Reese arches a brow at him and Savage immediately adds, "But of course, she will *never* be mine."

We all laugh again and soon I'm in the courtroom with Lauren by my side. "I heard everything about everything." She hugs me and then whispers, "I can't wait to see how this plays out."

And she doesn't have to wait long. The judge and jury enter, and it's minutes before Martha takes the stand and Reese steps in front of her. Once she's stated her name and swears her oath, Reese takes control.

"Why did you lie yesterday?" he asks.

"I was scared," she replies.

"Of what?" Reese presses.

"I was afraid if anyone knew I was in a relationship with Mr. Warren, they'd consider me a suspect."

"How long were you in a relationship with Mr. Warren?"

"Three years."

"Describe that relationship," he says.

"We were close," she says. "He wasn't the bear to me that he was to others."

"Did you fight?"

"Never."

Lauren and I look at each other, and Lauren whispers, "There is no couple that doesn't fight."

"Did you fight the night before he died?" Reese asks, ignoring her "no fight" reply.

"No. We didn't fight."

"Did you see him that night?" Reese asks.

"Yes. I did."

"And what happened?"

"I told him that Reginald Hicks came to me and wanted me to help kill him." The courtroom blows up into a gasp that explodes into murmurs.

Reginald jumps to his feet. "She's lying! She's lying."

Dana gasps and actually turns to try to find me in the audience. When her eyes meet mine, I mouth, "Easy. Let him do his job."

She inhales and turns around, but her fingers are squeezing the wooden chair arms, her knuckles white.

The judge does a lot of banging on the desk and finally, Reese can continue questioning Martha. "Why didn't you tell someone else? Like the police?"

"Mr. Warren, Nelson, didn't want me to. He said he'd handle it himself."

"How did he plan to handle it?"

"He wanted to confront Reginald. He said he was going to confront him."

"Did he?" Reese asks.

"I don't know," she whispers. "He died the night he was supposed to talk to him."

Reginald is on his feet again, screaming. "Liar!"

More chaos ensues, and finally, Reese asks, "Did you consider Reginald's offer?"

"No!" Martha shouts. "No. I would never do that. I loved Mr. Warren. I loved him."

"Did he love you?" Reese asks.

"Yes. He loved me." Martha replies.

I lean over to Lauren and whisper, "She told us sleeping with him was her job."

Lauren eyes me with an arched brow. "And now he loved her?"

"Exactly," I whisper.

"But you weren't in his will," Reese points out.

"I didn't want his money," she snaps. "I didn't care about his money, but he was very generous. I'll never find a job that pays that well. He took care of me."

"And yet you're not in the will," Reese comments.

"Is there a question?" Milton demands, in his first objection.

"I'll withdraw," Reese says, looking at the judge.

"What did Reginald offer you, Martha?"

"Money," she says. "He said he'd marry Dana, inherit, and pay me. He said Dana was going to walk away from the money, and he couldn't let that happen."

"What do you think he thought was your motivation to help?"

"I guess money," she says.

"Did he know that you weren't in the will?"

"He might have. Dana knew."

"And he believed since you were cut out of the will, you might want to kill your lover to ensure your good job continued to pay."

"I don't like how that sounds," Martha says. "I didn't want a payday."

"Everyone just thought you did," Reese comments.

"Objection," Milton shouts. "Again. Is there a question?"

"Did everyone think that you wanted a payday?" Reese asks, rephrasing.

"I don't know," she says.

"What did you tell Reginald when he offered you money to help kill your lover?"

"I told him I'd think about it. I was scared of him. I was afraid to say no."

"To clarify," Reese says. "You said you'd think about killing your lover, the deceased, who was murdered?"

"I—it wasn't—"

"Yes or no?" Reese presses.

"I was—I—"

"Yes or no," the judge demands.

"Yes."

"I'm through with this witness," Reese says and walks back to his table. Milton doesn't cross-examine. He can't. Anything he'd ask would just make Dana look more innocent.

Reese has won this case long before the trial ends.

Lauren leans close. "He made that look easy."

I smile, pride filling me. "Yes. He did." I lean close and whisper. "That's the father of my baby."

She grins. "Yes, he is." She reaches in her purse. "I got you this to give him." She hands me a long, narrow box that might be a pen box. I open it to find a cigar that has pink and blue ribbons on it. Girl or boy. Which will it be? Which will he want?

My stomach knots. What if he doesn't want this now? If he's shocked, if he's hesitant, this isn't the birthday present I want it to be. He won't be hesitant. Will he? I need to feel him out before his birthday. I have to know he wants this.

Chapter Eighty

Reese

The minute I finish with Martha and return to my table, Dana is tugging on my arm. "What just happened?" she whispers leaning in close. "Did Reginald do this?"

Milton stands up. "I'd like to request a short recess, judge."

"Once again," the judge says, "I imagine you do. Fifteen minutes." He pounds the gavel and the room erupts into more of the noise Martha's testimony delivered.

"What's going on?" Dana demands again.

"Let's go to our private room," I say.

"Dana!" Reginald screams. "I didn't do it. I swear to you. I love you. I wouldn't hurt your father!"

She presses her hands to her face, upset when she has reason to be happy. She has her reasonable doubt, and any jury doing their job will acquit her. My hand settles on her back and I twist around to find Cat, thankfully, at the railing. She has a way with Dana that I'm going to need right now and I motion for her to meet us in the back room. She nods and stands up, heading toward the door.

Elsa kneels next to Dana and says something to her, and Dana nods then stands up. I intentionally allow Elsa to guide Dana forward, while Richard and I fall into pace behind them. "Nailed it, boss."

"If I nailed it the trial would be over," I say. "I didn't get my confession."

"Close enough to win," he assures me, but that's not good enough.

"The longer the trial," I say, reigning myself in right along with him, "the more chances to have it turn against us. Never be overconfident."

We exit to the hallway and I hear Reginald shouting again, "Dana! Dana, please talk to me."

The man must have run from the courtroom to get here this quickly.

Dana bursts out of the conference room where Elsa has just managed to lead her. "I need to talk to him."

"No," I reject instantly. "Not now."

"I have to talk to him," she insists. "I need to hear the truth directly from him. Please."

"You'll know the truth when he testifies," I say. "If he turns on you, he killed your father."

"And if he doesn't?" she asks.

"That doesn't mean he didn't do it," I say, and silently add: It just means he's gambling on her protecting him with her money.

"I'm here!" Cat calls out.

I turn to find her and Savage rushing in our direction while Reginald's voice fades as he's clearly ushered away. "Our team took care of him," Savage confirms as he and Cat join us.

"I don't want him taken care of," Dana growls. "I wanted to talk to him."

I turn to face Cat, giving a barely-there shake of my head, letting her know how against that idea I am. She gives me a tiny nod. "Not if you want to help him and you," she says, stepping around me and taking Dana's arm. "Let's go into the conference room. We don't want to be overheard." Cat ushers her into the room.

"Jesus," Elsa murmurs. "Can't a client just be glad you saved her ass? Thank God for Cat."

"Agreed," Richard adds. "You saved her. She's losing her shit. That's not how this is supposed to play out."

No, I think, and that doesn't sit well with me. "Give us a few minutes with Dana," I say, but I don't wait for an answer. I enter the room.

"Right now," Cat says, as I shut us inside. "The prosecution believes you're going to get a ruling in your favor. They're scrambling to either convict you or save face. Anything you do will be suspect."

"If you're talking to Reginald," I say, "you could be coordinating lies. The police are watching right now. You're protecting you and him by staying away from him."

"Why didn't you warn me about that in there, Reese?"

"I needed you to be just as shocked as the jury," I reply. "And I needed Reginald to give us an honest reaction, not one you prepped him for."

"I don't like that you didn't tell me," Dana snaps.

"That testimony," Cat says, her tone angry now, my wife rising up to protect her husband, "was your ticket to freedom. Reese set you free. He saved decades of your life."

Dana presses her hands to her face and then looks at me. "I'm sorry." Her voice cracks. "I know you protected me. I just don't want him to be guilty. I love him. He's all I have."

"Which is another reason to give yourself some space," Cat says. "You're vulnerable with him right now."

"What happened to keeping him on our side?" she demands.

"Martha turned herself and him into the reasonable doubt we needed," I say. "If he's going to turn on you, he's going to turn on you. He'll be in desperate mode right now and we can't let him take you down with him."

"What if he's innocent?" she says. "What if Martha's lying?"

"We think she might be lying," Cat replies. "But we don't know. You're so very close to freedom." Cat walks up to her and settles her hands on Dana's arms. "When you're free, if he's innocent and needs a lawyer, you can get him one. You can help him, but you can't help him if you're disinherited and behind bars."

I don't miss the fact that Cat didn't suggest I become his lawyer, but Dana doesn't catch the inference that I won't be offering my services to Reginald. Dana breathes out and nods. "You're right. You're so right."

I take the opening I'm given. "Then you won't mind if I keep you under lock and key for the next few days." Cat steps back to allow me direct eye contact with Dana. "I want you in a hotel room with Walker Security protecting you."

"You think I'm in danger?"

"More from yourself than anyone else," I say. "One wrong conversation or move could ruin this for you and us."

"Do you think I'm in danger?" she presses.

"There's a killer on the loose," I say when I'm really just trying to keep her away from Reginald. "I'm not taking any chances. Desperate people do desperate things," I repeat. "Do we agree on the hotel and the security?"

Dana hugs herself. "Yes. Yes, okay."

"I don't even want a text message exchanged with Reginald," I add. "I mean it. Nothing. Agreed?"

"Yes. Agreed."

I study her a few beats, ensuring she really does agree. "Give me a moment," I say, motioning Cat to the hallway.

We step outside and shut the door. Richard, Elsa, and Savage join us. "I need her in a hotel with protection tonight," I tell Savage.

Savage nods. "I'll get a plan in place now in case court adjourns early." His phone beeps and he grabs it, glances at a text message and then at us. "Royce has an insider who told him the DA just submitted for a search warrant for Martha and Reginald's homes and offices."

"They know they're going to lose," Cat says. "They're trying to either connect Dana to the murder, via an accomplice, or make a new arrest before they look like fools."

"In other words," Richard says, "you didn't get your confession, but you might have caught a killer."

"Don't tell Dana," I say. "We do not want her warning Reginald."

Savage looks at me. "You don't think she's afraid if he goes down, she goes down, do you?"

"No," I say. "Do you know something we don't know?"

"We searched his place," he says. "We pulled random samples to look for DNA evidence. We didn't find anything, but the police will do what we couldn't do. They'll tear his place apart."

"That's not an answer," I say. "Do you know something I don't?"

"No," he says. "But you're worried. I see it in your eyes."

"There's not an attorney on the planet that isn't worried they've misjudged a client."

Savage nods. "I'll take care of the hotel arrangements." He looks at Cat. "Page me when you're ready to leave. I'll be at the end of the hallway." He walks away.

I take Cat's arm and motion to the office we met in yesterday. We step inside and I shut the door. "Was she too damn worried about him considering the revelations on the stand or am I being paranoid?"

"I thought the same thing. She was too worried. For the first time since you started this trial, I'm worried she's guilty."

I rest my head against the door and breathe out. Cat is quickly in front of me, her hands on my waist. "We're both being paranoid about your perfect record and our dislike of helping killers get away with murder. Let's consider option number two: She loves him. The idea that he is guilty, that he used her for money, on top of her father's death, makes her feel really alone. And once you have someone in your life that you love, the idea of losing them destroys you."

I cup her head and pull her lips to mine. "Are you telling me you thought you were going to lose me over Debbie?"

"No. Not really."

I pull back. "Not really?"

"I had fleeting moments that I felt those things. They were so very fleeting, but I think it's natural in such a situation. The point isn't about us, but rather that Dana's afraid of losing everything. I get that because of my fresh feelings over Debbie. Let's not decide Dana's guilt, based on her confused, emotional state of mind. She might just really need what I did. For the man she loves to tell her he's innocent."

"You needed to hear me say it?"

"I didn't think I did, but when I looked in your eyes and you assured me you were, I knew you were. It's like I could breathe again. We're denying Dana that chance and for good reason. We have to. I mean, if Reginald is guilty, for all we know he could turn dangerous and suicidal. I'm just saying, we believed in Dana. You believed in her and I don't think you should stop now. That will affect how you defend her. Stand by your client and win with your client."

I digest those words and they feel as right as everything with Cat always feels. This woman understands me in ways no other human ever has or could. She is truly my partner in this life, and she's right. If Dana felt Reginald could be that for her, she's going to resist losing him. "The questions is," I say, "what will she do to protect him? She was ready to turn on him only days ago. She's erratic and all over the board."

"My mother stayed with my father even when he cheated. The fear of being alone is powerful."

I cup her face. "That will never be us. You know that, right?"

"I know that, Reese Summer. We're going to grow old together. We're going to have babies together."

I pull back and look at her. "Babies? You're thinking about babies?"

"We've talked about it."

"Yes," I say. "We have. We should talk about it again."

"You still want babies, right?"

I kiss her. "I want everything with you, Cat," I assure her, but now she's got me thinking. She's been sick. She's different right now. Did my wife just tell me she's pregnant? Surely not. She wouldn't tell me here and now, but if she is or if she's just got the idea on her mind, I want her to know I'm all in.

There's a knock on the door and I quickly kiss her again. "Just to be clear, Cat," I promise. "Everything means everything," I say before I'm forced to leave this conversation for later.

Chapter Eighty-One

Cat

Lauren doesn't stay for the afternoon in court, but I'm feeling pretty good about the cigar in my purse that she gave me for Reese. I settle into my seat, waiting for the courtroom to come to order. After Reese and I had our little talk about babies and everything, he might have a little idea I'm pregnant, but he'll have to wait for the birthday surprise and I know it will be a really special day. Especially when Reese reclaims his spot in the courtroom and winks at me. There are a few murmurs in response that tell me we most likely got the attention of the press but I'm not complaining. Mr. Hotness winked at me, and I'm the lucky girl in the room.

The rest of the morning, the prosecution seems to stay on safe territory. They call non-consequential witnesses and fill up time. Come lunchtime, I reluctantly allow Savage to walk me to the food truck. "How long do you think it will be necessary to have you by my side?"

Savage holds his heart. "You wound me. I thought I was too good to let go of."

I laugh and Reese steps to my side, wrapping his arm around me, and eyeing Savage. "I'll take it from here."

Right at that moment, Reginald steps in front of us. "I didn't do it," he says. "I didn't fucking do it."

Savage steps between us. "You need to back away, man."

"I just want to talk. Please, Reese! Please, just talk to me."

Reese looks down at me. "Stay away from him and with me or Savage at all times." He then refocuses on the two men and calls out. "Savage, I'll talk to him."

Savage pulls Reginald in front of him and holds his arms. "As long as Reginald here doesn't mind being friendly with me while you do," he says, towering over Reginald and Reginald is not a small guy.

Reginald doesn't even seem to notice. "I didn't do it. Tell me what I need to do to prove I didn't do it."

"Tell the truth on the stand," Reese says. "Martha didn't and that didn't go well for her."

"Can *you* be my attorney?"

"That's a conflict of interest." Reese says.

"You think I'm guilty."

"It wouldn't matter either way," Reese replies. "It's a conflict of interest."

"I'll protect her. Put me on the stand, and I'll protect her."

"I intend to," Reese says. "When it's our turn which could be a long way off."

"What if I get Martha to confess? I'll confront her. I'll record her."

"We could make that work," Savage says.

"Talk to Savage, Reginald," Reese replies. "But don't talk to Dana. You're going to make her look guilty."

"Because I look guilty?" he demands.

"Because she looks guilty," Reese says. "She's the one who was charged. Don't give anyone a chance to question her. As long as there's no evidence against you, they won't charge you to just charge." He eyes Savage. "We're going back."

Savage nods and Reese wraps his arm around my shoulders and turns me back toward the courthouse. "First thought?"

"I hope he doesn't get an attorney. That could work against us."

"Agreed," I say.

"Maybe he'll deliver us Martha and save himself and Dana."

"Desperate people do desperate things," I remind him. "This feels volatile to me. It feels like a problem."

"That's why he's with Savage and on another note: Your brother texted me. Debbie is on an airplane and I talked to Royce. Wilson is stable. I think for now though, we'll keep Walker in place through the rest of the trial."

"Because of Reginald?"

"Because I want you safe."

We head back into the courthouse and I think about the baby in my belly and decide not to argue. I'm not taking any chances with our child and maybe on some level Reese senses that he needs to protect more than me. He needs to protect his child.

The afternoon is slow. The prosecution calls a number of police officers who are so uneventful that Reese allows Elsa to cross-examine them. It's four o'clock when Savage enters the courtroom and delivers a note to Reese. Reese reads the note and nods to Savage. "Judge, can we approach please?"

The judge motions him forward and he and Milton are quickly in front of him. Both are clearly arguing before the judge bangs his gavel. "Counselors, in my office. Court is adjourned until eight am tomorrow."

Savage is waiting on me at the end of the aisle, and we don't speak until we're outside. "What's going on?" I ask as soon as we're out of the cluster of people.

"The police raided Martha and Reginald's apartments an hour ago," he says. "Things are heating up."

"That's doesn't mean they won't find a way to connect Dana," I say, hurrying toward Reese's private hallway.

"An insider told Royce to expect an arrest," Savage tells me as we turn down the hallway.

"One arrest?"

"One."

"Which one?"

"He wouldn't say more," Savage says, "but after dealing with Reginald this afternoon I vote for Martha."

"Why do you say that?"

"He was willing to be recorded setting her up," he says. "If he had something to hide he wouldn't be that stupid. Well, not likely. I've met some really fucking stupid people."

"What's the plan on that anyway?" I ask.

"Reginald is with our team, but Martha is MIA. No one has seen her since she left court."

"Dana's in freak out mode," Richard says, rushing toward us. "She's afraid Reginald is being arrested."

"Isn't that adorable," Savage says dryly. "I just love when a woman on trial worries about her money-grubbing boyfriend."

"I thought you thought he was innocent," I say.

"Of murder," Savage says, "but I know men, and that man is in love with money, not the woman with the money."

I don't get time to ask where this assessment comes from. Reese exits to the hallway and we all wait eagerly to hear the news. "Well?"

"Milton tried to blow off the warrants as unimportant, but the judge wasn't convinced," he says. "We're meeting him in chambers for an update before court tomorrow morning."

Dana appears at the conference room door. "Well?"

Reese turns to look at her. "Warrants were issued for Martha and Reginald's apartments which are currently being searched. Time to get to that hotel room and wait out any news. No conversations with Reginald. Don't break that promise."

Dana hugs herself. "I want this to be over."

"Even if there's an arrest and your case is dismissed," Reese says, "it's not over until the killer is proven guilty. That means you need to trust cautiously and protect yourself."

"That's not easy to do with someone you love," Dana says, shoving her blonde hair from her face, her blue eyes bloodshot, as if she's fighting tears.

"Good news," Savage says. "That's why you have us right now." He wiggles an eyebrow. "And beyond our reasonable charges, we don't want your money."

"But Reginald does?" Dana asks.

"That's between you and him, ma'am," he says. "But we can talk about it over a ten-dollar deal night pizza, if you like."

"Go have pizza," Reese says. "And try not to overthink what comes next. It's going to happen no matter what."

"You really think my case will be dismissed?" Dana asks, sounding hopeful now.

"Unless there's evidence in Martha or Reginald's apartments to convict you," Reese says. "Then yes, I do."

Her eyes go wide. "What if one of them sets me up?"

"The only one that could set you up is Reginald," I say. "He came to us today and swore he'd protect you. We'll know soon if he meant those words."

"You have to wait this out," Reese says. "There's no way to take the hard part of that out of the equation."

"Sure there is," Savage says. "Ten-dollar pizza and cheap wine, the likes of which a rich Princess like you doesn't understand." He motions her forward.

Dana stares at Reese a moment. "You'll call if you hear anything tonight?"

"I will," he promises.

She gives a sharp nod and joins Savage who eyes Reese. "I'll have one of my men get you two home."

Reese nods and looks at Richard and Elsa. "Go eat pizza and drink cheap wine. Our job here is done for now."

They say they're goodbyes and Reese pulls me to him. "How about ten-dollar pizza and cheap wine for us, too?"

"No olives and no wine—I have to write my column—but I'm all in for the pizza,"

His lips quirk and he studies me. "No olives and no wine. Deal." He wraps his arm around my shoulders and we start walking. "If I guess the birthday present do I get it early?"

Chapter Eighty-Two

Cat

I'm saved from Reese's birthday inquiry when one of Savage's men joins us, but I am fairly certain that my need to feel Reese out on the topic of babies has blown my surprise. He knows. Or he suspects. I don't want to tell him. Not until his birthday. It's only two weeks. I'll let him wonder until then. He has to wait. We head out to the SUV waiting on us and despite a swarm of press that tries to get to Reese, we're on the road without any real trouble. On the ride home, Cole calls Reese to talk about the developments with Debbie and the call is over by the time we're at our apartment door.

We walk in the door with a sense of relief between us. The Debbie situation is all but behind us and so is this trial. For Dana, I'm not sure the problem is gone. Reginald may or may not be guilty, and her case being dismissed doesn't answer that question. "Pizza, no olives?" Reese asks as we walk into the bedroom and I kick off my heels.

I glance over at him, as he shrugs out of his jacket, that perfect chest of his stretching with the action. I wonder if pregnancy makes you want your man more because I'm not lacking in the want my man scenario despite my sickness. "No olives," I say. "I think it will be a while before I venture down that path again." I head into the closet via the bathroom and strip off my dress.

Reese appears in the doorway, and he's now wearing sweats and a snug tee. "No wine, right?" he asks, and he's looking at my stomach.

I point at my boobs. "They're right here, in case you didn't notice."

His eyes meet mine. "Cat—"

The doorbell rings. "Damn it," he murmurs, grabbing me and pulling me to him. "I'll finish that sentence when we're alone." He kisses me and heads out of the closet.

Damn it is right. He's going to make me tell him because if he asks me directly, I won't lie even if it is to save his surprise.

Reese

My wife is pregnant. I know it. I feel it and my excitement is dashed when I reach for the front door to open it and pause with a thought. She's been nursing this news, while Debbie was claiming that I cheated on her. I press my hands to the door. "Damn it," I whisper. No wonder she hasn't told me. I need to think about this. Where does that put her head right now? Do I push her to tell me?

The doorbell rings again and I grimace but push off the door. "Who is it?"

"Royce," comes the deep reply.

I open the door. "I hope this is good news."

"It's not bad news," he says.

"What's happening?" Cat asks from behind me.

I back up and allow Royce to enter, my gaze sweeping over my wife, who's in baggy sweats and a T-shirt and still looks sexy as hell. Pregnant. With my child. I can't even get my head around this really happening for us. I really don't want to get my head around the timing.

"Let's go to the kitchen," I say, motioning him forward, and joining Cat, but I don't let her follow him.

I pull her to me. "Cat," I whisper.

"What?"

"I'm so fucking sorry about Debbie. I hate you had to go through this."

"It's not your fault." Her hand settles on my face. "Why are you saying this right now?"

"It just hit me walking down the stairs, how shitty this really has to be for you right now."

"It's over and it was bad for both of us. This isn't your fault, Reese."

I rest my forehead against her. "I know, but that almost makes it worse. I couldn't protect you from this." I kiss her temple. "Come on. Let's talk to Royce." I take her hand and lead her into the kitchen.

Royce is helping himself to a bottle of water from the fridge. "Thanks," he says, shutting the door and holding it up. He takes a big swig and sets the bottle on the counter while Cat and I take up the spots at the island across from him. "They're arresting Martha," he announces. "They think she not only did the crime, they believe she acted alone, though they aren't prepared to fully rule out Reginald's involvement."

My phone rings in my pocket and I pull it out, glancing at the caller ID and the unknown number. "I have no idea who this is." I answer, "Reese Summer."

"It's Milton. We're dismissing the case in the morning, but if I find a connection to her, I *will* recharge her." He disconnects.

I slip my phone back in my pocket. "They're dismissing the charges," I say. "Reserving the right to recharge if they find new evidence."

"You don't look pleased," Royce comments.

"An acquittal means your client can't be recharged," I say. "This doesn't."

"It's still a good thing," Cat says. "They have a weak case that you exposed in court. They really would have to have something big to recharge."

"My source is good," Royce says. "Martha did it. They found gun residue and DNA. That said, Dana needs to proceed cautiously with Reginald until he's officially cleared. He could plant evidence on her."

"Does that mean that you think he's involved?" I ask.

"I don't," he says. "But we can't know for sure. Martha linked them. We have to be sure that link is broken before we call him innocent."

"I need to go talk to Dana," I say. "Which means I need to change."

"I'll give you a ride," Royce says. "I can share my concerns if you think it helps."

"Cat's the one that gets through to her," I say, eyeing her. "But you have a deadline, right?"

"I really do," she says, "but if you need me once you're there, call me and I'll come over." She frowns. "I'll just ride with you. I can sit in the hotel lobby and write, and then if you really need me I'll be there."

"You sure?" I ask, concerned that she's pushing herself, on top of all the stress. I don't want to lose this baby or her. "You've been really sick."

"I'm good. I feel okay right now."

I eye Royce. "Give us ten minutes to change again."

He nods. "I'll meet you downstairs."

I give him a wave and Cat and I head to the bedroom. Once we're there, she steps in front of me. "What was that down there?"

I cup her head, wanting to tell her I know, but now isn't the time. "A husband who loves his wife and wants everything with her?" I kiss her. "Let's go and get back. We have a date for pizza, no olives or wine, and I intend to keep that date."

She laughs. "Suddenly I think I might want the olives."

And I think I might just want her. Forget the pizza, no wine. We can't get this meeting over and back home soon enough for me.

Chapter Eighty-Three

Cat

"How much can I reveal?" I ask as Reese and I settle into the back seat of Royce's SUV, both of us now in jeans and button-down shirts. "I need to call my editor."

"Scoop it, baby," I say, squeezing her. "It's out tomorrow anyway."

"Don't name me as a source," Royce says. "But otherwise, go for it."

I grab my phone. "My editor is going to have an orgasm with no man present."

Reese and Royce both laugh. I punch in my editor's number and she answers immediately. "I was about to call you. Word is they're searching houses."

"And dismissing the charges against Dana tomorrow. I'm going to tell all. I'll have my column to you in about an hour." I think about Dana. "Actually, I need two."

"We'll make it work. Write it, baby!" She hangs up. I pull out my MacBook and I have a brief moment when I think of Reese in the hallway of our apartment earlier, worried about me and us. What I felt in him and from the experience with Debbie helps me connect to all the things Dana must be feeling. I start to type:

Lies never end well. People suffer. People hurt. In the end, though, we all hope that the truth wins. It has. The truth has won.

Reese leans close and studies my words. His lashes lower and there is this new torment in him that I don't understand. I touch his cheek and give him a questioning look. "And we're here," Royce says. "I'm going to valet."

Reese kisses my hand and my door is open by a hotel employee. Reluctantly, I shut my MacBook and suddenly wonder if Reese has guessed I'm pregnant and read something bad into my silence. Oh

God. He has. I know him. I scoot out of the vehicle and before I can even speak to Reese, Royce is by our sides.

We head inside and I spy a seating area. "I'm going to park myself right there." I push to my toes and kiss Reese, and stay right there, close to him. "Whatever is bothering you, you're overthinking it. Be as confident in us as I am."

He cups my head and despite the busy lobby and his preference for privacy, he kisses me. "I love you, Cat. I'll be back soon." He starts to move away and I catch his arm.

"I love you, too."

His lips curve and he leans in and kisses me again before he joins Royce at the elevator. I watch him disappear into the car and then claim my seat to start typing, certain that every word will be motivated by the ironic way the lies that have attacked our lives, have attacked Dana and this trial.

Reese

"I think she's pregnant," I say when the elevator doors shut. "I think she's pregnant, and she has regrets about it because of Debbie. I need that DNA test, Royce. Whatever it takes, however much it costs."

Royce glances over at me. "You think she has regrets? Why?"

"She hasn't told me. How can she want to be pregnant after another woman just claimed I fucked around on her?"

"I know people, and on top of that, your wife is close to my wife. Cat is not filled with any kind of regret." The elevator halts and we step into the hallway, but we stop right there.

"I didn't think so," I say. "But why the hell hasn't she told me?"

"Lauren and I had two pregnancies and one failed," he says. "The second time she waited a few weeks to tell me because she knew I'd be crushed if we lost the baby. I guessed just like you seem to feel that you have and that's when she told me. Maybe she just wanted out from under all of this before she told you."

"Well," I say. "I can't blame her for that." I think of her birthday surprise. Maybe that's why she's waiting, but I need to fucking know. "Let's go deal with this."

We head down the hallway and knock on the door. Savage answers quickly. "Bossman one and two," he greets. "We have pizza. Come. Eat. Talk."

We join him just inside the doorway, a hallway separating us from the living area where Dana is likely waiting. "She's feeling thankful and reasonable," Savage murmurs softly.

Royce glances at me. "We'll stand outside. I'll join you when you're ready."

I nod and round the corner to find Dana standing, now in sweats and a tee, her arms crossed in front of her. "Tomorrow in court the charges will be dropped."

Her eyes go wide and she starts to cry. "Oh my God. Oh my God." She races forward and hugs me. "Thank you. Thank you so much." She pulls back to look at me. "Did Reginald do it?"

"Let's sit," I say and she claims a chair while I claim the couch.

"Well?" she asks, nervously.

"Martha is being arrested, but they aren't ruling out Reginald. They could still re-charge you. This isn't an acquittal. That means you can't leave yourself exposed. Get on a plane and go somewhere where you and this case have distance. Keep me informed so I can reach you."

"And don't take Reginald," she says.

"Distance yourself and let this play out. I don't think Reginald will be charged but give this time to tie up. If he loves you, he'll wait. If you love him, this is better for him, too."

She presses her hands to her face and then looks at me. "I'm going to go to Paris. I have a friend there. Now that it's over, I want it to stay over."

"Good decision," I say.

"When can I have Reginald join me? When is it safe?"

"When they clear him. I'll let you know." I then make an attempt to escape. "I'm going to have Royce update you with a few more details."

"Can you please stay? I feel like I need your input on any question I might have."

"I can't. I need to take care of some things, which is why I'm going to let Royce answer your questions on his own."

She ignores my reply and then proceeds to ask me a good forty minutes of questions before I'm finally standing. "Thank you, Reese," she says. "You're worth every penny you charge."

I give her a nod. "I try to be." I walk to the door and exit to the hallway. "She's in a good place," I say. "I just need to have you, Royce, give her a chance to ask questions. And then I need your team to make sure she gets on a plane out of the city once she's released tomorrow."

"Done," Royce says, his eyes narrowing. "You're not going to wait on me, are you?"

"No. I need some time with my wife." I eye Savage, "Without you or your men."

"Understood," both men murmur, and they've barely spoken the word before I'm walking away.

I impatiently step onto the elevator and punch the lobby button. If my wife is pregnant, I not only need to know. I need to know that she's happy. That's not a conversation that can wait until my birthday, if that's her plan.

Chapter Eighty-Four

Reese

The minute Cat sees me she shuts her computer. "Perfect timing. I just sent my column to my editor. Where's Royce?" she asks, stuffing her MacBook into her briefcase.

"I left him to talk with Dana," I say, helping her to her feet.

"Is she okay? Is she thinking straight?"

"Remarkably clear headed. She's going to visit a friend in Paris. I'm past due some quality time with my wife."

"I'm with you all the time," she says, her hand settling on my chest, those beautiful green eyes of hers searching mine. "What's going on with you, husband?"

"We need some time together without everything else suffocating us. And now it's all but over with the exception of a few loose ends. The case. Debbie. All of it." I bring her fingers to my lips and kiss them. "Let's go home. I ordered a car on the ride down." I wrap my arm around her and we start walking. I have a moment when I consider that maybe she's not pregnant, but if she's not, she's not. She'll know that I very much want her to be the mother of my children. She's the entire reason I want children. This world needs more people like Cat.

The car is waiting for us outside, and we're inside and at our apartment in a few short minutes. Once we're inside the building, I think about feeding my wife. "Pizza, no olives?"

"Pizza *with* olives," she laughs. "I'm suddenly really wanting olives again."

The elevator opens and once we're inside the apartment, I start to order pizza and hesitate. We need to talk. I link our fingers and lead her to the bedroom, sitting her down on the couch where I proposed, that overlooks the city. We both sink down into the cushion, our legs connected. And as we do often, especially as we shift from one challenge to another, we stare out at the city. Parenthood would certainly be a new challenge.

"When do you go back to the doctor?"

She looks over at me. "Who said I do?"

"Do you?"

"Yes. Monday."

"Good. I'll go with you."

"You're not going to the doctor with me, Reese," she says, looking away. "I'm fine."

"And if I want to go?"

I glance over at him. "Why would you want to go?"

He stares at me several long beats before he says, "Because I love you. Because I'm worried about you. Why else would I want to go, Cat?"

"Whatever your question is, the answer is yes."

I arch a brow. "Yes?"

"Yes."

"Don't ask it though," she warns. "It's your birthday present."

"Holy fuck." I go down on a knee in front of her. "Are you pregnant, Cat?"

"Reese!" She leans forward and presses her hands to my face. "I told you not to ask."

"Tell me," I order.

"Reese—"

"*Say it,* Cat."

"Stubborn man. Okay. Yes, I'm pregnant."

I bury my face in her lap and press my hand to her belly, emotions sideswiping me, momentarily overwhelming me. I look up at her. "You're sure?"

"I'm sure. How do you feel about it?"

"Blessed. Happy, Cat, I'm happy but it's you I'm worried about. How do you feel about it? You didn't tell me."

"Blessed. Happy. Of course, I wanted to tell you. We've always talked about this, but I found out right before your opening statement. I wasn't going to distract you from that and then I was going to tell you once you were past that, but then Debbie—"

"You had to deal with Debbie, while you were pregnant. Please tell me you haven't been regretting this, Cat."

"My God, no. Regret your child, *our* child? *Never.* I knew Debbie stole a little of my joy and I didn't want her to steal yours. I wanted this moment to come when we were past her threats and I wanted it to be special. Why do you think I did the whole 'end this in one week' demand? That's not like me. I kept telling myself I could make it until your birthday, which I was going to tell you then no matter what, but it was killing me to hold it back."

I lay her down on the couch on her side and go down with her, facing her. "I understand why you held it back. I do. You tried to protect me and something special between us."

"Yes. Very much."

"And you succeeded. Now we don't have to think about Debbie or Dana." I laugh. "Let's stay away from names that start with a D. Boy or girl?"

"I don't know. I don't even know when we'll know. I had to see the nurse. The doctor is gone until my next appointment."

"Due date?"

"June 11th."

"Do you *want* a boy or a girl?" I ask.

"Either, but a boy that can be just like you would be very special. You?"

I stroke hair from her eyes. "Either, but a girl that can be just like you would be very special."

She smiles, but it fades quickly. "This wasn't how we planned this," she says. "We were waiting a while. I was on the pill. I don't know how it even happened but it did. Are you sure you're okay with this?"

"It seems to be that little one in your belly made that decision for us and yes, Cat. I'm fucking perfect."

"You're not scared?"

"Should I be?"

"Well, I wasn't, but now that we're talking about it, it's hitting. There's a baby in my belly and we're responsible for that life. That feels intimidating."

"If it didn't," I say, "you wouldn't be the perfect mom I know you're going to be."

"Even that statement feels like pressure. Is there such a thing as a perfect mom or dad?"

"Perfect is you and me doing this together and we're good at doing things together, Cat. We'll figure it out and even if we get it wrong, our child will feel loved."

Her hand comes to my face. "I need to tell you something. Lauren knows. I was freaking out over holding this back, but afraid of messing with your opening statement. Royce walked in. He overheard. He knows. No one else knows."

I laugh. "I put Royce on the spot in the elevator. I told him I thought you were pregnant and that I needed the DNA test from Debbie. Cat, I started thinking that you were—"

"Not telling you because I doubted you?"

"Yes. Exactly."

"I didn't think of how my silence might create those feelings for you." Her fingers trail over my lips. "I just wanted this to be special for us. I promise."

I catch her hand and kiss it. "It is. We are." Her stomach growls and we both laugh.

"The baby isn't even born yet, and she's making herself known," Cat says. "I'm starving."

"She?"

She smiles. "That slipped out, but maybe it's instinct. I need that pizza, with olives."

"How about half and half in case you change your mind?"

"I like that idea. I do believe, you, Reese Summer, will be quite skilled at negotiating with a toddler."

I laugh and half an hour later we sit at our window eating pizza, and Cat decides she only wants the olives. "I think we need to name this kid Olive."

"That's a bad joke. We will not name our child Olive. What's the middle name going to be? Branch?"

We laugh through a selection of names until we close up the pizza box. "When and who do you want to tell?"

"Lori and Cole should know, I think," Cat says. "Don't you?"

"Agree but what about family?"

"Can we wait until at least twelve weeks? Just to be sure everything is okay?"

The tentativeness in her voice draws an instant reaction from me. I lay her down again and settle my knee between hers, my body on the couch next to her. "We will tell people when you want to tell people." I stroke her cheek. "Cat, I know how disconnected you've always felt from your family, and how important ours is going to be to you but know this: That family starts with us. If something were to happen, which it won't, we still have us. And that will always be the start of good things."

Tears pool in her eyes. "Yes. Yes, you're right. I won't forget that. That's why Debbie couldn't get to me. I know how good we are."

I stroke away the dampness on her cheeks. "We're going to think only good things. Okay?"

"Yes. Okay."

I slide down her body and lift her shirt, pressing my lips to her belly. "Our baby."

She smiles and laughs. "Little Olive."

"Little Olive," I jokingly approve. "Now," I reach for her zipper. "I'm going to need to kiss you from head to toe, just to make sure you know how happy I am about this news."

Chapter Eighty-Five

Cat

The morning after Reese learns he's going to be a father, we wake to the news that Martha has officially been arrested. Everything is going as expected which means Reese and I are in the back of Savage's SUV on our way to court when my agent calls. "Your publisher read your column this morning along with the rest of the world. They want a book. Ten percent higher than the last deal."

"Send me the contract to review," I say.

"To review?" Liz demands. "Are you crazy?"

No, I think, *just pregnant.* I have a baby to think about, which means deadlines and due dates, have to be considered.

"Do you know how much money this is?" she adds.

Since I keep reading about how expensive babies are, I decide the offer is a good offer. "I'm always cautious. I need to review the contract but it's probably a yes."

"Probably?"

"I need to go," I say, as we pull up to the courthouse. "I'll call you later."

Reese arches a brow. "Book deal?"

"College fund."

He laughs, and a few minutes later, with Savage still by my side, through at least today, I enter the courtroom. Not much later, there's a press conference with Reese and Milton, and Dana as the special guest. It's hours before the crowd thins and Dana is so ready to be away from it all that we discover that she's already packed and Savage is dropping her off at the airport. "Savage talked to Reginald for me," she says as we walk her to the side exit with Savage moving on ahead to clear the exterior of the building. "He seems to understand why I can't talk to him."

We stop at the doors to wait on Savage and Dana hugs me and Reese. There are lots of happy words. Finally, Savage waves her onward to join him outside. We've just sealed her inside the SUV when she rolls down the window. "Maybe I'll take Savage to Paris."

We both laugh and the SUV pulls away. "You think Savage will go?" I ask.

"Not Savage. He's not about money."

"She's a pretty woman."

"She's not a Savage woman. You are, but we took care of that with the lipstick." He wraps his arm around me and another SUV pulls up in front of us. Reese grabs the back door and once we're inside, we find Royce is our driver.

"They just cleared Reginald," he announces as he set us into gear.

"Dana is on her way to the airport," I say. "She might want to wait on Reginald."

"Savage told her right as they pulled away," Royce says. "And the evidence against Martha is damning. This is over for Dana. It's over for you two."

"And yet so much more has just begun," Reese says. "I know. You can stop playing dumb."

Royce glances at me in the mirror. "We're not telling anyone but Lori and Cole right now and not until after my appointment on Monday."

"Understood," Royce says.

A few minutes later we exit at our apartment and Royce meets us at the door. "Congratulations you two. If you need survival tips. Well, I have survived. You will, too. That's about the best I got other than calling my wife."

Reese and I enter our building with smiles on our faces. "Do you think it's that rough?"

"Of course not," Reese says. "People always try to scare expectant parents."

"Expectant parents," I repeat. "Okay, I'm scared."

He leads me into the elevator, folding me against him even as he punches the elevator button. "Don't stress. I'll find a way to keep your mind off your fears once we're alone."

"That's a big order."

"I'll practice until I get it right," he promises.

⚬⚬⚬

480

Monday arrives and Reese and I attend my doctor's appointment together. By the time we leave, we do so feeling more like official parents-to-be than ever. We are also weeks from knowing the sex of the baby and we decide when we are that far along, then we'll announce. For now, we're going to Lori and Cole which is exactly what we do. I join Reese at the office, and we call them to the conference room. Once they shut the door, I just can't wait to get it out. "We have an announcement," I say, grinning. "We're pregnant."

"Oh my God," Lori says, her eyes going wide. "I knew it. I had a gut feeling." She hugs me as Cole does the same to Reese, because apparently, the baby thing takes away the macho in them, at least a little.

Telling them feels good. It makes the baby feel real and instead of staying at work, Reese and I take a trip to a baby store and start planning for the nursery. It becomes immediately obvious that Reese wants nothing less than everything for this child and it's really adorably sexy. When I get home, and he's forced to return business calls, I write all about his sexy, adorable shopping in the journal I still plan to give him for his birthday.

One week before Reese's party I have to tell him about that, too. He's too attentive right now and without a case that has his interest, for me to pull off the surprise. Instead, I let him help me pick the food and plan, but I pick the cake. It's a surprise. It's his mother's recipe that I've had the local bakery recreate with her permission.

What's interesting is that my brothers are both attentive as well, though Reid's version of attentive is cranky and quick, but there's something different about him I can't quite understand. I'm a little weird with Gabe, I decide after several calls over several days. I just can't get over him being so willing to let Wilson be hurt, even if it was to protect me.

Finally, the night of the party arrives and I'm dressed in jeans and a blouse, ready to receive our guests, only to be surprised when Gabe shows up early to help me setup. Together we force Reese to go downstairs to have a drink in the bar while we ready the house for about thirty friends which means Gabe moves furniture while I watch. "Reid's coming," Gabe announces after the catering company arrives and we retreat to the kitchen island with coffee in hand. "And bringing a woman."

I blanch. "Reid? A woman?" I'm stunned.

"She came in like a hurricane, and I do believe he's recovering from the storm."

"Now I know why he seems different." I narrow my eyes at him. "Is she nice? Pretty? Successful?"

"All of the above and tough as nails. She can handle him and then some."

"That's good. Really good. What about you? Any special woman these days?"

"Never. I'm not that guy."

"Reid said the same thing," I remind him.

"Reid and I are not as alike as Reid likes to think."

I'm curious about all that I obviously don't know about my brother. He's a funny guy and yet, he's clearly cold beneath that humor. Reid is Reid. Hard and harder, but Gabe's not that simple. He's right. They aren't so alike. The sound of the front door opening has me standing up as Reese calls out, "I'm here!"

I shove off my stool and race to greet him, finding him positively perfection in faded jeans and a T-shirt. I push to my toes, kiss him and then lower my voice to say, "Your last birthday before you're a father."

"I wouldn't have it any other way."

Gabe rounds the corner and greets Reese, and I leave the two men to chat. I have a gift to add a few final touches to. I hurry upstairs, shut the bedroom door, and pull out the bound notebook I had all of my journal entries laminated inside. I then go to the bed and pull out a custom-made box that has "Dad to Be" all over it, insert the notebook and then seal it with a combo of pink and blue ribbons.

I didn't give him his baby news for his birthday. but I'm going to give him the gift of knowing that nothing he feared was on my mind over Debbie was really on my mind. Everything I was thinking was about us and our growing family.

***

Two hours later, the party is in full gear, my gorgeous husband is the center of attention, and we are surrounded by friends; Lauren and Royce, Cole and Lori, being the ones who stay close to us, above all others. It's almost time for cake and gifts. I want mine to come first. I grab his hand. "Come with me," I say.

His eyes light with mischief. "Why?" he whispers, leaning in close. "What are you going to do to me?"

I laugh and give him my back while tugging on his hand. With a quick rush through the crowd, I lead the way to our bedroom and once we're there, I point to the chair. "Go. Sit. Shut your eyes."

"Should we do this while the guests are downstairs?"

"Yes. Because we aren't doing what you keep hinting at. Go sit, husband."

He kisses me and does as ordered. "Shut your eyes."

"Okay. Eyes shut, sweetheart."

I grab the box and set it on Reese's lap. I sit down next to him. "Okay. Your gift that was supposed to be part of the baby news."

He opens his eyes and smiles at the box. "Future dad. That I am."

He opens the lid and pulls out the book, giving me a curious look. "When I found out I was pregnant and decided not to tell you right away, I started writing down all of my thoughts so you'd know you didn't miss anything."

He flips it open and starts to read before glancing over at me. "This is perfect, Cat. Absolutely perfect."

"Now you know Debbie wasn't on my mind."

He leans over and kisses me. "Perfect. Like you."

"Some of my thoughts are pretty silly when I read them now. You'll get a few laughs."

He refocuses on the book and flips to a random page and gives me one of those laughs now. "You wondered if you tasted differently?"

My cheeks actually heat on that one. "I—well—yes. I did."

He sets the book aside. "No, you do not, but why don't I make sure right now."

I squeeze my legs together. "No. Not now. And it's your birthday. I do you."

He stands up and pulls me to my feet. "We do us, sweetheart."

"And baby Olive."

"And baby Olive."

Two months later...

I open the new journal I've been keeping to document my pregnancy and start to write:

Today I'm thinking about the night of Reese's birthday, my father showed up and he could have ruined the night. He was rude and horrible to Reid's new woman and he had me shaking all over. I think of this today because my father has never been a man to show love and affection, and while yes, this causes me pain, it also drives home the contrast between him and Reese. Sometimes it's what we don't have that makes us appreciate what we do have. And if we don't, we should. I hope that one day my child will read this and remember to appreciate what she has. Yes, she. We found out today that we're having a girl. For now, we're calling her Olive, for fun, but we're torn between the names Ashley and Heather.

Reese appears in the doorway and holds up an envelope. "A gift from your brother Reid, delivered by courier."

"A gift from Reid and he doesn't even know I'm pregnant yet."

Reese sits down next to me. "He said to open it together."

I grab it, unseal it and pull out a document. "It's the paternity test. You're not the father. Well, not of Debbie's baby." I set the document aside. "Just the father of Heather."

"Heather."

"Yes," I say. "I like Heather."

"As long as it's not Olive," he teases, and pulls me down on the couch with him, where we do not keep our clothes on, nor do we shut the door, though those days will soon be history, once baby Heather arrives. Which is exactly why Reese seems to believe we should spend as much time without clothes as possible now, while we can.

Six months later...

I wake in the hospital bed to find that Reese has snuck into bed with me, and our daughter, baby Heather, is asleep in a bassinet next to us. I smile and tangle my fingers in my husband's hair, but he doesn't wake up. I snuggle closer to him and close my eyes right as Heather makes a soft sound. Reese is up in an instant, awake for our daughter, then he didn't even notice me playing with his hair. That tells me he's that comfortable with me touching him, and that he's going to prove me right and be an amazing father. Which makes me wish that for my daughter, that all of her dreams come true, and that she ends up with a man just like her father.

The End

Read more in the Scandalous Billionaires series:
https://www.lisareneejones.com/scandalous-billionaires.html

Be the first to know!

Be the first to know!

The best way to be informed of all upcoming books, sales, giveaways, and to get a FREE EBOOK, be sure you're signed up for my newsletter list!

SIGN-UP HERE:

http://lisareneejones.com/newsletter-sign-up/

Another surefire way to be in the know is to follow me on social media:

a

amazon.com/Lisa-Renee-Jones/e/B001TXMWU/?tag=lisrenjon-20

♪

tiktok.com/@lisareneejonesbooks

f

facebook.com/AuthorLisaReneeJones/

Also by Lisa Renee Jones

Also by Lisa Renee Jones

THE INSIDE OUT SERIES

If I Were You
Being Me
Revealing Us
His Secrets*
Rebecca's Lost Journals
The Master Undone*
My Hunger*
No In Between
My Control*
I Belong to You
All of Me*

THE SECRET LIFE OF AMY BENSEN

Escaping Reality
Infinite Possibilities
Forsaken
Unbroken*
Damages (2025)

CARELESS WHISPERS

Denial
Demand

Surrender

WHITE LIES

Provocative
Shameless

TALL, DARK & DEADLY / WALKER SECURITY

Hot Secrets
Dangerous Secrets
Beneath the Secrets
Deep Under
Pulled Under
Falling Under
Savage Hunger
Savage Burn
Savage Love
Savage Ending
When He's Dirty
When He's Bad
When He's Wild
Luke's Sin
Luke's Touch
Luke's Revenge

LILAH LOVE

Murder Notes
Murder Girl
Love Me Dead
Love Kills
Bloody Vows
Bloody Love
Happy Death Day
The Party Is Over
The Ghost Assassin
Agent vs. Assassin

DIRTY RICH

Beautiful Betrayal
Filthy Deal
Naked Truth
Dirty Lawyer
Dirty Boss
Dirty Enemy

DIRTY RICH

Dirty Rich One Night Stand
Dirty Rich One Night Stand: Two Years Later
Dirty Rich Cinderella Story
Dirty Rich Cinderella Story: Ever After
Dirty Rich Obsession
Dirty Rich Obsession: All Mine
Dirty Rich Betrayal
Dirty Rich Betrayal: Love Me Forever
Dirty Rich Secrets

THE FILTHY TRILOGY

The Bastard
The Princess
The Empire

THE NAKED TRILOGY

One Man
One Woman
Two Together

THE BRILLIANCE TRILOGY

LISA RENEE JONES

A Reckless Note
A Wicked Song
A Sinful Encore

NECKLACE TRILOGY

What If I Never
Because I Can
When I Say Yes

THE TYLER & BELLA TRILOGY

Bastard Boss
Sweet Sinner
Dirty Little Vow

WALL STREET EMPIRE

Protégé King
Scorned Queen
Burned Dynasty

STANDALONE THRILLERS

You Look Beautiful Tonight (L.R. Jones)
A Perfect Lie
The Poet
The Wedding Party (L.R. Jones)

eBook only

About the Author

About the Author

New York Times and *USA Today* bestselling author Lisa Renee Jones writes dark, edgy fiction including the highly acclaimed *Inside Out* series and the crime thriller *The Poet*. Suzanne Todd (producer of Alice in Wonderland and Bad Moms) on the *Inside Out* series: *Lisa has created a beautiful, complicated, and sensual world that is filled with intrigue and suspense.*

Prior to publishing, Lisa owned a multi-state staffing agency that was recognized many times by The Austin Business Journal and also praised by the Dallas Women's Magazine. In 1998 Lisa was listed as the #7 growing women-owned business in Entrepreneur Magazine. She lives in Colorado with her husband, a cat that talks too much, and a Golden Retriever who is afraid of trash bags.